The Lost Sister

KATHLEEN McGURL

ONE PLACE. MANY STORIES

HQ
An imprint of HarperCollins*Publishers* Ltd
1 London Bridge Street
London SE1 9GF

www.harpercollins.co.uk

HarperCollins*Publishers*
1st Floor, Watermarque Building, Ringsend Road
Dublin 4, Ireland

This paperback edition 2021

First published in Great Britain by
HQ, an imprint of HarperCollins*Publishers* Ltd 2021

ISBN: 9780008380526

For my son Connor McGurl, who helped develop this plot on many walks during lockdown.

Chapter 1

Harriet, 2019

How she would ever thin down her possessions enough to allow a move into a much smaller property, Harriet had no idea. She wandered from room to room, touching ornaments, stroking the backs of armchairs, running her hand along polished tables and sideboards. Everything was infused with so many memories of her seventy years. The little Toby jug on the mantelpiece that had been her mother's and she remembered loving as a child. The dining room table and chairs that she and John had saved up for in the early years of their marriage, determined to buy decent furniture that would last them a lifetime. The large, squishy sofa, much more modern, bought only about ten years ago and so comfortable and perfect for stretching out on when reading a book. It would never fit in the kind of two-bedroom bungalow her daughter Sally thought she should buy. Neither would the dining table. But how would she ever part with them? And all this stuff was just downstairs. Upstairs she had four bedrooms and a study filled with more stuff. And then there was the attic – huge, and filled with endless boxes of who knew what.

That's what they were due to start tackling today: the attic. Sally had suggested it when she'd phoned the previous evening. 'I'll go up there with you, Mum, and we'll just do it bit by bit. Once we get started you'll find it easier but I know how daunting it must feel.'

'Are you sure you can spare the time, love?' Harriet had asked. 'What about Jerome?'

'He's doing well today. He's in school, and he should be well enough to go to school tomorrow. So I'll have time. See you around ten; get some chocolate croissants in for me from McKinley's bakery, will you?'

'Sure, of course, love,' Harriet had replied. And now the croissants were warming in the oven, the coffee was made and at any moment Sally would arrive and they'd have to get started on the attic, going through the forty years' worth of junk and memories that were stored up there. Outside it was a blustery March day, raining on and off. The perfect day to tackle an indoor job, even one that was likely to be difficult and emotional.

The doorbell rang and Harriet rushed to answer it, smiling as she greeted her eldest daughter, the one who'd stayed living close to her home in Bournemouth, the one she saw every week, who'd supported her when John died so suddenly and throughout the nine long months since, as Harriet adjusted to life without him. And all this even though Sally had so many troubles of her own. She gathered her daughter into a hug and kissed her cheek. 'Hello, darling. Thank you so much for coming round to help.'

'No problem, Mum. If I'm honest, it's good to have a few days when I'm not just looking after Jerome. Did you get those croissants in?'

'Of course! I was outside McKinley's before it had even opened. We'll have coffee and pastries first, before going up into that hideous attic.' Harriet gave a fake shudder at what was ahead, and Sally laughed.

'You know what, I reckon you'll quite enjoy it once we get started, Mum. It's quite cathartic, throwing out rubbish.'

Harriet nodded, and poured out the coffee. It wasn't the rubbish she was worried about finding up there. It was the memories. 'I'm sure it is. Anyway, sit you down and tell me, how's my little grandson?'

'On good form.' Sally took a mouthful of warm pastry and had to immediately reach for a paper napkin Harriet had piled on the table, to mop up some escaped chocolate from the corner of her mouth. 'Wow, these are as excellent as ever. He's at a point in his treatment cycle when he has more energy than usual, enough to do a few days in school. I'm so glad. A bit of normality for him, a chance to play with his friends; and for me, a chance to do something else other than constantly change the DVDs while he lies on the sofa.'

'Poor little mite. Is the chemotherapy working?' Six-year-old Jerome had been diagnosed with an acute form of leukaemia a couple of months earlier. It had knocked them all for six. It just seemed so unfair.

'I'm really, really hoping so, Mum.'

Harriet glanced at her daughter. Sally's voice had cracked a little and there was a tell-tale glistening in her eyes. Time to change the subject, then. She knew that Sally hated showing how vulnerable she was, and found it hard to talk about Jerome's illness. Even in the early days when he'd just been diagnosed, she'd struggled to put into words what the consultant had told her. Half the point of today was to give Sally a chance to take her mind off Jerome for a few hours. 'Shall we get going then, if you've finished your coffee? I've pulled the loft-ladder down already.'

'OK. Let's do this.' Sally stood up abruptly and rubbed her eyes, which Harriet pretended not to notice as she led the way out of the kitchen and upstairs. The hatch to the loft was above the landing, and they had to duck around the ladder. 'You go up first, Mum, and be careful.'

3

'I'm perfectly all right on the ladder, love,' Harriet said. She might be seventy but she was fit and active, doing Pilates every week and cycling everywhere. Even so she climbed the ladder with care. It'd be mortifying to trip and fall with Sally here. Her daughter would never forgive her.

She flicked the light switch as she emerged into the attic. It was a large space, boarded over, and with a murky skylight set into one section of the sloped roof. There was very little free floor space – boxes were piled on top of boxes, carrier bags tucked into corners, small pieces of furniture stored haphazardly. John's set of golf clubs leaned against a chimney breast. Half a dozen framed pictures were balanced against the golf clubs. Boxes of Sally's and Davina's old schoolbooks were tucked deep under the eaves. Three boxes of books and bric-a-brac she'd once sorted out to sell at a car boot sale that somehow she'd never got round to doing, were stacked in the middle. A pile of crates that she'd brought from her own mother's house twenty years ago, meaning to sort them out, had never got further than her own attic and now sat in what had once been intended as a clear walkway through the space.

'Well. Where shall we start?' said Sally, as she emerged through the hatch and stood beside Harriet, hands on hips, gazing about her and trying unsuccessfully to hide her astonishment at the amount of stuff there was to deal with. 'This is, I hate to say it, even more cluttered than I remember.'

'I know. But I kind of know where things are – there's sort of a system,' Harriet said, sounding uncertain even to herself. 'Over there's Christmas decorations. All that lot is from your nan's house. Stuff relating to you and Davina is in that corner. Photos and slides and the projector and whatnot over there.'

'What's this pile?' Sally had her hand on a precariously stacked pile of boxes. The bottom one had 'old stuff' helpfully written on the side in marker pen.

'No idea,' Harriet had to admit. She had a horrible feeling

4

the 'old stuff' box might have remained packed and sealed since she and John moved out of their last house and into this one, nearly forty years ago.

'Well then, shall we start here?' Not waiting for an answer, Sally heaved the top box off the pile, opened it and peered inside. 'Vases. Salt and pepper shakers in the shape of church towers. A picture of the Coliseum.'

'Ah. Mum's old bits and pieces. I thought it was just that pile.' Harriet gestured to boxes that sat on top of an old travelling trunk. 'But yes, we can start here.'

'So what's the plan?' Sally asked, holding the cruet set. 'One pile for keep, one to go to charity or car boot sale, one to go to the tip? And only keep what's valuable or really sentimental?'

Harriet smiled. Sally was so much more efficient than she was. Her daughter's house was always tidy and clutter-free. 'That sounds good to me. For a start, you can put that cruet set in the charity pile. I always loathed it. Mum bought them when on holiday in York many years ago.'

'I quite like them,' Sally said, 'but I'm not keeping them.' She looked around her, found an empty box that had once held an old cathode ray tube television set, and put them in. With a marker pen she pulled from her pocket she wrote 'Charity' on the side, then held up an ugly green glass vase with a crack down one side.

'Bin,' said Harriet, and Sally nodded. That was put into a different box.

They progressed quickly through the first pile of boxes, and by the end Harriet was pleased to find she was only keeping two small items: a pie funnel in the shape of a blackbird that she remembered her grandmother using, and a framed photo of her parents in their wedding outfits. The boxes marked 'For the Tip' and 'Charity' were full. 'Let's get these downstairs to give ourselves more space, have a cup of tea and then get back to it,' Sally suggested.

Harriet agreed, and stayed in the attic while Sally went down, then passed the boxes down to her daughter. 'The deal is,' Sally said, 'you need to dispose of these boxes as you go along. So when we're finished today, drop those off at the charity shop and those at the tip before you do any more sorting.'

'Yes, boss,' Harriet said, making a mock salute. It was always easier to just go along with whatever Sally suggested. She had to agree with the sense of the system however. Little by little, bit by bit, was the only way, as Sally had told her. And actually, it *was* cathartic. With five boxes sorted there was a long way to go, but it was actually quite fun doing it with Sally. It'd be harder once they got to things that held all the memories of her life with John, she suspected. Though most of that was downstairs still, anyway. She'd be better off doing that herself, taking her time over it, enjoying the memories as she sorted through. Sally would make her rush it too much, and there'd be a danger she might throw away things she'd later regret.

After a reviving cup of tea (and after Sally had eaten another chocolate croissant), they returned to the attic.

'What next?' Sally asked.

Harriet looked around. It hardly looked as though they'd done anything, despite having worked for a couple of hours. 'I suppose that lot. Keep going with Mum's old stuff. Unless you want to tackle your old toys?'

Sally laughed. 'Don't say you've still got our old dolls up here! Surely they could have gone to a school fete or something?'

Harriet shrugged. 'I always meant to. But then ...' She sighed. 'Davina had her daughters, and I suppose I thought I'd keep the dolls ...'

'In case she ever turned up here with your other grandchildren in tow?' Sally snorted. 'Unlikely. She's so bloody selfish. Those kids must be, what, eight and ten by now? And you've never been allowed to even meet them?'

'I know, I know.' Harriet waved a hand to stop Sally saying anything more. If she dwelt too long on the facts, she inevitably

6

found herself sobbing. It hurt, it really did – the way Davina had left home as a teenager and cut off all contact other than occasional calls from a withheld number. How she'd let Harriet know by postcard about the birth of her first grandchild, *two months* after the event. How ten years on, she still had not met little Autumn, or her sister Summer. And that horrible day … the event that had hardened Davina's resolve to stay away. The estrangement wasn't entirely down to Davina's selfishness, if she was honest. They'd all played a part in it.

But Sally kept talking. 'Has she even called you recently?'

'Not for a bit, no,' Harriet had to admit.

'Does she know? About Jerome, I mean?' Sally's tone was confrontational.

'No. I haven't had a chance to tell her.'

Sally rolled her eyes. A muscle twitched in her jaw as though she was trying to get her anger under control. A moment later she sighed and shook her head. 'You're right, Mum. We'll not think about her any more. Let's just get on with sorting out Nanna's things. Right then. This box next.' Sally opened a box marked 'Ornaments' and they continued the process of separating them into keep, charity, and tip piles.

Three boxes later they had finished all of Harriet's mother's stuff. Harriet was pleased to find she had only decided to keep half a dozen items from it all for sentimental purposes.

'So now, this? What is it, some sort of travelling trunk?' Sally patted the trunk that the boxes had been stacked on top of.

Harriet nodded. 'That was my grandmother's sea trunk I think. Mum had it stored in her attic and after I cleared her house, I just moved it here.'

'What's in it?'

'No idea. I've never looked. It's locked, and I don't have a key. But we'll never manage to get it downstairs and out of here. Maybe we can just push it to a corner of the attic and leave it here when I sell up.'

7

Sally stared at her mother, an expression of utmost horror on her face. 'Absolutely no way, Mum. We are not just leaving this. There could be some real gems in here. What do you mean, her sea trunk?'

'My grandmother worked on board ocean liners when she was young,' Harriet replied. 'I guess this is what she packed her stuff in, to take on board ship. Grandpa worked on them too – it's where they met.'

'Yes, there are labels on it – White Star Line. That rings a bell,' Sally said, frowning as she peered at the sides of the trunk.

'That's the one. Gran worked on the *Olympic*, which used to sail back and forth across the Atlantic from Southampton to New York.'

'Hmm. But you say you don't have the key?'

'Not anywhere I know of. Shame.' Harriet ran her hand across the top of the trunk, feeling its scratched and battered surface. Finding it had piqued her curiosity about her grandmother's early life. As a child she could remember sitting on her grandmother's knee, listening enraptured to tales of life at sea. She'd loved gazing at Gran's wrinkled and powdered face, watching her eyes light up as she told her stories. She could remember the feeling of Gran's arms wrapped around her, the smell of her perfume and powder, the gentle sound of her voice. But she couldn't remember much of the detail of Gran's stories – just vague impressions of her talking about her job as a stewardess on board ocean liners, being run off her feet by spoilt and demanding passengers.

And now here, in her attic, was Gran's old sea trunk. Harriet sighed. How she'd long to see inside it!

'Mum?' Sally was on her knees in front of the trunk, looking closely at it. 'Thought you said this was locked?'

'It is.'

'No, it's not. It's just held by a catch that's a bit stiff. Look.' Harriet watched as Sally prised open the catch then pushed the lid up with both hands. It made a cracking sound as it rose, as if decades of dirt that had sealed it were being broken, but then it was open, the lid leaning back on its hinges, and the contents of the trunk exposed for the first time in many decades.

Chapter 2

Emma, 1911

Emma Higgins' earliest memory was of being on board a ship. Well, it was not really a ship, she supposed. It was a ferry, a steamer operating between Southampton and Cowes, on the Isle of Wight. She'd been about four years old, her sister Ruby just a babe in arms and her sister Lily not yet born. She'd been so very excited to be on board a boat, amazed that such a huge thing could float, and astounded at the views from the deck as Southampton faded into the distance and Cowes loomed ever closer.

The family were on the ferry because they were moving to the Isle of Wight, where Emma's father, George, had secured a job working in a new hotel in the fashionable resort of Sandown. 'There'll be a beach for you to play on,' he'd told Emma, 'and the sea for you to paddle in. We shall have a wonderful life in Sandown!' But it was the sea crossing – steaming down Southampton Water and then across the Solent – that had captured little Emma's imagination. When she looked back on it, she thought that was probably the moment that determined her lifelong fascination with being at sea.

They had lived in Sandown, George working in the hotel and Emma's mother Amelia taking in sewing, for almost ten years, until George had fallen prey to a gang of ruffians one stormy afternoon when he had been carrying the hotel's takings to the bank to lodge. They'd beaten him and stolen the money, leaving him lying in a ditch with broken ribs and a smashed skull. He was found some hours later by a passing policeman but did not recover from his injuries. Amelia, on hearing the news, had collapsed and taken to her bed for a week, by which time the rent was due and there was not enough money to pay it.

Emma's second sea crossing, therefore, was the return trip from Cowes to Southampton, where the now-fatherless family stayed for a while with Amelia's sister until Amelia felt able to leave her bed, take on work as a laundress and seamstress, and move herself and her daughters into a tiny terraced house near the Southampton docks.

Now, as Emma hurried back to that same terraced house, bursting with her news, she wondered what her mother and sisters would make of what she had to tell them. Would they be pleased? Or fearful? She had no idea. All she knew was that this felt like her destiny. A chance to go to sea again – properly to sea! – and actually live on board a ship. It felt so right. It seemed like a job that had her name on it; a job she'd been meant to do since she was four years old and had marched onto the bridge of the paddle steamer on the way to Cowes, demanding to see the horses that powered the ship. Her father had been simultaneously mortified and delighted by her audacity, she recalled, and the ferry's skipper had picked her up and let her hold the wheel for one brief, glorious moment.

She turned a corner, passed the small grocery shop where Ma went every day to buy the family's dinner, waved to the little girl who lived across the street and was playing out with a hoop and stick, and found herself running the last few yards to her front doorstep, where she almost tripped over her sister.

'What are you doing sitting out here, Ruby? You'll make your skirts all dirty and Ma'll be furious.'

'Huh. I scrubbed the step this morning so it's clean as anything. Sitting out here because it's better than being in *there*.' Ruby pointed over her shoulder with her thumb at the house.

'Oh dear. What's happened now?' Emma sighed. Her news would have to wait a while. She nudged Ruby with her foot to make her move over, and sat beside her.

'Ma. That's what's happened. Making me scrub steps and wash clothes and sweep floors. I ain't a general skivvy, Ems.'

'We need to share out the jobs. Especially when Lily's ill and Ma needs to nurse her.'

'Where was you, then? Where was you this afternoon? You could have done your share of the jobs.' Ruby glared at Emma. 'I do enough blinking work at the hotel every morning without having to do more when I come back home.'

'I swept upstairs and did all the grates this morning before I went out. While you were still abed,' Emma replied. Part of her wanted to be furious at Ruby for suggesting she, Emma, didn't do her fair share of the chores. But another part felt for her sister. Of course Ruby wanted more from life than to spend her days scrubbing floors. At 17 she deserved fun and happiness and sunshine and laughter. But with their father dead, their mother's fading eyesight meaning she was struggling to sew her piecework, their little sister Lily's precarious health requiring her to frequently spend days in bed … well, it was essential that Emma and Ruby have jobs and bring in some money. They'd both worked since leaving school at 14.

'Yes, I know.' Ruby leaned against Emma as a gesture of apology, and Emma smiled to show it was accepted. 'But I wish there were some way out of this. Where's my knight, riding over the horizon on his glossy black steed, come to sweep me off my feet and take me to his castle to live in luxury?'

Emma laughed. 'You've been reading too many romances, Ruby. Life's not like that.'

'I know. I just wants something a bit different. Less scrubbing, more love and laughter with some lovely-looking fellow.'

'You're so pretty, Ruby, it'll happen in time. You're still young.'

'Wish it would hurry up and happen.'

'Ah, pet. Don't wish your life away. Come on. Let's go inside and make tea for us all. I have some news to share.' Emma stood and held out her hand to haul her sister to her feet. Ruby followed her in, looking curious as Emma called for Ma and Lily to come to the kitchen and listen to what she had to say. As she passed through the hallway it dawned on her that her news would mean Ruby would have more work to do at home, as Emma wouldn't always be there. With a pang of anxiety she wondered how her sister would take the news.

'There's a possibility of me getting a new job,' Emma announced, when Ma, Ruby, and Lily were all sitting at the kitchen table, looking at her expectantly.

'What, on top of the one you already have, in the Star Hotel?' Ma looked surprised. Emma already worked six days a week cleaning hotel rooms.

Emma shook her head. 'Instead of it. I wouldn't be able to do both – listen while I tell you.'

'Get on with it, then,' Ruby said, rolling her eyes.

'There's a new ship coming in, next month. A big one. The biggest ever built, they say. It's sailing down here from Liverpool, and then a week or so later it's off on its first proper trip – the maiden voyage, they call it.'

'So what?' Ruby shrugged.

'You want to get a job on it?' Lily said, her eyes shining. 'Will you be climbing the rigging?'

Emma laughed. 'You're right, Lils, I do want to work on it. But not on the rigging. She's a steamship. An ocean liner. Her name is RMS *Olympic*.'

'You, work on a ship?' Ma said. 'Doing what?'

'As a stewardess, I hope. Looking after the rich people in their cabins. Or cleaning if I can't get a stewardess job. Or in the kitchens.'

Lily looked vaguely disappointed that Emma wouldn't be climbing the rigging. 'Do you work on the ship when it sails away or only when it is in port?'

'When it sails, dear Lily. The staff need to go on board before the passengers to make everything ready, and then stay on board as it sails across the ocean. All the way to New York, imagine that!' Emma could barely imagine it herself. New York seemed so far away, but here was a chance that she might actually go there, herself, on board the world's newest and largest ocean liner.

'How can it go so far in a day?' Lily still looked confused.

'It doesn't,' explained Emma. 'It takes many days to get there. But they think the *Olympic* might be able to beat the record and make the crossing faster than any ship ever has done before.'

'Never mind about records and speed and whatnot. How are you going to get a job on board, I wants to know?' questioned Ruby.

'There's interviews for posts on board starting next week, down at the docks. At the White Star Line's shipping office. I have the right experience, and they need loads of people. I think I stand a good chance. And if they like me, I then sign on for the first voyage, and after that … well, who knows?'

'How long would you be away for?'

'About three weeks I think, for the first voyage, and then if I like the work and sign on for another, I'd be away again.'

'Ems, don't go! I'll miss you!' Lily climbed off her chair and clung to her big sister.

Emma wrapped an arm around Lily's waist. 'Ah now, pet. Just think of all the stories I'll have to tell you when I come back! Three weeks would go by so quickly, and then I'd be home on leave for a few days or a week, before sailing again. You're almost grown up now. And you'd still have Ma and Ruby here.'

'Huh. Yes. Leave me with all the work, why don't you? What if I runs off and gets a job on this ship as well, eh? What then?' Ruby put her hands on her hips and glared at Emma.

'Ruby, you need to be over 18 or they won't employ you. But maybe next year ...'

A thoughtful expression flitted across Ruby's face, and Emma smiled. Her sister was always looking for more from life, adventure, something out of the ordinary, and this just might be the perfect solution. Let her, Emma, work on board ship first to find out what it was like, then if Ruby still liked the idea next year perhaps they could work together on board the *Olympic* or some other ship.

'Well, I think it's a marvellous idea,' Ma said. 'Is the pay good?'

'Better than I am getting now, plus of course board and lodging is included. I'll be able to save nearly all my pay and bring it home to you, Ma.'

'Oh, no you won't. Your pay is your pay. All I will need is a tiny bit to cover your food when you're back home, and the rest is your own. You earn it, you keep it, lovey.' Ma nodded decisively and folded her arms across her chest.

Emma smiled. One way or another she'd get her mother to accept some of her earnings, when the time came. The family needed it. 'So is it all right? May I apply for a job on the ship? You don't mind?'

'I don't mind at all, lovey,' Ma said.

'I mind.' Ruby glared at Emma. 'With you away for weeks on end I'll have to do your share of the housework as well as my own, as well as my job. I'll have no free time to myself. But you don't care about that, do you?'

'I can do Emma's chores,' Lily said. 'I'm old enough now.'

'Huh. Half the time you're too poorly to help with anything. And with Emma away I'll end up having to nurse you on top of everything else.'

Lily pouted. Emma sighed. It was true that she tended to be the

15

one who looked after Lily most whenever she had one of her frequent bouts of ill health that had plagued her since she'd had tuberculosis at the age of seven. Ruby had always done the minimum.

'Lily's not so often sick these days, Rubes. Not now she's growing up. It'll be all right, if I go away, I'm sure. And I'd be back every few weeks.' *And it's my chance to do something different with my life*, she wanted to add. *My life, my choice.*

'Of course it will be,' Ma said. 'Now then, how about a nice cup of tea? I hope they'll have tea on board the ship. I know how much you like a cup in the mornings.'

'Of course they'll have tea,' Emma said. 'And I'm sure I'll get a few breaks in the day in which I can drink a cup. At least I hope so!'

'When are the interviews?' Ruby wanted to know.

'Tomorrow. I have a half day, so I'll go down in the afternoon. Wish me luck!'

'Good luck, lovey.' Ma smiled but there was a sadness in her eyes. Her first daughter to leave home, even if it was only for temporary periods. But Emma knew Ma would miss her. As Emma was the eldest, Ma had leaned on her heavily since Pa had died. She'd helped nurse Lily. She'd counselled Ruby many times, doing her best to curb her middle sister's wayward nature and spare her mother's grey hairs. She'd taken on as much of the day-to-day housework and cooking in the home as she could. She'd been working in the Star Hotel since they'd returned from the Isle of Wight when she was 14, giving up most of her wages to help keep the family. None of it was what she'd dreamed of, but it was her duty as the eldest to take care of the family. And now, there was a chance to have some adventures of her own, while still helping provide for the family's needs. It was perfect. If only she could get the job!

The following afternoon Emma changed quickly out of her work uniform, put on a neat brown dress and re-pinned her hair, then hurried down to the docks to the shipping offices of the White Star Line. There were people milling about everywhere; she had expected it to be busy and indeed there were hundreds of people, mostly men, hanging around in and outside of the offices. Emma approached a young woman who was waiting patiently inside the offices, sitting on a plain wooden bench that ran along one side. The woman, pretty with dark hair, was neatly dressed in a tweed coat and hat.

'Hello,' Emma said. 'Do you mind if I sit with you? Am I in the right place for interviews for a job on RMS *Olympic*?'

The other woman smiled. 'Of course, sit down. Yes, this is the right place to sign on. Is this your first time?'

Emma nodded. 'I heard about the possibility of work and thought I would quite like it. I'm Emma Higgins, by the way.' She held out her hand for the other woman to shake.

'Violet Jessop. Good to meet you, Emma. Stick with me and I'll help you out.' She looked kindly at Emma, who felt relieved to have found a friend so quickly.

'Have you done this before? Been to sea, I mean?' Emma asked.

Violet nodded. 'Several times, yes. I've been with White Star for a while and they asked me to come and sign on for the *Olympic*. But they're short so they are needing to recruit more.'

'All those men out there? Are they all trying for jobs?'

'Some of them will be signing on, yes. As engineers, stokers, crew, able-bodied seamen, stewards, deckhands. There's a lot more jobs for men than women. But they need stewardesses too to help look after the female passengers. That's what I do. Is it what you are hoping for?'

'Yes. I've been working in a hotel for a few years,' Emma replied, as she looked around at the people milling about in the waiting area. 'Should I be giving my name or something?'

'Oh, heavens, have you not done that? Yes, go over there and give your name to the clerk at that desk.' Violet gestured to where a man with greased-down hair was sitting behind a desk, fending off enquiries from several men at once.

Emma felt nervous as she approached. Some of the men looked rough – they must be hoping for work as stokers or engineers rather than as stewards. The man at the desk looked up at her.

'Can I help?'

'My name is Emma Higgins. I am looking for work as a stewardess, please.'

'Very well, Miss Higgins, I'll put your name down and if you can just wait over there until you're called.' He gestured to the bench where Violet was still sitting, and Emma returned to her seat gratefully.

A few minutes later a door opened, and a man in a smart suit came out and nodded to Violet. 'You're next, Vi,' he said. 'Glad to see you'll be joining us on board.' He tipped his hat to Emma and sauntered out, whistling.

'Good luck getting the job,' Violet said to Emma as she stood up. 'Hope to see you when *Olympic* sails.' She went through the door the man had left open and closed it behind her. Emma felt a little alone now, with nothing to do other than sit quietly, back straight, knees pressed together, observing all that was happening around her. Some of the men seemed to know each other – she guessed from previous voyages. These people seemed to only need sign some sort of form and have an entry made in a book they each carried. But they weren't leaving immediately, and Emma overheard two men wishing 'they'd hurry up and read out the Articles so's we can go home for our tea'.

At last Violet emerged from the inner room once more, and nodded to Emma. 'In you go. Chin up, look confident.'

Emma swallowed her nerves and tried to do as Violet had said. The inner office was a plain room with wooden wall panelling, a battered desk and two chairs. The man behind the desk was of middle age, with an impressive set of grey whiskers.

'Miss Higgins? Your discharge book, if you please.' He held out a hand.

'Yes, sir. I mean, yes, I'm Miss Higgins but please, what is a discharge book? I don't have one ...'

'Ah, a first timer.' The man leaned back in his chair and looked appraisingly at Emma. 'Tell me about your experiences and background, if you would.'

Emma launched into the little speech she'd prepared to introduce herself and talk about her years of hotel work. 'And I have always wanted to work on a ship,' she finished, 'ever since I was very little and sailed over to the Isle of Wight.'

The man threw back his head and laughed at this. 'Well, being on board the world's finest liner is a little different from the steam packet over to Cowes. But if you can supply references and pass the medical check I think you will do very nicely, Miss Higgins. Now then, through there to see the doctor, bring me your references tomorrow and then we'll have you sign the Articles and be issued with your very own Seaman's Discharge Book. It's used to log all your voyages, and rate your work on each one,' he explained.

'Sir, I have references with me already,' Emma said, pleased with herself for organising that beforehand, even though it had meant admitting to her employer that she was thinking of leaving them. She took the papers out of her pocket and handed them over.

'Excellent. Then see the doctor, come back straight after and we'll sort you out.' He smiled at her and gestured to another door. She thanked him, went through the door, and found herself in a room with a kindly doctor who carried out what she thought was a rather cursory health check.

A few minutes later she was issued with her discharge book, signed a paper called the 'Ship's Articles' and was told to wait with the other successful applicants. There she found Violet talking to the man who'd recognised her.

'Well?' Violet said, smiling. Emma guessed Violet must know she'd been successful, as she had joined all the other people being taken on.

'I'm in!' Emma said, and was delighted when Violet gave her a quick, spontaneous hug.

'I'm so glad. There won't be many women on board, and so us girls have to stick together. Now, in a little while they will read out the Articles of Agreement – that's what we've all signed – so they know we've heard them. Just rules and regulations, really. We'll be issued with uniforms when we go aboard. All new for a new ship! So pleased you're on board, Emma. It's a hard life but an exciting and rewarding one. You won't regret this.'

At that moment, with a grin threatening to split her face in two, Emma felt Violet was absolutely right. She would never regret her decision to go to sea. This was the start of a new and wonderful life.

Chapter 3

Harriet

Harriet moved over to peer into the trunk. It was packed with clothes – grey uniforms, white aprons and caps, knitted stockings. All moth-eaten and mildewed. A hairbrush was tucked down one side. And two framed photos lay face down on top of the clothes. She reached in and picked up the first one.

'Look, it's my gran and grandpa. They look very young here – must be when they'd just become engaged.'

'They look so happy,' Sally said, taking the photo from her and inspecting it. 'I'm guessing you'll want to keep this, then. What's the other picture?'

Harriet picked it up and turned it over. The frame was a pretty one in carved wood with a black edging that might be badly tarnished silver. And the picture was a sepia image of three girls, the youngest wearing a smock with her hair tied loosely in a ribbon, the older two wearing plain dark dresses, their hair pinned up. The three had similar faces with long noses and gentle smiles, though there was something about one girl's expression – defiant, as though she was issuing a challenge to the photographer – that made Harriet think she'd be trouble.

'Who are they, Mum?' Sally asked, taking the picture from Harriet to look more closely at it.

'Well, that's Gran again,' Harriet said, pointing at one of the girls. 'And I assume one of these other girls must be her sister. But I have no idea who the third one is.'

'They look like they are all sisters.'

'Gran only ever spoke of one sister. She was very fond of her when they were young.'

'Only when they were young? Don't tell me, it's like me and Davina, is it? Great friends till adolescence then that's it. And you and your brother who you hardly ever see, too,' Sally said, shaking her head. 'Does falling out with your sibling run in this family?'

'Matthew and I didn't fall out. We just drifted apart, I suppose. Gran's sister died young. Gran used to tell me tall tales of how her sister had saved her life somehow, but I never quite believed her.' Harriet smiled at the memories. 'She used to love telling me stories.'

'Ah, that's sad that her sister died young.' Sally turned the picture over and began carefully opening up the back of the frame, twisting the little catches that held the back board in place. Behind it, a slip of paper was glued to the back of the photo. 'The Three Higgins Sisters, 1911,' Sally read out. 'So there were three of them. I wonder why your grandma never spoke of the other sister?'

Harriet widened her eyes in surprise. 'Well I never! I wonder, too, why she never mentioned her. You know, sometimes I wish I could go back in time, just for a day, sit at my gran's knee again and then I could ask her. And this time I'd write everything down so I wouldn't forget it. She told me so many stories when I was little but I only have such vague memories of them now. I'd love to ask her about this lost sister. What happened to her? What was her name?'

'I'd love to know too,' Sally said. 'Anyway. What do you want to do with all this stuff? It's mostly clothes underneath.'

'I'll throw out the clothes, I think. Look, they've had the moths at them.' Harriet held up a chemise that was full of holes. 'I'll keep the pictures. Maybe I can find out this other girl's name and details. My friend Sheila knows how to check the old census returns – she's really into all that genealogy stuff. I'll get her to show me how. If I check on the census returns from the beginning of the century I might be able to find out.'

Sally laughed. 'Beginning of *last* century you mean. Maybe the 1901 or 1911 censuses would help. Can I have the trunk, if you don't want it? It'd be great for storing some of Jerome's toys, if I clean it up a little.'

A perfect use for it. 'Of course you can. Right, we'll need your Charlie to help get this trunk down, next time he's here.'

'Sure, I'll ask him to come round at the weekend. We'll bring Jerome who's been begging to see his Nanna again soon.'

'I'd love to see him, too. Right, what are we tackling next then? Or have you had enough for one day?'

Sally smiled. 'I'm all right, Mum. Still got time before I need to pick up Jerome. Let's have a go at some of the old toys, shall we?'

'OK. Those should be quick to deal with. Keep any you want for Jerome and the rest can go to charity.'

Sally looked at Harriet, tilting her head to one side. 'You've given up on Davina ever bringing her girls here then?'

Harriet bit her lip and shrugged. 'I'll never give up. Your dad always said we must never give up on her. But the girls are probably already too old for some of the stuff I kept.'

Sally was already opening a box and tugging items out. She held up a doll, whose hair had been messily cut. 'Oh my God. Belinda! I haven't seen you for years!'

Harriet chuckled. 'I remember when you gave her that haircut then cried because the hair wouldn't grow back.'

23

'That wasn't me, Mum. That was Davina. I was bloody furious with her for doing it.'

'No love, it was you. You came to find me, sobbing like the world was ending, and said you'd cut Belinda's hair but now you wanted it to be long again. It was definitely you.'

Sally shook her head. 'We thought you'd be cross, so I took the blame. Davina always thought you'd be more angry with her than with me.'

'That's not right – I treated you both equally!' Harriet was astonished. Had Davina really thought that?

'I thought so. But she didn't. So when we were little if she did something stupid like this,' Sally glanced at the mutilated doll, 'we'd tell you I did it.'

'You thought I'd be less angry with you because you were the older one?'

Sally shrugged. 'That might have had something to do with it. I felt protective of her back then.' She scoffed. 'Looking back I don't know why I bothered. She's not been much of a sister to me for the last fifteen years. Haven't seen her in all that time.'

'Yes you have. Briefly, anyway, at your dad's funeral. Less than a year ago.' Davina had turned up out of the blue. Harriet had had no way of contacting her younger daughter to tell her her father had died, but she'd put a notice in the *Guardian*, John's favourite paper, on the off-chance Davina might see it. And although Sally had refused to, Harriet knew some of the girls' schoolfriends had posted the news publicly on Facebook, in case Davina was keeping tabs on them quietly.

'Doesn't count. She didn't say two words to me, that day.' The hurt in Sally's voice was evident. 'She sat at the back of the church, hung back at the graveside, then left as soon as Dad was in the ground. Wouldn't even come back for a cup of tea.'

Harriet remembered all too well. She'd been glad that the news had reached Davina, and pleased that her younger daughter had made the effort to come to the funeral. But her hopes that the

24

occasion might be the start of a reconciliation had been dashed when she'd gone over to give her daughter a hug afterwards, and Davina had stepped away. 'I just want a moment alone with Dad, then I'll go. I'll ring. Hope you're OK.' That was all she'd said, those three short sentences. Harriet had gone over the words endlessly, trying to draw comfort from the fact Davina had said she'd ring, that she'd hoped Harriet was OK, that she'd cared enough to come. In the end she'd had to step back and give Davina space to pay her silent respects to her father with whom she'd always got on better than she had with Harriet, especially as a teen. She'd watched as her daughter stood, head bowed, at the graveside for a minute before walking away to a waiting taxi without so much as a farewell or a backward glance.

'Yes, I know. It hurt me too. But she came. And she did ring me, after.'

'Two months later, wasn't it?'

Harriet nodded. 'And then again a month after that.' But the last phone call from Davina was four months ago now. Harriet had no number, no address, no email or anything else for her daughter. She'd tried to find her on social media with no luck.

Sally flung a pile of doll's clothes and a couple of Barbies into the 'charity' box. 'I hate her for what she's done to you. I thought her running off like that at 17 with that ridiculous rock band was bad enough. It hurt so much when she didn't come back for my graduation. Or my wedding! But to refuse to talk to us at Dad's funeral – that was unforgivable.'

Harriet sighed. 'I suppose she was grieving too, and didn't want to deal with any kind of emotional reunion on top of it all. Maybe she was thinking of us, that we had enough to cope with, without adding her arrival ...'

'If she really thought that then she shouldn't have turned up at all. She never bothered at any other family occasion.'

Harriet had to agree. It was Davina's failure to come to her sister's graduation that had been the final straw for Sally. And once

Sally had made up her mind about something it was very hard to make her change it. She refused to cut Davina any slack at all now. Davina had asked for Sally's phone number once, but Sally had told Harriet on no account was she to let her sister have it. 'She made it clear she wanted nothing more to do with me years ago, so therefore she has no right to have my phone number.'

Harriet had pleaded with Sally. 'Maybe she wants to make up. Maybe she wants to rebuild some bridges; won't you give her a chance?' But Sally had been immovable. Even so, on the rare occasions that Davina phoned Harriet, Harriet would pass on news, and Davina would listen politely, sometimes asking a question or two. It wasn't much, but it was all Harriet could do to keep a fragile thread of relationship alive between her two daughters. She had no idea though, whether Davina had ever forgiven her or Sally for what they'd done on that awful day, just before Davina's eighteenth birthday.

'Well, we can chuck this out, for a start.' Sally was holding up a battered old teddy bear. It had been Davina's – her inseparable companion from birth till the age of 12. Oddly, when Davina had left home so abruptly it had been the fact she'd not even taken the bear that had cut Harriet the hardest.

'Pass it here,' she said, holding out her hand. The bear was missing an eye, and one leg was badly sewn on with pink knitting wool – Davina's own attempt to repair him after he'd been in an altercation with a visiting puppy.

'You're not keeping it, are you?' Sally's tone was incredulous.

'I remember John buying it for Davina, and bringing it into hospital just after she was born. It holds memories for me. I think I will hang onto him.'

'For God's sake, Mum,' Sally muttered, shaking her head. But she continued with the task, finding a stuffed elephant that had been her own that she put aside for Jerome.

A little later Sally glanced at her watch. 'I'm going to have to go soon, Mum, and fetch Jerome. Shall we get these charity and tip boxes downstairs or do you want to continue a while on your own?'

'I'll do a little more,' Harriet replied. 'I feel I'm on a roll. Maybe Charlie will help take the boxes down at the weekend. Do you want a cup of tea before you go?'

'No, I'm all right, thanks.' Sally descended the loft ladder and waited at the bottom as Harriet climbed down. 'Not sure I like the idea of you going up by yourself though, Mum. What if you fell?'

'I go up all the time by myself, Sally. Fetching suitcases and Christmas decorations, storing stuff away. I'm fine. Honestly. I'm not that old.'

'Hmm. Well.' With that, Sally went downstairs and picked up her jacket and handbag.

'Thanks so much for helping, love,' Harriet said to her back.

Sally turned with a smile. 'No problem, Mum. Good job one of your daughters stayed close to help you in your old age, isn't it?'

'Seventy's not that old. Not these days,' Harriet replied. She didn't feel old. At least, as long as she didn't dwell too much on Davina. Or on Jerome's sickness.

After Sally had left, Harriet returned to the attic to sort through a couple of boxes that she knew contained Davina's things. She sighed. She'd long since reconciled herself – as far as it was possible to – to the idea that she might never again have a close relationship with her younger daughter. Davina was a very private person, and had always had an independent, unconventional streak. She'd chosen a different path to Sally, and although Harriet couldn't say she approved of it, she respected Davina's right to make her own choices. As a small child Davina had deferred to her bossy older sister, but as she'd grown she'd begun pushing back, rebelling first against Sally and later against her parents. At 15 Davina had met a boy who played rhythm guitar in a band called Hades Rising. He was 17 at the time, and clearly talented. At 16 Davina had informed Harriet she was going on the pill so she could sleep with Jez. John had been furious about this, but

Harriet had convinced him it was good that Davina was being responsible, and they'd do better to support her than fight her.

At 17, when Jez's band were asked to go on tour as supporting act for an up-and-coming rock band, Davina had dropped out of her A-level courses, packed a rucksack and gone with them, leaving Harriet a note on the kitchen table. The day before she'd rowed with Harriet when she'd announced she didn't see the point of staying on at college when she knew she wanted to work with Hades Rising.

'Oh, why can't you be more like your sister?' Harriet had eventually snapped. 'She just gets on with it, does what's expected. Never causes any trouble.'

'I'm not my sister. I'd *hate* to be like her. She's so fucking conventional,' Davina had shouted, and then the next day she was gone. She'd phoned home weekly to start with, but then the calls had dropped to just monthly.

'She'll return at the end of the tour. You'll see. Let's allow her to have her wings. Give her space,' John had counselled, but Harriet had found it hard.

'I miss her so much. I worry about her. I'm not sleeping for worry,' she'd confided in Sally, who'd put her arms around Harriet and held her, whispering, 'We'll get her back, somehow, Mum.'

But Davina had never come back, and a year later she'd sent a photo showing her and Jez getting married on a beach in the Bahamas. This was just after a phone call in which she'd promised to come home for Sally's graduation, but then she hadn't turned up. Sally had been furious with Davina – for missing her big achievement and for not inviting Harriet and John to her wedding. And Harriet suspected Davina was equally furious with Sally. Worse – for Harriet – was to come, when Davina sent a postcard announcing the birth of her first child, and then a couple of years later another one. And then the phone calls had dried up. It felt like the rebellion had gone too far.

'I have two granddaughters, and I don't even know which

country they live in,' she'd wailed to John, while Sally, three years older than Davina, who'd had a traditional church wedding and was now trying for a baby, had miscarried her first pregnancy. Looking back, Harriet wondered if that was what had made Sally decide never to accept Davina back in her life, even if Davina was willing. She always said it was Davina's broken promise regarding her graduation ceremony, but maybe it was the heartbreak of that miscarriage, compared to Davina's obvious ease at having children. 'If only I could turn back time,' Harriet had said to John, 'and do things differently.'

'But Davina always had her independent streak,' John had replied. 'What could you have done differently?'

She'd shaken her head sadly. 'That day in Weymouth. I'd have done things differently then.'

John had had no reply to that, other than to take her in his arms.

Davina's girls would have been 2 and 4, by Harriet's calculations, when Davina resumed her sporadic phone calls home. She'd split up with Jez, it seemed, but was now with the band's drummer who went by the name of Sticks, and was still touring. And then she split up with that fellow when Hades Rising broke up, moved into a campervan with the children and drove around Europe to wherever took her fancy. She lived off money she'd earned when she was with Hades Rising and had worked as their tour manager and publicist, and home-schooled the girls.

Every time she phoned, Harriet would ask where she was and when she was coming home, and Davina would answer, 'in the land of the living' and that she'd come home when she was ready.

'When's that, then?' Harriet would ask.

'When you start treating me as an adult.'

'I'll do that when you grow up,' she'd say. The same argument, every time, round and round. John would end up taking the phone off Harriet, and try to have a gentler, less confrontational conversation with Davina instead. She'd always got on better with her father.

The girls – named Autumn and Summer after the seasons they were born in – were now 10 and 8, attended a school, and Davina had moved into her latest boyfriend's house. That was all Harriet knew and all Davina would tell her. Davina had once sent a photo, a couple of years ago, of the two girls standing side by side under a tree. It was the only photo Harriet had of her granddaughters. It hurt, but she was growing used to it after all these years.

Harriet found herself keeping more than she'd intended from Davina's boxes. A tiny pink leotard from when Davina had attended ballet lessons aged five. An envelope full of certificates – cycling proficiency, swimming, piano grades one to five, summer-term star pupil for year seven. A handful of CDs that Davina had loved – mostly edgy rock, the kind of thing that Hades Rising played. Two of the CDs were by the band. Harriet hesitated over those, tossing them into the 'throw out' pile in the end. She didn't blame Jez for taking her daughter away. It had been Davina's choice. If only Davina would choose to come back again. Just a day – an hour, even! – in her company was all Harriet longed for.

As soon as she thought this she stopped herself. No. It was not all she longed for. Far more important was for little Jerome to get better. He was Sally's only child, and for him to have developed leukaemia so young had been devastating news for all of them.

At the weekend, as promised, Sally visited again, this time with Charlie and Jerome in tow. Jerome seemed on good form – pale as usual but happy to see his Nanna. Harriet had bought in stocks of his favourite biscuits and sweets. If she only got to see one of her grandchildren she was definitely going to spoil him, the way grandparents should.

'Three Freddo frog chocolate bars and two packs of chocolate digestives – for one small 6-year-old boy who's visiting for one day. Mum, I think you may have gone a little overboard,' Sally said, laughing.

'You can take the rest home with you,' Harriet said, passing Jerome one of the chocolate bars.

'Thank you, Nanna,' he said, giving her legs a hug. She stroked his little head – smooth as silk after his cancer treatment had meant he'd lost his hair.

'Now then, I've put the wooden train set in the sitting room. Would you like to play with it?'

Jerome nodded and Harriet took his hand and led him through. 'Can you make it up for me?' the child asked.

'In just a minute, pet. First I need to make your mummy and daddy a cup of tea, and Daddy is going to help carry some boxes down from the loft. Then we'll all come and play.'

'All right.' Jerome seemed satisfied with that plan, and sat down beside the box of train set pieces and began rummaging through, pulling out the engines and carriages, and a few track pieces to clip together.

Harriet watched him for a few seconds. He was coping so well with his illness. He never complained when he had bad days, and made the most of the good ones. She prayed that his treatment would work, and soon he'd be fully well again.

'So, tea? Or shall we get the boxes down first?' she said to Charlie and Sally.

'I'll put the kettle on, you two sort the boxes,' Sally suggested, and Harriet nodded, leading Charlie upstairs to where she'd already got the loft ladder down.

'Sally and I managed most of the boxes, but there's a wooden trunk. If I go up and pass it down to you ...'

'It's all right,' Charlie said, 'I'll go up and get it.'

'If you're sure – it's to the left of the hatch,' Harriet said, as Charlie climbed the ladder. Her daughter had married well, she thought. Charlie was one of those people for whom nothing was too much trouble. He'd do anything if asked, and he'd do it with a smile. He was the perfect son-in-law. Much better than that Lucas whom Sally had gone out with during her student years.

Thank goodness Sally hadn't married him. Harriet was convinced it was largely *his* fault that Davina had never returned at the end of the band's first tour.

'Gorgeous trunk,' Charlie said, as he began backing down the ladder, pulling the trunk after him, resting a corner of it on each step of the ladder. 'Really old. Sally said it was something to do with the White Star Line?'

'Yes, it was what my grandmother used when she worked on the *Olympic*. Careful now,' Harriet said, putting out a hand to steady the trunk as Charlie reached the bottom of the ladder and lifted it off.

'Oof. It is quite heavy, I'm glad you ladies left it to me. Shall I take it downstairs?'

'Yes, Sally said it might do as a toy chest for Jerome.'

'That'd be fantastic,' Charlie said, carrying it downstairs as Harriet pushed the loft ladder back up again. She followed him down to the sitting room where Jerome had begun a railway layout covering half the floor space.

Charlie was looking something up on his phone. 'So your grandmother worked on the *Olympic*, which was taken out of service in … let's see … 1935. Did she work on any others after that?'

'No, I remember her saying she and Granddad retired from life at sea the same year the *Olympic* did.' Harriet opened the chest and lifted out the old uniform. 'Which means it's been eighty-four years since these were packed away. No wonder it all smells a little musty.'

Sally came through with a tray of tea. 'Oh, well done. Wow, that will make an excellent toy box. Jerome, what do you think?'

'Huh? Yeah,' he said, clearly not wanted to be distracted from the train set for more than a second.

Sally rolled her eyes. 'I'll clean it up and polish it. He'll no doubt want to put stickers all over it. What are you going to do with the uniforms, Mum?'

'They're in terrible condition. I'll have to throw them out.'

'You sure you don't want to keep the trunk? I mean, even just to use it on your cruise?' Charlie asked. 'Might be fun to pack your stuff in this.'

Harriet laughed. 'It's far too heavy for me to manage. I'll stick to my nice modern suitcase with wheels, thanks.'

'When is the cruise?' Sally asked, her eyes narrowing.

'Only a week away, now.' Harriet smiled. 'We are so looking forward to it, Sheila and I.' Sheila was Harriet's best friend, who had surprised her by booking them both on a short cruise on board the *Queen Mary II*.

'It was a good idea of hers,' Charlie said. 'You're due a break. It's your first holiday since John died, isn't it?'

'I do kind of wish you weren't going,' Sally said, quietly. She nodded at Jerome. 'In case I need any help with him. It'll be hard, knowing you're not around.'

'Sal, it's only – what, six days?' Charlie said, looking at Harriet for confirmation.

'Five nights. Yes, just a short cruise. Do you really want me to stay home? I could cancel …'

'Well, I …' Sally began, but her husband held up his hand to stop her.

'Not at all, we wouldn't hear of it. You deserve a break. You've had a tough time, and you've done so much for us. Jerome's doing fine at the moment. You go and enjoy the cruise, and make sure you bring back lots of photos. Don't worry about us.' He glared at Sally who'd looked as though she was about to say something else about it.

Harriet sighed. She wanted to enjoy the cruise, but she knew she would worry that something might happen with Jerome and Sally would need her help while she was away. Sheila had booked it back in January before she knew about the little boy's diagnosis, and while Sally had been originally enthusiastic about the idea, now she seemed to be against it. But it was only five nights. And Charlie was right – she was more than ready for a break.

Chapter 4

Emma, 1911

Emma rushed home feeling as though she could burst with her exciting news. As she turned into the familiar street, she paused for a moment. Ma would be pleased for her but also sad that she was leaving home. Ruby would be jealous, wanting excitement for herself, and resentful that she'd have to take on more responsibility at home. And Lily would be excited but would miss her. Perhaps Emma should tone down her enthusiasm a little. There were two weeks left until the ship was due to arrive in Southampton. She had to work out her notice at the hotel, and put together a trunk of personal things to take on board. She'd been given a list of suggested items. She'd been advised she would be issued with a uniform when she first went on board. Violet had been helpful – adding a few essentials to the list ('Bring a photograph of your family,' she'd suggested, 'in case you feel homesick') and crossing off things she said she'd never seen the need for.

Emma arranged her face into an expression of quiet, under-stated happiness as she approached the house. Today there was no grumpy Ruby on the step. She opened the door – it was rarely locked – and stepped inside. Ma was in the kitchen, elbow deep in pastry-making and Lily was helping her.

'Well?' Ma said, pausing in her kneading of the pastry mix. 'Any luck?'

'She's got the job, you can tell by her face!' Lily squealed with excitement and jumped up to give Emma a hug.

'Did you, lovey?'

Emma nodded, unable to stop herself breaking into a huge grin. Well, Lily was excited for her at least, Ma looked pleased, and there was no sign of Ruby. Perhaps she was out with her friends. She wouldn't be at work at this hour. 'I certainly did, Ma, and I start in two weeks when the ship arrives here from Liverpool after its ocean tests.'

'Oh, that's marvellous! Very exciting, and I am so pleased for you, really I am. Two weeks!' Ma rinsed her floury hands, wiped them on her apron and enfolded Emma into a hug, but not before Emma had caught the tell-tale glint of tears in her eyes.

'The maiden voyage is over to New York and back. I'll be away only about three weeks on this first one, and back before you know it,' Emma said, hoping this would settle Ma. 'The lovely thing about living in Southampton is that as soon as the ship's docked and my duties are done I'll be able to get back here in minutes.' Emma smiled at Lily. 'And I'll be full of stories of life at sea, just you wait!'

Lily clapped her hands with glee. She was almost 12 but still loved it when Emma came to sit on her bed at bedtime and tell her stories, either made up or anecdotes of things that had happened in the hotel. 'It will be so wonderful! Oh, I wish I could go!'

Ma smiled. 'You're too young, Lily. Thankfully, so is Ruby, though I would lay good money on the idea that she'll follow you to sea in a year or two, Emma.'

Emma hoped so. Ruby tended to want to go her own way, rather than follow in Emma's footsteps but perhaps the lure of the excitement of crossing the ocean would tempt her. 'Where is Ruby, Ma? I want to tell her my news.'

Ma rolled her eyes. 'She's out somewhere. I don't know where and I don't know who with. She came home from work, changed into her blue dress and dabbed a bit of my rouge on her cheeks. Then she sang out, "see you later, Ma" and was gone before I could say a word to her.'

'Want me to go and look for her?' Emma really didn't want to go out again that day, especially as it had started to rain, but if Ma was worried she'd do whatever she could to help.

'Ah no, lovey. You sit down and let me put the kettle on. Ruby'll be back soon, no doubt, in time for her tea at least. She's wayward, but not daft.'

Emma smiled, and pulled out a chair from under the kitchen table. She should make the most of being at home with Ma and her sisters, Lily at least, while she still could. She'd miss them when she was away, she knew it. That thought reminded her of Violet's advice. 'Ma, I would like a photograph taken of our family, that I can take to sea with me, to look at if I feel lonely. I know it's expensive, but I'll pay … could we do this, please?'

She'd assumed her mother would dismiss the idea as frivolous and too expensive, but to her surprise Ma nodded. 'What a wonderful idea, lovey. I'd like a photograph of my three girls too, to sit on my mantelpiece. Shall we see if we can arrange it all this week? Ruby has a day off on Friday.'

'That would be lovely. I'd like you in the picture too, Ma,' Emma said.

But Ma shook her head. 'Ah no, not me. I'm too old, and have nothing I could wear for a photograph. Just you three pretty girls, I think.'

'Me, in a photograph!' Lily was delighted by the idea. 'May I have a copy of it too?'

'Yes, I think we should have a copy each,' Emma said, though privately she wondered whether Ruby would cherish the picture quite as much as she, Lily, and Ma would.

*

At last, in the early hours of June 3rd, RMS *Olympic* docked at Southampton. Emma had decided to stay up and see its arrival – after all her home was only a few minutes' walk away so once the ship had docked she would be able to go home and catch some sleep. To her surprise she was far from being the only person waiting at the dockside. She estimated there must have been a few thousand people thronging the roads and quayside, all waiting for that first glimpse of the famous new liner. For Emma, of course, there was the additional thrill of seeing for the first time the ship that was to be her home, for a few weeks at least, possibly for years if she decided to sign on for further voyages – and of course if the White Star Line wanted to keep her on. She knew she was tremendously lucky getting a place on this maiden voyage. 'Usually they only take experienced people for first voyages,' Violet Jessop had told her, 'but I know they are short, as this ship is so large and needs so many staff and crew. And you have the right experience from your hotel work.'

Emma found a spot to stand on the new dock that had been built specifically to accommodate the enormous new liner. It had not quite been completed yet but was to be used for the *Olympic*'s berth anyway. She watched as the huge ship made its way slowly up Southampton Water, accompanied by five tugboats. Even in the dark, what a tremendous sight it was – the long, sleek hull of the ship, the several decks of the superstructure lit up from within, all topped by four backwards-leaning funnels.

'Magnificent,' she whispered to herself, as inch by inch the tugs manoeuvred the ship into position alongside the dock. Now it was towering over her, and she had to crane her neck to see the top decks. How on earth were people to get on board, she wondered. As the ship berthed a huge cheer went up from the waiting crowd.

'That was worth staying up for,' said a woman standing along-side Emma. 'Something to tell the grandchildren about in years to come. Marvellous, isn't it, that they can build ships as big as this, sail them all the way across the ocean and back. They say nothing can sink this ship, or its sisters that are still being built. My, how I'd like to see what it's like on board!'

Emma smiled to herself. In two days' time, when the crew and staff were due to board, she would see for herself the grandeur of the ship. How lucky was she? All those years ago, when she'd been a child living in Sandown on the Isle of Wight, she'd so often watched the great liners as they made their way around the island at the start of their long journeys to exotic places all over the world. She'd stood on the beach there so many times, waving and jumping up and down, even though she knew the ships were too far off for anyone on board to see her. Still, she'd tell herself, maybe someone on board had binoculars and would spot her and wonder who she was.

And now, it would be Emma herself rounding the island on board a great ship. She resolved to wave in case a child was watching from the beach. Maybe they too might then grow up to a career at sea, just as she had.

The farewells to Ma, Lily and Ruby had been an odd mixture of joyful yet tearful, with the expected touch of resentment from Ruby that Emma had forced herself to ignore. Lily had coughed a little as she hugged her goodbye, and Emma had prayed her little sister wasn't about to have another relapse while she was away. But as she strode along the street towards the docks, carrying a bag that contained her personal items, she found herself looking only forward, to her great adventure. Once on board ship she'd be reunited with her trunk and would be issued with her stewardess's uniform. Her stomach flipped with excitement as she imagined herself getting settled in a cabin, putting on her uniform, reporting for duty.

As she neared the great ship, which managed to look even more magnificent in the daylight, she wondered how on earth she'd ever learn her way around it. Hopefully there'd be a comprehensive tour for the crew, and maybe she'd be issued with a map. She hoped too, that she would quickly manage to meet up with Violet Jessop again. It felt good to know there was a friend on board.

A clerk from the White Star Line was standing by one of the gantries that provided access to the ship for passengers and crew. He was ticking off names from a list as people approached. Emma followed a couple of men, hoping they were crew like her and she wasn't about to make a huge mistake and try to board by a passenger entrance.

'Name?' asked the clerk as she came alongside him.

'E-Emma Higgins,' she stuttered, and the clerk scanned through his list of names, before making a tick beside one.

'Stewardess, second class. Inside, turn left, report to the chief steward Mr Latimer. Next!' and with that, the clerk turned to a man behind her, who gave his name and occupation as stoker and was directed down to the boiler rooms.

Emma walked across the gantry, not daring to look down into the cold dark depths of the harbour. To think, the next dry land she trod on might well be in New York! That is, if she didn't leave the ship again before it sailed. She followed the clerk's instructions and found herself in a large room where many men and some women were standing, waiting. There was a hubbub of conversation going on, and an air of excitement at being on board the largest, newest liner in the world. Emma cast about looking for Violet, or failing that, any friendly looking face. In the end she found herself staring at a young man with blond hair and the beginnings of a moustache, who looked as lost as she felt.

'So many people!' he said to her, catching her looking his way. 'My name's Martin, by the way. Martin Seward. I'm a steward.'

'Emma Higgins, stewardess,' she replied, shaking the hand he'd offered. He grinned at her, and she felt that here too was someone she might be friendly with.

'What class?'

'Second, I think,' she replied. 'You?'

'Same. Only those with lots of experience get to work first class. Mind you, from what I hear the first-class passengers are much harder to manage.'

'Have you been to sea before?' Emma asked, feeling vaguely disappointed that he seemed to know more about it all than she did. She didn't want to be the only person new to this work.

'Only a couple of times, on the *Majestic*,' he replied. 'It's nothing like this. Not that we've seen much of the *Olympic* yet. I can't wait for the tour ...' He broke off as a bearded man in a smart uniform had climbed onto a small platform and was calling the gathering to order.

Emma listened closely as the various speakers introduced themselves. The first man was none other than Captain Smith, who was to command the ship on her maiden voyage. He seemed to inspire awe and respect in the crew members who'd met him before. 'An excellent captain,' Martin whispered to Emma. And then there were a few words from Thomas Andrews who had designed the ship, Purser McElroy, and the chief steward Mr Latimer, explaining what was to happen over the next few days as the ship was made finally ready to greet its first passengers.

At last the speeches were over, and after a smattering of applause the crew were split into groups according to their role. Emma and Martin went to the side of the room with the other second-class stewards. Emma caught a glimpse of Violet across the room, but she had joined the group of first-class stewards and hadn't seen Emma. Emma hoped she'd find a chance later to track Violet down.

And then it was time for the long awaited tour of the ship. They went in groups, concentrating on the areas they'd need to know best, but were taken to all main areas. Emma's head spun as she was shepherded through room after room, all decorated and furnished sumptuously. The second-class smoking room, with its geometric patterned carpet, oak panelling, and leather armchairs. The second-class dining salon, its ceiling of patterned

40

plaster and its snowy white tablecloths echoing each other. 'If these are the second-class rooms, what on earth are the first-class ones like?' she whispered to Martin, as they were led past a well-equipped gymnasium, a Turkish bath and even a swimming pool. 'A swimming pool! In a ship!' Emma was astounded by the very idea of such a thing.

A little later they were taken into the first-class lounge, furnished in what they were proudly told was Louis XV style, with elegant sofas, chairs, and coffee tables arranged in groups and moulded wall panels surrounding gilt mirrors. It took Emma's breath away. She had never seen anything as grand and opulent before. There were more smoking rooms and dining rooms, a library, a barber's shop, and magnificent staircases leading from one deck to another. They were shown a glimpse of some first-class cabins. 'In case you are asked by your second-class passengers what they could expect if they ever travelled first class,' explained the chief steward. These were gloriously decorated, in Queen Anne style, Louis XVI style, or what Mr Latimer described as 'modern Dutch' style. All held beds adorned with thick satin eiderdowns and the plumpest pillows Emma had ever seen. As well as beds and wardrobes they contained armchairs and writing desks in separate sitting rooms, and each had its own private bathroom.

The second-class cabins were decorated in a more restrained manner but still to Emma's eyes looked the height of luxury. Bathrooms were shared here, but had heating and electric lights that came on automatically when the door was opened.

At last they were taken to see the crew's quarters and allocated to a cabin. Emma felt she must have walked several miles down endless corridors by the time she reached the one she was to share with another girl. ('They're not called corridors on a ship, they're galleys,' Martin had corrected her, 'and not walls – bulkheads.' She'd smiled and thanked him, and he'd blushed in response.)

The girl sharing her cabin introduced herself as Mary, and like Martin she'd worked on RMS *Majestic* before being picked to work the maiden voyage of the *Olympic*. 'I'd rather have stayed on the *Majestic*,' she confided. 'Smaller ships are less work. I fear this one's going to be tough.'

'Are you first or second class?' Emma asked.

'First.' Mary rolled her eyes. 'The fussy ones who seem to think stewards and stewardesses need no sleep whatsoever. "Oh, be a love and get me a gin and tonic, ice and lemon, and a slice of strawberry gateau," they say, "and bring it to my cabin." At midnight! And then at six o'clock in the morning they'll be wanting you to take darling Poochikins for his morning constitutional on deck, while they have a lie-in. You're lucky to be working second class. Those people are so much more reasonable in their demands, and they do seem to remember that we lowly stewards are human too.'

Emma laughed at Mary's mimicry of the spoilt first-class ladies, and felt thankful she had not been assigned to them. Second class she'd be able to deal with, she thought.

Her trunk had been delivered to her cabin, and she spent the next hour unpacking and making friends with Mary, who also knew Violet Jessop from previous ships. That was three people she knew and felt could be her friends, already! As Emma placed her copy of the photograph of Ruby, Lily and herself that they'd had taken the previous week on top of her night-stand she knew she'd made the right decision taking this job.

The days passed quickly on board the ship, as it was made ready to sail. Emma and a few other new stewards were given intensive training in what their duties were. On the 10th of June, the public were allowed on board to view the ship, and Emma was kept busy showing people around and serving refreshments, then clearing up after them. That night she was exhausted and fell into bed with burning feet.

'We're lucky – they've all left the ship now. Wait till we have passengers staying on board, and still ringing for us after we've gone to bed,' Mary said, with a roll of her eyes.

When the passengers boarded, Emma introduced herself to those in the cabins she was assigned to look after – she was working alongside Martin, she was pleased to note. He was responsible for the male passengers in their set of cabins, while she looked after the females. They had a mixture of elderly couples, young newlyweds looking to make their home in New York, and a few families with children. When she first met them Emma thought all of them seemed pleasant enough people. One or two of the older women might perhaps prove to be a little harder work than the others, but their early requirements seemed no more excessive than she'd been used to from her job in the hotel.

And finally, the big day came. On the 14th of June, a band played, and a huge crowd turned out to see the ship leave its berth and set sail on its maiden voyage. A deafening blast on its foghorn announced the departure. Five tugs were needed, just as when the *Olympic* had docked, less than two weeks earlier. To think, back then she'd watched the ship come in, and now she knew her way around it, and had lived aboard it for a week! Emma was on deck along with almost everyone else as the ship inched its way backwards, down Southampton Water until it reached the mouth of the Itchen, in which it was able to swing round, be freed from the tugs and make its way down towards the Solent, around the Isle of Wight past Sandown and out into the English Channel. Emma stayed on deck as long as she could – she could make out Ma and her sisters waving at her from the dock – but once the ship had turned she knew she had to go below and attend to her duties. The ship was due to put in at Cherbourg in France and then Queenstown in Ireland before setting off across the Atlantic. Emma could not believe that by the time she returned to Southampton she'd have had sight of three other countries – France, Ireland, and the United States of America! Not only that, but there were rumours the *Olympic* was going to try to beat the record for the trans-Atlantic crossing. And Emma was on board, playing her own small part in making sure everything went as smoothly as possible. She needed a far bigger word than 'excited' to describe the way she felt.

'Isn't it all stupendous?' Martin had appeared alongside her at the deck railing.

Emma grinned and nodded. Yes, stupendous. That was the word.

Chapter 5

Harriet

After Sally, Charlie, and Jerome had left, taking the old trunk with them, Harriet spent a little while going through another box Charlie had brought down for her. It contained mostly framed pictures from her mother's house. Many of them would be destined for the charity shop, but buried deep in the box was a photograph of Harriet and her brother Matthew as teenagers. She gazed at it wistfully, remembering how much she'd worshipped her older brother in those days.

She placed the photo on her mantelpiece along with the ones from her grandmother's trunk and was sitting down with a well-earned cup of tea, when her phone rang. The display announced the call was from a withheld number. 'Either a cold call or her ladyship,' Harriet muttered as she answered it, but inside her stomach was in knots as she fervently wished it would be Davina. It had been several months since she'd heard from her.

'Harriet? It's me. Davina.' As always, it grated a little that Davina would not call her 'Mum' but nevertheless Harriet was delighted to hear from her, even if she felt the familiar little pang of dread that maybe Davina was phoning with bad news.

'Hello, love. Lovely to hear from you. Is everything all right? How are the girls?'

'They're fine. How are you?' It was typical of Davina to give minimum information about her daughters, and instantly change the subject. Harriet had tried hard over the years not to push her, but just to chat normally and hope Davina would release a few more snippets about the girls. The best thing she could do was give Davina space and time, as much as she needed, but always to let her know she'd be welcomed if or when she wanted to return. But it was so hard, especially after all these years.

'I'm fine, too. Sally's helping me clear out the attic. She thinks I should move to a smaller house.' As soon as she said this she regretted it – it made Sally sound too controlling, and was just the sort of comment that would wind Davina up.

'That's just like Sally. She's so bossy. What do *you* want to do, Harriet? I mean, don't move house if you'd rather stay there, with all the memories of Dad.'

Harriet flinched as Davina referred to John as 'Dad', despite refusing to call her 'Mum'. 'Well, there are lots of memories here, it's true. But this is a big house, as you know, and I'm rattling around in it on my own, and it takes so much effort to maintain it. So I suppose she's right – I should sell up and buy something smaller. It'll only get harder as I become older. Anyway, it's not on the market yet but she's helping me thin everything down, on the days when Jerome's ... well enough to be at school.' As she spoke she remembered that Jerome's diagnosis had come since Davina's last phone call.

'Well *enough*? What's wrong with him?'

Harriet took a deep breath. 'Davina, there's some bad news. Poor little Jerome – he's 6 now, you know – has been diagnosed with leukaemia. Acute lymphoblastic leukaemia, to give it the full name.'

'Oh no! Poor little thing. How's Sally taking it?'

'Badly, as you might imagine. He's on chemotherapy and sometimes he feels too tired and ill to go to school. But when he's between cycles he goes back to school, which he loves, and it gives Sally a bit of a break as well.'

'Must be horrible. God I can't imagine how I'd cope if Autumn or Summer got something like that. They're everything to me.'

'Yes, Jerome's everything to Sally and Charlie. But we're praying for the best for him.'

'Of course.'

There was a moment's silence, and Harriet let it last, allowing Davina time to absorb the news about Jerome. When she heard Davina sigh, she broke the silence. 'So, where are you living now, Davina?'

'Oh, just … in a house.'

'Whereabouts? Anywhere near me? I'd love to visit, meet my granddaughters …'

'Ah, no. Too far for you to visit. I'm not in the UK.'

'Where, then?'

'Well … France.'

'Whereabouts in France? I mean, it's easy to fly to Paris or Nice, or I could drive to one of the Channel ferry ports if you're in the north …'

'Just France. Does it matter?'

This was what happened every time, Harriet knew, and yet she still could not stop herself getting angry. 'Of course it matters, Davina. You're my daughter, your daughters are my grandchildren, and you've never even let me meet them. It's so unfair! I mean, why can't you at least phone me weekly, or let me have your number so I can call you. Jerome's diagnosis came months ago and I've only just been able to tell you. He's your nephew! Why can't you come over and visit us now and again – not often, I know you like your independence, but would it be too much for you to come a couple of times a year? Even just once a year?

Maybe drop the girls off to stay with me for a few days in the summer holidays – all my friends who are grandmothers have the kids to stay. I'd love to be able to take them to the beach, buy them ice creams—'

'Summer hates ice cream,' Davina interrupted. 'The only kid ever to hate ice cream.'

'You see? I didn't even know that. I should know that sort of thing about my 8-year-old granddaughter.' Harriet took a deep shuddering breath. 'And your dad died without ever meeting them.'

'Yeah, I'm kind of sorry about that,' Davina said quietly.

'So you should be. At this rate *I'll* die without meeting them too. Will you bring them over? Or at least call me more often, maybe fortnightly?'

There was a long drawn-out sigh from the other end of the line. 'Harriet, the reason I don't call very often is because you always get upset. Like you are now. I find that hard to handle.'

'I'm only upset because I don't get to speak to you often enough! If you phoned regularly, I wouldn't get upset!'

'Yes, you would. You'd get upset about something else. Me not visiting, perhaps. And if I visited you every year, you'd be upset because I didn't come every month. And if I came every month you'd be upset because I didn't live round the corner from you. I can't win, you see?' Davina took a deep, shuddering breath. 'You and Sally – you were always nagging me to do what you wanted. What you expected. Take my A levels, go to university, have a big white wedding and settle down in a semi. I didn't want all that. I wanted freedom and adventure and to be my own person. But you wouldn't accept it. Christ you even tried to *force* me to come home that time. That was unforgivable. Even now you won't accept me living my own life, the way I want to. That's why I'm better off keeping my distance.'

Every phone call went this way. Every single time. It was mostly Davina being selfish, but Harriet knew the only way through this was for her to take the blame herself. And to be fair, she wasn't entirely blameless anyway. 'All right, I'm sorry. I shouldn't have pushed you. Maybe though, can we compromise? If you promise to ring every two weeks, I'll promise not to ask for more. At least so I can update you about Jerome.'

'Three weeks.'

'You'll ring every three weeks?' That was much more often than had recently been the case.

'If you promise not to nag me for more.'

'I promise.' Harriet was relieved – she hadn't thought for a moment Davina would agree. But maybe her daughter was mellowing, at last. A little. 'So, tell me a bit about your life at present.'

'What do you want to know?'

'Anything you're happy to share.' *There's no point asking questions*, Harriet wanted to add. Davina would only close up, as she had done when Harriet had tried to find out where she was living.

'Well, I've moved in with James. In France, as I said. He works for an international company. He's an accountant.'

'An accountant!'

Davina laughed. 'Yeah, I know, a bit different to dating a rock musician. He's nice, though. Good with the girls.'

'I'm so glad. They need …' Harriet trailed off, thinking but not wanting to say 'a father figure' or 'a bit of stability' for fear of upsetting Davina.

'And the girls are in school, now. No more home-schooling. Didn't I tell you that last time?'

'You did, yes. Is it a French school?'

'International. They are learning French but take most lessons in English.'

'So they'll be bilingual.'

'They already are, more or less. Their French is a lot better than mine. And I'm fairly fluent now.'

Harriet was surprised – at school Davina had never paid much attention to languages. Perhaps she'd lived in France for some time. She sighed. There was so much about her daughter that she didn't know.

'Well, if you're back to sighing at me I'll say goodbye. I'll ring again in three weeks. Hope Sally's kid gets better. Cheers, then.' And Davina hung up before Harriet had a chance to say goodbye herself.

She sat cradling the phone for a moment, remembering all that Davina had told her, wishing she'd kept her temper and not criticised Davina – maybe she would have stayed on the phone longer if Harriet had been calm. She let the tears fall down her cheeks but at the same time felt hopeful that with calls every three weeks perhaps Davina was softening a little. Possibly beginning to forgive them for trying to make her conform when she was a teenager. Growing up. Maybe this new chap – James – was a good influence. Part of her wanted to call Sally and tell her what she'd heard from Davina, but then she imagined Sally scoffing and complaining that Davina still hadn't given Harriet a way of contacting her, even in an emergency, so she decided not to. When Sally next came round she'd tell her then.

She glanced at the photo of Gran and her two sisters. Had they had some sort of rift, like Sally and Davina? Harriet had always got on well with her own brother. They'd been great friends as children. Somehow, though, as adults they'd drifted apart. Now she struggled to remember the last time she'd actually seen him, though they sent each other Christmas and birthday greetings and occasional letters.

As well as rebuilding a relationship with Davina for herself, to regain her daughter and see her granddaughters, Harriet's deepest wish was that her two daughters would eventually become close again. Sisters – siblings – were important. You shared so much with them when you were young. No other friend could ever replace them. But for that to happen, there'd be a lot of forgiveness needed first. On both sides.

Even now, so many years on, Harriet still found it hard to think about that day. She was ashamed at her part in it, however minor it had been. She never spoke about it with Sally – of course they had back then, when it happened, but never now.

It was about two months after Davina left with Hades Rising. Two months of sporadic phone calls and a couple of postcards. Two months of missing Davina so much that it hurt, but still expecting that she'd come back at the end of the tour. Letting her have her freedom, as John put it, allowing her to spread her wings and find her own way.

But Sally hadn't seen it like that. Looking back, Harriet wondered if there'd been a touch of jealousy. Sally had never done anything so dramatic as run away with a rock band. Her life had always been planned in detail. She'd always known what her future held – school, university, get a job, marry and settle down, have kids. It was as though she had a mental tick-list that she was working through, whereas Davina had a set of dice that she rolled to make her life choices.

Sally was 20 at the time. She had a boyfriend she'd been with since sixth-form college days – a young man named Lucas who'd completed a couple of years as an apprentice plumber and now was setting up in business by himself. Harriet had never been quite sure how much she liked him. He was too brash for her liking. He was, she suspected, the kind of man who secretly would prefer women to be kept indoors, cooking meals and raising kids, rather than having careers of their own. He was good-looking and charming though, and this was, she assumed, what had attracted Sally. Nevertheless, she harboured hopes that the relationship would not last. Sally could surely do better, and find a man who would appreciate her abilities and allow – no, *expect* – her to be independent.

That day – that awful day – had begun when Sally received a phone call from Lucas. She was home from university for the summer, staying in her old childhood bedroom and seeing Lucas

51

several times a week. Sally had taken the phone into the sitting room, away from Harriet who was still clearing up after breakfast. She'd returned flushed and excited.

'Lucas has found out where Davina is. For tonight, anyway. Hades Rising's tour has brought them to Weymouth – they're playing some small venue in the town. We're going to go – see the band, try to go backstage after and find Davina. At least talk to Jez and find out how she is.'

'Oh my word!' Harriet had clapped a hand to her mouth. 'That'll be lovely for you. There's another month left on the tour, Davina said when she last called. It'll be wonderful if you can see her today. Ask her if she's coming home. And let me know if Hades Rising is any good!'

'You could come with us, Mum. It's not far to Weymouth. Lucas said he'll drive, in his van. It fits three on the bench seat.'

'Oh, I'd love to ...' Harriet considered. John was not at home – he'd gone to spend a few days with his elderly and ailing mother, in north London.

Sally grinned. 'Right then. I'll call Lucas back, and we'll sort out the details.'

And so, later that day, the three of them set off in Lucas's battered white Transit van, for Weymouth. They found a parking spot near the venue, and had a late lunch in a nearby pub. Sally seemed on edge – nervous, Harriet assumed, at how Davina would react to them just turning up like this. Lucas seemed to be trying to calm her down. When Harriet returned from a visit to the ladies' he had his hand on her shoulder and was whispering intently to her. He broke off as soon as he caught her eye.

'So I'm thinking,' Lucas said, 'that they'll be in there, setting up by now. It probably takes a while, getting all the amps and mics and everything sorted. So we could see if we can get in. I bet Davina'll be there. Didn't she say she helps the roadies?'

Harriet felt a flutter of excitement at the idea she might see Davina in potentially a few minutes. There might be awkwardness

– but if they didn't talk about the way Davina had left so suddenly, without warning, then maybe all would be well. John had said: let her be, let her do her own thing, and in time she'll come back. And that was what she'd tried so hard to do, these last couple of months.

They went around to the back of the theatre, and found the doors by which equipment was taken in and out. They were standing open, and a couple of vans were parked nearby. A man in a black T-shirt and ripped jeans approached. 'Excuse me, this area is not open to the public ...'

'Ah, sorry mate. We were just looking for someone. Jez Trethgow, if he's around, or better still, Davina Wilson. We're family.' Lucas sounded confident and friendly, and Harriet felt glad he'd come. She'd probably have stuttered and apologised and ended up leaving without seeing her daughter.

'Oh, right. I'll just see ...' The man gestured inside and headed towards the door. 'Wait here.'

A few moments later Jez emerged, clutching a takeaway coffee. He frowned when he saw them. 'Oh. You want Dav, then. Not sure if ...' He waved his hand vaguely in the air.

'Please Jez. If she's there, let her know we're here,' Sally said. 'Tell her ... I have something for her. For her birthday. It's next week. She'll be 18. Can't let that pass without ... presents from her family.'

Harriet was surprised – Sally hadn't said anything about bringing presents for Davina. For herself, she'd planned to transfer money into Davina's bank account as her present, thinking that money was probably what she would most need.

'Oh. Well, I suppose.' Jez shrugged moodily and went back inside.

The wait, wondering whether Davina would come out, was tough to bear. Harriet wanted to dart inside the theatre, following the roadies who were still unpacking equipment and throwing them puzzled glances now and again. Lucas moved close to Sally and muttered something, and Sally, looking anxious, nodded.

Finally, there she was. Dressed in a tight sleeveless top with 'Hades Rising' printed across her chest, and jeans even more ripped than Jez's had been. Hair with a bright pink streak down one side, and sporting a nose piercing she hadn't had before. Davina. She smiled nervously when she saw them, as though wondering how she'd be received. But Harriet held out her arms and Davina ran the last few steps across the yard and into them.

Harriet revelled in the embrace for a moment, ignoring the distinctive scent of cannabis smoke that clung to her daughter's clothes. 'Good to see you, love. How is the tour going?'

'Oh, you know. Good, mostly. Hard work. I'm not coming home, Mum – not now, you get that, right?'

'Of course. We've come to see the gig, and see how you are.' Sally had stepped forward. Davina didn't hug her though, just looked at her quizzically.

'You were never interested in Jez's music, Sal.'

'I am now though, now that you're touring with them,' Sally said. She glanced at Lucas. 'Hey, listen, I've your present in the van. Come and see.'

'In the van? Couldn't you—'

'Wasn't sure if we'd find you, so I left it in there. Come on, come and get it then we can perhaps have a drink or something before the gig.'

Davina shrugged. 'OK then.' She followed Sally down the side of the theatre and back to the quiet side-street where Lucas had parked the van. Harriet followed them and Lucas, wondering what this present was that Sally had kept so quiet about.

'What is it, then? I'm all on tenterhooks!' Davina gave a little laugh. 'Come on, Mum, spill the beans.'

'I don't know, love.' She genuinely didn't.

'It's a secret from Mum, too. You'll see.'

They'd reached the van, and Lucas unlocked the back doors. 'It's in there,' he said.

'Can't you bring it out?'

'Easier if you get in, to see it,' Lucas said, with a twisted smile.

Davina glanced at Sally who nodded, biting her lip. Harriet frowned. What was in the back of the van?

Davina put her hand on the van's door, and lifted a leg to climb in. At that moment Lucas shoved her hard, bundling her into the back of the van, and Sally stepped forward, blocking the way and pushing on the other door. Davina screamed. 'What the fuck? Sally, what's going on?'

Harriet cried out, too. 'Lucas, stop it, you'll hurt her. Sally, what is this?' She caught Sally's arm and tried to pull her away, but Sally shook her off. Davina was kicking and screaming, and Sally was looking scared, glancing along the street as if checking no one was near.

Lucas grunted in pain as Davina's foot caught him on the knee cap. 'Bitch! Just get in there!'

'No, I fucking won't! Help!' Davina shouted out, and at the same time Sally hissed urgently, 'Lucas, there's someone coming!'

Harriet turned to see a young couple hurrying up the road towards them.

'What's going on? Did someone shout for help?' the man called out.

Lucas had stepped back, letting go of Davina when Sally warned him. 'It's nothing, we're cool, thanks mate.' The couple stood a little way off, watching, as though they'd step in and help if needed.

Davina climbed out and glared at Lucas, Sally and Harriet. 'I don't know what game you were playing, but it's over. I'm going back to Jez. You're not going to fucking *abduct* me. For God's sake, Mum, I can't believe you went along with this – *you*? I bet Dad doesn't know. Christ, you're all so … just …' She shook her head, as though she'd run out of words, and began walking towards the young couple.

'Davina, I knew nothing of this,' Harriet began. 'Whatever they'd planned, it wasn't anything to do with me.'

'Mum, we were doing it for you,' Sally said, her voice sounding distressed that it had all gone so wrong. 'You've said so many times you just want her back.'

'Not like this, love, not like this.' Harriet was sobbing. How had this happened, how had she allowed it to happen?

Davina reached the watching couple and reassured them she was all right, and that she didn't need the police. She turned back for a moment. 'That's it, Mum. That's it, for good. Have a good life, all. I'm done.' Head high, she marched off, the witnesses walking with her as escorts.

Sally sat in the back of the van, head in hands. 'We messed that up, Lucas. We really did.'

He shrugged. 'I tried, Sal. Bitch kicked me in the knee. The one I injured playing footie. That'll be more physiotherapy I need.' He rubbed his kneecap and stared at Harriet and then Sally. 'So, I guess we're not going to the gig after all then. I'm driving back to Bournemouth now, if you want a lift.'

Harriet was still staring after Davina as she walked away from them, down the road and round the corner. She willed her daughter to look back to see how anguished she was, how sorry, even though it hadn't been anything to do with her. But Davina did not look back, not even the slightest glance, and Harriet knew in that moment that she'd lost her. They'd all lost her.

Chapter 6

Emma, 1911

Emma could not believe how quickly her first voyage on the *Olympic* had gone by. On the one hand it seemed like months since she'd sailed out of Southampton, first waving at her family, then watching as they passed by Netley Abbey and the huge military hospital, then marvelling at the white cliffs of St Catherine's Point on the Isle of Wight … and then all the countless other sights she'd glimpsed from portholes and when she'd gone out on deck to assist her passengers. Cherbourg, Queenstown, the long days crossing the north Atlantic, then the excitement of spotting land once more and finally docking at New York to as much fanfare as there had been in Southampton. So much had happened. She'd been kept very busy by her passengers, and had rarely managed more than about five hours' sleep a night.

Her day would start at six o'clock, when she'd rise, wash and dress, have a quick breakfast in the stewards' canteen and then set off to her passengers' cabins. She was looking after a couple of families who always wanted help dressing their children each day. How they managed when at home she had no idea, but on board ship they seemed unable to find shoes, to buckle belts or fasten buttons. Then an old lady who was travelling alone would need her to pick out an outfit and jewellery for the day, before escorting her to the breakfast salon. With everyone up and dressed and at breakfast, she'd then need to go to each cabin and tidy up – rehanging clothes, straightening bed clothes, and once, mopping up a pile of vomit from beside the bed.

By lunchtime she'd be tiring, and more than ready for her brief break and a few minutes chatting with Martin, comparing notes about the day so far. He'd make her laugh with his tales, and she'd feel invigorated and ready to face her afternoon duties after a little while in his company.

The passengers tended to spend afternoons on deck, and she'd be kept busy running back and forth fetching them cups of tea, biscuits, coats from their cabins. Or walking their little dogs up and down the decks, while they reclined on deckchairs sipping cocktails. And then it was the children's teatime, followed by their parents needing help dressing for dinner. Emma would snatch a meal for herself once everyone was dressed and heading to the restaurants, but sometimes she'd be kept back babysitting, or tidying cabins. With luck she'd get a couple of hours' leisure time in the stewards' mess, before needing to help unclasp rows of pearls or hang up evening gowns. Undoubtedly one of her passengers would want an item of clothing cleaned before the morning, too. It was often midnight before they were all settled and she could collapse onto her own bed, exhausted.

'It's tough, isn't it?' Mary said, on the third night. 'But in a funny sort of way I do enjoy it, even though the passengers drive me mad at times.'

Emma smiled and nodded. 'Yes, me too. It's hard work, but fun.'

As the ship returned to Southampton and docked once more it seemed like only hours since she'd left. Everything looked just the same. There were some people gathered to see the ship come in, though not nearly as many as had waved her out. Emma had a number of duties to attend to before her contract for this voyage was finished, and as the ship tied up and the passengers got ready to disembark suddenly it seemed as though the time could not go quickly enough. She could not wait to leave the ship, run home to Ma and her sisters, hear all their news and tell them all about her adventures. She'd been able to leave the ship for a few brief hours in New York, and had walked up and down streets marvelling at the enormous buildings soaring above her as she tried to find affordable mementos to bring home.

The passengers' mood was a mix of excitement to have docked and regret at leaving the ship. The *Olympic* had indeed crossed the Atlantic in record time, and the maiden voyage had run smoothly and been a huge success. Many of the passengers who'd been on the outbound crossing were still on the ship for the return, although some had stayed in New York and the ship had picked up some new people. Emma was kept busy tracking down lost items for them as they prepared to disembark – stray shoes, bags, coats, and in one instance, a child who'd taken it upon himself to go and explore the third-class lounge while his frantic mother searched everywhere for him.

At last, with the passengers disembarked, the cabins tidied and awaiting cleaning, and a debriefing session over, it was time to return to her own cabin, pack and say farewell to Mary, Violet, and Martin, and leave the ship herself. She had enjoyed working with Martin.

'Will you sign on again with the *Olympic*?' he asked her.

'I think so, will you?'

'Yes, if you will,' he replied with a smile, and she found herself looking forward to seeing him again.

Her trunk was being kept at the White Star offices until the next voyage. Her discharge book had been stamped and marked 'very good', ready for her to present the next time she signed on.

As Emma walked down the gantry and onto the quayside,

breathing in the salty tang of Southampton's air, she could not stop herself from grinning broadly. She'd done it – she'd been to sea, and she was in all likelihood going to do it again, very soon. This job suited her so well. As long as she wasn't needed at home, she would keep signing on for more and more voyages. Maybe she'd be promoted to first class. Despite Mary's moans about the first-class passengers, she was sure it couldn't be as bad as Mary said. Violet seemed to enjoy working first class, and had nothing but good words to say about her passengers.

There'd been no one to welcome Emma as she stepped off the ship – Ma and her sisters had not known how long it would be before she could disembark. She walked home alone but excited to see her family once again. She had sent a letter from New York but suspected it might have been carried back over the Atlantic on the same ship she was on anyway.

She turned into her street, and was met by a neighbour, Mrs Williams. 'Welcome home, Emma. Good job you're back. Your ma needs you, I'd say.'

Emma's heart gave a lurch. 'Why, Mrs Williams, what's happened? Is it Lily?' Oh God, no. Please let Lily not be sick again. She thought her little sister had fully recovered from the tuberculosis that had plagued her on and off since childhood.

Mrs Williams shook her head. 'No, it's your Ruby's the problem.'

'What is it? Please tell me?'

But Mrs Williams pursed her lips together. 'You'd best just get home and let your ma tell you her worries. Not for me to gossip.'

Emma set off at a run, her overnight bag banging against her hip. She barged in through the front door. 'Ma! I'm home! Is Ruby here? Is she all right? And Lily?'

Her mother emerged from the kitchen, wiping her hands on a tea towel. Was it Emma's imagination or did she look older than when Emma had left? Greyer, more lined? 'Ah lovey, you're home, how wonderful! Lily, your sister's here!' Ma enfolded Emma in a tight hug.

60

'How's Ruby?'

'Ah you know, lovey, she's the same as ever.' Ma looked away as she answered. Emma didn't want to say she'd seen Mrs Williams who'd been gossiping. Whatever it was it couldn't be too serious or Ma would have told her. It was probably just Ruby being Ruby – going her own way, making life hard for herself and the people who loved her.

'And Lily?' Her little sister hadn't come downstairs to greet her, which was worrying.

'Ah, she had a little turn. She's over the worst now, but I've said she's to stay in bed. Go on up, she'll be longing to see you. I'll put the kettle on.'

Emma remembered how Lily had coughed a little as she said goodbye, and felt guilt wash over her. Hopefully Ruby had done her share of nursing and not left it all to Ma. She went upstairs and into Lily's room, where her sister was tucked up in bed, sleeping. She sat for a moment on the end of the bed watching her, and then Lily woke, breaking into a huge smile when she saw Emma there. She sat up and crawled over the bed into Emma's arms.

'You're back at last! Have you stories to tell? What were the cabins like? Was it very beautiful on board? How fast did you sail? Did you get seasick?' Lily's eyes were bright and wide and although she was pale, Emma was pleased to see she had no cough so was definitely recovering.

Emma hugged her sister. 'So many questions! Yes, I have plenty of stories to tell. I will tell you them all, over the next few days. How have you been?'

'I'm fine. Ma's been fussing too much. I'll be back at school next week.'

'Has Ruby helped look after you?'

Lily shrugged. 'A bit. Not the same as having you here though.' She bit her lip. 'That doesn't mean I want you to stay, Ems, and not go on the ship again. I like having a sister who's travelling the world. I can't wait to be back at school and tell my friends!'

'Well, I'm back home for a few days now.'

'What happens after that?' Ma entered the room, carrying a tray holding a tea pot, cups and a plate of biscuits.

'If it's all right with you, Ma, I'd like to sign on for another voyage. I like the work, and enjoy being at sea. But if you need me here …'

Ma turned away, putting the tray down onto Lily's bedside table, and poured out the tea. Emma felt vaguely embarrassed that she was using the best tea pot and not the chipped brown one they usually brought out when it was just for the family. 'Of course you should go again, lovey. Now you're trained and everything, it'd be a shame to waste it. We're all right here, aren't we, Lily?'

Lily nodded. 'As long as I get to see Ems every few weeks.'

'How's Ruby?' Emma asked again.

Ma sighed and sat down heavily. 'That girl. She'll be the death of me, she will.' She shook her head.

Lily stared at her mother. Emma tried to catch her eye, to see if that would give her any clues as to what trouble Ruby might be in but Lily just shrugged. Whatever it was, Ma must have kept it quiet from her youngest daughter. Emma's guess was confirmed when Ma looked at Lily as if remembering she was there, and then closed her mouth firmly. She didn't look as though she'd say anything more about it now. Emma made a mental note to catch her later, or perhaps when Ruby came home, ask her sister herself what was going on.

Ruby didn't return home until the dinner had been cooked, eaten, and cleared away. A plate of mutton stew with dumplings sat cooling beside the stove for her. Lily had been down and eaten a reasonable amount before going back upstairs to bed.

'She's better now you're home,' Ma said. 'Ruby spends no time with her, the poor thing. She's been so lonely.'

Emma sent Ma to relax in the front room while she cleared

up, and washed and dried the dishes. She was just finishing when Ruby finally came home.

'Ah, you're back,' Ruby said, as she entered the house through the back door, from the alleyway that ran behind the row of houses. 'Where's Ma?'

'In the front room,' Emma replied.

Ruby nodded and sat at the kitchen table, watching Emma work. 'So, how was life on board ship? Did you get lots of tips from rich passengers?'

'It was good. I told Ma and Lily lots of stories about it all over dinner. Which you missed.' Emma nodded to the congealed stew. 'Put that in the oven for a bit, it'll be all right then.'

Ruby glanced at the plate of food and shook her head. 'Don't fancy it. I've already eaten something anyway.'

'Where've you been? Ma said she was expecting you hours ago – weren't you on a morning shift today? You should let her know you're back. I think she'll be beginning to worry.' Emma picked up the plate and scraped it off into the scraps bucket. What a waste of food, that they could ill afford.

'I was out. With … friends. Ma won't be worried. I'm often out. Might have escaped your notice, Emma, but I'm a grown woman now. I can make my own decisions.'

'You're 17. Still a girl.'

'A girl who deserves some fun! While you've been away I've had to do all the work here, and nurse Lily who decided to be sick as soon as you went away. I swears she does it on purpose.'

Emma was astounded. 'What a thing to say! She can't help it.' She softened her tone. 'Look, I'm sorry I wasn't here to help with Lily but I wasn't to know that would happen.'

Ruby pushed her chair violently back from the table, knocking it over. 'Right. I'll go tell Ma I'm home, then I'm off upstairs. To get away from *you* and your endless bossiness.' At the kitchen door she stopped and turned back. 'By the way, you're sharing with Lily. I have a room of my own now. Makes

63

sense as you're hardly ever here.' She slammed the door closed on her way out.

Emma realised she was still holding the dirty plate and the knife she'd used to scrape the food off it. She felt stunned. She and Ruby had fallen out before, though never for long. They'd exchange a few cross words and then immediately make up. Never like this. Never door slamming and marching out. She didn't mind Ruby taking over her old room and having it for herself – it did make sense, and it'd be nice to share with Lily who always loved her company. But what was wrong with her? Why was she so aggressive? Just as Ma seemed to have grown older in the few short weeks Emma had been away, so Ruby appeared to have become even more difficult than she had been.

She finished the washing up, put away the plates and wiped the table. Removing her pinny she went through to the front room. Ma was sitting beside the unlit fire, staring at a point on the wall. Although it was dusk the gas lamps were not yet lit. She was alone.

'Did Ruby come in here to see you?' Emma asked, taking a seat opposite her mother.

'She did, yes. For a minute.' Ma let out an enormous sigh.

'She didn't want her dinner. I assume she's gone upstairs? Ma, what's going on with her?'

'Wish I knew, lovey. She's out till all hours – believe me this is early for her to come home. She won't talk to me. She just walks out if I ask her where she's been. I've no control. But if I push her too hard, she might walk out and never come back.'

'She seems resentful that she's had to help look after Lily. Ma, I'm sorry. I won't go back to sea if you need me here.' It broke Emma's heart to say this, but if Ma wanted her, she'd stay.

Ma stared at her. 'What rubbish. *I've* nursed Lily, not Ruby. She did the least possible. And Lily wasn't too poorly this time. I think she's growing out of it.' She sighed. 'I wish I knew what Ruby gets up to when she goes out. Ask around for me, lovey? See if you can find out what she's up to. Maybe she'll talk to you.'

Emma took her mother's hand and squeezed it. 'Of course I'll try. I'll go up now, shall I?'

Ma nodded, and Emma left the room. She held little hope of being able to get through to Ruby. Her sister had not even welcomed her home.

Upstairs, she found Ruby lying on her back on her bed, in the room she and Ruby used to share. That meant Lily was still in the small room, and if Emma was to share that with her it'd be a tight fit. Best not to complain, though, and risk Ruby shouting at her again.

'Rubes? Can I come in?' Emma tapped on the open door.

'Suppose you can.'

Emma slipped through the door, closing it behind her. She'd caught a glimpse of Lily's face, wide-eyed, peeking out from her room. She wanted to talk to Ruby alone, first.

She moved a pair of boots off an old bentwood chair and sat down. 'Rubes, what's happening? Ma seems unhappy. Is there anything I can help with? I don't want to be … bossy … but if I can help at all?' She let the sentence tail away, hoping it might encourage Ruby to open up.

'You can't help. I'm just trying to have a life, that's all. You've got one – you're away on your ship, having adventures, seeing the world. I'm stuck here in dull old Southampton, working my fingers to the bone scrubbing floors in that grotty old hotel, coming home to do the same here as well as play nursemaid to my sister. All I does, that makes Ma so despairing of me, is go out after work with a few friends, when I can.'

'Going out where?'

'Not that it's any of your business, but we goes out for tea, or for a walk in the park, or sometimes to a pub.' Ruby lifted her chin high on the last word.

Ah, Emma understood now. It was the idea of Ruby, who was still just 17 even though she looked much older, going to a pub that Ma would be objecting to. Pubs were for men. Working men, with dirty clothes and blackened hands, men who went for a few pints after their shifts ended, before going home to their worn-out wives and snot-nosed children. Men who kept everything going – miners, shipbuilders, road-menders, labourers. Men whose work was essential, but who were not what Ma considered suitable companions for her daughters. Pa had been that little step up – having a 'clean' job as a hotel porter – and now Ma liked to think she was better than the other women in the street, better than the wives of those men. And yet she worked as a laundress and had encouraged her daughters to work in hotels, as chambermaids.

'It's the pub that's upsetting her, is it?'

Ruby shrugged. 'That and the crowd I goes with.'

'Who are they?'

'Some people from the hotel. And some people they knows. Big crowd.' Ruby turned away, and it was clear Emma would get nothing more from her now.

'All right. Well, I've done what Ma asked and had a chat with you. Maybe all that's needed is you tell Ma if you're going to be late home so she doesn't worry. I can't see what's so bad about going around with a group of people, or going to the pub with them now and again. Just maybe try not to do anything that makes Ma worry, especially if Lily's having a bad day.' Emma tried not to let her tone become bossy, but as the eldest sister it was her place to advise her younger siblings and help them steer a safe path through life. She wanted only what was best for them.

But Ruby, it seemed, was taking her good intentions the wrong way. She was staring at Emma, a look of disdain on her face. 'Ems, you have no bloody idea, and no right to go telling me what to do. If you'll *kindly* leave me alone now, so's I can sleep. And hurry up and bugger off back to sea, out of my life, would you?'

Emma stared back at her sister, wondering where she'd learned to swear like that, but realised there was nothing she could say to make things better. She stood wordlessly and left the room, closing the door firmly behind her.

On the landing Lily was hovering, half in and half out of her room. Her eyes widened as Emma came out of Ruby's room, and she beckoned Emma across into her room – which had an extra bed crammed in under the window. Emma realised that was for her, as Ruby had said she would no longer share a room. 'Ruby's like that all the time now,' Lily said. 'Won't talk to anyone. Gets really cross if you ask her who her friends are. Hates doing anything for me, and I wasn't even that ill this time. Ma's been trying to hide it all from me, but I'm not stupid and I can see what's happening. I thought Ruby might talk to you – I've been longing for you to come back.'

'She won't talk to me,' Emma said.

Lily nodded. 'I heard. Wasn't listening, Ems, but couldn't help but hear.'

'I'll try again in a day or two. Maybe she'll talk to me before I go back to sea.' Emma sat down on the extra bed and smiled at Lily. 'Meanwhile, it's going to be fun sharing a room with you, isn't it?'

'Midnight feasts and pillow fights?'

'If you're well enough ...'

'Course I am!' Lily grabbed her pillow and swung it at Emma, but Emma had anticipated this and managed to get the first hit, eliciting a squeal of excitement and a retaliatory bash with Lily's own pillow. As the fight escalated Emma resolved to enjoy her stay at home as much as possible. If Ruby wouldn't take any well-intentioned advice then so be it. She'd just have to find her own way in the world.

Chapter 7

Harriet

'It's odd,' Harriet said to Sheila on the phone the day after the phone call from Davina, 'the effect finding those photos and the other stuff has had on me.'

'In what way?' Sheila asked, sounding concerned.

Harriet sighed. 'I mean, I should be used to it all by now. And I was prepared to feel emotional going through memorabilia of my life with John, but it's Davina's things, and the photos of me and my brother as children that have really got to me.'

'You weren't prepared to find those, I guess, so they caught you unawares.'

'But I was – I mean, I knew all that stuff was there. It's just that I keep looking at those old photos of my gran and my brother, and the other ones of the four of us – me and John, Sally, and Davina. And then I get all depressed, and feel that I've lost so much. I keep disappearing into memories of old times, wallowing in the past.

'Oh love, shall I come round? You sound like you need cheering up.'

68

Bless Sheila, Harriet thought. A good friend indeed. 'Ah, it's all right. I'm just feeling a bit maudlin I suppose, going through this old stuff. I mean, it's triggering lots of happy memories too. I just wish that there'd been more memories, and that we were still making them now. I miss my family.'

'There's still a chance, always a chance, that Davina will come back to you one day. Never let go of that hope, Harri. What was it you told me once – love is always open arms.'

'Yes, those were John's words.' Harriet smiled at the memory.

'He was a wise man – it's so true. Meanwhile, make the most of Sally and Jerome. The little lad will pull through – I'm sure he will. Bless him.'

'He'd better do. I can't bear the thought that he might not.'

'He will. I looked it up. The odds are good. So, would you like to meet for a coffee soon? Or come round for lunch? I'm at a loose end for most of the week so it'd be nice to see you. And you'll need a break from all that sorting out!'

'You come to me, for lunch. Monday or Tuesday – either. We can discuss our cruise – it's not long now.'

'Perfect, Tuesday works for me,' said Sheila. 'I shall see you then. And you can show me some of these old photos you've found.'

It had become a regular thing for Harriet – once a week she'd take a walk along tree-lined streets of inter-war housing, across a busy shopping street, up a side street past Victorian terraced houses, and into the cemetery. Tucked away on the edge of a large park it was a peaceful spot, as long as you picked a time to visit when Bournemouth weren't playing at home – the foot-ball stadium was on the other side of the park. Wide paths led between trees through the middle of the cemetery. Today was a pleasant day with warm sunshine and enough birdsong to lift her spirits, as Harriet took the familiar right then left turns to the section where John's grave was. She put the pot of purple hyacinths that she'd been carrying beside the headstone, and spent a few minutes tidying the grave up – pulling out a few weeds, gathering up fallen leaves.

'There, John. Those hyacinths should look nice for a few weeks, as long as there's some rain.' She smiled as she put a hand on the gravestone. John had never liked cut flowers. 'Waste of money,' he always said. 'They only last a few days. They're dead when you buy them, and you're then just watching them decay. I much prefer living plants.' And so Harriet had made a point of putting only potted plants on his grave, bringing a plastic bottle of water with her each visit to water them, replacing the pot when the plant stopped flowering. Then she'd bring it home and transfer the plant into her garden.

There was a bench nearby where she often sat to have a conversation with John, as long as there was no one around. It was quiet today, so she took her seat. 'Well, John, here I am again, another week has passed. Actually, it's eight days – I didn't come yesterday because Sally and her family were visiting. And I won't be able to come next week because guess what – Sheila and I are going on a cruise! Isn't that exciting?' She chuckled, as she imagined John rolling his eyes at the news. Cruises had never been his idea of a good holiday. Harriet had always hoped that as they aged she might have been able to talk him into trying one, but she suspected he'd never have agreed.

'Davina rang me again. So good to hear her voice. She's well, and so are her girls. They're living in France now, you know …' Harriet tailed off. There wasn't really much else she could report – Davina had given her very little real news as usual. She sighed. 'Oh John, we ended up rowing. Again. Every time. I know, I know – I must let her take her own course through life. She's an adult. She's free to do whatever she wants, including keeping away from me and keeping her daughters away from me. But, oh John, it does hurt so much.'

It wasn't the first time she'd sat on that bench saying much the same thing. And she suspected it wouldn't be the last. But sometimes it felt as though it helped a little – admitting out loud how difficult it all was and how much it hurt. She sat in silence for a few minutes, listening to a blackbird singing its heart out somewhere high in a tree above her. A tiny wren flew down and landed near the bench, pecking around on the path and she watched its little tail bobbing up and down. Was there any bird more adorable than a wren? John had liked magpies, she remembered. Their personality, the way they asserted their authority over other birds in their territory, the way they'd see off a cat that was threatening their nest. 'Birds are such fabulous parents,' he'd say. 'They protect their chicks; keep them safe in the nest. And then they let them go. When the fledglings are ready to leave the nest, they let them fly high and free, to make their own way in the world. As Davina has.' But that was the hard part, with Davina having flown so distant.

'Love is always open arms. We have to let her go,' he used to say. He'd counselled this the first time back when Sally was 17, beginning to go to parties and come home late and Harriet had fretted about it. He'd said it again when Sally left home to go to university and Harriet had felt like her world was crumbling without her older daughter there. And when she'd spent so much time with Lucas. Perhaps she'd then clung to Davina to make up for missing Sally so much. Looking back, she could see that possibly she'd kept Davina too close, restricting her freedoms more than she had with Sally at that age. Easy to see with hindsight, but at the time Harriet hadn't felt ready to be the mother of two grown-up women. She understood now that in trying to hold on to Davina's childhood, she'd only managed to push her daughter away. She'd wondered if John had been wrong, and that you should hang on to those you love and never let them go. That hadn't worked either. She'd wrapped her arms too tightly around Davina, when she was a teenager. And now she was left holding only herself.

'I don't know what the answer is,' she said to John's gravestone.

71

'I don't know what's best to do. I try to let her lead the way, but in all these years she's made no effort. To think, you never saw her again after she left home at 17. And I only saw her for a couple of minutes at your funeral. She's not been fair to us. If I think about it, it makes me so angry. And that just bubbles up every time I talk to her. I can't help myself. It makes Sally so angry too. I can't even talk to her about it.' She fell quiet, listening, wishing that in the sigh of the wind in the trees, in the song of the blackbird there'd be some comforting words from him. She missed him so much.

'I know we were wrong, trying to force her to come back that time. I mean – Sally and Lucas were wrong. I'd never have let them do it if I'd known! Oh, if I could turn back time to that moment and stop it happening ... Davina might have come home after the tour. Gone back to college. At least stayed in touch more.' As she spoke, the wren looked at her quizzically then flew away.

Her eyes were filling with tears. Realising that there were people approaching – a middle-aged couple meandering their way through the cemetery hand in hand – she quickly dabbed at her eyes with a tissue and took a deep breath. She wasn't in the mood for explaining to well-meaning strangers that she was OK, really she was, and thank you but no there was nothing they could do for her. She smiled at them as they passed, then stood up, bade John's grave a silent farewell, and went on her way.

On Tuesday as planned, Sheila came to Harriet's for lunch, so they could discuss their upcoming cruise. Harriet had no idea what to pack to wear on board, and they needed to arrange travel to the cruise liner terminal.

Sheila arrived with a bottle of wine in her hand. Her hair was wound up in a colourful scarf and her lips were painted her trademark pillar-box red. Harriet smiled as she welcomed her inside. Seeing Sheila always lifted her spirits.

'Come in! I hope you're hungry!'

'Absolutely starving, my dear. Let me get the cork out of this little beauty first, and you can tell me all your news. After that we can talk about the cruise. I can't wait, can you?'

Harriet served up lunch of a quiche and salad and while they ate and sipped a glass of wine, she updated Sheila about Davina's phone call, and the old trunk she'd found in the attic. She fetched the photo of the three girls to show Sheila.

'It seems my gran had a second sister, one she never talked about. I know one died young, but what of the other girl?'

'Hmm. They certainly look alike,' Sheila said, pulling her specs from her handbag for a closer look. 'Well, it should be easy enough to find out her name. Can I take the photo out of the frame? There might be something written on the back, or at least a date.'

'There is. It says, "The Three Higgins Sisters, 1911".'

'Well, that's excellent,' Sheila said. 'The 1911 census is available online, and this photo dates from that year so all three girls should be mentioned in the census. We just need to find your grandmother and see who is listed as living with her. They look young – so I think they'd all be still living with their parents at that time. Do you know where your grandmother lived as a young girl? I could borrow your laptop, log into my Ancestry account and have a quick look.'

'That'd be amazing! But look, let's finish lunch first and then start digging into history.'

Half an hour later, with lunch eaten and the dishes cleared away, Harriet topped up their wine and leaned back in her chair. 'I have a dessert for you too, but honestly I can't eat another thing. What about you?'

'Not for me, thank you. At least not just yet. Come on, I want to start investigating your mystery great-aunt!'

Harriet fetched her laptop for Sheila to use. 'Gran lived in Southampton – somewhere in Northam though I am not sure which road. And her maiden name was Higgins.'

'Perfect, I bet I can find them,' Sheila said, stretching out her arms in front and cracking her knuckles. 'Right then, here we go.'

Harriet watched over her shoulder as Sheila logged onto the Ancestry website and entered details on the search page. She was right – within a few minutes Harriet found herself looking at an entry from the 1911 census that listed Amelia Higgins living with her three daughters, Emma, Ruby, and Lily. 'There they are!' she said excitedly. 'No father – I seem to remember Gran saying he'd died when she was a child and the family struggled to make ends meet with just her mother's income.'

'Amelia's profession is given as laundress and seamstress,' Sheila said, pointing at the screen. 'She probably took in washing and mending for other people. I can imagine it'd be hard to keep four people on that – but look, by 1911 both the older two girls were working as hotel chambermaids.'

'So that must be before Gran went to sea. And this defiant-looking girl, who looks to be the middle one in age – must be Ruby, the sister I never knew about. She's really pretty. I keep wondering why Gran never spoke about her.'

'What a mystery! Look, let me show you how to use this site – you should be able to find their birth and death registrations, and find them on the 1901 census. Maybe their dad was still alive then – and then you can go back in time. Once you've got the family, if they stayed in more or less the same area it's quite easy to trace them backwards. It can be fascinating.'

'I know – you've told me about your research so many times!' Harriet laughed. 'Yes, go on, show me. I'd love to see more.'

They spent a happy hour trawling for more details, with Harriet jotting down all the findings in a notebook. Later, over a cup of tea, Harriet told Sheila what she could remember of her grandmother's tales of life at sea.

'It sounds amazing, doesn't it?' Sheila sighed, staring off into the middle distance. 'Sometimes I wish I'd done something like that – gone to sea, seen the world, instead of leading such a boring life.'

'You, madam, could never be described as boring,' Harriet said.

'I was an accountant for thirty years! The definition of boring!'

'An accountant who also spent her summers at music festivals, who's run marathons, who brought up three sons more or less on her own, who's survived cancer, who's written a book on how to stay fit after 50 ... I could go on!'

'Ah, piffle.' Sheila shook her hand dismissively but Harriet noted the little smile of pride at the corners of her mouth. 'But I haven't travelled. I've never been to sea, unless you count taking the ferry to Calais once or twice. That's why I'm so excited about going on this cruise, especially when we got it for such a bargain price. You've never been on one before either, have you?'

Harriet shook her head. 'No, it'll be my first time, too.'

'It might give you a bit of an insight into your grandmother's life. She worked on the cruise ships for many years, didn't she?'

'She and my granddad worked on the *Olympic* until it was decommissioned in the mid-1930s,' Harriet said. 'And you're right, I have never been on a cruise before. John wasn't into them – he preferred activity holidays. We'd go camping, cycling, hill-walking – that sort of thing.' She frowned, remembering Sally's objections to her holiday.

'What is it, Harri?' Sheila said, putting a hand on Harriet's arm.

Harriet shrugged and forced a smile to her face. 'Oh, nothing really. Just that ... I had a bit of a run-in with Sally about the cruise. She ... doesn't think I should be going away, not while Jerome's ill.'

'But we booked it before we knew about him. And it's only five nights. You're not thinking of cancelling, are you?'

'No, no. I definitely want to go. I just didn't want her to be upset with me. Charlie – you know, her husband – he thinks it's all right to go. It's just Sally.'

'Sally being Sally, I suppose. She does tend to boss you around a bit.'

'She's good to me, though. She's been helping me so much with everything.'

'Of course. But don't listen to her about the cruise. You deserve it, you know. And, God forbid, if anything happened with Jerome and Sally needed your help, it is only five nights away. You could probably jump ship and fly home quicker, if absolutely necessary. But he's stable, isn't he? And doing all right with the treatment? So it'll all be OK, just you wait and see.'

'Thanks, Sheila. I suppose I just need a bit of reassurance that I'm not being selfish.'

'Not in the slightest bit selfish. You've been here for her and Jerome, right from the moment he first became ill. You deserve a bit of fun for yourself, especially after losing John like that so suddenly last year. So – how are we going to get to the cruise terminal on Friday?'

'Train to Southampton and a taxi, I thought. Although it's probably walkable from the station, but with luggage it might be hard work.' Harriet smiled, grateful for Sheila's wise counselling.

'Definitely a taxi. I'm not turning up on the *Queen Mary II* all sweaty from having hauled a suitcase across Southampton,' Sheila said firmly. 'I'm so glad we picked a cruise on a proper, big, beautiful liner. Your grandmother's ship, *Olympic*, was the pride of her time, the sister of *Titanic*, so it's right that we should sail on one of the really gorgeous iconic ships of today.'

'And we're sailing out of Southampton too, just like Granny did on *Olympic*.'

'Dahling, it's the *only* way to travel,' Sheila said, picking up her wine glass and waving it around. Harriet laughed. The cruise, with Sheila as companion, was going to be absolutely fabulous.

Chapter 8

Emma, 1911

A few days after Emma returned home from the *Olympic*'s maiden voyage, she was back at the docks, signing on again for the next voyage, which was to depart less than a week later. As she came out of the White Star offices, she spotted a familiar figure on his way in.

Martin broke into a broad grin when he saw her. 'You've signed on again?'

His smile was infectious. 'I certainly have!'

He flung his arms in the air and gave a little cheer. 'I'm so pleased. We worked well together, didn't we? I'm looking forward to having the chance to do that again.' He blushed a little then, as though embarrassed by his exuberance, and Emma laughed.

'I'm looking forward to it, too. So, in you go, get yourself signed on and I'll see you in six days. Got to get home now.' She waved goodbye and walked home with a spring in her step.

Ma had given her blessing for Emma to return to sea, though she looked worn and worried. Lily was excited for her of course, and thankfully fully recovered, and Ruby was ambivalent, simply shrugging when Emma announced she'd signed on again and would be boarding the ship in another six days.

'Do what you want. You always do, anyway,' she said, and Emma had turned away.

She'd barely seen Ruby since her first day back home. Her sister went out to work every day, stayed out late and came home only to sleep. Even on her day off Ruby had left the house early in the morning and not returned until past eleven at night, when the rest of the family had long since retired for bed. Emma had heard her come in that night, slamming the front door, clattering up the stairs and into her room.

'Why's she so noisy?' Lily had whispered from the other bed.

'Shh, sleep now, she's home safe,' Emma had responded. Her sister was probably drunk, she'd thought, but no need to tell young Lily that. She'd heard Ma go into Ruby's room, hold a whispered conversation, and then leave. And then she'd thought she heard stifled sobs from her mother's room.

In some ways it broke Emma's heart to leave Ma and her sisters again, especially when things were so difficult at home. But in other ways she couldn't wait to be back at sea, with her friends Violet, Martin, and Mary who she knew had all signed on again. She was looking forward to the excitement of another Atlantic crossing and another visit to New York. And the prospect of spending more time with Martin, if she was honest with herself. This time, on her brief visit onshore in New York, she'd planned to walk up Fifth Avenue and gaze in the windows of the huge department stores she'd heard lined that street. And to tell the truth, she was looking forward to being away from the worry of Ruby for a while. On the *Olympic* there was nothing she could do to try to change Ruby's behaviour, so there was no point worrying. Not until she was next home, anyway, in about three weeks' time.

The day that she boarded ship, a day before the passengers embarked, was a glorious, hot summer's day. How lovely it would be, Emma thought, to be able to sit in a deckchair all day, soaking up the sun and watching the activity on the quayside. But of course she could not do that. While there was less to do than at the start of her last voyage – no tours, no training, no days when the public were allowed on board to view the ship – there was still plenty of work to complete before she met her passengers for this voyage. Firstly, she needed to take her trunk to her cabin. She'd been assigned the same one as before, and was delighted to find she was sharing with Mary once more. 'Oh, once they know a couple of girls get on all right, they'll put us together every time we're both on board,' Mary said, after Emma arrived in the cabin and hugged her. It had only been days but felt like a lifetime since the last voyage.

She changed into her stewardess's uniform and got started on the pre-voyage tasks, excited to be on a ship once again, though also feeling a little daunted by the anticipation of the hard work ahead. Last time she hadn't known quite how hard she'd have to work but this time she knew exactly how arduous the job was.

'Here we are again,' said Martin with a smile, when they passed in a galley-way later that day. 'Gluttons for punishment!'

'I love this job,' Emma replied, laughing. 'I'll keep signing on for as long as they'll have me.'

'You know the White Star Line is launching a new ship next year? A sister ship to this one, only it's going to be even more opulently furnished? I think I might try to get on the maiden voyage again. Maiden voyages are more exciting than regular ones. Will you sign on for it too, when the time comes?' Martin's expression was hopeful, and it made Emma's heart take a little leap of joy. She liked Martin. He was funny and kind, and his eyes were a deep brown, the type of eyes you wanted to dive into and swim around in.

'I might,' she replied. She still felt too new to the job, unsure whether White Star would take her again on another maiden voyage. Also, it wouldn't hurt to keep Martin guessing. She didn't want to seem too keen. 'A sister ship to this one. What's it going to be called, do you know?'

'RMS *Titanic*, I believe. A fine name for a ship. And they're building a third of the same design.'

Three sisters. Just like herself, Ruby, and Lily. Emma smiled at the thought. She hoped that none of the sister ships would provide as much heartache as her middle sister was causing her family.

The second voyage passed smoothly, with Emma settling into the routines of the job and getting to know Mary and Martin better. She didn't see so much of Violet who worked the first-class state rooms. The highlight of the trip was a few hours spent onshore in New York, when Emma and Martin had walked through Manhattan to Central Park where they had bought hot dogs from a stall and sat on a bench to eat them, watching rich women with parasols strolling past on the arms of smart young men.

'How the other half live!' Martin had said, and Emma laughed, leaning slightly into him.

'I'm perfectly happy with my own life, thank you. Honestly, today's been marvellous. And I love this.' She'd waved the hot dog in front of him. It was the first time she'd ever eaten one.

'Well, it's traditional now. We must sit here and eat hot dogs every time we come to New York,' he'd replied, and she'd smiled, beginning to wonder about the future, imagining visiting Central Park in all seasons with Martin at her side ...

On the way home they slipped into a comfortable routine of meeting up in the evenings, when their passengers were all at dinner. They'd eat something quickly themselves, then rather than stay in the stewards' lounge they'd grab their coats and go out on deck. It was so peaceful without the passengers, and pleasant to stroll up and down. If questioned by an officer they'd say they were searching for some small item a passenger had mislaid, but most evenings they saw no one else at this time.

'Look at the moon,' Martin said one evening, as they leaned

on the railings. 'It's as though it's lighting a path for us, across the ocean. Showing us the way home.' There was a trail of silvery moonlight glinting on the sea ahead of them, a twinkling path through the blackness either side.

'It's so beautiful,' Emma whispered. Beside her, Martin moved a little closer, so that his arm pressed lightly against hers. She could feel its warmth through her coat sleeve.

What would it be like if he put his arm round her now, and maybe pulled her towards him and kissed her? She dared not turn to look at him, but kept her gaze focused on the moonlight. She barely knew him, and they were here to work. It was good that they were friends, but for now, that was all it could be.

He must have thought the same, for after a few minutes he coughed slightly and moved away. 'They'll be coming back to their cabins soon, I think. Mrs Winters will be wanting her bath run. And the Skinners' Cairn terriers will be wanting their evening constitutional.'

'You're right, we'd better go in.' The spell was broken and in any case, a cloud had drifted across the moon. She smiled at him and followed him back inside to resume their duties.

All too soon they were back home again in Southampton, and Emma was bidding farewell to her friends once more.

'You'll sign on again for the next one?' said Martin, as they stood on the quayside preparing to go their separate ways. 'The *Olympic* is sailing again in a week.'

'Possibly. If Ma's happy to do without me for another three weeks,' Emma replied. It depended on how things were with her sisters – whether Ma needed her at home for a while to try to keep Ruby in check, and whether Lily had been well. She smiled; Martin looked so crestfallen that she hadn't said she would definitely sign on again that she felt she must offer him some hope. 'If not the next voyage, then definitely the one after. Keep an eye out for me, eh?'

He grinned. 'I will. Look after yourself, Emma. If I didn't have to get the train to Salisbury to see my folk I'd be asking if we could meet up during the week in Southampton. But my ma will kill me if I don't go straight home now I'm onshore. Hope to see you on board next week then.' He gave her a cheery wave and strode off, whistling.

Emma set off for home. Maybe Ruby had settled down since Emma's last shore leave. She certainly hoped so. Ma didn't deserve to have to worry about any of her daughters.

Back home, just as last time she passed Mrs Williams in the street. Their neighbour was coming out of her own house – if Emma was feeling uncharitable she'd say Mrs Williams had been watching out of the front room window, waiting for a chance to pounce when she saw Emma.

'You're back again then. Not before time. Better have words with that sister of yours, before she gets herself into real trouble.' Mrs Williams nodded knowingly, her arms folded across her ample bosom.

'Hello Mrs Williams. Beautiful day, isn't it?' replied Emma, without breaking stride. She wanted to be home, not gossiping in the street with an old busybody.

'Ask her about her *friend* Harry Paine,' Mrs Williams called after her. Emma waved in response without looking back. She did not recognise the name but didn't like the way Mrs Williams had stressed the word 'friend'. What was going on? She hurried the last few yards to her home and rushed in without knocking.

Ma was in the kitchen, angrily pummelling away at some dough to make bread. 'Ah, you're back, lovey. I hope you had a good trip.'

'It was good, thanks Ma.' Emma gave her mother a kiss, being careful not to lean against her or the table and cover her uniform with flour. 'Lily around? Ruby?'

'Lily's at school. She's been fit as a fiddle while you were away this time, I'm glad to say. As for Ruby, who knows where that girl is. Supposed to be at work, isn't she, but according to Mrs Williams she's out with that man again.' Ma punched the dough with her fist then picked it up and flung it back down onto the table. Her face was red and sweaty with the effort.

'What man, Ma?'

'Don't know his name. Ruby calls him Harry but I don't know his surname. I think he's a bad lot. She's out till all hours with him and his pals. I don't like it, Emma, not one bit. T'ain't right for a girl of that age to be out in all the pubs and bars till all hours, with a man. I tell her this and she tells me I'm Victorian and everything's different now, and girls can go about as they please with whoever they please, and I'm to keep my nose out.' The dough took another beating, then Ma sat down suddenly and heavily on one of the battered old kitchen chairs, and covered her face in her floury hands. 'Truth be told, lovey, I don't know what I'm to do with her. What would your da have done? Mrs Williams says I should throw her out on her ear. But she's my girl. I can't do that, can I?'

Emma sat beside her mother and wrapped her arms around her, no longer caring if her uniform got covered in flour. Ma's needs were more important. 'No, Ma, you can't throw her out. It'd just send her into the arms of this chap, anyway.' She sighed. 'I'll try to talk to her again. Can't quite promise anything though – I tried last time I was home and got nowhere.'

Ma sniffed. 'I know you did, lovey, and I'm grateful to you for trying. I only wish she'd listen.'

'And I can try to find out something about this Harry. Maybe he's all right after all. Harry Paine, is it? Mrs Williams said—'

Ma stared at her, horrified. 'Harry *Paine*? No. Can't be him. Even Ruby wouldn't … sure she wouldn't …' She shook her head, disbelieving. 'No wonder people are gossiping.'

'What, Ma? Who's Harry Paine?'

But Ma wouldn't say any more. She stood and continued pummelling the dough, her expression even more furious than when Emma had entered. Emma watched for a moment then put the kettle on, making a pot of tea for the both of them and resolving to say no more about Ruby or this Harry to Ma until she'd had a chance to speak to Ruby.

Ruby was late home that night, and Emma, exhausted after the voyage, was fast asleep in the room she shared with Lily by the time Ruby returned. She did not even hear her sister come in. The following morning, Emma awoke late to find Ruby had already gone out to work.

'Ma, I'll go and catch her when she leaves work this afternoon, and speak to her then. I can wait outside the staff entrance,' Emma said, when she went downstairs to find her mother already up and fretting about Ruby once more.

'Shall I come with you?' Lily asked.

'Haven't you got school today?'

Lily pouted. 'Suppose so. Wish I was old enough to leave school and do something useful.'

Emma hugged her sister. 'Don't wish your life away, Lily. Go to school, learn everything you can, and that'll help you get a good job in the future.'

'Like you. I'd rather work on a ship than in a hotel, and go to all those exciting places.'

'So far I've only been to one exciting place, and the work is hard, but it's good to have ambitions, Lily.'

'You tell that to our Ruby,' Ma said. 'She needs ambitions that'll take her away from that Harry Paine.'

'I'll talk to her later,' Emma said. 'Come on Lily, isn't it time you were off? I'll walk you to school if you like.'

'Yes! Like old times!' Lily leapt to her feet and grabbed her satchel, stuffing the pack of sandwiches wrapped in greaseproof paper that Ma had made for her inside.

Emma pushed her feet into her shoes and followed her sister out of the house. It had been many years since she'd walked to the school with Lily – once Emma had left aged 14 she'd got a job almost straight away and had been rarely able to spare the time to accompany her little sister. Lily skipped along happily, acting younger than her twelve years, making Emma smile. It was good to see her so well this time. Lily had always been such a sunny child; even during her many bouts of sickness she'd always had a smile on her face. It was as though all the goodness in the family had flowed into Lily … and the badness into Ruby.

'Work hard, Lily,' she said as she kissed her sister goodbye at the school gates. 'You've two more years. Learn everything they can teach you.'

'Will do, Ems. See you later.' Lily skipped into school, spotted a friend and linked arms with her, waving to Emma as she began the walk home.

On the return walk, Emma debated how best to approach Ruby. By the time she reached home she'd decided the best way was to take Ruby out – offer to buy her tea and cake at a Lyons corner-house, maybe even offer to buy her a present somewhere. Get her onside, happy and friendly, gain her confidence and then perhaps she'd be a little more receptive to sisterly advice. Yes, it was a plan, and it might just work.

Emma spent the day helping her mother with chores around the house – taking over the cleaning and grocery shopping so that Ma could put her feet up and rest awhile. It helped, Emma thought – by mid-afternoon Ma was looking happier and less stressed.

'So Lily gets out of school at four, but I need to go and meet Ruby at that time. I thought I'd try to talk to her somewhere away from home, but we'll be back in time for dinner.'

'Thanks, lovey. Lily will help me make the dinner. It'll be on the table around six o'clock.'

As it always had been, all Emma's life. She finished her chores, took off her pinny and went upstairs to wash her face and comb her hair. She felt strangely nervous and had to remind herself it was only her sister Ruby she was going to meet, and it had only been three weeks since she'd last seen her.

It was a twenty-minute walk to the hotel where Ruby worked, but Emma allowed herself half an hour. It was a warm day and she didn't want to work up a sweat, not if they were going to go out for tea. Also, she wanted to take a longer route, via a park, and enjoy the walk. She reached the hotel at five to four, and went around the back to the staff entrance. There were a few kitchen staff standing around outside in the sunshine, smoking and chatting, and another man dressed in a lounge suit with a straw boater on his head, stood leaning against a fence, a cigarette dangling from his lip. Emma took a position a little way away from him. Something about the way his gaze had appraised her as she approached unnerved her. She hoped Ruby would come out on time.

It was just after four o'clock, by Emma's watch, when the staff door opened and a stream of chambermaids began pouring out of the hotel, chatting and laughing. Emma stood upright, watching for Ruby, and then spotted her near the back of the group. She raised a hand to wave to her sister but then dropped it as she realised Ruby was heading over to the man in the suit. Ruby approached him, leaned towards him for a kiss and then linked arms with the man as they turned to leave the hotel. A couple of other girls glanced at Ruby, then turned away whispering to each other, their expressions harsh and disapproving. It was only then that Ruby spotted her, Emma, waiting.

'Ems! So you're back again? I thought it was next week.' Emma noticed her sister had let go of the man's arm and taken a step away from him.

'Hello Ruby. I got back yesterday. I was hoping to see you last night, but I was so tired …'

'I was working late yesterday. I'll see you tonight? Ma doing dinner for six, is she? I'll be home by then, I think … something I was going to do first. See you later then, eh?'

'Rubes, I came to meet you hoping we could perhaps go out for tea, just you and me? I'm paying.'

'Ah, but … I've got to …' Emma noticed her sister glance towards the suited man, who was still nearby, watching and listening to their conversation. There was an amused smirk on the man's face. Emma assumed this was Harry Paine. Ruby clearly did not intend introducing him.

'Come on, Ruby. I haven't seen you for weeks, we've got loads to talk about, and I've got my wages from the last voyage to spend. Tea and cake, on me. What's so important that can't wait another day?'

'This your sister?' the man said, stepping forward.

Ruby blushed and half turned towards him. 'Um, yes. This is Emma.'

'Pleased to meet you. I'm Harry.' He held out his hand for Emma to shake. His hand was warm, his grip strong, and he held on just a fraction too long for Emma's liking. His eyes were a cold blue-grey and although handsome, he had a couple of missing teeth and those that were present were blackened. 'Looks like you aren't free today, Ruby,' he said. 'Go and have fun with your sister. I'll see you tomorrow.' He didn't wait for an answer, but strode off, hands in pockets, whistling.

Ruby watched him go, an expression Emma couldn't quite read on her face. Was she disappointed not to be spending time with her boyfriend? Or annoyed that Emma had now met him, and her relationship with him was a secret no longer.

'Ready?' Emma said, and Ruby turned back to her with a too-bright smile.

'Tea and cake, you said? Yes, I'm always ready for that.' Ruby linked arms with Emma and they set off towards the nearest Lyons corner-house.

'So that man was …?' Emma asked, when it seemed Ruby wasn't going to offer up any information.

'That was Harry, as he said.'

'Harry Paine?'

'How did you know his surname?'

'Something Ma said,' Emma replied.

'Ma? I've not told his name to Ma. How can she know?' Ruby sounded worried.

Emma silently cursed herself. She'd heard Harry's surname from the gossiping Mrs Williams. They crossed a road, and she tried to change the subject. 'How did you meet him?'

'Oh, he's just one of the crowd that I goes around with. Remember when you were last home and you was telling me off for going to the pub? Well, if I hadn't have been going to the pub I wouldn't have met Harry.' Ruby smiled triumphantly.

'So are you … stepping out with him?' Emma asked cautiously. There'd been something about Harry she hadn't liked. He was too old for Ruby. Too worldly-wise.

'I'm … seeing him, is probably a better way of putting it. But we don't want anyone to know.'

'Why not? Wouldn't it be better to bring him home to meet Ma? Then she'd know who you're out with and perhaps worry less about it.'

Ruby shook her head violently. 'No. You don't understand. I can't do that. God, I wish she didn't know his name. It could ruin everything.'

'How can just knowing his name be a problem?'

'She knows him. Or knows of him.'

'So?' They were almost at the corner-house. This conversation felt like one that had to be completed in private, not sitting in the bustle of the tea-shop.

Ruby stopped walking and turned to face Emma. 'Ems, Harry and I can't be together openly. Not now. Not for ages – not until he leaves his wife. There. I've told you now. So you'll understand why it all has to be kept as much a secret as possible?'

Chapter 9

Harriet

Friday inched around at last. Harriet had packed and repacked her suitcase at least a dozen times. It was mid-spring: warm enough in the daytime but evenings on deck might be chilly, so she needed to take some warm clothing. Dressy clothes for the dinners. Light comfortable items for daytime. Walking shoes for the excursions on shore – the ship was calling at Rotterdam, then Zeebrugge from where you could take a trip to Bruges, and St Peter's Port on Guernsey. And she'd need swimwear for the pools, loose clothes in case they decided to take an exercise class, and something to wear travelling to and from Southampton. Finally, after much soul-searching and a dozen phone calls to Sheila, she had a selection of clothes she was happy with. Why had it been so much harder than packing for a week's camping with John?

The night before, Sally had phoned. 'Are you all packed, Mum, for your big trip?'

'I am, at last. But it's not that big a trip, honestly. I'll be back before you know it. How is Jerome?'

'Tired. Missed school today but I'm hoping he can go tomorrow. How are you getting to the docks?'

'Taxi to Bournemouth station, train to Southampton Central, taxi to cruise terminal is the plan.'

'If Jerome's in school, I'll pick you and Sheila up and take you to the station, if you like.'

'Oh, that would be fantastic! But only if you're sure …'

'It's no problem. The sooner you go, the sooner you come back, in my strange, stressed and warped mind. What time do you need picking up?'

Harriet frowned at Sally's odd logic, but the lift would certainly help. 'Oh, I suppose around 9.30 would work?'

'OK. I'll let you know by 8.30 if there's a problem – if Jerome can't go to school. You'll still have time to book a taxi then.'

And now, here Sally was, on the dot of 9.30, all smiles because Jerome was having a good day. She grimaced as she hefted Harriet's suitcase into the boot of the car. 'It's five nights, right? Feels like you've packed for a month!'

'I tried to keep it down, but it was difficult!' Harriet laughed. 'Once we get to the cruise terminal the luggage gets taken from us and put in our cabin. So it'll be all right. OK, so I have turned off the gas and double checked it, and locked the door, and checked that three times. My neighbour's putting the bin out on Monday. Sheila lives about five minutes away, and she's texted to say she's ready.'

'You sound as excited as a kid going on a school trip,' Sally said with a laugh, and her comment brought to Harriet's mind a day long ago when both her daughters went on a Guide camp together for the first time, leaving her and John alone for a week. Sally and Davina had been best of friends in those days, and had been jumping up and down with excitement about the trip when they were dropped off at the campsite. Harriet had assumed then that they would always be friends, all their lives. But Davina had come home sullen, complaining that Sally had bossed her about all week. Sally had insisted she'd only been trying to *instruct* her sister, as the older and more experienced Guide. But as usual Davina would have preferred to work things out by herself.

Sheila was waiting by her garden gate for them, and the two of them did a good impression of Sally and Davina going on Guide camp while Sally stowed Sheila's suitcase in the boot of the car.

Sally laughed. 'You two kids. I hope you have a fabulous time.'

'I'm sure we will,' Sheila said.

'I'll ring you every day,' Harriet added. 'Shall we go? Train to catch!'

An hour later they'd arrived at the cruise terminal, checked in, handed over the suitcases which would be put in their cabin for them, and were standing in front of the *Queen Mary II*, gazing up at it and admiring the ship's size and splendour.

'She's beautiful, isn't she?' Sheila said. 'So glad we picked this ship.'

'Yes. Gorgeous.' Harriet was imagining how her grandmother must have felt the first time she boarded a liner for work. The great liners of those days were far smaller than today's ships of course, but must still have been awesome to see. She'd read up a little on the *Olympic* and the White Star Line – and the *Titanic* tragedy, of course – since finding the old trunk. The *Olympic* had been the largest liner of the day, when she was first built. Just as the *QM2* was the largest at the time of her launch. There was a pleasing symmetry about that fact, though Harriet was glad she was going on board as a passenger, not working as a stewardess.

'Shall we board, *dahling*?' Sheila said, arching her eyebrow.

'Yes, why not?' said Harriet, taking Sheila's arm, and giggling, they walked over to the covered walkway that sloped up and onto the ship. Soon they'd found their cabin, unpacked their cases, peered out of the porthole at the tugs that were getting ready to pull the ship away from the dock, and were heading up to be on an outside deck as the ship set sail. They were halfway up when the ship's foghorn sounded – so loud it startled Harriet and she clutched at Sheila's arm. Laughing, they reached the deck just as the tugs began to ease the ship away from the quay. There were quite a few people on the quayside – some working and some who'd come to see friends and relatives off. Harriet spotted a family including three very small children waving madly, the mother holding up a hand-made, coloured-by-children sign that read 'Happy Cruise Granny!' She felt a pang of self-pity that no grandchildren were there to see her off, but then remembered it was a school day and Jerome, thankfully, was well enough to be at school. And as for Summer and Autumn – she could only assume they too were at school, somewhere in France.

'Shall we get ourselves a drink?' Sheila said, when they'd pulled away from the quay and begun the journey down Southampton Water.

'Absolutely!' Harriet grinned, and they went in search of the nearest bar.

'Champagne is called for, I'd say,' said Sheila, ordering them a glass each. 'To our first cruise!'

'First of many!' Harriet said, clinking her glass against Sheila's.

They stayed on deck sipping their drinks, at the stern so they could cross from the port to the starboard side to see the views in both directions, pointing out landmarks to each other as the ship made its way along Southampton Water. 'There's the mouth of the Itchen river,' Harriet said. 'Northam, where my grandmother lived, is just up there. She'd have been within walking distance of the liner terminal.'

'Perfect job! Look, that's Hythe, with its marina and pier,' Sheila said, pointing the other way. 'I have a cousin who lives there. Cute place.'

'We'll pass Netley in a moment on the left,' Harriet said. 'Might be able to get a glimpse of the Abbey ruins. I've never been there, have you?'

'Yes, and I also visited the Royal Victoria country park where the huge Netley military hospital used to be. Always felt it was a shame they tore that building down. These days I would think it would be converted into apartments or something.'

They watched as Netley passed by on the port side, followed by the mouth of the river Hamble, with the huge oil refinery at Fawley on the other side, looking like a dystopian city skyline. And then the ship emerged from Southampton Water into the Solent, passing Portsmouth harbour and rounding the eastern tip of the Isle of Wight and eventually out into the wider English Channel where they soon lost sight of land.

'Well, next stop Rotterdam,' Sheila remarked, and as the wind was picking up they decided to go and explore the interior of the ship.

There was no doubt about it – the ship was vast. They'd wanted to explore all of it that first day, but Harriet's feet were soon hurting, necessitating a visit to their cabin to change shoes. Once there she collapsed onto the bed. 'Whew! It's enormous. I mean, I knew it was, but it's even bigger than I'd thought it would be.'

Sheila was tapping something into her phone. 'It's about three times the size of the *Titanic*. And they thought that was a big ship!'

'Biggest for its time,' Harriet said. 'I suppose it's all relative. Well, look, I've put my trainers on. I don't care if they don't go with my outfit. Let's continue with our exploration!'

'You're on. And maybe we'll stop somewhere for a cup of tea.'

Restaurants, gyms, swimming pools, theatres, cafés, lounges and of course plenty of boutiques – there were endless facilities on board. The afternoon passed quickly and they still hadn't seen it all. 'But it's time we changed for dinner,' Sheila said. 'And then there's the cabaret. I want the full cruise ship experience!'

'Shall we call a stewardess to help us dress for dinner? I need help fastening my pearls, you know!' Harriet giggled. 'I can't help thinking of Granny and how hard she had to work. Of course, the *Olympic* was mostly used to shuttle back and forth between Southampton and New York, so many passengers were on board as a way to cross the Atlantic rather than as a holiday in its own right. What a way to travel, eh?'

'Certainly beats flying,' Sheila agreed, as they re-entered their cabin and began deciding on an evening outfit.

It was an amazing evening, Harriet thought, as she settled down much later that night to read a few pages of her book before sleep. They'd had a sumptuous meal where white-jacketed waiters provided unobtrusive but perfectly timed service. They'd taken the rest of their wine into a lounge where they'd leaned back against plush upholstery, listening to a jazz trio. And then they'd gone to the second performance in the main theatre, where they'd been entertained by singers and dancers. It was the kind of night out you'd pay a fortune for in London, she thought, and here it was all part of the package.

'Enjoying it so far?' Sheila asked sleepily.

'Oh God, yes!' was the only reply Harriet could make, before settling down to sleep. They'd be docked at Rotterdam when they woke, and there was a day trip to Amsterdam booked.

Harriet and Sheila were up early the next morning, not wanting to miss a minute of their experience.

'We'll be docking in a short while,' Sheila said. 'Shall we grab a coffee and a pastry and go up on deck to watch? There'll be time for a proper breakfast afterwards, before the excursion to Amsterdam begins.'

'Great idea,' Harriet said, and donning a warm fleece she followed Sheila through the ship and out to an open deck.

They watched through early morning mist as the ship entered the harbour. 'Hard to see much with all this mist,' Harriet commented. 'I just hope the captain can see more than we can.'

'I'm not entirely sure he can,' Sheila said. 'Is it just me or are we a bit close to that other ship?'

Harriet gasped as she looked where Sheila was pointing. Looming out of the mist was a container ship, tied up at the dock. The *QM2* was veering dangerously close to it. There was the sound of the ship's engines and churning water below, as though the captain was doing all he could to make the liner turn away from the other ship. It seemed so close – Harriet felt as though she could almost touch the containers if she reached out.

'Are we going to hit that other ship?' she said, turning to Sheila who was watching intently.

'I don't know. It's bloody close. Actually I think we should move away from the railings, just in case. Maybe go back inside.'

'I agree, come on, it'll be safer if anything happens.'

They went back inside but continued watching, along with many other passengers, through windows on that side of the ship. People were muttering excitedly about how close they were, and would the ships touch, and if so would the collision damage the *QM2*, would they have to disembark onto lifeboats?

'Good grief, I can't imagine it'd be that bad,' Sheila said, as Harriet raised her eyebrows after overhearing another passenger say the ship was going to sink.

'That's what they all said when the *Titanic* first hit the iceberg,' the woman said sharply. 'I'm going to pick up my valuables, just in case.' She marched off, and Harriet stifled a giggle.

'This is hardly the north Atlantic, is it? Even if the ship's damaged we are more or less in port.'

Sheila nodded. 'And we have enough lifeboats, and there are no icebergs. Anyway, look.' She pointed, and Harriet could see that the gap between the *QM2* and the container ship was definitely widening.

'Just hope the stern doesn't swing round too much and hit it anyway,' she said.

It was close, but it missed, and there was a collective sigh of relief from all who were watching.

'Imagine being in an actual shipwreck,' Sheila said. 'I'd be hopeless. Can't row, can't even swim.'

'With life jackets you don't need to be able to swim,' Harriet replied. 'Anyway, the excitement's over. The mist is clearing just in time for our trip into Amsterdam. Shall we get some breakfast?'

'Ooh, yes. I'm more than ready for it now.' Sheila took Harriet's arm as they made their way to a restaurant serving breakfast.

While they ate – yogurt with granola and fruit for Harriet and a full English fry-up for Sheila – Harriet found herself remembering the nearest she'd ever come to being ship-wrecked once before, many long years ago.

It had happened when Harriet had been sailing a small dinghy, with her brother. Harriet and Matthew, then in their teens, were on holiday with their parents and some old family friends, camping in a field beside an estuary in Cornwall. The other family had brought a couple of sailing dinghies on a trailer, and the father of that family – whom they called Uncle Pete – spent much of the week teaching the children the basics of sailing, assigning one of their boats to Harriet's family for the week. Harriet's parents had not wanted to trust the rather battered-looking wooden dinghy, but Matthew had taken to it like a duck to water. By the end of the week he was competent enough to be helmsman, with Harriet alongside as crew. Her job was to handle the small jib sail, untying it when Matthew said 'ready about' then hauling on the sheet – she'd learned not to call it a rope – to pull the sail across to the other side, remembering to duck under the boom as it swung over, when Matthew gave the command 'lee ho'. He managed the mainsail and the rudder.

Out on the water, with the little dinghy skipping over small waves as they tacked back and forth across the estuary, always within sight of the small shingle beach they'd launched from, there'd been a feeling of freedom that Harriet had never forgotten. Just her and her brother, the boat responding to their commands, the wind and water at their service, the sun on her face and her hair flicking about her shoulders, Matthew grinning as they set a course for the opposite bank of the estuary – magical times. Even then she knew they were special moments that she would remember for ever, and wished they could live like that always – camping, cooking on small Primus stoves, their parents managing the practicalities of shopping and cooking while the two of them mucked about on the water all day.

'It's like we're the children in *Swallows and Amazons*,' Harriet said, and Matthew laughed.

'We could do with an island, and some buried treasure, and maybe an evil pirate to do battle with,' he replied.

'We can always pretend,' Harriet said. 'Look, that other dinghy over there – perhaps they've captured that girl on board and mean to sell her into the slave trade. We have to stop them. After them!'

'All right! Let's get tight into the wind and see if we can outrun them!' Matthew adjusted his sail and told Harriet to pull hers in a little, and soon the boat was sailing faster than ever before, leaning over so much the centreboard was almost out of the water. Harriet and Matthew sat on the very edge, leaning back, to stop it from capsizing. There was a fine line to judge to keep the speed up but also keeping the boat upright. They were gaining on the other dinghy, then passing it, and Harriet waved and whooped as they did so, and then the wind veered round a little and suddenly the boat was over, capsized, and she found herself floundering in the water. She was thankful for the life jacket she was wearing as she bobbed to the surface, spluttering and laughing. Matthew was near, already standing on the centreboard and pulling with all his weight on the side of the boat until it righted itself, river water running off the sails.

'Come on, climb in. We're true sailors now, having capsized. Well done!'

She hauled herself over the side and set to work bailing water out of the bottom, using a plastic container that Uncle Pete had tied to the boat with a piece of string. The sails flapped uselessly while they worked to make the dinghy shipshape again.

'Everything all right?' yelled an occupant of the other dinghy that floated nearby.

'Yes, we're fine, thank you,' Matthew responded, and soon they were under sail again, more sedately this time, tacking back and forth towards the little beach so they could land and dry off.

'I saw what happened. You did well, to right the boat,' Uncle Pete said, clapping Matthew on the back.

'Oh my goodness. You could have been drowned! You're not to go out in that boat again unless you're with Pete,' their mother said, fussing around Harriet with a towel.

'Mum, I can swim,' Harriet said, as she went back to their tent to change her clothing. Behind her she'd heard Uncle Pete comfort her mother, telling her they'd been in no real danger, and that capsizing and learning how to handle it was all a part of sailing and Matthew had handled it very well indeed.

They were good days – their teenage years, when Harriet and Matthew had been great friends. He'd looked out for her and protected her, as all big brothers should, but they'd also had fun together, and that holiday of sailing and camping was, looking back on it all, the highlight.

Sailing on the *QM2* was of course a very different experience, Harriet thought, smiling, as she finished her breakfast.

'What are you grinning at?' Sheila asked.

'Oh, just remembering happy times from long ago,' Harriet replied.

'With John?' Sheila's expression was sympathetic.

'With my brother, actually. I hardly ever see him these days. I miss him.'

'Why don't you see him?' Sheila asked gently.

Harriet shrugged. 'Don't know, really. We just drifted apart over the years. He lives a long way north, in Cumbria.'

'You could always invite him down for a visit.'

She could, she knew it. Or she could wait for an invitation to visit him.

Chapter 10

Emma, 1911-12

Life was settling into a pattern – three-week voyages across the Atlantic then a week at home with Ma, Ruby, and Lily. Emma's wages weren't enormous but they were good enough and better than she'd had from her hotel work, which helped with the home finances. Ma had finally agreed to accept a portion of her wages. On board ship she spent her limited spare time with Mary or Martin. Mary had become a good, solid friend, always prepared to listen to Emma's worries (which were mostly about Ruby) or advise her on her slowly blossoming relationship with Martin.

It was a tough decision to sign on for the voyage that sailed to New York over Christmas and New Year, but after being sure that Ma was happy for her to do it, Emma signed on, promising to bring back Christmas presents from New York for the family. Lily hugged her when she left. 'Your first Christmas away from us. You're really a grown-up now, you know?'

'There'll be extra Christmas pudding for you, Lils,' Emma replied. 'And we can celebrate again when I get back in January.'

Ruby had simply shrugged at the news Emma would be away

for the festive season. 'You're away all the time anyway. Makes no difference to me.'

Even so Emma felt a pang of guilt at leaving them all – but it was short-lived. As soon as she was back on board, in the cabin with Mary and working with Martin, she felt nothing but excitement.

There was a festive atmosphere on board, with all the state rooms sumptuously decorated. Several huge Christmas trees had been brought on board and decorated with glass baubles. There was even one in the stewards' lounge, and a party for the crew scheduled for Christmas Eve. Emma had packed her best dress to wear to the party, and was very much looking forward to it.

Somehow the demands of the passengers seemed more reasonable with everyone in such a cheerful mood, and the first few days sped by. At last it was Christmas Eve, and Emma had checked in on all of her passengers. 'Enjoy your party my dear,' one had said to her, pressing a small gift into her hand. 'You look after us so well. You deserve your night off.'

The gift was a little box of Turkish Delight, tied with a satin ribbon. Emma was delighted and a little overwhelmed, but it turned out not to be the only present from her passengers. Most of them had brought something small for her.

'I wasn't expecting that,' she said later to Martin, as they made their way to the crew party. 'They're so kind.'

'I know. It's lovely. I've more new handkerchiefs than I know what to do with,' he replied, and Emma laughed.

'Stitch them together to make a shirt.'

'Might just do that.'

Emma enjoyed the party more than any other evening in her life, she thought, as it drew to a close. She'd eaten far too much, drank a couple of glasses of wine that had made her feel pleasantly light-headed, danced until her feet were sore – mostly with Martin but also with a couple of other stewards who'd shyly asked. There'd been music and laughter all evening. Mary and Violet had danced too; there was a young man named Ned that Violet seemed keen on, and Emma had seen them sneak away together, returning later to the party with flushed faces.

'Shall we go out on deck?' Martin said in her ear, after one energetic dance that had left them both hot and sweaty. 'To cool off?'

'It's freezing out there! But yes, let's.' She'd followed him out of the stewards' lounge and up through the ship to the boat deck, where the lifeboats offered a little shelter from the cold wind.

'I was so hot in there!' Martin said, turning his face to the breeze to cool off.

'So was I. But it's pretty cold out here,' Emma replied, wrapping her arms about her.

Martin turned to her, concern in his eyes. 'We should go back in, then.'

'In a minute. It's a lovely night.' Emma glanced up to the sky, where the Milky Way shone in all its glory. A shooting star caught her eye, but was gone before she could draw Martin's attention to it. 'So transient.'

'What is?'

'A shooting star. This beautiful night. Our lives.'

He chuckled softly, and put an arm around her shoulders. 'Very philosophical! We should enjoy every moment that we are here then, shouldn't we?'

'Mmhm.' She nodded and let him pull her closer to him. He wrapped his arms round her and she leaned her head against his shoulder. She felt him rest his cheek on her hair. If she looked up, he'd kiss her.

It was Christmas Eve. It was a beautiful night. Life was transient.

She twisted in his arms and lifted her face. He was gazing down at her. She parted her lips slightly and he accepted the invitation. His lips were warm and soft against hers. If only she could bottle this moment and keep it for ever!

But the kiss had to end, and the night was indeed very cold. He pulled her tight against him once more. 'Miss Higgins, that was the most wonderful thing ever, but I think we should go back inside before we freeze. It wouldn't do for the officers to find us here frozen together on Christmas Day.'

She smiled. 'It certainly wouldn't. Maybe there's still some dancing going on. Shall we see?'

He kissed her once more – a brief peck this time. 'Yes, let's. And, happy Christmas, my dearest Emma.'

'Happy Christmas, Martin.'

There was just a week left of 1911, the year that had changed Emma's life. They'd see the New Year in when they were on the return voyage. What would 1912 hold for them? It would bring them closer, she was sure. It would be their year.

Back home, Emma held back from telling Ma about Martin. She didn't want her mother to worry about another daughter's suitor. Ruby, now 18, had spoiled things for all of them, through her relationship with Harry Paine. She was still seeing him, and seemed not to care any more who knew it. Ma had been spat at in the butcher's shop, by a friend of Harry Paine's wife. And several neighbours were no longer talking to the family. 'Not as long as you've still got that brazen husband-stealing hussy living with you,' Mrs Williams had said, but she was still prepared to talk to Ma if she thought there was any chance of hearing more gossip.

On every visit home in early 1912, the situation had become worse. Ma told her in hushed tones that there had been some nights when Ruby had not come home at all – and these had coincided with a period when Mrs Paine had gone to visit her sister in Portsmouth who needed nursing. 'If we can at least keep that quiet it'd be something,' Ma said. 'But honestly I am despairing. If he leaves his wife for Ruby then she will always be known as a marriage-breaker, and if he doesn't then she is soiled goods and no one will have her. She's done for in this town, lovey, but she can't seem to see it.'

Ruby remained defiant, telling Emma she loved Harry and

that was all that mattered. 'Does he love you too?' Emma asked, and Ruby shrugged then said, 'Yes, well, he must do, mustn't he?' Emma wasn't sure why he 'must' but had not wanted to say anything. She and Ruby had been getting along reasonably well, as long as Emma didn't say anything critical of Harry.

Ruby's other friends had dropped away. 'I don't care,' Ruby said. 'They was happy to be part of the group when Harry paid them attention, too. Now he's picked me over all of them they don't want to know.'

Or were they ashamed of her, Emma wondered but didn't say.

Arriving home at the end of March, Emma was excited to see Ruby again, resolving to tell her about Martin, but also nervous to find out what had happened over the last three weeks. Her sister was in a precarious position in her relationship with Harry, and Emma was terrified that she'd push it too far. She'd had nightmares on the ship that she'd come home to find Ruby out of work or fighting in public with Mrs Paine.

She hugged Martin goodbye as they left the ship. 'Signing on again tomorrow, then?' he said.

'I certainly am,' she replied.

'I might see you there, but then I'm rushing up to Salisbury to see my folk for a few days before we embark. Next time we're between voyages, I'll stay in Southampton.'

'And I'll take you to meet Ma and my sisters.'

'I'd like that. Very much.' He bent over her then, and kissed her, tenderly, on the lips, just as he had on Christmas Eve, but this time in full view of so many people leaving the ship. He blushed, turned away and hurried off, waving over his shoulder at her. Emma stayed standing where she was for a moment, her fingers on her lips where he had kissed her and sent a thrill through her. Was this how Ruby felt when she was with Harry? If so, Emma thought maybe she could understand why Ruby was prepared to take risks with her reputation. She resolved to be kind to Ruby, to talk to her and see if there was any way out of this mess that would leave Ruby happy, with the man she loved.

She hurried home, expecting to find only Ma and Lily there, for although it was after the time Ruby finished work she'd no doubt be snatching a few hours with Harry while she could. He finished his shift as a department store stockroom clerk half an hour before her shift finished, and always met her after work. His wife thought he was doing overtime, Ruby had told Emma. At least she had thought this, until the gossip-mongers began spreading the word about Ruby. Now, who knew what Mrs Paine thought.

But Ruby was in the house, sitting at the kitchen table in her work uniform, with a cup of tea in her hand and a sour expression on her face. Ma was seated opposite, wringing her hands.

'Emma, lovey, thank goodness you are home. I hope you had a safe trip. I'll make you tea – you sit there with your sister.' The sub-text was clear. *Talk to Ruby. Find out what's happened now. Knock some sense into her.*

'Hello, Ma.' Emma kissed her mother's cheek. 'Tea would be lovely. Ruby – how are things?'

But before Ruby could answer the kitchen door was flung open and Lily bowled in, arms outstretched. 'Ems! You're home! Tell me it's for more than a week this time!'

'Lily, sweetness, you've grown again!' Emma kissed her little sister. 'But I'm sorry, I only have a week off this time. *Olympic* sails in a week, then her sister ship *Titanic* sets off on her maiden voyage in about ten days' time.'

'Sister ship! Just like we're sisters!' Lily giggled.

'Yes, just like us!' Emma said, giving her sister a squeeze.

'Which ship are you signing on for?' Ma asked.

'I'll stick with *Olympic*. I know it well now. Maiden voyages are lovely but the passengers can be a bit over-excited, which makes them more difficult to look after.'

Ruby had listened in silence, but now she got up and walked

105

out. A moment later Emma could hear the clump of her feet on the stairs. 'What's up with Ruby? I thought she'd be out?'

'You'll have to ask her,' Ma said, tight-lipped.

'She's in trouble, as always,' Lily said, 'but she won't talk to me, hardly at all. I might as well have only one sister, not two. She's never taken any notice of me, not like you, Ems.'

'I'll go up.' Emma took the cup of tea Ma was handing to her and left the room. Upstairs, Ruby was lying full length on her bed, her forearm draped across her eyes. She shifted it slightly to see who'd come in, and Emma was pleased to note she then moved over a little in the bed so that Emma could sit down. It was as near as she'd ever get to an invitation to sit and talk. 'All right, Rubes? Seems like ages since I saw you last.'

'Three weeks. So much can happen in three weeks though, can't it?' Ruby sighed, and reached out a hand to Emma, who clasped it with both of hers.

'Oh Rubes, what's happened?' Emma could see her sister was fighting back tears.

'Harry bloody Paine, that's what's happened.'

Emma felt as though all her nightmares were about to come true. She waited, heart in mouth, for her sister to continue.

'So – we've been seeing each other for ages now. Nearly a year. And people know. They all gossip about us, and someone threw a rotten tomato at me, and Mr Biggins at the hotel – you know, my boss – calls me into his office and says word has reached him that I'm running about with a married man, and that if it continues he'll have to let me go as it's bad for the hotel's reputation. Huh. As if they don't have unmarried couples staying there all the time – the number of Mr and Mrs Smiths that check in is ridiculous.'

'Oh Rubes, you don't want to lose your job,' Emma said, hoping that her sister hadn't already lost it. Family finances were tight enough without having Ruby out of work for a while.

'I don't care. I'm going to hand in my notice anyway. But that's not the worst of it. So I said to Harry, it's been a year, it's time you made an honest woman of me. I wants him to divorce Celia and marry me.'

'Divorce! That's a big step.'

Ruby shrugged. 'Not really. Just means he made the wrong decision five years ago. You shouldn't be forced into staying with the wrong person if you don't love them any more. Anyway, it isn't going to happen. Harry told me yesterday he's not going to get divorced. They've got three little kiddies and he doesn't think it's right for them to have to grow up with divorced parents. One of those kiddies is only three weeks old. That means he'd already started seeing me when he got Celia pregnant. He'd told me they was estranged and sleeping apart. He's a bloody liar.'

'Oh Ruby.' Emma leaned over and gathered her sister into her arms for a hug. 'I'm so sorry this has happened.'

Ruby pulled away. 'I haven't finished yet. There's been a few days lately when Harry was supposed to meet me but didn't turn up. Then Ellie Carter told me today she saw him, down at the Crown and Anchor, chatting up some girl with red hair. Don't know who she was, but he was supposed to be with me that evening.' She scoffed. 'Ellie Carter took such glee in telling me.'

'He's let you down.' *Just like he let his wife down*, Emma wanted to add but stopped herself in time. Men like that let everyone down.

'I never wants to see him again. To think I let him …' Ruby tailed off, and turned over, her face to the wall. 'I hates him. I wants to get myself as far away from him as possible. I hate it here. There's nothing for me in Southampton any more. No one will talk to me. They all think I'm a … slut.' She spat the last word out, her tone a mixture of shame and defiance. 'Even Lily hates me. Says I never talk to her. Says she don't care if I never sees her again.'

'Oh, she's just at that difficult age,' Emma said, soothingly. 'She doesn't mean it.'

Ruby nodded. 'I think she does. She told me her school friends

107

were making fun of her for having me as a sister. I've got to get away from here.'

'What will you do?' Emma asked.

'D'you reckon they'd take me on *Olympic*?' Ruby asked, twisting back to look at Emma hopefully. 'I'm old enough now. Or that new ship, *Titanic*, is it?'

'Worth a try,' Emma said, with a smile. 'Sign on day is tomorrow. Come down to the docks with me.' *There's someone I'd like you to meet*, she almost added, but thought better of it. No need to show off her own boyfriend just as Ruby had lost hers, even if she would be better off without hers in the long run. 'Does Ma know?'

'Not really. I said he upset me, that's all. She's probably hoping it's all over, so she'll be delighted when she finds out it is.'

'She'll be sad for you, though. She only wants you to be happy. Same for all of us.'

'No, Ems. She wants more than that, don't she? She wants us to be *respectable*, not to embarrass her, to make her proud. I haven't done that, have I? I needs to get away. Away from him, and from this city. Really hope I can get a job like yours.'

'I hope so too,' Emma said. She tried, but failed, to imagine working alongside Ruby on one of the ships. It might be better if they signed on for different ships. 'Come on. Let's go downstairs and tell Ma your plan. It'll make her feel better.'

As expected, Ma was thrilled by the idea of Ruby getting a job on board a ship. 'I'm losing another daughter but it'll be so good for you, lovey,' she said, though tears sparkled at the corners of her eyes.

Emma guessed Ma was most pleased by the idea of Ruby being far away from Harry Paine. 'You'll be all right here with just Lily, will you? What if Lily's sick again?'

'I'm not going to be ill again,' Lily said. 'I'm out-growing it. So I can help Ma in the house, and we'll be fine. Rubes never did much anyway, and you'll be back every few weeks.'

'I does my share,' Ruby said, glaring at her younger sister, and it took all Emma's and Ma's diplomatic skills to avert an argument.

Later, when Ruby and Lily had both gone through to the front room and Emma was helping make the dinner, Ma turned to Emma. 'You said there were two ships?'

'That's right – *Olympic* and *Titanic*.'

'Will you and Ruby be on the same one?'

'I don't know – depends which one she signs up for. As I said, I want to stick with *Olympic*. My friends are probably going on that one.' *And stick with Martin*, she thought.

Ma took a step towards Emma and clutched at her upper arms. 'Promise me, lovey, that you'll persuade her to sign on for *Olympic* as well? So you can keep an eye on her? You know what she's like … I'd feel so much better if I know you're there with her, to stop her getting into any trouble …'

Emma hugged her mother. 'All right. I'll take her to the *Olympic* signing-on. I'll look after her, no matter what.'

Inwardly she sighed. She'd enjoyed keeping the two parts of her life separate. Her time on board ship was busy but it was hers, there was no need for her to worry about Ma or her sisters while she was at sea. Now those two lives were going to collide, if the White Star Line took Ruby on. But she'd have to do what she'd promised Ma.

The following day Ruby and Emma headed down to the docks together. 'What about the hotel? If you aren't taken on by White Star you'll need to go back to your old job, and they'll be cross you didn't turn up today,' Emma cautioned.

'I'll tell them I was at home, sick.' Ruby shrugged. 'But anyway I wants to give up that job, whatever happens.'

'But you'll need references.'

Ruby pulled a sheet of type-written paper from her bag. 'I have those.'

Emma tried to take it from her sister to look more closely, but

Ruby tucked it away again quickly. 'How did you get a reference when you haven't told them you're leaving?' Emma asked.

'Never you mind,' Ruby said. 'Just need to hope they don't check the references too thoroughly.'

'You forged it?' Emma was aghast.

'I didn't, no. Let's just say Harry has his uses. We'd talked about going away and starting again somewhere new. Until he decided he couldn't leave his kiddies.' Ruby's tone was bitter.

Emma said no more. It was clear Harry had strung Ruby along with promises that he'd had no intention of keeping. When he'd bored of her, he'd dropped her. And he'd do the same to some other poor gullible girl, like the one Ellie Carter had seen him with in the Crown and Anchor. She prayed silently that the White Star Line would give her sister a job, despite the faked references, so Ruby could rebuild her life. She needed a second chance. Whether she deserved it or not was another matter.

They reached the White Star offices, where dozens of people were milling about as was usual on signing-on day. Emma kept scanning the crowds for Martin, Mary, and Violet. Mary and Violet usually came later, but Martin was due to travel to Salisbury to his folk that afternoon so she'd expected him to be there early on.

'There are a lot of rough-looking chaps about,' Ruby commented, gazing at a group of men in scruffy, coal-blackened clothes.

'They'll be firemen and engineers. A lot of men are needed to keep those steam engines going,' Emma replied, enjoying the chance to show off her knowledge of how the liners operated.

'Do they mix with the stewardesses much?' Ruby wrinkled her nose in distaste.

'No, hardly at all. Stewarding staff have no reason to go to the engine rooms, and we have our own cabins and rest areas.'

'Good. So where do I sign on?'

The offices were even busier than usual as they were dealing with both the *Olympic*'s next trip across the Atlantic, and the

Titanic's maiden voyage that was due to depart a few days after the *Olympic*. Emma was amazed that there were enough rich people to warrant two such enormous ships plying the same route. And Martin had said the Harland and Wolff dockyard in Belfast was building a third ship, too. She glanced up at the signs. 'Through here to sign on for the *Olympic*.'

'I fancy the *Titanic*,' Ruby said, turning towards that sign.

'I'm not sure they're taking people with no experience as it's a maiden voyage,' Emma said, catching her sister's arm to stop her. 'Come with me on *Olympic*.'

'Your first voyage was a maiden voyage,' Ruby reminded Emma, pulling her arm free. 'Why do you always have to try to control me? I'd love to be on *Titanic*'s first voyage – and the papers are saying *Titanic*'s even more luxurious than *Olympic*. I wants to be on the best ship.'

Emma let out an exasperated sigh. 'Just sit here, Rubes. Ma wants us on the same ship, and that'll be *Olympic*. It's the ship I … oh, there's …' She'd spotted Martin across the hall. 'Wait there, Rubes. I'll be just a moment.'

She hurried over to Martin, and only just managed to stop herself from flinging her arms around him and kissing him. Here was not the right place for all that! 'Martin, come and meet my sister Ruby. She's hoping to sign on as well, today.'

'You said she might. I've already signed on for *Olympic*, as we agreed. I was here early. Been waiting around hoping to see you.'

'And here I am.' Emma caught his hand and pulled him back through the throngs of people to where she'd left Ruby. 'Where is she? She was here …' She looked around, but there was no sign of Ruby. 'Just like her to wander off,' Emma grumbled.

'She'll not have gone far. Not if she wants to sign on.'

He was right. Emma sat down to wait for her name to be called, with Martin beside her chatting happily.

A few minutes later a triumphant-looking Ruby came striding across the hall to them, waving a brand new Seaman's Discharge book. 'Done it! They've taken me on. You're looking at Ruby Higgins, stewardess second class, RMS *Titanic*, sailing 10th April, 1912.'

'*Titanic!* But we said—'

'*You* said. I wants to be on the new ship. You do what you like. Who's this?' Ruby indicated Martin, who'd stood as she approached.

'Ruby, this is Martin Seward. He's a second-class steward I've been working with, and have become, er, friends with. Martin, my sister Ruby.'

'Delighted to meet you,' Martin said, shaking Ruby's hand.

'Likewise. Ems, why have you not mentioned Martin at all?'

'Haven't I? Oh, well …'

'Miss Emma Higgins, please,' a clerk called out. Emma hesitated. If Ruby was on the *Titanic*, then she too would need to sign on with that ship, to keep her promise to Ma. But Martin was going to sail with the *Olympic*. She felt torn. The thought of being on board without Martin, not seeing him for a month or more … but then, she'd promised Ma, and Lord knew Ruby needed watching …

'Martin, I—'

'You want to stay with your sister?' he said quietly, taking her hand.

'I promised our Ma. I have to.'

He nodded, his eyes full of understanding. 'So you must. Go on – explain to the clerk, they'll switch you over.'

Emma squeezed his hand and hurried over to speak to the clerk. It was not a problem. They were grateful to have more experienced stewards and stewardesses on the *Titanic*. Soon her discharge book was stamped, she'd signed the Articles for the new ship, and was returning to Ruby and Martin.

'I'll be with you,' she said to Ruby. 'On *Titanic*.'

Ruby's expression was an odd mix of annoyance and relief. 'Well, I don't need babysitting, but it'll be fun to be together, I suppose. Grand name for a ship, isn't it?'

Chapter 11

Harriet

The cruise was over all too quickly. Harriet and Sheila had visited the Rijksmuseum in Amsterdam, and strolled alongside the city's canals. They'd skipped the excursion to Bruges from Zeebrugge as both had been there before; instead they'd decided to spend the day on the ship doing various different activities. At Guernsey the ship docked at St Peter's Port, and it was a short stroll into the tiny town centre.

'What a dear little place!' Sheila remarked to Harriet. 'And so much history all around. Definitely somewhere I want to come back to for a longer visit.'

Harriet had agreed. A week touring Guernsey followed by another week on Jersey would make for a perfect summer holiday. Maybe Sheila would accompany her. This cruise had proved it was possible to have a fun holiday without John, even though she still missed him so much.

They disembarked in Southampton and waved goodbye to the ship. 'Until next time, dear *QM2*,' Harriet said.

'Or we could try the *Queen Victoria* next time,' Sheila said. 'It'd be fun to compare the Queens.'

They travelled home by taxi and train, and en route Harriet phoned Sally to find out how Jerome was and invite them for dinner on Sunday.

'He's much the same as when you went away,' Sally said, 'and thank you, we'd love to come for Sunday lunch.'

Harriet was pleased to hear Jerome was no worse. 'I'd have felt so guilty,' she said to Sheila after the phone call. 'I'll be glad to see him and judge for myself at the weekend.'

'Ah, bless him. He'll like the bits and bobs you've bought for him, won't he?'

Harriet had been unable to resist buying several small toys and trinkets from each place they'd visited, plus a toy model of the ship itself. She couldn't wait to see him again, her dear little grandson.

When Jerome was feeling up to it, Harriet promised herself that she'd take him to the beach again. She lived only a ten minute walk from the golden sands of Bournemouth – along a couple of tree-lined streets, cross the Overcliff road and down a zig-zag path that led to the promenade. At the bottom of the zig-zags at the end of a row of beach huts was an ice-cream stall that was open all summer and also sometimes out of season at the weekend if the weather was good. Jerome could never be persuaded to set foot on the beach until she'd bought him a cornet. 'It's not a proper beach without ice-cream,' he'd say with a laugh.

The last time she'd taken him to the beach was the previous summer, before his diagnosis. It was only a couple of months after John's death, but Harriet had insisted she keep to the tradition of having Jerome to stay for a few days during every school holiday. On the first day it had rained so they'd stayed indoors and baked chocolate chip cookies, then played games and watched DVDs, and had burgers with oven-cooked chips for tea. On the second day the sun had come out so they'd gone to play crazy golf on the cliff top, then made their way down to the beach for a picnic, which of course had to start with an ice cream.

Harriet remembered how she'd helped Jerome build a sandcastle. That had usually been John's role, and it had been at least fifty years since she'd made one herself. But it had been surprisingly enjoyable, the sand at the perfect degree of wetness to stick together. They'd dug a traditional mound with a moat, decorated it with stones and shells, then as the tide began to come in Harriet, remembering something John had done with Davina and Sally, suggested they dug a channel to the sea to let waves come in to fill the moat. She'd been amazed to discover they'd spent hours at it – happy, joyful hours of digging and excavating and laughing as the incoming waves swamped the moat and began to undercut the castle itself.

It was a perfect day – cloudless blue sky, stunning views of the Purbeck hills in one direction, and the western tip of the Isle of Wight in the other. When the sun shone on the white cliffs of Alum Bay it took on the shape of a polar bear, from their viewpoint on the eastern end of Bournemouth's beach. 'Can you see the polar bear?' she'd teased Jerome, and he had spent five minutes scanning the beach, cliffs and horizon before gleefully spotting it.

At last, recognising that Jerome was beginning to tire, she'd packed up the rug, picnic bag and buckets and spades, and taken him home where she'd put on a Disney DVD while she cooked something for tea. He'd fallen asleep on the sofa. She'd found him curled up cuddling a cushion when he didn't respond to her calls that tea was ready. She'd spent a minute just gazing at him, his sun-lightened hair that was clumpy with dried saltwater, his face with a hundred times more freckles than he'd had that morning, his little bronzed arm curled around the cushion. What was it about children that tugged so at your heartstrings? She loved this child so much; she'd do anything to keep him safe.

It had been a wonderful day. Would her unknown granddaughters have enjoyed that kind of day on the beach? Would she ever get the chance to take them, to jump the waves with them, treat them to ice cream – Autumn at least. She remembered that Davina had said Summer didn't like ice cream. Would the girls ever play with their little cousin in the sand? She pictured the three of them, heads together, digging a moat around a huge castle while she, Sally and Davina watched, chatting happily. Would that, could that ever happen?

Back home after the cruise, Harriet unpacked and put a load of washing on, then spent a while sorting through the many photos she'd taken on the trip. She picked out the best ones and transferred them to a file on her laptop, ready to show Sally and Charlie at the weekend. There were a few of ships and tugs she'd taken especially for Jerome too.

She realised with a pang of pain that these were the first photos she'd taken since John had died. In the past, they'd have sorted through holiday snaps together, putting together albums of each trip, each photo neatly labelled. How she would love to be able to show him this set of pictures! Once the sorting was complete, she decided to take a walk to the cemetery. She could tell his headstone all about the cruise, at least.

It had been so sudden, John's death. One day they'd been settling into their new lives as retirees, spending time pottering in the garden, visiting local places of interest or planning weekend breaks away. And the next – he was gone. Harriet woke up one morning beside him, and instantly realised something was horribly, terribly wrong. The lack of warmth from his side of the bed, lack of movement, of the sounds of his breathing; she turned over and propped herself on one elbow, and saw that he was gone. A massive heart attack that probably killed him instantly, the post-mortem later concluded. Harriet blamed herself. Why hadn't she woken, when the heart attack hit? She'd always thought they would be noisy affairs, accompanied by groaning and thrashing by the victim. How could he have had such a large one and it not have woken her? She might have been able to do something – call the paramedics, resuscitate him, something, anything.

But by the time she'd woken, that bright early-summer morning, he'd been lying dead beside her for several hours. Long enough for his body to have cooled and stiffened. As the initial shock gave way to dawning of the awful truth she felt an astonishing sense of calm – realising these would be her last moments with him. There was no point rushing to call anyone – there was nothing that could be done for him. She should make the most of the time, say goodbye to him properly, spend a few minutes remembering. She leaned over and kissed his forehead, then his lips. 'Goodbye, my love. Thank you for our life together. I wouldn't have changed a moment of it. Sleep well.' She lay down again, her head against his stiffened shoulder and draped her arm across his chest. So many times she had lain like this, held him like so. And this was to be the last time.

She stayed like that for a minute, or was it an hour – time seemed to have stopped. The tears came, silently flowing down her cheeks and onto John's chest. She thought about the last words he'd said to her the night before, as they put down their books – his Lee Child thriller he'd never now finish – and turned out the lights. 'Love you, love you, love you – is that enough to last you the night?' It was one of their little nightly routines. She'd replied, as she always did, 'It'll have to do. Love you too.' And now those words of love had to last the rest of her life, for she would never hear them from him again.

The bedroom window was open, and outside she could hear birds singing and the bin lorry making its way down the street, collecting the recycling bins. John had put theirs out as usual the previous night. Life was continuing as usual for everyone else, but not for John. And her own would be very different from now on.

It was time. She sat up, got out of bed and pulled the duvet up to John's chin. At a casual glance he looked as though he was simply sleeping, but the greyness of his skin, the stiffness of his features gave away the terrible reality.

Her phone was downstairs. 'I'm just going to go and call someone,' she said to him, as she pushed her feet into slippers and put on a dressing gown. Ambulance or Sally, first?

She decided to call 999 first, and get the ball rolling. As John had died so suddenly no doubt the police would need to come too. She explained to the emergency operator what had happened, and a sympathetic voice confirmed that both police and ambulance would soon turn up. And then she took a deep breath and called Sally.

'What? He can't have … are you sure? Have you tried heart massage? I mean … he was fine yesterday. Oh God. I have to get Jerome to school. I'll come round. I'll get Elaine from across the road to take Jerome. I'll … Oh Mum! I'll be there, I'm coming. Hold on.'

As she hung up and waited in the last moments of quiet for the emergency services and Sally to arrive, Harriet's thoughts turned to Davina. Davina who had not seen her father for fourteen years. Davina, for whom she had no contact details, so no way of letting her know her father had died. Harriet felt a wave of anger at her younger daughter wash over her as she thought how John would have hated going to his grave without seeing Davina again – but that was what was happening. And it might be months before she could even tell Davina what had happened.

It wasn't long before the doorbell rang and everyone seemed to arrive at once. First a paramedic, who she ushered upstairs. And the police and Sally arrived at almost the same time, shortly followed by an ambulance.

Sally bustled through, her eyes red, and gathered Harriet into a hug. 'Oh, it's so awful, I can't believe it! He was so well!'

'Do you want to see him?' Harriet said gently.

'Yes, no, oh goodness, I don't know.' Sally sat down heavily on a chair in the kitchen and covered her face with her hands. Harriet knelt beside her and wrapped her arms around her daughter.

'It's terrible, but you know, it's not a bad way to go. He wouldn't have suffered. Just went to sleep and didn't wake up. Better than a long, slow death of cancer or something.' She wasn't sure if her words were intended to comfort Sally or herself more.

'But he was only 70. Too young. And no warning.'

'I know. I know.'

'Ahem.' A cough from the kitchen doorway alerted them to a police officer standing there. 'I am sorry to intrude, but I will need statements from you. Just a formality, but as your husband died at home there will need to be an inquest.'

Sally sniffed, wiped her eyes and stood up. 'Of course. Mum, why don't you sit here with the policeman, and I'll make some tea.' She'd gone into her organising mode, taking charge. Harriet was grateful for it; she knew it was Sally's way of coping.

The morning passed in a whirlwind. It seemed a long time before the ambulance took away John's body, and the police left, having taken photos and statements. Finally Harriet was alone with Sally, with the chance to get dressed at last. The first set of clothes she'd worn after John's death, she realised. There were going to be a lot of firsts, and it didn't seem fair that she hadn't realised the last times for everything with John had been the last.

It was Sally who largely organised John's funeral – both the humanist service and the buffet lunch in a pub that followed. She did a good job. It was just, Harriet thought, as John would have wanted, and as he'd have organised himself. Sally had clearly inherited her tendency to take charge from him.

Sally phoned all Harriet's local friends and told them of John's death and the funeral arrangements. She'd borrowed Harriet's address book and written to everyone on the Christmas card list to inform them.

'I can phone some,' Harriet said, but Sally waved her away.

'Mum, it's too distressing for you. Let me do it.'

And Sally had written the eulogy for John before Harriet had a chance to. At least she let Harriet approve it and amend a few

119

sections. Sally read it out at the service – and for this Harriet was truly grateful, knowing she would never have been able to get through it without sobbing.

'It's nice that she's doing so much to help you,' Sheila said, but she frowned as she said it. Harriet nodded, not wanting to think too hard about whether in fact Sally was taking over too much, taking on tasks that actually Harriet would have liked to have done herself. For now it was easier to sit back and let Sally take charge, but a small part of her worried that looking back, she might wish she'd had more say in it all. But she knew too, that being busy, organising the practical aspects of it all, helped Sally come to terms with her loss.

'You're grieving, Mum. You're the widow. You have to look after yourself, let other people do things for you. That's what grown-up kids are for, after all.' Sally sniffed. 'Well, this one, at least. Not that you're getting any help from your other daughter.'

Then Davina had turned up, all too briefly, at the graveside, and Harriet had been glad to see her, even though it was only for a moment. She'd wondered if she was being unfair – in some ways she'd felt more grateful that Davina had turned up than for everything Sally had done for her.

All that was almost a year ago, now. A year in which she'd tried to come to terms with John's loss but sometimes still felt as though the wound was too deep, too raw to ever heal. A year in which his loss was not the only upheaval – Jerome's diagnosis had hit the family even harder, in some ways, and left them all reeling yet still trying to act as though everything was normal. It'd never be 'normal' again, she realised, as she sat on the bench near John's grave. A new normal, perhaps, but things could never be the same. 'As long as Jerome recovers, I think we'll cope, though,' she said out loud, as a breath of wind blew around her head, as though John was ruffling her hair in response.

Chapter 12

Emma, 1912

There were ten more days at home before the *Titanic* sailed. It was a busy time – Emma helped Ruby organise her sailing trunk; went with her when she handed in her notice at the hotel; and watched the *Olympic* sail with a pang of disappointment that she wasn't on it alongside Martin, mixed with excitement that she was to sail on another brand new ship. The *Titanic* arrived in port at midnight on the very next day, sailing down from Belfast after her sea trials had proved her seaworthy. She took the *Olympic*'s usual berth. Emma had heard that using some new technology the two ships had been able to send messages to each other as they passed.

As with the *Olympic*'s arrival there was a huge buzz about the city. Many notable personages were arriving to sail on the *Titanic*'s maiden voyage, including Bruce Ismay the Managing Director of the White Star Line, and Thomas Andrews the chief engineer and designer of the *Titanic* and her sisters. Some had been on the *Olympic* too. The stewarding crew were due to board the ship on the same day as the passengers, early in the morning.

As most of them were experienced and it was the second ship of its class, it had not been thought necessary to have several days of training as Emma had had on the *Olympic*.

'You'll pick it up quickly,' Emma said to Ruby. 'And I'll be there to help you and advise you.'

Ruby had scowled at this, and walked off, leaving Emma shrugging. She was only trying to help her sister.

On their last night at home Emma and Ruby prepared the dinner for Ma and treated her to a bottle of wine. Ma was in tears as she raised her glass to her two eldest daughters.

'I'm so proud of you both, you know. Emma you've been such a support to me, and Ruby, now that you've sorted yourself out and got this job, I couldn't be prouder. I told Mrs Williams, they're both off on the *Titanic*, all the way over the sea. And who knows, if you do your jobs well you might be promoted to first class and I've heard those first-class passengers tip their stewards and stewardesses handsomely.'

'Some do, but not all, and my, you have to work for it, so Violet tells me!' Emma said. 'Anyway, I like second class.'

'I just want to be on a ship,' Ruby said. 'Ma, I'll miss you, and you too, Lily.' She got up from her place at the table and hugged each of them, crying openly. Oddly, Ruby had been making more of an effort with Lily since she'd signed on. Emma watched, slightly bemused. She had not been this emotional when she'd left on the *Olympic* for the first time.

Lily looked surprised at the rare show of affection from Ruby but returned the hug. 'I'll miss you too, Rubes.'

'Ah, come on, Ruby,' Emma said, trying to lighten the mood a little. 'We'll be back home again at the end of the month, and it'll feel like no time at all has passed.'

Ruby sniffed loudly and composed herself. She gave a weak smile. 'Yes, I suppose you're right, and you'd know. Just – my first time away, and after all that's happened, it feels like such a big step.'

Emma patted her hand. 'I know, and it is. Come on, let's pour out the rest of the wine, and toast the *Titanic*, and all who sail in her.'

Ma and Ruby raised their glasses. 'To the *Titanic*.'

'Can I have some wine?' asked Lily, her eyes wide and hopeful.

'Just a tiny taste of mine, lovey, and only because both your sisters are going away and you're going to have to be my big grown-up girl and help me around the house.'

'I am almost grown-up and I already help you, don't I?' Lily looked a little put out, as she often did when she was treated as a baby. She was almost 13 now, and not far off leaving school. Emma realised they'd often treated her as younger than she was, because of the recurring illnesses she'd had. It was time they treated her as an adult, or a near-adult.

'Of course you are, sweetie,' Emma said, giving Lily a hug, 'and yes you do help Ma. You might have to do a bit more now there's only two of you.'

'I'll miss you both,' Lily said. 'When I'm old enough, I think it's the job I'd like to do, too.'

'We'll keep a place warm for you on the ship then,' Emma said with a smile.

'Early start tomorrow?' Ma asked.

'Yes, the stewarding crew need to be on board before the passengers embark, and that starts at half past nine,' Emma said. 'So we'd better be packed tonight and ready to leave at seven.'

'I'll be up to see you off,' Ma said.

'So will I,' chipped in Lily.

Emma smiled. Both Ma and Lily seemed excited for them, and not bothered at all by the idea of them both going away. So different to when she'd first gone to sea. It was only Ruby that was tearful today, but Emma supposed that was natural as Ruby was leaving home for the first time.

As planned, early the next morning the sisters hugged Ma and Lily goodbye then made their way to the docks. At the end of the street

Ruby turned and looked back at the house. There was something wistful in her expression. It was her first time away from home, Emma realised. She linked arms with her sister. 'Come on. You'll feel better once you're on the ship and the adventure has begun.'

Ruby smiled and walked on, and soon they boarded the *Titanic*. The quayside was teeming with people – passengers and crew, sightseers wishing to see the ship leave, journalists hoping for quick interviews with notable passengers. Carriages and motor-cars delivered first-class passengers and their huge volume of luggage. Many brought their pets with them – pampered lapdogs who'd be largely looked after by the stewards while on board.

On board Ruby was shepherded off for a tour and initial training immediately, along with a few other people new to the job. Emma had a little longer to settle into her cabin, down on 'E' deck. She was sharing with Ruby this time – it had made sense for the sisters to be together. Mary was along the galley-way sharing with another stewardess named Ann – an older woman who'd been working on the liners for many years. Emma noted there were a few improvements in the layout of the staff cabins compared with the *Olympic*. Thomas Andrews had asked the *Olympic* crew for any recommendations they'd like to make, and it seemed he'd listened to them. In the stewards' cabins, there were now two separate, small wardrobes rather than a shared larger one, and the bunks had been placed in a way that gave more privacy.

Violet was also on board, and she came to knock on Emma's cabin door to say hello.

'Good to see you here,' Violet said. 'Another maiden voyage – we'll be experts at them soon! I hear your sister has signed on too?'

'Yes, Ruby's here, and sharing with me. She's just gone for her tour and initial training.'

'They're not getting much training this time, are they? We're sailing later today. You had much more, on the *Olympic*.'

'I did, yes. But this time nearly all the stewards worked on *Olympic* so we know the layout. I suppose they think that us old hands can help the new ones out.' It felt strange to consider herself an 'old hand' but after eight voyages on *Olympic* Emma supposed that she was. She'd only missed one voyage – and felt herself lucky to have missed it. It was the one where the *Olympic* had collided with HMS *Hawke* in the Solent. The ship had to go back to Belfast for major repairs after that. Violet had been on board and told her all about the sickening crunch of the impact, and the fear that although the *Olympic* was supposed to be unsinkable, was it really? The crew had been relieved when the ship managed to limp safely back to Southampton to be patched up enough to allow her to sail back to the Harland and Wolff shipyard in Belfast. Emma had a long break between voyages in autumn 1911 as the full repairs had taken six weeks to complete. She'd enjoyed the time off, glad she hadn't had the traumatic experience of being on board during the collision, but had missed the wages.

'Well, I'll see you later. I've still my cabin to sort out, and it's not long before the passengers come on board. My first-class people won't be here till later though – they're embarking third class first as there's so many of them. All looking to start a new life across the Atlantic, I suppose. I'll call by later to meet your sister.' Violet waved a hand and hurried out, leaving Emma to finish her unpacking.

It didn't take long – she had packed and unpacked her trunk so many times now she knew exactly where she wanted to put everything. She placed the photograph of her sisters beside her bed as usual – even though on this voyage she had one of her sisters with her. Once finished, she gazed at Ruby's trunk, and decided she might as well help her sister out and unpack that one too. She felt a pang of guilt as she opened it, but reasoned that as the old hand on the ship, she knew best where everything should be put. It wasn't as though it was a stranger's trunk – it was only her sister's.

She was halfway through when she found something

unexpected. A cream knitted shawl that she recognised – Ma had used it to swaddle Lily when she was a baby. Emma hadn't seen it for years. It was too small for a grown woman to wear on her shoulders. Why had Ruby packed it? She was mulling this over, still holding the shawl, when the cabin door opened and Ruby returned, looking flushed and happy. 'What a ship! It's so beautiful – those first class staterooms … wait, what are you doing? Why are you going through my things?' Her mood switched instantly and she grabbed the shawl out of Emma's hands.

'I was just unpacking your trunk.' Emma waved a hand in the direction of the cupboards. 'Trying to be helpful.'

'Well, don't. They're my things, I'll unpack them myself.' Ruby threw the shawl back into her trunk.

'Why have you brought that shawl?' Emma asked.

Ruby's chin went up defiantly. 'Because I like it.' She turned her back on Emma and began flinging items into drawers. After a moment she turned back again, her face red with fury. 'Honestly, Emma. You're so controlling. I'd never open *your* trunk and go through it. It's private. Yet you thinks nothing of rummaging in mine. You treats me like a 6-year-old. I'm only three years younger than you, and now we're both grown women that means nothing.'

'Rubes, sorry, I didn't think you'd …'

'You didn't think. Listen, Emma, if we're to get along while we're both on this ship you needs to start acting as though I'm your equal. Who's the girl you used to share with? Mary? Treat me as you would treat her. You wouldn't have gone through her trunk, would you? So don't go through mine. Otherwise we'll fall out, you and me. And that would be a shame, especially as we're stuck here together now.'

'All right. I do take your point. Calm down, Ruby. I won't touch your things again.' Ruby was overreacting, Emma thought. They were sisters, for goodness' sake. They had no secrets from each other. At least not now all that trouble with Harry Paine was over.

'Just go away, will you, Emma, while I finish this? Give me a bit of space?'

Emma stared at her sister, then turned and left the cabin. If Ruby was going to be like that there was no point staying. She had so much she wanted to tell Ruby about life on board ship, but clearly Ruby wasn't in the mood to hear it now. You'd have thought she'd have made the most of having a sister who knew the ropes, but no. Ruby, as usual, seemed to want to do things her own way. Well, at least Emma had tried to help her. She wandered off in search of Mary or Violet. Anyone from her previous voyages.

Halfway along the galley she spotted a familiar face, but not one she'd expected to see. She broke into a broad grin. 'Martin! What on earth … I thought you'd sailed on the *Olympic!*'

'Hello, Emma my love. After you left with Ruby on sign-on day, I pleaded to be allowed to swap. The clerk grumbled a bit but when he realised how experienced I am he agreed I'd be of more use on this ship. So here I am!' He took a quick look up and down the galley as if making sure they wouldn't be seen, then flung his arms around her. 'We're together again! I hated the idea of being apart from you for weeks.'

She snuggled into his embrace. 'So did I. I'm so glad you're here with me.'

'Always.' He kissed her, then let go quickly as a nearby door opened and another steward came out of a cabin. 'See you later. I think I'm working with your sister on this voyage. I can help look after her.'

'Thanks.' Maybe Ruby would settle down with kind, steady Martin at her side showing her the ropes.

It wasn't long before the first- and second-class passengers began to embark, and the stewards and stewardesses had to be on hand to greet those they'd be looking after. The Captain – Emma was pleased to see it was the jolly, bearded Captain Smith again who'd been in charge on a number of *Olympic* sailings – greeted all the first-class passengers personally. A nice touch, Emma thought. It made those who'd paid such a lot of money for the crossing feel special and secure in the knowledge that the Captain himself was looking out for them.

As they set sail, it seemed as though everyone was on deck, including the crew. The first- and second-class passengers and their stewards were on the promenade deck, the third class thronged the poop deck, and what must be half the population of Southampton were on the quayside waving the ship off – more people than had come to see the *Olympic* sail, a year before. The *Titanic* had been billed as being even more luxurious than her sister and the publicity had obviously paid off. Emma spotted J.J. Astor and his new wife on board – Violet had told her he was one of the richest people in the world. She also saw a young woman in first class who looked familiar. 'Why do I feel like I recognise her?' she said, as she pointed the woman out to Ruby.

'Because you've seen her at the pictures,' Ruby answered. 'That's the film actress, Dorothy Gibson. My, the rich and famous really are on board, aren't they?'

'Told you they would be,' Emma replied, with a triumphant smile, glad that she and Ruby seemed to be friends again, after the argument over unpacking.

That first evening in their cabin, Emma smiled at her sister. 'Like old times, isn't it, you and me sharing a room?' She'd shared with Lily on her visits home ever since her first voyage. It felt good to have the chance to reconnect with Ruby.

'Yes, I suppose so.' Ruby flopped down onto her bed, looking exhausted. 'Did you forget to tell me it was so tiring, or had I forgotten?'

'I think I mentioned it. Don't worry, you'll soon get used to it,' Emma replied. She wasn't sure whether Ruby had forgiven her yet for the incident with the trunk. Maybe she'd forgotten all about it. That was the thing with Ruby – her moods could change in seconds, from happy, loving, and friendly to wilful, grumpy, and stubborn. You never knew how she'd react to anything you did or said.

'I hope so. Your friend Martin's been helpful.' Ruby rolled onto her back, an arm flung across her face.

'Good, I knew he would help you. You're very lucky being paired with him.'

'Mmm. Yes, I think I am. He's a bit of a dish.'

Emma's mouth dropped open. Was there a danger that Ruby would flirt with Martin and turn his head? Ruby was prettier than her, and livelier, and maybe he'd think her more fun to be with. Had Ruby not realised how important Martin was to Emma? 'You know that he and I are … stepping out?'

'I know. But it's not like you're engaged, or anything. So I'm allowed to fancy him if I want to.'

'For goodness' sake, Rubes. About 80 per cent of the crew on this ship are men, and you set your sights on my man?'

'Your man? Like I said, you're not even engaged, so he's hardly yours, is he?'

'Even so, leave him alone.'

Ruby turned her face and stared at Emma. 'You don't sound very confident that he wouldn't stray. If you're sure of him, you wouldn't care if I flirt a little, as you'd know he wouldn't do nothing. But if you're telling me not to flirt, that means you're not so sure of him. Hmm. Maybe it's time you listened to advice from me, Ems. I've had more experience with men, after all.'

'With a married man! A married man with young children, who ended it with you at last, thank goodness.'

'What do you mean, thank goodness? Don't it even matter to you that I loved him? I was heartbroken. And he's left me with …'

She tailed off, biting her lip. Emma looked at the way her sister's hand had moved to lie protectively over her midriff. Oh God, she wasn't, was she? She opened her mouth to say something, but Ruby got in there first.

'Look, I've even had to run away to sea to get over him. So let me have a little flirtation with the good-looking man they've paired me up with. It's only for this week, after all, then you gets him back.'

'Only for this week? And the week it'll take for the return voyage. They don't swap crew around while we're in New York.'

Ruby pressed her lips together. 'Hmm. I might not be on the return voyage.'

'What?' Emma stared at her sister. 'What do you mean? You're signed on for both directions.'

Ruby sighed. 'I suppose I'll have to tell you my plans. You can't stop me now, anyway, and you'd find out soon enough. Just remember you're my sister, you wants me to be happy, so you won't do nothing to mess this up.'

'What are you talking about?' Emma was getting worried now. She was trying to think of some way that she could ask Ruby if she was pregnant, without being too blunt about it. She needed to know, didn't she, as Ruby's sister, the only family member on board. But she couldn't ask outright, in case she was wrong. She hoped Ruby would confide in her.

'I'm going to leave the ship in New York. This job was just a cheap way of getting across the ocean. I'm going to start again, over there.'

'But ... but ... you won't be paid for this trip if you don't go back to Southampton and get your discharge book stamped!'

'I have some money. Enough to keep me going for a little while. I'll get a job in New York. There are lots of hotels there, Martin says. I'll easily find work like I was doing in Southampton, to get me started.' Ruby sat up and looked directly at Emma. 'So no, I'm not going back to Southampton. I'll write Ma a letter that you can take back to her.'

'She'll be heartbroken.' Emma tried and failed to imagine telling Ma that Ruby was not coming back. Even worse, that she was not coming back and pregnant with a married man's child.

That explained why she'd packed the shawl. It was intended for her own baby.

Ruby laughed. 'She'll be glad to see the back of me. She says I've brought her nothing but worry. But look, I can't live in the same town as that bastard Harry Paine any longer, can I? And he won't move – not with his wife and kiddies. So I've no choice, really. Besides, I quite fancy trying my luck in New York. Perhaps I'll meet some nice rich American. Maybe someone on board – one of the passengers. Violet said some passengers try to recruit their stewards as their own staff, if they've been impressed with them.'

Emma had heard this too. 'Only in first class, though. And as this is your first voyage …'

'I know. Unlikely to happen. But a girl can dream, can't she? So now you knows my plans. And don't you dare try to do anything to stop me.'

'I promised Ma I'd look after you,' Emma said quietly.

'That's just it, don't you see? You're always there, fussing around, claiming to be keeping an eye on me. I'm fed up of it, Ems. Fed up of Lily holding us back, always having to tread on eggshells around her in case she gets sick again. And Ma, always looking at me with disappointed eyes. My friends – well, I don't have any, do I? I'm staying in New York, and nothing you say will stop me. I'm a grown woman and I can and will look after myself.' With that, Ruby stood up, grabbed her wash things and headed off to the bathroom along the galley-way that they shared with several other staff cabins.

Emma sighed. She'd have to leave it there. But she resolved to have another talk to Ruby about her plans, before they docked in New York. She owed it to Ma to at least try to talk Ruby out of jumping ship. And she had to know – was Ruby carrying Harry Paine's child? It would certainly explain her need to get away and stay away from Southampton, but how on earth would Ruby cope alone and pregnant in New York?

Chapter 13

Harriet

On the Sunday after the cruise Harriet cooked lunch for herself, Sally, Charlie, and Jerome. She'd bought a rib of beef – a real treat as there was never any point buying a large joint for just herself. It had always been a favourite dinner of John's. She spent the morning cooking, preparing a tray of vegetables to roast, whipping up a batter for Yorkshire puddings, and making homemade horseradish sauce. There was trifle for dessert – already made and setting in the fridge. She had the table set and the toys she kept for Jerome in a basket in the sitting room, plus his gifts from the cruise laid out on the coffee table ready for him, when the phone rang.

'Mum? It's me. Sally. God I'm so sorry to leave it this late, but we're not going to be able to come today. Jerome's not so well.'

'Ah no, love. What's happened?' Harriet suppressed the pang of annoyance – she had so much food and now who would eat it? If Sally had called earlier, before she'd put the roast in the oven, she could have frozen it for some future occasion.

'He just seems really fatigued today, and he's saying his joints hurt. I can't persuade him to get out of bed – he's just lying there and shaking his head if I suggest he comes down to watch a DVD. Oh Mum, I'm so worried about him.'

'When is his next appointment with the haematology clinic?' Harriet did not know what to say to comfort Sally. Was there anything she could say that would help? It was all so unfair, poor little Jerome.

'Tuesday. Mum, will you come with me? Charlie will be away on some conference he's speaking at and can't get out of. And I'm scared.'

Harriet's heart broke for her daughter. 'Of course I'll come, love. Meanwhile, is there anything Jerome can take for the pains?'

'I've given him Calpol. But it all seems so inadequate. He had three days at school last week and two this week, and I honestly thought he was getting better, and that the chemotherapy was showing signs of working, and now … God, now I've no idea.'

'Do you think you should call a doctor today?'

Sally sighed. 'I'm not sure there's any point. We're following all the advice we've been given for when he has bad days, and with the appointment coming up so soon, there's not really anything they can do. But it's heartbreaking to see him like this.' Her voice caught on the last words.

'I know, love. I know. If there's anything I can do …' Harriet's voice tailed off. How many times had she said that to Sally since Jerome's diagnosis? Too many to count, and yet there was so often nothing she could do.

'Just, be there on Tuesday to keep me together. Look I'm so sorry about today. Hope you hadn't bought anything special for our lunch.'

'No worries about the food – it'll keep.' She'd be eating roast beef for a week but that couldn't be helped.

'Well, Tuesday, then. The appointment's at 11.15 – I'll pick you up at 10.45, assuming I can get Jerome up and in the car.'

'Shall I come round before to help with him?'

'I'll ring you in the morning if I need you. Thanks, Mum. See you then.'

'Bye, love.'

Harriet replaced the phone and went to check on the roast and the vegetables. Enough to feed an army. She sighed, then on a whim picked up the phone again and called Sheila. If Sheila was on her own today, maybe she'd come round and help make a dent in the food.

'Roast beef, you say? Better than the cheese on toast I was planning! On my way, Harri. I've a Pinot Noir needs drinking – I'll bring that.'

Harriet smiled. That was the response she'd hoped for. It had only been a few days but they could reminisce about the cruise.

And she could confide in Sheila her worries about Jerome.

Sheila arrived within half an hour, all trailing scarves and glittery nail polish. She went straight to the kitchen to open the wine she'd brought, pouring some for Harriet before asking after Jerome. It was as though, Harriet thought, she could see straight into Harriet's soul and could read the anguish there. With a glass of wine in hand and the roast out of the oven and resting, Harriet felt strong enough to tell Sheila what Sally had said.

'And now I am so worried. Oh Sheila. I've lost so many of my family. I never see my brother. I cope, kind of, with Davina's estrangement. I've lost John which hurt more than I can say, but … God … if we lost Jerome too, I can't even …' She shook her head, unable to express how she felt. 'It's like my family's dwindling, piece by piece. I want a large family all gathered around me, huge family celebrations at Christmas and birthdays. But every year there's fewer people, not more.'

'Harri, love, you've only properly lost poor John. The others – there's still chance. Hang on in there.'

'I'm trying. It's so hard. And Sally needs me to be strong. As does Charlie – his own parents are gone, he has to lean on me too. How do I do it, Sheila? How am I going to be strong for them, if the worst happens and Jerome …' She could not bring herself to say the word 'dies' after Jerome's name. Those two words did not belong in the same sentence.

Sheila put down her wine glass, crossed the kitchen and gathered Harriet into her arms. 'The worst is not going to happen, Harri. Trust me on this. Jerome is going to pull through, one way or another. I have a direct line to the Almighty, you know, and I've had words with him. Now's when you need to be strong for Sally and Charlie. On Tuesday when Jerome goes for his appointment. There will be other treatments they can try, if the chemo isn't working. Bone marrow transplants, radiotherapy, whatever – I'm no doctor. There is *plenty* of reason to be hopeful.'

Harriet allowed herself a few tears onto Sheila's velvet-clad shoulder, but then in a gesture worthy of Sally, who rarely let herself crumple for more than a minute, forced herself to smile and wiped her eyes. 'You are so wise, Sheila. Where did all that come from?'

'No idea. Whatever happens, Harri, remember I am here for you to lean on. So when Sally leans on you, you lean on me, and somehow there'll be enough strength to hold everyone together. You were there for me through my messy divorce and again when I had breast cancer – I am here for you now, and always.'

'You are such a good friend. Anyway, I think that beef's rested long enough now. Shall we?'

Sheila grinned. 'Thought you'd never ask. Let me at that beef. I've been eating vegetarian all week and it's lovely but right now I could murder some red meat.'

'You are in the right place, then.' Harriet ushered Sheila to the table and brought out the food, while Sheila topped up their wine glasses. Midday wine was such decadence but she felt she deserved it. There might be rough days ahead.

On Tuesday, the day of the appointment with the haematologist, Sally picked Harriet up as planned, with Jerome sitting in the back seat of the car tucked up in a blanket.

'Hello, my favourite little man,' Harriet said, leaning over from the front seat to kiss him. 'How are you today?'

Jerome pushed his bottom lip out into a pout and turned away, leaning his cheek against the back of the seat.

'He's tired, the poor thing. Didn't want to have to come to hospital today. But we have to go, don't we, Jerome? To find out how we can make you better.' Sally's voice was artificially bright, and Harriet could hear the agonised worry behind her words.

She smiled at her daughter and caught her hand to squeeze. 'Shall we go, then? And afterwards, when we get back, I've got some little presents from the cruise for Jerome, if he's been good. How about that, eh?' But Jerome just shrugged, uninterested. Harriet bit her lip. For him not to care about the offer of new toys he must be feeling very poorly indeed.

Sally started the engine and drove them to the hospital. Harriet tried to keep up a stream of light conversation for the whole journey, telling Sally about the cruise, the near miss with the container ship, and the genealogical research she'd been continuing with. She could tell her daughter was only half listening but if it helped her to keep her mind off Jerome's sickness then it was a good thing.

At the hospital, Sally dropped Harriet and Jerome off at the entrance while she went to find a parking space. 'Come on then soldier, let's go and sit in the waiting room,' Harriet said to her grandson. He leaned against her leg and looked up at her, his eyes looking far too large for his head. 'Can you carry me, Nanna? My legs hurt.'

'Of course I can,' she said, leaning down to scoop him up. Just as well he was small for his age, she thought, as he wrapped his arms around her neck and his legs around her waist. His weight was at the limit of what she could carry, but she was not going to show that she was struggling. Thankfully the haematology department's waiting room was not far and she was soon able to put him down on a chair and sit beside him. 'Phew! You're growing into such a big boy, you know.'

Jerome gave her a small smile and cuddled up to her, his thumb in his mouth just as he used to do when he was a toddler. Sally came in a moment later, registered their arrival with the reception desk, and sat on the other side of Jerome. Harriet reached over to her and squeezed her hand.

It wasn't long before Jerome's name was called, and this time it was Sally who scooped up Jerome to carry him through to the consulting room. In the room, the consultant Dr Windletter sat, perched casually on the corner of his desk. To one side was a support nurse – a blonde woman who smiled reassuringly as they came in and took their seats. Her name badge read 'Alison'. She handed Jerome a picture book to look through, but he just tucked it under one arm and made no effort to open it.

Harriet glanced at Sally. She'd gasped when she entered the room, as though she'd sensed there was going to be bad news. Usually, Harriet knew, it was a registrar that they saw – not the more senior consultant. Perhaps that in itself meant that things weren't going too well?

'So, young man, how are you feeling today?' the consultant asked.

Jerome put his thumb in his mouth and climbed onto Sally's lap in response.

She shook her head. 'Not good. He's very tired. Didn't want to get out of bed at all today. He complains of pains in his arms and legs. He'd had a good couple of weeks when he was well enough to go to school, but we seem to have … gone backwards.'

Harriet noticed the way her voice caught on the last word, and how she'd dipped her head, pressing her lips against Jerome's head, to hide the fact tears had come to her eyes. Alison silently handed Sally a tissue which she took with a weak smile.

'Hmm. Well, we have the results of his last blood tests here,' said the consultant. 'And I'm afraid it does show that the chemotherapy has not had as much of an effect as I'd have liked to see …'

The rest of the consultation passed in a blur. Harriet tried hard to take in everything Dr Windletter said, knowing that Sally might well be missing some of the important points. Usually when Charlie was with Sally, he would make notes and ask questions and ensure they got as much from the appointment as possible, but today it was up to her to listen properly. But it was so difficult – if the chemotherapy wasn't working, what did that mean for Jerome's chances? It was unthinkable that he might not make it …

Thankfully afterwards Alison led them into a quiet room, offered them tea, and then talked it all through with them once more.

'Are you happy that you understood everything?' Alison asked, after she'd handed them cups of tea and made sure Jerome was comfortable.

'Chemo not working, something about bone marrow transplant,' Sally said. 'And he asked if we had any more children.'

Alison nodded. 'Siblings are usually the best match for bone marrow transplants. But as Jerome hasn't any, we can test you and your husband. I must warn you, it's rare for a match to be found in any family member other than a sibling, but we can try. And of course we'll look at the donor registry.' Alison smiled, and laid a comforting hand on Sally's shoulder. 'Listen, there are many thousands of people on that registry, and we've never yet failed to find a match. I know it's hard, but you must try not to worry. We're a long way from being out of options here.'

As they drank their tea, Alison repeated the new treatment plan. They'd test family members and then search the donor database for a match. Once one was found, Jerome would be brought into hospital to start a course of preparatory treatment, before having the transplant itself. 'That part's quite hard,' she said, 'but the good thing is you know you're moving forward. And of course we support you at all stages.'

They left the hospital armed with leaflets to read at leisure, when it had all sunk in. Sally carried Jerome out to the car, holding him tightly against her.

'We'll soon be home, soldier. You can go back to bed if you want. I'll set up the iPad so you can watch CBeebies.'

'Mmm-mm,' was all the response she got.

'God, Mum, I'm so glad he's not having to stay in hospital right now. At least we'll have time to go through it all with him so he knows what's ahead.'

'Yes, and Alison mentioned play therapy sessions to help him understand. Hang in there, Sally. It'll be all right, I'm sure of it.' She wasn't at all sure, but right now she knew she had to say what Sally needed to hear. Just as Sheila had said what Harriet needed to hear, at lunch on Sunday. Each person in the pyramid of support doing their bit.

Sally put Jerome into the car on his booster seat. Almost immediately he leaned his head back and fell asleep. She turned to Harriet, tears flowing down her face. 'Can you drive, Mum? I'm in no fit state …'

'Of course.' Harriet held her hand out for the keys. 'Let's get you home, tuck Jerome into bed and I'll make you some lunch.'

The drive back to Sally's house was accomplished largely in silence, as Harriet concentrated on driving the unfamiliar car. She could get a taxi home from Sally's, or walk – it'd take her about an hour but it'd do her good and it was a fine day. But first, she needed to do what she could for her family, for this side of her family – the people who needed her. Truth was, she was more worried than she wanted to let on about Jerome. It was rare, the consultant had said, for a suitable bone marrow donor to be found amongst relatives who weren't siblings. But they would all be tested, just in case, and meanwhile they would start the search through the bone marrow donor registry.

Chapter 14

Emma, 1912

In the morning, Ruby came back from the bathroom smelling of vomit. 'Seasick,' she said, in response to Emma's enquiring look. 'That's all.'

'Is there anything I can do?' Emma asked. 'If you want to talk …' *Confide in me*, she wanted to say.

Ruby let out a harsh laugh. 'What about? The consistency of my vomit?'

At the end of the second day, Ruby returned very late to the cabin, hiccoughing and smelling of whiskey. The following morning she was sick once again.

'Maybe I drank too much,' she said to Emma. 'So what? You're not my keeper, as I am bored of having to tell you.'

Over the next couple of days, with the ship following the northern route across the Atlantic, the temperatures dipped substantially. Passengers on deck were huddled in overcoats and scarves, and Emma was sent back to cabins several times to fetch extra layers for her charges. On one trip back to the promenade

140

deck she passed Ruby, who was carrying a tray of tea things to a passenger's cabin.

'How are you getting on?' she asked her sister.

'My feet are killing me,' Ruby replied, leaning against the galley wall. 'I've been back and forth, up and down stairs all day. These people are always calling me – *fetch me this, get that, do the other.* Driving me mad. There is no way I will do this job again. There have to be easier ways to make a living.'

'You're still planning on leaving the ship in New York?' Emma asked in a whisper. It wouldn't do for a senior steward or purser to hear this.

'Either that or I'll throw myself off this ship. That would solve a lot of problems,' Ruby said, and with that remark she pushed herself back upright and headed along the corridor, the things on her tray rattling alarmingly.

Emma gasped and hurried after her. 'Rubes, don't be daft, you don't mean that?'

'I'm so blinking fed up of it all, Ems. The way I've been treated, by Harry, by the passengers, by *you*! I've got to do something.'

'Don't you dare jump overboard. Stay in New York if you must. Think of Ma! Think of the baby you're carrying!' Emma couldn't stop herself from blurting it out.

Ruby span around to face her. 'What? H-how did you know?'

'I guessed. Look, if I can help at all ... money, anything ...'

Ruby cut her off. 'I want to do things by myself. I don't need you, Ems. You'll just judge me. I want a new start, alone.'

'Then if I can at least meet up with you, whenever I'm in New York?'

'I knew you'd come round to my way of thinking of leaving the ship,' Ruby said with a grin.

Emma snorted, exasperated, and turned to walk the other way, back to the passengers who'd sent her to fetch their coats. It would soon be dark and they'd all come inside anyway.

*

That evening, once more Emma found herself alone in her cabin with no sign of Ruby. Her sister was probably drinking again, though where, she wasn't sure. Not in any of the crew areas – Martin had searched for her and reported back to Emma. Possibly she'd gone to the third-class lounge and was even now chatting up some Irish or Polish emigrant, searching for a potential father for her baby, perhaps. Maybe she wanted to find someone who'd take her and the baby on. Or maybe – Emma could scarcely believe she was thinking this of her sister – maybe Ruby wanted to trick someone into believing they were the father. No. Surely she wouldn't stoop that low. She'd turn up eventually. Emma readied herself for bed and settled down to read a magazine that one of her passengers had finished with and handed to her.

There was a jolt, a bump, a grinding, crunching, ripping sound. And then it stopped. Emma sat up in bed, wondering what she should do, wishing she was sharing with Mary. Mary would know what to do. A moment later she noticed something else – the engines had stopped. The ship was quiet – too quiet. And still. The constant vibrations from the engines were gone. She decided to investigate, and dressed quickly. Her passengers would be wanting to know what was happening, so she'd better find out and then be on hand to tell them. Where was Ruby? No doubt she'd come running back in a moment, to ask Emma what they should do.

But by the time Emma had dressed there was still no sign of her sister. She hurried out of the cabin, bumping into Martin on the way. 'What was that noise?'

'I don't know. Sounded like we hit something.'

'But what? There are no ships anywhere near, surely?'

'Come on. Let's find out.' He grabbed her hand and they hurried up the nearest stairs to the passenger decks. Emma thought the galley-ways would be thronging with worried passengers but they were quiet. There were just a couple of men wandering up and down looking for crew.

'What's happened, miss?' one asked her, clutching at her arm.

142

'I don't know. I'm going to find out. I'm sure it's nothing to worry about, sir,' she replied, and walked briskly after Martin.

She went up to the promenade deck, where Martin was already talking to a couple of officers. Pushing open a door to the outside deck, she gasped as the cold air hit her, and wished she'd put on a coat as well. Martin turned as she approached. 'We've hit an iceberg, Officer Boxhall says. There's a hole in the side, under the waterline.'

'Oh my God.' Emma clapped a hand to her mouth. 'So water is coming in?'

Martin nodded. 'But we're not to worry the passengers. The ship's unsinkable. The bulkheads will hold.'

'All right. I'll go down to answer questions and reassure people then. Any sign of Ruby?'

'No.' Martin caught hold of Emma's arms and pulled her into a hug. 'I don't like this. Not at all. Whatever happens, Emma, be strong tonight. And remember, I love you.'

She gasped. He'd never said that to her before. She raised her head and stared at him, and in response he dipped his head and kissed her – not the chaste little pecks he'd given her on occasion before, but a deep, firm kiss that sent shivers through her.

'Ahem, to your duties, stewards.' One of the officers was hovering nearby, a smirk on his face.

Emma broke away from Martin, blushing. The situation couldn't be that serious if the officer was laughing at them kissing, could it? But he was right – they had duties to attend to, and she also needed to find Ruby. She'd promised Ma she'd look after her sister, and if the ship was holed, that was surely an occasion when she should keep her sister by her side until the emergency was over?

As they went back along the promenade deck Emma noticed the calmness of the sea – it looked like a silken sheet, a lake of molten silver.

'So beautiful,' she whispered. She wished she could fetch a coat then just stay there for a while, gazing at the stars and the sea and wondering at the sublime loveliness of it all.

'I'll see you later,' Martin said, grinning at her as he pushed open the door and went inside. 'If I find Ruby I'll keep her with me.'

'Thank you,' she replied, hurrying after him. On 'F' deck he turned left to his allocated cabins while she turned right to hers. There were a few more passengers milling around, wanting to know what was happening. Most were in their night clothes. She reassured people as much as she could, fetched them drinks, and generally carried out her usual duties for a little while.

And then one of the officers came along the galley-way and told her to get everyone up, dressed, and into their life jackets.

'Life jackets! Is it that serious then?'

'Just a precaution, tell them. But everyone should dress warmly and come up on deck now.'

'Are we … are we in trouble?'

The officer gazed at her as though assessing how much to tell her. Finally he nodded, and leaned in close to speak into her ear. 'Yes. We are sinking.'

She widened her eyes and held his gaze for a moment. He was serious. Deadly serious. She wanted to gasp and scream that it wasn't possible – the ship was supposed to be unsinkable. But she couldn't react like that – she was crew, she had duties to attend to. With an effort she gathered herself, nodded, and left him to follow her orders. There were lifeboats, there was time to get everyone into them. She'd do her duties, and keep an eye out for Ruby, who surely had to turn up sooner or later. Passing along the galley-way she knocked on doors and called out to the passengers. 'Everyone, please get dressed in warm clothing, put on your life jackets and go up to the boat deck. This is just a precaution, but please do it now.'

'What? But my children have just gone off to sleep,' protested one woman.

'You must wake them and dress them. I'll come back and help you in a minute.'

'This is nonsense,' said a man. 'The ship can't sink. If it's only a drill I'm not doing it.'

'Sir, it's not a drill.' Emma put as much authority into her voice as she could. 'It's Captain's orders. You must comply.'

'But you said it was just precautionary. So there's no real need to do as you say.' The man shut his cabin door in her face, and she heard a click as he locked it. She banged on it and shouted her message once again – but there were plenty of other cabins she needed to reach, lots more people she needed to help. She continued down the corridor, helping people dress their children, assisting them putting their life jackets on, telling them that no, they shouldn't bring their luggage up but by all means put their valuables into pockets and lock their cabins as they left.

'We'll be back in our cabins soon, won't we?' one woman asked, her eyes filled with fear.

'If or when the Captain says we can return,' Emma replied, not wanting to lie but not wanting to worry the woman further. 'And meanwhile the life jackets will help keep you warm on deck.'

At last she'd sent all her passengers upstairs, except for the few who'd refused to go. And all the while she'd been thinking about Ruby – where was she? Did she know the seriousness of the situation? For a brief moment she let herself wonder about the hours ahead. It was hard to imagine that this great ship would sink. Perhaps it wouldn't, after all. Perhaps it would stay afloat, even though it was holed, and they could all stay aboard. They'd be laughing about it in a couple of days when they limped into New York, no doubt. But then she recalled the seriousness of the officer's expression, and his certainty that they were indeed sinking, and she found she did not want to imagine what lay ahead. It was better to focus on what she needed to do *now*. Deal with the passengers, and find Ruby.

As soon as she'd cleared her corridor, Emma rushed back to

her cabin, hoping that Ruby might be there. She banged open the door, shouting Ruby's name, but the cabin was empty. She grabbed her coat and hat, noticing that Ruby's were still there. Should she take those too, find her sister and give them to her, or would Ruby come back here herself at some point? As she crossed the cabin floor to Ruby's wardrobe she tripped – something was wrong with the floor. And the photograph of her sisters was sliding across the top of the bedside cabinet. She stopped and looked around – there was a definite tilt. The ship was dipping down towards the bow. 'That's not good,' she said to herself, and hurried out of the cabin, leaving Ruby's coat where it hung. She needed to find her sister, and fast.

She ran to the row of second-class cabins that Ruby and Martin were assigned to. He was still there, remonstrating with a passenger who was refusing to leave his substantial amount of luggage in his cabin. Eventually Martin physically pulled the man out and locked the cabin door. 'I'll unlock it when the emergency is over and not before. Now go up to the boat deck.' The man took a step forward as though to fight Martin but Martin held his ground and the man backed off, muttering curses.

'God, this is hard,' Martin said to Emma. 'Half of them don't want to go, the other half want to do their packing first, as though we're docking in New York, not adrift in the mid-Atlantic.'

'I know. Have you seen Ruby?'

He shook his head sadly. 'Maybe she's already up on the boat deck? I'll see you up there.'

'All right.' She ran off to search the open decks. Out there, everything was chaotic. The lifeboats were being filled – she peered over the side and saw a couple already in the water. They did not look full, which confused her. Officers were supervising the loading of them, and there was a crush of people by each.

'Women and children only!' came the cry, over and over. She recognised Second Officer Lightoller and First Officer Murdoch – they were pushing back men who were surging forward and trying to pull the women through the crowds, some of whom were holding small children. She watched as the millionaire J.J. Astor helped his wife into a lifeboat and then stepped back.

'Miss, go through, get on the boat,' a man said, pushing her through the crowd. It was Thomas Andrews, the White Star Line's chief engineer. He looked fraught, and was rushing from boat to boat, urging people to get on them quickly. There couldn't be much time left, Emma realised. Of all people, Andrews would know how long the ship could last in this state.

'No, no, I must find my sister first,' she said to him. She could not get on a lifeboat without Ruby! She'd promised Ma. She turned away, and crossed to the other side of the ship, standing on lockers and coils of rope and anything that allowed her to look over the heads of the people, scanning for Ruby. She spotted Mary and asked her, but no, Mary had not seen Ruby.

'There are a lot of people downstairs still – in steerage,' Mary said. 'Maybe she's helping down there?'

Emma nodded and ran off, down the stairs back to 'F' deck. The third class, or steerage cabins were on the lower decks towards the stern of the ship. There were hordes of people in the corridors and bottlenecks at some of the stairs. 'Go up to the boat deck or promenade deck,' she yelled to people.

'But that's only for first and second class,' a woman said. 'We're not allowed up there.'

'Yes, you are. Captain's orders – up you go. With your life jackets on.'

Some of them did as she said, but others stayed in the galleyways, looking confused. She realised that not everyone spoke English and tried to gesture towards the stairs to get the message across. There was a definite tilt towards the bow now, and on 'F' deck she was terrified to see water beginning to pool at the forward end of the corridor.

There was still no sign of Ruby. Emma was beginning to feel panicky – where could her sister be? She checked the third-class lounge and bar, and the staff areas, but all were deserted. A steward urged her to go up to the boat deck. She went to check her cabin once more – Ruby's coat still hung in the wardrobe. Ruby must have gone up early on, without her coat and perhaps got in one of the first lifeboats, Emma told herself. She must have. And now there was water in the corridor on this deck, lapping into her cabin even. This was no place to be, now. She ran out, meeting Martin in the galley-way.

'Thank goodness! I came back looking for you. We've got to get up to the boat deck, now. There's no one else on this deck.' He grabbed her hand and tugged her after him. She didn't resist. The water soaking through her shoes was freezing.

'Ruby?' she gasped at him as they ran up a set of stairs.

'I expect she's either already on a lifeboat or about to get on one.' He pulled her close. 'If … anything happens, go and see my parents for me, will you? Tell them …'

She forced herself to smile reassuringly at him. 'We'll go together.'

'Of course.' He returned her shaky smile. 'Now come on, we need to get you onto a lifeboat.'

'And you, too,' she said, but Martin didn't seem to hear her.

Up on deck, the band were playing a lively ragtime tune. How they could keep playing at a time like this she had no idea. Nearby she spotted Captain Smith talking to Bruce Ismay, the managing director of White Star. They seemed remarkably unconcerned. A firework went up – no, when she looked at it, she realised it was a distress flare. So the *Titanic* was trying to contact other ships in the vicinity. On the horizon there were lights – that must be a ship, within reach! People on board it must be able to see the flare! That ship would come over and take the *Titanic*'s passengers off. Then even if the *Titanic* sunk – and she still couldn't quite believe that would happen; the ship seemed too large, too stable to go down – all the people would be saved.

'Go on – get on that lifeboat,' Martin was saying, pushing her through a crowd of people. As Emma looked around she realised it was the last lifeboat on this side. Violet was standing near, and grabbed her hand.

'We have to get on this one, Emma. Come on.'

'Women here – let them through!' Martin shouted, and some of the men stepped aside to let them pass. Emma heard shots being fired somewhere nearby, though who had fired them and at what she had no idea. It all just added to the escalating chaos around them.

'Where've you ladies been hiding?' an officer said, as Violet and Emma approached the lifeboat. The officer was standing with one foot in the boat and one on the deck rail. There was a makeshift ladder made of deckchairs that people were climbing up to board the lifeboat, helped by a couple of seamen.

Emma glanced back at Martin. He waved and smiled. 'I'll get on another boat. Take care, my lovely girl.'

'But Ruby – I can't …' she began saying, but the officer grabbed her arm and another man pushed her roughly, and before she knew it, she was sprawled in the bottom of the boat.

'Get up, sit here,' another woman said, and Emma recognised her as the stewardess Ann, Violet's roommate. And then Violet was on board too, clutching a bundle of something, and the boat was being lowered down the side of the *Titanic*, and Martin's white face was peering over the deck rail, still smiling, still waving, and Emma knew there were no more lifeboats for him or the other men, or the hundreds of people from third class who'd still been wandering in confusion around the lower decks as she and Martin had come up.

Chapter 15

Harriet

A few days later, at the weekend, Harriet had a visit from Sally. 'Charlie is staying home with Jerome today, and I feel the need to get away for a bit. Can I come round?' she'd asked on the phone that morning. 'We could continue with your sorting out.'

Harriet was delighted to hear from her. 'Of course, come round. But no need for us to work – it's a lovely day. We could go for a walk, maybe do some shopping or something.'

'I'd rather be doing something useful,' Sally said. 'See you in half an hour or so.'

Harriet hurried out to the bakery for a batch of chocolate croissants, and had a pot of tea standing ready by the time Sally arrived. 'This is getting to be a tradition,' Sally said with a smile when she saw the kitchen table set ready for her.

'I love having you here. How's Jerome?' Harriet asked.

'Much the same. No worse, which is good, but no better. Charlie and I have appointments to give a blood sample which the doctor will test to see if either of us are a good match for bone marrow

150

donation – that's on Monday. Apparently it's unlikely we will be, but we have to try.'

Harriet poured Sally some tea. 'Here. And please take a croissant. I want to be tested too, to see if I can be a donor.'

Sally pulled a card out of her handbag and passed it over. 'I remember you said you would. Here's the number to call to make an appointment. They only need take a blood sample at this stage to see if there's any chance. And if none of us match, then they can look through a national database of people who've signed up to be potential donors. If I'm not a match, I'm going to sign up to that database to see if I can help someone else at least.'

'That's a lovely idea,' Harriet said, taking the card. 'I'll call this first thing on Monday. I'm probably too old to go on the national database but I will enquire.'

Sally smiled. 'Thank you, Mum. God I really hope one of us will be a match. Remember the support nurse said that the donation procedure can be quite painful for the donor. I'd rather it was a family member that had to go through it, than a stranger.'

Harriet glanced at her daughter, judging whether to say out loud the thought that had crossed her mind. Yes, she decided. Why not? 'When Davina next rings … I could ask her … whether she would go to be tested?'

'Huh. No, don't bother, Mum.' Sally gave a hollow laugh. 'She's never done anything for me.'

'She'd be doing it for her nephew, though.'

'There's no point. It's too unlikely that she or her kids would be a match, and it'd only wind her up, asking. No, Mum. I don't want her involved. She's out of my life.'

Harriet sighed. 'Do you think you could ever forgive her?'

Sally shrugged. 'Don't know. But it's irrelevant – I don't suppose she'll ever forgive *me*. That day in Weymouth, with Lucas.'

'Yes. That was … misguided.' To put it mildly, Harriet thought.

'Mmm. Seemed like a good idea when Lucas suggested it. But it fucked everything up, didn't it?'

Harriet stared at Sally, astonished to hear a rare swear word from her. There were tears in Sally's eyes, too. It was time to steer the conversation away from Davina. 'Anyway, they said they always manage to find a match on the register. And I'm sure that if someone's altruistic enough to sign up for it, they'd be only too delighted to have the chance to save a child's life at the expense of a little discomfort. I know I would.'

Her daughter dabbed at her eyes with a tissue, took a second croissant and smiled through a mouthful of pastry. 'You are probably right. And of course we'll take any donor that's a match. It's not a time to be fussy. Then there's treatment to prepare Jerome's body for a bone marrow transplant. I don't know the details, but Charlie has read up on it all and understands what's going on better than I do.' She smiled tightly. 'And now let's change the subject, or I'll get all tearful again. How's your house-clearing going?'

'Slowly but surely,' Harriet replied. 'I've done a bit more in the attic – there are some more boxes of stuff to throw out or give to charity that I need you to help me bring down. But I must admit,' she looked sheepishly at Sally, 'I came across an old photo album which kind of distracted me for a while.'

'What kind of photos?' Sally asked. 'Your grandmother again?'

'No. John and me, in the early days of our marriage. We had a camping and cycling trip in northern France – carrying everything in panniers on our bicycles. I'd never done anything like it before. We'd cycle about forty miles, then find a field or a cliff top or something, and set up our little tent. We had a little Primus stove to cook on but mostly we ate bread, cheese, tomatoes, and melon bought locally. The way I remember it the sun shone every day but the photos definitely show cloud and rain one day so my memory's definitely a bit off.'

'Wow. I don't think I've ever heard you mention that holiday before,' Sally said. 'Sounds awesome. So, shall we get on with stuff in the attic?'

'In a moment. Let me show you these photos first.' Harriet went through to the sitting room where she'd left the album after finding it the previous day. There was a pile of photo albums strewn across the coffee table and sofa – she'd forgotten she'd left so many out. And not just photo albums – there'd been a box of souvenirs amongst them. Bits and bobs they'd bought or picked up on their travels. The old Primus stove itself. A little flag they'd made with their initials entwined that they'd attached to the tent pole. A collection of stones from beaches they'd visited. All of it was spread across tables and the floor of the room.

Sally had followed her through to the sitting room. 'Good grief, Mum! You're supposed to be sorting stuff out. This is a terrible mess in here! Remember what I said about only handling each item once – pick it up, make the decision whether it's to keep, give to charity or chuck, and then box or bag it accordingly. Not spread everything all over the place and wallow in memories. You were better than that when we started a couple of weeks ago.'

'Yes, but that was my mother's old stuff. This,' Harriet waved a hand at the memories strewn across the room, 'this is John. Our marriage. My life. And, well, it's a lot harder to throw these things out.' She picked up a postcard that John had sent her when he'd been away for a few days on a training course.

Sally snatched it off her and glanced at it. 'You see, if you keep every last little memento, you'll never get rid of enough stuff to allow you to downsize. This is just an old postcard, Mum. It's of no value and says nothing of importance. It needs to go in the "bin" pile.' She dropped it into a wastepaper basket.

Harriet's instinct was to retrieve it immediately. Maybe she would throw it out but she'd like to read it one more time first. But she stopped herself. She'd end up having a row with Sally if she picked it out of the bin now. She could always go through everything Sally threw out later on, and hide away anything she really wanted to keep. It seemed weak though – this was her home, these were her belongings, her memories – why could she not stand up to Sally and say, *no, I want to keep this*? Deep down she knew Sally was right. She needed to downsize, she needed to thin down her possessions, she needed to sort everything out. But – one postcard? How much space did that take up?

Making a decision, she got up and picked the postcard out of the bin. 'I know I probably shouldn't keep this, love, but it doesn't take up much room. I'm going to find a box and put the things I can't bear to throw out for sentimental reasons in it. Just one box, for things like this.'

'It'll just clutter up your new place, though,' Sally said, sounding a little petulant.

'I'm sure I'll be able to tuck it away somewhere, on top of a wardrobe or under a bed, or in an attic,' Harriet said decisively. She was going to win this battle.

But then, to her dismay, she realised Sally was sobbing. Head in hands, tears running down her cheek, shoulders heaving. Harriet sat beside her and wrapped her arms around her. 'Oh, love, what's wrong?'

'Sorry Mum, it's just … so hard. Trying to help you, worrying about Jerome, worrying about you. Bloody Davina. And Charlie had a go at me this morning, too.'

'Whatever for?'

Sally shrugged. 'Oh, nothing really. I threw out half a pot of coffee, and it turned out he'd wanted more. He snapped at me. I know it's because he's under so much strain too, but honestly, he could be a little more forgiving. It's so bloody hard, Mum.'

'Of course it is – what's happening with Jerome is terrible, but why are you worrying about me? There's no need to. And Davina – well, she's made her own decisions. Best to put her out of your mind – there's nothing you can do.'

'I can't help it, Mum. It just bugs me so much that she's not here to help. If she was here, she could be helping you to downsize while I concentrate on Jerome.'

'Love, you don't need to do so much for me if it's making you

154

too stressed,' Harriet said, anguished to think she was adding to her daughter's problems.

'I do, though. It's my duty to.' Sally pulled a tissue from a box on a side table, dabbed at her eyes and gave herself a little shake. She smiled at Harriet. 'Sorry for that little meltdown. I'm OK, and I do want to help. I'd feel so guilty if I didn't do what's best for you, as well as what's best for Jerome. Just feel a bit stretched at times, is all.'

'Shall we leave it for today, though? We could go for a walk instead. The fresh air would do you good.'

Sally shook her head. 'No, I'll feel better if we achieve something today. If we move things along a little. So, let me make us some more coffee and we can get on.' She went out to the kitchen, and Harriet heard the sounds of the coffee machine being switched on. She left her daughter to it, recognising that Sally needed a little time alone. Looking around the sitting room, she realised her mistake. These items, these memories of John – she needed to sort through this stuff herself, alone. Only she could decide what she wanted to keep. Sally was helpful when sorting out the less sentimental items. She quickly boxed up everything again, and pushed the boxes behind a sofa, to deal with later, then she followed Sally to the kitchen.

'I've been thinking, let's leave that old stuff for now. I'll get on with it this evening. Maybe you could help me with the books? I must have hundreds, and there's no guarantee I'll have space in a new place for the six bookcases I currently have.'

'Six?' Sally widened her eyes.

'Four in the dining room and two upstairs in Davina's old room,' Harriet replied. 'So if you don't mind, can we start with the dining room? I thought I could get rid of any I know I won't read again and wouldn't want to lend to anyone. I imagine the charity shops will take them.'

'Yes, or I know of a charity library that will take them too,' Sally said, looking much brighter, Harriet thought, now that she had a purpose. She picked up the coffee Sally had made her, and

155

led the way to the dining room, where four full height bookcases groaned with hundreds of books crammed into every available space. It was going to be a big job.

Harriet took the plunge a week later: with the boxes of books donated to a charity library and the boxes of memories of John sorted, thinned down and stored back in the attic for now, she contacted estate agents and had the house valued. It was worth more than she'd thought, and after consulting Sally, who she knew would want to be involved, she decided on a local agency and instructed them to put the house on the market. An estate agent called round to take measurements and photos, and Harriet had to admit the house looked good, when she browsed the online listing later.

'I need to do this, John,' she said to his gravestone on her next visit. 'It's a wrench, but the place is too big for me. It needs a young family in it once more.' Oddly, having made the decision to take the first step, she felt better about it all and excited about the prospect of living somewhere new.

And then, of course, she had the job of finding a suitable property to move to. In spare moments she began working her way through listings of local properties. She wanted two bedrooms, possibly three. A small garden. Something easy to maintain and in good condition, though she'd be happy to paint a few rooms if necessary. Somewhere not too far from Sally, so that she could easily pop round at a moment's notice to help out as necessary, for who knew what the future held, or how much support Sally might need in the months and years to come?

Thankfully there were plenty of suitable properties in her price range, and it was just a case of viewing the best options and making a decision. The estate agent had advised her it may take some time to sell her large house, but there was no shortage of the type of place she wanted to move to, so it was probably wise to wait for an offer on her house first.

Sally was pleased when Harriet phoned her to say the deed

was done, and the 'for sale' board had been erected in the front garden. 'Well done, Mum. It's a big step, but in the right direction. And it's one less thing for me to worry about.'

Harriet was pleased to hear that, although for herself, despite knowing it was the right thing to do, deciding to sell the house had been hard. In some ways, living in the place where Davina had grown up had been a way of keeping her younger daughter close. How many times had she walked into Davina's old bedroom, even though it looked nothing like it had when the teenage Davina had lived there, just to look around and bring to mind Davina sitting at her homework desk, lying on her bed reading a book, sprawled across the floor playing with her toy farm? Moving would cut that last little tie with Davina. At least she wouldn't need to change her phone number. These days Davina called Harriet's mobile, withholding her own number.

A few days after the house went on the market, and after a handful of unsuccessful viewings (people who seemed simply curious about the house rather than serious potential buyers), Sally called with the terrible news that neither she nor Charlie were bone marrow matches for Jerome.

'Oh love,' Harriet said. 'I know it was always a long shot, but I did hope it'd work. I have my test later today. Maybe, just maybe, I'll be a match.'

'God, I hope so,' Sally replied. 'Otherwise it's the national database. They've started searching it anyway, but I'm just so worried about whether even the most altruistic stranger will be prepared to go through with the procedure.'

'Someone will. I'm sure of it.' Assuming they could find a match on the national register of course, but Harriet didn't want to say this and worry Sally any more.

Later that day, Harriet drove to the hospital to give a blood sample, to be tested to see if she was, by some wonderful fluke of nature, a match for Jerome. She crossed her fingers and muttered prayers under her breath as the blood was taken. The hospital would test it, and let Sally and Charlie know within a couple of days if it was any good. Harriet had read up on what was involved when donating bone marrow. It didn't sound pleasant – it involved a general anaesthetic and then long needles inserted into the donor's pelvic bone to extract a litre or so of bone marrow. Afterwards the donor would feel sore and bruised, and have a dull ache in their lower back. They might also suffer from anaemia for a while, and recovery could take a couple of weeks. Of course, if it was your own family member you wouldn't care at all – what was a bit of soreness and a few weeks feeling tired compared with the life of a 6-year-old child?

With the blood sample taken, Harriet left the hospital armed with a few leaflets. All she could do now was hope and pray.

Chapter 16

Emma, 1912

The lifeboat hit the surface of the water with a thud, jolting them all and eliciting some squeals from the women on board. It was full to bursting – Emma wasn't sure how many it was supposed to take but there was certainly no room for more. They already had people sitting on the floor between the seats. One of the two crewmen on board shouted, 'Oars out!' as soon as the boat stabilised, and they began rowing away from the *Titanic*, the crewmen muttering about not wanting to risk being sucked down with the ship.

Emma looked back at the mighty liner. It was much lower at the bow now, and was also listing to port. She counted the decks, each still brightly lit. Six above the waterline. Only six! She checked again, and now could only count five. 'E' deck, her cabin, would now be underwater completely. She leaned her head back and offered up a silent prayer that Ruby had got away safely on an earlier lifeboat.

'She'll be all right,' Violet, sitting opposite, said. 'Your sister can take care of herself. Try not to worry.'

Emma looked at Violet, grateful for the other woman's reassuring tone. She noticed once again that Violet was carrying a bundle, and only now realised that it was a baby. 'Whose is that?' she asked.

'I don't know,' Violet said, tucking the shawl the child was wrapped in more tightly around it. 'A man thrust it into my arms as I climbed into the lifeboat.'

'What will you do with it?'

'I don't know,' Violet said again. 'Keep it alive for now, is all. What else can I do?' She looked at Emma with dark, sad eyes, and Emma found she had no response. Keep the baby alive. Keep themselves alive. What else could any of them do now?

The night was bitterly cold. Emma turned up her coat collar and wrapped her scarf around her head. The sea was still flat calm, black, and glassy, and in the distance she could see starlight glinting off an iceberg. Whether it was the one they'd hit or not she didn't know. It was a beautiful thing to see – beautiful but deadly.

Other lifeboats were dotted around, she could see the glow of cigarette tips and torch beams here and there. All were keeping their distance from the *Titanic* which was inexorably sinking, slowly but steadily, tilting further and further nose-down. It must be hard to stand on deck by now, she thought, and worried that Martin might slip and fall.

Martin. What would become of him?

'Sir, was this really the last lifeboat?' she asked the crew member sitting at the stern of the boat. He'd shipped his oars for now, but was keeping hold of the tiller. She noticed he was wearing only a vest.

'Yes, miss. The last wooden lifeboat. There are four canvas collapsibles on board. I imagine they'll be launching those now.'

So there was hope yet, for Martin, and some of the others who'd still been on board. Mary too – Emma had not seen whether she'd got into a lifeboat or not. But – only four collapsibles? She did not know what a collapsible lifeboat would look like, but imagined it would not hold as many as the main wooden lifeboats. And if there were only four, yet still so many men on board ... She shook her head. The horror of what was unfolding around her, what was inevitably going to happen when the ship finally sank, was unthinkable.

And now she could only count four decks above the waterline.

All they could do was watch and wait. Somewhere on the horizon there'd been the lights of another ship, she remembered. It must have seen the distress flares, and would be on its way, to take any remaining passengers off the *Titanic* before she sank. So there was hope, still. Emma scanned the horizon but could not see the lights. Of course, in the lifeboat she was much lower than when she'd spotted the other ship, from the *Titanic*'s boat deck. The other ship was coming, and would be here soon, no doubt. It had to.

There was a grinding crash and screams, from the now distant *Titanic*. One of its four funnels had broken off. The ship's bow was now completely submerged, she looked like she was trying to stand on end. The lights flickered off and back on, and then off for the last time. The *Titanic* began settling back down in the water, and for one glorious moment Emma thought it would be all right, the ship would stay afloat after all, but no, it was just for a minute, and then there was the sound of tearing metal and the front of the ship once more plunged downwards. This time the stern rose right up, vertical, and seemed to hang there, lit by starlight, for a few seconds before it too plummeted down.

She expected there to be silence once the ship had sunk, but instead the air was filled with a sound that she knew would stay with her for the rest of her life – the sound of hundreds, maybe thousands of people, struggling to stay afloat in the freezing water, screaming, crying, calling for help, calling for their loved ones, pleading, splashing, drowning, dying.

'We should go back, we could pick up some more people,' she said. But the crewman nearest her shook his head.

'We're full as it is, miss. Any more would swamp the boat and we'll all go down. Better to save some souls than try to be heroes and lose us all.'

'But those people …'

He just shook his head once more and looked away.

Those people. All those people. Some of them her friends, her loved ones. Martin.

She caught Violet's eye. The other woman was crying openly, and clutching the baby tightly to her, as though trying to derive some small crumb of comfort from its little, warm body. Ann too, sitting next to Violet, was weeping, her head in her hands. Others in the boat were sitting quietly, staring back at where *Titanic* had been, in shock, unable to comprehend what was happening. *Titanic* was gone. All those people were in the water, and unless help came quickly, how were they going to survive?

Ruby. Martin. Mary. Her thoughts ran from one to the next to the next, round and round. Ruby and Mary might have got themselves onto earlier lifeboats. Martin might be on a collapsible. Or they might not. All she could do was to hope and pray.

'I wish,' said a woman near her, 'that those cries would stop.'

Emma opened her mouth to agree – it was heartbreaking to listen to – and then she realised that the anguished cries only stopped when the person could cry no more. Already the shouts were dying away, and she knew it was not only the shouts that were dying. When at last the cries finally subsided, the silence was far, far harder to bear than the screams had been.

There was a glimmer of light on the eastern horizon. Emma stared at it, trying to work out what it was. Dawn. They'd been in the lifeboat for hours, drifting. For the most part they'd sat quietly, everyone lost in his or her own personal hell. Now and again the baby Violet held whimpered, and she held it tighter and murmured to settle it. There was no drinking water or food on board. No torches. Just them, on the little boat, under the most glorious canopy of stars. How could the night be so beautiful when such a tragedy had occurred? It made no sense.

Icebergs, when they drifted past them, were no longer things of beauty but objects of terror. Sinister hulks, looming over them as they passed, the crewmen taking care to steer a wide berth.

The sea was no longer as calm as it had been. Small waves lapped at the lifeboat, making it rock a little. The crewmen tried to keep the little boat pointing head on to the swell to lessen the effect, but they were tired and cold and Emma could see it was increasingly too much effort to do anything. The man who'd been in only a vest was now wearing a woman's coat across his shoulders. Someone from first class had been wearing two when she boarded the lifeboat, and had insisted he take one.

Emma welcomed the rougher sea. The movement, the sounds of the water splashing on the side of the boat – all were a reminder that they were still alive, that for their little party on board Lifeboat Sixteen, there was still hope. They could no longer see any other lifeboats, but they were out there, somewhere. Was Ruby on one of them? Please God that she was!

A memory surfaced – of the day Emma and her sisters had posed for their photograph. Smiling and happy, before she'd gone on her first voyage on the *Olympic*. Before Ruby had been caught up with Harry Paine. That lovely photograph, of the three of them. It would be at the bottom of the sea now. As would Ruby's copy. Just two copies remained of that photo – Lily's and Ma's. It was this thought, of all the thoughts and images that had run through her mind, that finally made the tears come. Emma covered her eyes with her hand and allowed herself a few moments to quietly sob. No one attempted to comfort her, and she understood – everyone was dealing with their own shock and grief and had no comfort to spare for anyone else.

'Look, a flare,' a woman said, without enthusiasm.

Emma looked where she was pointing, and spotted a green flare, a hundred feet above the water. Had it come from a ship?

Or another lifeboat? Did they need help? As the lifeboat bobbed up and down in the waves she scanned the horizon to see where the flare had come from. At last she spotted the lights of a ship. Definitely a ship. Was it the one she thought she'd seen from the *Titanic*'s deck, or another? As she watched she realised it was coming closer. It really was – every minute brought it closer. 'A ship,' someone said, and all eyes raised to look at it, although the mood in the lifeboat was unchanged. Everyone was too tired, too shocked to respond, Emma thought. And Violet's attention was still on the tiny baby she held.

'It's *Titanic*,' one woman said. 'It didn't sink, after all. We'll soon be back on board, with our men.'

No one answered her. No one wanted to tell her the men were dead.

Now Emma could see other lifeboats, rowing towards the ship. 'We should row too,' she said to the crewman who sat huddled in his woman's coat. 'That ship won't be able to come too close. Look at all the ice around us.'

The seaman roused himself and nodded. He and the other seaman wearily began to row towards the ship. Emma could see that it had now stopped, more or less, and was waiting for the lifeboats to reach it. There were three, four ahead, that had almost reached the ship. Too far away to see who was on board, even though the sky was gradually lightening. One of the collapsibles was being towed by a wooden lifeboat. They were being rescued. They were all being rescued, but would Ruby and Martin be among them?

Even after the long cold wait of the night, these minutes as dawn broke and they rowed agonisingly slowly towards the rescue ship seemed to last even longer. Inch by inch the ship came closer as the day became gradually lighter. Sounds from the ship began to reach them, shouts from the other lifeboats. Emma kept up a mumbled prayer under her breath, that her loved ones might turn out to be among those on the other lifeboats. She'd find out soon, once she was on board. All she could do now was hope and pray.

Chapter 17

Harriet

The morning after giving her blood sample, Harriet had a call from Sheila.

'Been thinking about your grandmother. I know she worked on the *Olympic* – I wonder if you'd like to find out more about that ship and what life was like on board? It was sister to the *Titanic*, and there's a new exhibition on, in Southampton, about the *Titanic*. Fancy going?'

'Oh! Yes, that sounds wonderful! When shall we go?'

'Tomorrow? Or even today – I've nothing on. I'll drive. Or we could take the train again, if you like.'

'Let's go today. Why not? But I'd prefer to go by car, if you don't mind. We could then stop for a meal in a nice country pub somewhere on the way home.'

'Great idea! Pick you up in twenty minutes?'

'Perfect!'

And so Harriet bustled around the house, drinking coffee, putting on some lipstick, deciding which jacket and shoes to wear, and texting Sally to let her know she'd be out for the day.

Just in case. She was ready at the door when Sheila pulled up outside, beeping her horn.

'A day out – what a treat!' she said, as she climbed into the passenger seat. 'Lovely idea.'

'Well, I've always been fascinated by what happened to the *Titanic*,' Sheila said. 'And now that we've been on a cruise ship ourselves, I thought it'd be fun to compare the pictures of the *Titanic* with our own experiences. Plus – your grandmother. It'll take us less than an hour to drive there. You ready?'

'Absolutely!'

The journey passed quickly – they took the scenic road that led across the New Forest and through the village of Lyndhurst. The two women chatted non-stop. Harriet updated Sheila on the latest news of Jerome, her forthcoming house move and her blood test. 'It all means I've not had the chance to do any more of that genealogy research,' she added. 'I was going to try to find out what happened to Gran's sisters. I know one died young but Gran never said how, or at least not that I can remember. And Gran never even mentioned Ruby, as far as I recall.' She sighed. 'You know sometimes you wish you could go back in time and simply ask someone about it? If I could see Gran again I'd pay so much more attention to her old stories. Her sister saved her life once, I remember her saying, but how, where, when I have no idea. I'm even wondering which sister it was, now that I know she had two. She just used to say "my sister".'

Sheila nodded. 'The problem is, when you're young and your life is ahead of you, you just want to look forward, not backward. So you don't really listen to the old people's stories. And then when you're old yourself and your life's mostly behind you, that's when you want to know about the past. But by then your parents and grandparents are gone, and their memories with them.'

'It's so sad. But there's no answer to it.'

'Yes there is. Do the research – we are the first older generation to have the internet at our fingertips. We must make the

166

most of it. And then write it all up. We should write our own memoirs too, so that when our grandchildren get to our age and are interested in the past at last, they've got access to our stories, told the way *we* want to tell them.'

Harriet considered. 'Nice idea. Though I'm not sure anyone would be interested in my life story.'

'Your grand-kids will – Jerome, and those two little girls who don't even know you. In fifty years' time. They'll be interested, trust me on this!'

'Hmm. Maybe I will, then. Never really considered myself to be much of a writer, though.'

Sheila laughed. 'Me neither, but I am writing my memoirs anyway.'

Soon they arrived at the exhibition, bought their tickets, had a quick cup of tea in the café to refresh themselves after the journey and began following the story of the *Titanic* from her earliest days in the Harland and Wolff shipyard in Belfast where she'd been built alongside the *Olympic*, through to the discovery of her wreckage at the bottom of the north Atlantic. Harriet loved seeing the photos of the part-built ships side by side, and the numerous photos of the luxurious interiors of both ships. There was a display board about a third ship of the same class – the *Britannic*.

'Look,' she called to Sheila, 'there was a third sister ship, too.'

'I hadn't known that,' Sheila said. 'Just like your grandmother then, keeping quiet about a third sister. Says here it was used as a hospital ship during the first world war.'

'Interesting. And only the *Olympic* continued sailing till the mid-Thirties. One thing I do remember Gran saying is that she retired from life at sea when the *Olympic* did, not wanting to work on any other ship. She hadn't worked on many voyages after my mother was born anyway – just a few when money was short and they'd leave Mum with Granddad's parents. Granddad got a job on land after the *Olympic* was decommissioned too.'

They moved on, peering at display cases of items retrieved from the *Titanic*'s wreck – crockery and cutlery, hairbrushes and vanity cases, glasswear and silverwear, shoes and gloves. A card printed with the menu for dinner on the 14th of April, 1912. A gold pocket watch, inscribed with the name of the owner – a man from first class who had perished. A doll. A set of keys. A life jacket.

Harriet shuddered at that last exhibit. 'I wonder if someone was wearing that when the ship went down. It's hard to imagine, isn't it, so many people in the water, unable to get onto the lifeboats.'

'Those scenes in the film *Titanic* are harrowing, aren't they?'

Harriet nodded. 'Yes. They certainly are.' She'd seen it many years ago, and the shots of people in the water, calling out for help as they clutched onto deckchairs or pieces of wreckage, had stayed with her ever since.

Sheila had moved on to a couple of display boards with lists of names. 'Look. There's a list here of all the survivors, and another of those who were lost. It says here the lists are not one hundred per cent accurate, as no one's quite sure how many people were on board.' Sheila tutted. 'Imagine that. These days at least the passenger lists would be complete. The list of survivors is very much shorter than the victims. So sad.'

Harriet went to stand beside Sheila in front of the lists, paying silent respect to those who'd died. She scanned down through the names – the boards also stated whether the person was a passenger and if so which class, or crew. 'So many dead. A child, here, aged just 6. Same age as Jerome.'

Sheila peered at the board. 'Third class. I don't suppose many first-class children perished.'

'No. There's definitely more third class here than first or second. If the *Titanic* film is anything to go by, they prioritised first and second class over third.'

'I think it varied, depending on which officer was in charge of loading up the lifeboats,' Sheila said. 'I have a book at home

168

somewhere about it. But of course there is still so much confusion over what happened, especially surrounding whether or not the—'

'Oh my God,' Harriet said, interrupting her friend. 'Look.'

She was pointing at the list of those lost. The list was alphabetically arranged, and there, under H, was the name Ruby Higgins.

'That's your grandmother's sister, isn't it?' Sheila clutched at Harriet's arm.

'Yes, the one I never knew about. I wonder if this was why Gran never mentioned her. Perhaps it was too painful, having lost her on the *Titanic*. She was crew – look. A stewardess, like Gran.'

'And she never made it onto a lifeboat. That's so sad. You said your gran's sister died young – you don't think she was referring to Ruby, then?'

'God, I don't know! I'm so confused about it all now – I wish more than ever I could just go back and ask her, or find a diary in which she tells all, or something.' Harriet shook her head. It was hard to believe that her great-aunt had died on board the *Titanic*, and no one in the family had ever spoken about it. Had her mother known? Or had Gran just kept quiet for ever?

'And look,' Sheila was saying, pointing. 'Emma Higgins, also a stewardess, is on the survivor's list.'

'Wow. Well, I never knew she'd worked on the *Titanic*,' Harriet said. 'Another thing that was kept quiet.'

'Perhaps the memories were too painful,' Sheila said gently. 'The family lost Ruby when the ship went down, so I can imagine they never wanted to talk about it again.'

'You could be right,' Harriet said. 'If they were both working on the ship, how come one survived and the other didn't? You'd think they would try to stick together as the ship was sinking.'

'Perhaps they had duties to attend to, passengers to help, and got separated. It must have been horrible for the survivors. That must be why it was never spoken about.'

Harriet nodded. 'So now I want more than ever to find out more about them all. As you said in the car – in the future my grandchildren might thank me for doing the research and writing it all up.' She was supposed to be concentrating on moving house, but it would be good to spend a little bit of time on this project too. Especially as there wasn't much more she could do on the house move until she had a firm offer on the table. And writing up the research for her granddaughters was a nice idea. Would Autumn and Summer ever see it, she wondered? Would there come a time when they, perhaps as adults, would read her research and wonder about this grandmother they'd never known? Or perhaps they *would* come to know her, eventually. Perhaps after they were 18 they might track her down – Davina would not be able to stop them then. Or perhaps, and she had to cling on to this hope, at some stage Davina might soften and allow Harriet to visit, or bring the girls to Harriet ...

'You OK?' Sheila was asking. 'You look miles away.'

'Sorry, yes I was. Just thinking about families, generations, loss ...'

'Wow, all that, just then.' Sheila looked at her with sympathy. 'You look like a woman who needs another cuppa. And a cake. Yes, cake is prescribed. If you've seen enough, shall we go to the café? We can always come back in if you like.'

'I think I've seen enough. Still processing the fact that the great-aunt I only discovered I had a few weeks ago, died on the *Titanic.*'

'It's terribly sad. And all that's left of her is her name on that board, and the photo you have of her. She was the cheeky-looking one, wasn't she? The one with a defiant look about her, as though she was daring the world to try stopping her from doing whatever she wanted.'

'Yes, that was Ruby. The middle sister. Prettiest of the three.'

'Died on the middle sister of the three sister ships. So tragic.' Sheila took Harriet's arm. 'So, then. Tea?'

'Yes please!' Harriet followed her friend out to the café, where they decided to have a late lunch as well as a cup of tea and cake, before heading home. Harriet had so much to think about, and found she could barely wait to get on with some genealogical research. She wanted to phone Sally later, to tell her what she'd discovered, but then thought better of it. Sally had enough on her plate at the moment. She might be upset by Harriet spending time doing something so trivial – looking into the past – when poor Jerome's whole future was hanging by a thread.

Chapter 18

Emma, 1912

Another hour, maybe two or three – Emma no longer had any idea of the passage of time – elapsed before her lifeboat was finally secured at the hull of the rescue liner. The day was fully light by then. RMS *Carpathia* was written on the ship's side, and she recognised it as belonging to the Cunard company. One by one the occupants of her lifeboat were helped on board, either climbing a rope ladder lowered down the ship's side, or for those too weak to do this, hoisted up in a sling. They were met by members of the *Carpathia*'s crew who issued each survivor with a blanket and told them where to go to get hot drinks and food or have any wounds attended to. *Carpathia*'s crew looked as disbelieving of the situation as the *Titanic* passengers were.

'How could it have sunk?' she heard one steward say. 'There's just no sign of it at all. We thought we'd arrive to see it taking on water, listing a bit but that would be all. But look, it's gone. There's only ice.'

No one from the *Titanic* answered him. They could not explain it either, even if they'd had the energy to try.

'What are you going to do with the child?' Emma asked Violet, as Violet was hoisted up, still clutching the baby in her arms.

'I don't know,' came the response, but by the time Emma had boarded the *Carpathia* Violet was no longer holding the child.

'Where did the baby go?'

Violet shrugged. 'A crying woman came and grabbed it from me. I think it was hers. She didn't even say thank you.'

'Well, it is good that the child was saved. You have done well,' Emma said, but Violet seemed too shocked to respond. Emma put a comforting hand on her friend's shoulder and squeezed, hoping the gesture said more than her woefully inadequate words.

Along with Ann they made their way through the ship, to the areas that had been made available for the *Titanic*'s passengers. Violet and Ann found a bench on deck and sat down wearily.

Emma wanted nothing more than to sleep, but first she had to search for Ruby. And Martin. But every time she thought of Martin she realised that there was little hope that he'd have survived. There were very few men amongst the *Titanic* survivors. Just the seamen who'd been assigned to the lifeboats, and the few officers who'd been in charge of each. But the *Carpathia* was still picking up lifeboats and there was talk that it would stay in the area and search for survivors in the water, so there was still hope. She forced herself to stay strong. Martin had told her to stay strong, no matter what happened.

And he'd told her he loved her.

She began a tour of the decks, calling Ruby's name. As she walked, Emma realised her feet hurt – there'd been a few inches of freezing water in the lifeboat. Her feet had been numb sitting in the boat but now were hurting as they warmed up. Gently she pulled back blankets from faces of women who'd lain down, sleeping or just staring blankly into space. She asked *Carpathia*'s crew members, describing her sister, and was directed to a make-shift hospital set up in what had been one of the ship's first-class dining rooms. There, a doctor was attending to a number of people with small injuries, sustained when they'd fallen into lifeboats. Some of *Carpathia*'s passengers were helping him.

'Sir, I am looking for my sister,' Emma said, and described Ruby.

He looked at her with tired eyes. 'I cannot recall each patient. Please, have a look around. There are more people from the *Titanic* in some of the cabins. Maybe she's there.'

'I'll take you,' said a young woman who'd been rolling bandages and placing them on a tray. She caught Emma's arm and led her along a galley-way. 'I'm so sorry for you all. It must have been awful.'

'It was,' Emma said, but found she did not want to say anything more. What she'd seen and heard was indescribable.

The young woman introduced herself as Caroline, a first-class passenger on the *Carpathia*. 'We are all doing our bit for you poor souls,' she said. 'Here are the cabins that have been turned into sick rooms.' She tapped on a door and opened it. Emma scanned the beds but there was no Ruby. She noted however that three extra makeshift beds had been crammed into the cabin. She had no idea how many *Titanic* survivors the *Carpathia* had picked up, but the rescue ship did look as though they'd done everything they could to prepare for the extra passengers and to do what they could for them.

'She's not there,' Emma said to Caroline, and the other woman closed that cabin door and took her to another. Still no sign of Ruby. Her feet pained her more and more with each step.

But further down the galley-way in another cabin, a woman in a *Titanic* stewardess's uniform lay huddled on a bed facing the wall. Emma darted into the room. 'Ruby? Oh, Ruby!'

The woman turned over, her face ashen. She had a large bruise on one side of her face and was nursing a bandaged arm. It was Mary.

Emma fell to her knees beside the bed and hugged her old friend, being careful of her injuries. 'Thank goodness you are alive!'

'I was on a lifeboat – I don't know which one. I fell as I jumped into it, did this.' She waved her arm feebly.

'You need to rest. You're safe now. Can I just ask – did you see Ruby at all?'

'Ruby?'

'My sister.'

Mary shook her head. 'I've not seen any others, only you.'

'Violet and Ann survived. They were on the same boat as me.'

'Thank God.' Mary leaned back and closed her eyes.

Emma kissed her forehead. 'I'm going to go now, and see if Ruby's anywhere to be found. I'll come back and see you later.' She hauled herself to her feet and left the cabin.

'Found her?' Caroline had been waiting outside and smiled as Emma came out.

'Found my friend, but not my sister. Is there anywhere else?'

There was, and Emma followed Caroline to several more cabins, then down into steerage where once again, *Carpathia*'s passengers had been condensed into fewer cabins to make space for those from the *Titanic*. Emma went from room to room, calling Ruby's name, but had no luck. Her feet were in agony, but she forced herself to keep going. She was looking out for Martin too, although she knew there was no real hope of finding him. At last, at the far end of the lowest deck her knees buckled and gave way. Caroline caught her as she fell.

'You're exhausted, poor love. Come on, if you can walk let me find you somewhere to lie down and get you a nice hot cup of tea with plenty of sugar. I'll keep asking for your sister. Ruby Higgins, is it? If she's on board, we'll find her, don't worry.'

But what if she isn't on board, Emma wanted to say, to scream at this kind and gentle young woman who was doing all she could for her. What if Ruby had not made it into a lifeboat? What if she was at the bottom of the sea, trapped inside the *Titanic*, or still out there in the water, floating frozen in a life jacket like so many other poor souls? 'I promised Ma I'd look after her,' she whispered, as Caroline hoisted her to her feet, an arm around her waist, and led her back up to an open deck where there was space for her to lie down on a bench.

Somehow she must have slept, for when she woke there was a cooling mug of tea near her, and Caroline was nowhere to be seen. Emma guessed she'd had other people to help. The *Carpathia*'s resources and crew must be stretched to their limits. It didn't seem as though there was any other rescue ship in the area. She gulped down the tea and decided to resume her search. Maybe while she'd slept more lifeboats might have been picked up.

She toured the decks and the requisitioned cabins once more, asking, pleading, and being answered only by sadly shaken heads and haunted eyes. All of the *Titanic*'s lifeboats had been picked up and accounted for, she was told, including the collapsibles. And although the ship was still checking for survivors in the water there was no real hope of finding any. 'Is there a list, at all, of the people you've picked up?' she asked one of the *Carpathia*'s officers.

'Of course, miss, have you not given your name?'

She had; she'd been asked for it when she boarded. 'I'm looking for my sister. Ruby Higgins. She was a stewardess like me ...'

'Come with me, miss,' the officer said, and led her to an office where a sheaf of papers lay on a desk – the names of the *Titanic* survivors. He ran his finger down each page, as Emma waited.

'Please, can you look for Martin Seward too,' she asked. The officer glanced up and began going through the list once more, from the beginning. When he reached the end of the last page he looked up at her and shook his head, compassion in his eyes.

'I'm very sorry. Those names are not on the list.'

Once more her legs gave way, and she crumpled to the floor. The officer ran round to her, scooped her up, and carried her to one of the sick-bay cabins where he laid her gently on a bed. 'There, miss – the doctor will come and see you soon. Try to stay strong. It's a terrible thing, such a terrible thing to have happened.'

He left her then, alone with her thoughts, her anguish. Ruby, dead. Her promise to Ma broken. Martin, dead. Her dreams for the future shattered. Might it have been better for her to have died, too?

But then no one would have gone back to Ma and Lily, to tell them what happened. And Martin's folk, in Salisbury. She'd go and see them too, when she got back, she decided. She could at least keep that promise, the one she'd made to Martin. Maybe she could offer some crumb of comfort, telling them of his bravery in those last hours, how he had worked hard to save as many passengers as he could, and had pushed her forward to get a place on the last proper lifeboat.

Ma would find no comfort, she knew. Emma would not be able to tell her anything of Ruby's last hours. She had no idea where her sister had been, that evening. Or why had she not come up to the deck when the *Titanic* was sinking. Why, oh why, had Ruby not got herself into a lifeboat? She remembered her sister saying she might as well throw herself overboard. Emma had thought she was joking, but now she wondered. Had Ruby perhaps not attempted to save herself on purpose? Had she felt it was better to allow herself, and her unborn child, drown as a way out of her mess? Emma could not believe it of her sister. Ruby had always been so vibrant, so beautiful, full of life and energy. No. It was not true. Ruby had been headstrong, foolish at times, but being pregnant would have made her want to live. Despite it all, she had wanted her baby. The shawl packed in her luggage was proof of that, wasn't it?

Ruby must have been trapped somewhere on the *Titanic*, unable to get to the boat deck. If only Emma had searched more areas.

At last, after all those hours of searching the *Titanic*, of being adrift at sea in the lifeboat, of being on the *Carpathia* hobbling around on swollen feet as her hopes gradually dwindled away, at last Emma gave in to the emotions that engulfed her and cried, wrapping her arms around her head, turning to the wall and sobbing, her body shaking, head pounding, throat raw. The tears were useless, pointless – they brought no one back to life, they brought Emma no relief from the pain of her loss. But they eventually allowed her to sleep, a long, dreamless sleep of exhaustion, that lasted until dawn broke the following morning.

It was two more days before the *Carpathia* docked at New York. Two days in which Emma couldn't help but keep searching the ship for Ruby and Martin, asking all the *Titanic* crew members she came across (so few!) if they'd seen or heard any more of them. Two days in which she found herself hoping that maybe there'd been another ship in the area that might have picked up survivors. Two days in which the faces of Ruby and Martin were always at the front of her mind.

Caroline came to see her a couple of times, but was busy doing what she could for other *Titanic* survivors. Emma spent most of her time with Mary, tending to her friend's injuries as best she could. The mood amongst those who'd been rescued was subdued, as almost everyone was missing friends and family.

'What will it be like when we reach New York?' Emma said, to Mary. 'I suppose the news will have reached them there. I suppose there will be lots of relatives of the American passengers, all hoping their loved ones are on board. Will they know, do you think, who's survived and who's been lost?'

'I don't know,' Mary said. 'Maybe they will have used the Marconi equipment to tell New York who's on board. I don't know if that's possible though. We will soon find out.'

Another ship escorted the *Carpathia* for the last leg of the journey, up the Hudson river. She was manoeuvred into the docks, after dark that evening. There were crowds of people waiting on the quayside, but the atmosphere could not have been more different to that of less than a week ago when the *Titanic* had left Southampton. There were shouts and cries, some from journalists on board small boats who were shouting questions at the passengers. Emma hated it all. Couldn't they just leave the poor survivors in peace for a while, until they'd come to terms with it all? And then she thought of how people would want to hear the news, would want to know the details of what had happened, would want to know the names of all those who'd been lost. Newspapers would be printing lists of names, once they had them, she supposed.

Ma, Lily. If the news had reached them, they must be in anguish waiting to hear if she and Ruby had survived. Emma could not bear to think about what they must be going through.

When the ship docked, Emma and the other survivors were helped onto the quayside. Dry land! Solid, beautiful, blessed land. 'I don't know about you,' Mary said, 'but once I get back to England I am never going to sea again. I shall find myself another job.'

Emma felt exactly the same. 'I agree. That's it for me. I'll need to stay at home with Ma, anyway.'

'She'll be heartbroken about your Ruby, but very glad to see you, I imagine,' Mary said.

'I was supposed to be looking after Ruby.' It was the thought Emma could not stop herself returning to, over and over again.

'You did your best. You did all you could,' Mary said quietly. 'You must not blame yourself.' Mary hugged her, as they made their way into the terminal building.

Inside there were tables of old clothes. It looked like a jumble sale, and Emma was confused for a moment, until she realised that it was clothes donated by the people of New York for the *Titanic* survivors. Some had been in their nightclothes when they'd evacuated the ship. Some children were clothed only in rough smocks hastily stitched together from the *Carpathia*'s blankets.

'Do you need anything?' Emma said to Mary, indicating the tables.

'Clean underwear,' Mary said, and the two women rummaged through to find something suitable.

Arrangements had been made for the *Titanic*'s crew to be put up in hotels for a few days, so that they could give their statements. And then they were assured that White Star would take them back to Southampton, and that there would be no loss of pay for this voyage. 'No loss of pay! I should think not!' Emma had said, outraged. But the more experienced Violet told them that normally if you did not complete a voyage, even if it was due to problems with the ship, you would not get your discharge book stamped and therefore would not be paid.

Emma and Mary were billeted together in a room in a downtown Manhattan hotel, awaiting their voyage back. As far as possible Emma tried to avoid the reporters who thronged the hotel's lobby as soon as they realised there were *Titanic* crew staying there. She gave her statement to the investigators, detailing her actions from the moment she'd heard and felt the impact with the iceberg to the time she'd boarded the *Carpathia*. Other than that, and for meals, she and Mary mostly stayed in their room, sitting silently but appreciating each other's presence. Emma tried not to think about the plans she and Martin had had, for their stay in New York on this trip. If only that iceberg had not been there, if only the *Titanic* had made its turn a little sooner and avoided the impact, if only there'd been enough lifeboats, if only that first ship they'd spotted on the horizon had come to the *Titanic*'s aid – if any of these had been true Martin and Ruby might be here with her now. She and Martin would be walking arm in arm through Central Park, or along Fifth Avenue, gazing through the shop windows, planning a future together. Ruby would be … well, who knew? Beginning to make a future for herself here in New York, perhaps. Emma would have helped her, she knew now. She would have done anything in her power to help her sister start a new life.

If only they'd signed on to sail with the *Olympic* again, not the *Titanic*. If only she hadn't encouraged Ruby to take a stewardess's job. If only Ruby had never met Harry Paine …

At last word came that passage home to Southampton had been arranged for the *Titanic* crew members on board the White Star liner *Lapland*. The ship would thankfully sail by a more southerly route, avoiding all risk of ice, in deference to its passengers who had suffered so much.

As Emma boarded the *Lapland* clutching her small bundle of belongings – mostly second-hand clothes donated by the good people of New York – she told herself that it was the last time she ever would go to sea, no matter what the future held.

Chapter 19

Harriet

Harriet had a clear day, the day after her visit to the *Titanic* exhibition with Sheila. Sally phoned in the morning to say Jerome was poorly but stable, and that the search for a bone marrow donor was ongoing. She also told Harriet that, as they'd sadly expected, Harriet had not turned out to be a match.

'So we are relying on the people on the bone marrow registry,' Sally said, sounding resigned.

'Someone will be a match. There are hundreds of thousands on that registry,' Harriet said, trying to sound positive and convincing.

'I know. They are all heroes. Every single one of them. But there are apparently millions of different combinations of tissue type. Anyway. All we can do is hope and pray. I'll let you get on, then. Bye.'

She'd rung off before Harriet had a chance to talk about what she'd learned about her grandmother's family. Of course, it was Sally's great-grandmother – another generation away, a generation Sally had never met. Unimportant to her, especially when

Jerome's future was so uncertain. But Harriet found the research helped take her mind off other things, so she decided she'd spend the day working on it. She could look for death registrations for her great-aunts. Maybe order copies of their death certificates, to get the full story. To think one had gone down with the *Titanic* – how horrible that must have been for the rest of the family to cope with! One sister dead, one sister surviving. Why had they not stayed together and got on the same lifeboat? Not for the first time Harriet wished she could go back in time and ask her grandmother these questions. There must have been so many stories.

She set her laptop up on the kitchen table, and made herself a coffee. But just as she sat down to get started on the research, her mobile rang; the number was withheld.

'Hello?' As always, she held her breath wondering whether it was a spam call or Davina.

'Harriet? Hello. Well, you asked me to phone more often, so here I am. I think it's only been three weeks since my last call. So I've kept my promise. Were you marking the days off in a diary?' Davina laughed, in a teasing, good-natured way.

'Davina! Lovely to hear from you. Yes, you did say you'd call every three weeks, so thank you. I hadn't been counting, though, in case you forgot.'

'If I say I'll do a thing I do it, Harriet. You should know that. Anyway, how's Sally's kid? I've been thinking a lot about the poor little fellow. Is he any better?'

Harriet took a sip of her coffee before responding. 'Well, no, sadly. He looked as though he was doing OK, and then he got ill again, and the latest tests showed he was not responding to the chemotherapy.'

'Oh no. That's … that's awful news. Is there any other treatment possible?'

'They're looking at doing a bone marrow transplant. But he has no siblings, who would usually be the best chance for a match.

Sally, Charlie, and I have all been tested and we're no good, so his only chance is an unrelated donor from a registry. If they find someone on the database who's a match, and who's prepared to go through with the donation, they'll then do some treatments to prepare him for the transplant. He'll be in hospital for a while then. Poor little thing.'

'Where's he being treated? Who's the consultant?'

Harriet gave her the name of the hospital and consultant. 'They're among the best in the country. He's in good hands. But it's all about finding a donor, now.'

'Well, I'm sure a match will turn up for Jerome. There are loads on that register, as I understand it.'

'Yes, we're all very much hoping so.' Harriet sipped her coffee. 'So, how are your girls? Looking forward to the summer holidays?'

'They're both fine. And they are, yes. Autumn is showing hints of the type of teenager she'll be in a couple of years.'

'Oh? What type?'

'Stroppy, argumentative, strong-willed, fiercely independent.'

Harriet could not help but laugh. 'Sounds like she's a chip off the old block, then. You've just described yourself at 15.'

'Hmm.' Davina was silent for a moment, as though considering this. 'I'm going to find out what it was like for you, parenting me, aren't I? Could be in for a bumpy ride.'

Yes, and maybe you'll realise just how I felt when you left home with no forwarding address and no way of contacting you, Harriet wanted to say. But she stopped herself in time. So many of their conversations had descended into arguments at this point. Instead, she tried to keep the conversation light-hearted. 'What about Summer, is she the same?'

'She's still at that lovely, sweet, middle-childhood stage. She was hard work as a toddler – she seemed to specialise in having daily tantrums – but now she's the easiest, sunniest child in the world. Mind you, so was Autumn a year or so ago, so things could all change. James is good with Autumn, thank goodness. He stands for no cheek from her, and she adores him so tries not to upset him in any way. It's a different story with me, though.'

'Tricky relationship, mothers and daughters.' The words slipped out before Harriet could stop herself. Covering up, she quickly asked, 'Do the girls get on with each other?'

'Yes, at the moment. Summer still looks up to Autumn, as the big sister who knows it all. I remember feeling like that about Sally when I was little, and then at some point I realised she was just a normal girl, like me, just a bit bossier, and that I didn't necessarily agree with her on everything. I keep watching for that moment to happen with Summer, wondering if I'll recognise it when it comes.'

'If it comes. Some sisters stay friends for life.' Harriet prayed her words had not sounded judgemental.

'Hmph. I think siblings always fall out. You hardly ever see your brother. I only remember seeing Uncle Matthew two or three times in my life.'

'We didn't fall out. We just … drifted apart, I suppose. We're still in touch. Still friends.' Davina was right, though. She and Matthew sent each other Christmas and birthday cards, and occasional letters, but whole years would go by without them meeting up or speaking. 'I probably should make more of an effort to see him, I guess. Speaking of getting in touch with siblings, what about—'

'Oh no. Here we go again. Well, we've been talking a good ten or fifteen minutes now, so you've done well, Harriet, to get this far without nagging me about coming to see you all. So, I'll say goodbye, and send my best wishes to my nephew. I honestly hope and pray they'll find a donor for him – tell Sally that, for me, will you? Bye then.'

And as usual, she hung up without waiting to hear Harriet say goodbye too.

Harriet sat staring at her phone for a couple of minutes, as if wondering whether it might ring again. It remained silent. At least they'd had a chat. They'd even laughed a little. And she'd heard a bit about what her granddaughters were like. She could picture them. She chuckled to herself imagining Davina coping with a stroppy teenage Autumn, receiving a taste of her own medicine. Maybe though, having been like that herself, she'd do a better job of parenting a difficult teenager than Harriet had.

Later, with another cup of coffee to hand, plus a cheeky chocolate cookie for fortification purposes, Harriet began the research she wanted to do. Ruby Higgins. What was her position on board the *Titanic*, and had her body been recovered? She searched for a death registration and there was one, from the second quarter of 1912. She'd have to order the death certificate to see exactly what it said.

And then she Googled 'list of victims of Titanic' and came across a website – the fabulously named 'Encyclopedia Titanica' – which provided just that. Better still, it listed bodies recovered, and which ship had recovered them, plus where the victims had been buried. Ruby was listed as a second-class stewardess, just like Emma, and missing. Her body had not been recovered. Harriet spent a while browsing the lists. There were thumbnail photos beside many of the names, and their ages were given. She was silent as she scrolled through, looking at the photos of young men, middle-aged women, babies. The photos made it all seem so real. These were not just statistics, not just names. They were people, and each loss was a tragedy in its own right.

There was no photo beside Ruby's name. Clicking on it, Harriet discovered the website listed a brief set of facts about her great-aunt:

Born in Southampton in 1894 to George and Amelia Higgins, the second daughter of three. Ruby Higgins was resident at 49 Albert Road, Northam, when she signed on as a second-class stewardess, and the Titanic voyage was her first. Her body was never recovered. Her sister Emma Higgins survived, and the family later placed a notice in the Southern Daily Echo *announcing Ruby's death.*

That was all there was to show for Ruby's life. Not much, really. Harriet closed her eyes in silent tribute to the great-aunt she'd never known existed. The young girl, who'd been just 18 when her life was cut short in such a tragic way. What might she have become, what could she have achieved in her life? She might have gone on to have children and grandchildren – her grandchildren would have been second cousins to Harriet.

Harriet pondered how Ruby's last moments would have panned out. She obviously had not been picked up by a lifeboat. Had she been trapped in the ship, or perhaps in the water, trying to stay afloat until she'd perished from the cold? Had she been injured in some way? Had she not managed to get hold of a life jacket and therefore drowned quickly? It was impossible to ever know. Harriet hoped that the end had come quickly and as painlessly as possible. And what of Emma? The website listed her as making it onto a lifeboat and being picked up by the *Carpathia* along with all the other survivors. Again there was a brief biography of her, but no photo. Harriet wondered whether to copy the photo of the three sisters, snip Ruby's and Emma's faces and send them in to the *Titanica* website, so they too could have a picture by their names.

Emma would have had to go back home to Southampton after her rescue and face her mother and remaining sister, and tell them about Ruby's death, Harriet realised. They might have asked why she hadn't stuck by her younger sister and made sure she got on a lifeboat. Had she rushed off to get on an early boat to try to save herself? Harriet didn't like to think so. She preferred to imagine Emma searching for Ruby, hoping that maybe she'd already got on a lifeboat, before getting on one herself. She was listed as having been on lifeboat number sixteen. In what order had the lifeboats been launched? That might give a clue as to whether she'd just saved herself or tried to search for her sister first.

Harriet ran some more searches, read some Wikipedia articles and eventually found herself browsing books about the *Titanic* on Amazon. One intrigued her – a memoir by a woman named Violet Jessop, who'd been a first-class stewardess on the *Titanic* and survived its sinking. She'd also worked on the *Olympic*, as well as on the third sister ship, the *Britannic*.

'Wow,' Harriet whispered. 'You survived *Titanic*'s sinking and then went back to sea. That's so brave!' She ordered a copy of the memoir, wondering whether Violet had known her grandmother at all. They'd worked different classes but it was possible they'd come across each other in the crew areas. In any case, it would be fascinating reading a first-hand account of both life at sea as a stewardess, and what it had been like surviving the *Titanic* disaster.

Harriet jotted down everything she found out, and kept a file of useful online links. The story of the three sisters was taking shape, but as always, the more she found out the more questions she had, and some, she knew, she could never find the answers to.

'Gran, I wish you could tell me your stories again. Just come into my dreams and whisper in my ear or something,' Harriet said, to the photo of the three girls. Then she laughed at herself, calling on a long-dead ghost to help her with research. She'd had a long career in IT, she was definitely computer-literate, and she had the whole of the internet at her fingertips. There could be a lot more out there that she could find.

She spent the rest of the day on the Ancestry site, plugging in all the details she knew about her parents, grandparents, great-aunts. She tracked her great-grandparents – George and Amelia Higgins among them – on the nineteenth-century censuses and added those details. The website flagged up matches between her family tree and others. Harriet was intrigued, but there was no time now to click on the links and follow them all up. She looked at the clock and realised it was mid-afternoon. She'd missed lunch, and really she ought to get some housework done today or it'd never be done, and there were potential buyers coming to view the house tomorrow. She snapped her laptop lid closed and stood up stiffly, to get a shift on, as her grandmother used to say.

Chapter 20

Emma, 1912

When the *Lapland* docked in Southampton there were just a handful of people on the quayside to see the ship arrive. Emma glanced around the cabin she'd called home for the week that it had taken to cross the Atlantic, and said a silent farewell to life at sea. Mary too had decided never to work as a stewardess again. She was returning to her home city of Liverpool.

'Will we ever see each other again?' Emma asked her, as the two women disembarked.

'I'm sure we will. When I've got a new job and have some savings, I could come down to Southampton to visit you.'

'I'd like that,' Emma said, giving her friend a hug. But privately she knew it was unlikely. Neither of them wanted to be reminded of their terrible ordeal, and Liverpool was such a very long way from Southampton.

As Emma walked down the gang plank clutching her bundle of old clothes, there was a squeal and a shout – Ma and Lily had come to meet the ship. Emma stepped off onto the quayside and dropped her bundle, opening her arms for Lily who was running over to her.

'Ems, oh Ems. Ma read a list of survivors printed in the news-paper, and it said you were coming back on this boat. But where's Ruby? What happened? Oh, Ems!'

And then Ma reached them. Emma gazed at her over Lily's shoulder. Ma's expression was one of regret and anguish, but with a tiny tinge of hope in her eyes – she was silently asking, Emma realised, if perhaps the newspaper had been wrong and maybe even now Ruby was preparing to disembark from the *Lapland* and join her family. Emma gave a little shake of her head, and Ma's eyes filled with tears.

'Lovey, I am glad you are home safe at last,' she said, putting a hand on Emma's shoulder. Emma caught hold of it, her arm still wrapped around Lily, and squeezed, trying to say with a gesture all that she could not put into words.

With Ma holding one arm and Lily the other, she walked home by the familiar route that looked somehow so very different now, in this post-*Titanic* era. She'd lost so much since she last walked those streets. As they turned into their road, Mrs Williams was outside, standing by her doorstep in her usual position. She shook her head sadly as they approached. 'It's true then, is it? All those deaths and your Ruby among them?'

None of the family answered her or even looked her way. It was their private time to grieve.

As they entered the house, which felt different, wrong, quieter without Ruby's presence, Ma spoke. 'There's five other families on this street alone who have lost someone on board that ship. All were men who worked in the boiler room. None of them stood a chance, did they?'

'No,' Emma said, 'they didn't.'

'But Ruby, *she* must have had a chance. The paper said it was women and children first. And you got off it all right ...' Ma's voice tailed away as she hung up her coat and turned to Emma. This was it. It was time she told them the full story of how she'd searched and searched and in the end had had to hope that Ruby had saved herself on an earlier lifeboat. She resolved, however, not to tell Ma of Ruby's plans to jump ship in New York, or about Ruby's pregnancy. Ma need not know that she had lost a grandchild too. Nor would she mention Martin. He was her own, private loss.

'You did your best,' Ma said quietly, when Emma finally finished her tale. 'You couldn't have done more, I can see that.' But there was an accusation in her eyes, and Emma could read it all too clearly. She had survived, Ruby had not, yet if Emma had not let Ruby go drinking in the evenings after their duties ended then they'd have been together when the ship struck the iceberg, they could have stayed together and they'd have been on the same lifeboat.

'I wonder where she was,' Lily said. 'You looked everywhere. I suppose we'll never know. I hope … I hope it was all over quickly for her.'

Emma just shook her head sadly. Lily had grown up, it seemed, since Emma was last at home. She'd been the only daughter at home to help Ma, and of course since news of the *Titanic*'s sinking reached Southampton she'd have had to support Ma through the agonising days and weeks while they waited for news of survivors.

Ma said no more. She rose from the kitchen table where they'd been sitting, turned her back and busied herself setting a kettle to boil. Only the slight heaving of her shoulders showed she was weeping silently, hiding it from her daughters. Emma wanted to go to her and wrap her arms about her, but felt the gesture would not be welcome. Ma needed to grieve in her own private way, for now.

Instead, she reached across the table to Lily, who had tears streaming down her face. Lily squeezed her hand, and gave a tiny, forced smile that Emma returned. They had each other, and together they would help Ma come to terms with Ruby's loss. Despite the troubles Ruby had brought to the family, Emma had always suspected she'd been Ma's favourite. And now she was lost to them forever.

*

That night, Emma decided to sleep in the little room she'd shared with Lily the last few times she'd been home. Somehow she couldn't bring herself to take Ruby's room. She stood by its door for a moment on her way to bed, looking in. Everything was just as Ruby had left it – her clothes still hung in the wardrobe, a dent in the pillow where her head had lain, a spare nightdress she'd not needed on board tucked under it.

'It's hard to believe she's never coming back, isn't it?' Lily said, coming to stand beside her. Lily's arm crept around Emma's waist, and Emma leaned against her younger sister, grateful for the support.

'It's impossible to believe. Even though I saw the ship go down and heard the cries of all those people in the water, I can't believe it.' She bit her lip to stop the tears coming – surely she'd wept enough? 'How's Ma been?' She whispered this last. Ma had gone to bed only a few minutes before.

'Up and down. One minute saying you'd both have been saved, the next saying she'd lost you both.'

'You've done a good job, supporting her.' Ma looked older, ill from the stress and worry, Emma had thought.

Lily shrugged. 'It's my job, isn't it? Glad you're back, Ems. I'd not have managed if I'd lost two sisters.'

In Lily's room Emma picked up one of the two remaining copies of the photograph of the three sisters and gazed at it – Lily's sweet shy smile, her own cheerful one, and Ruby's defiant, chin-up glare at the camera. Such a precious picture – the only one there would ever be of Ruby. She held it against her heart, and mouthed a silent apology to Ruby that she had not been able to save her.

The next day Emma took the photo to the photographic studio where it had been taken. 'Is it possible to get more prints of this made?' she asked. Ma and Lily still had theirs, but she wanted a copy for herself.

The photographer checked the number printed on the back of it, and thumbed through his records. 'I am afraid we no longer have the negative. We only keep them for six months, and this was taken a year ago. But if the three of you return to the studio, we can take another picture at a reduced rate.' He smiled at her expectantly.

She could not bring herself to tell him that was not possible, but just nodded, thanked him and left the studio quickly.

It was one of the hardest things she had ever done. In some ways, it was even harder than facing Ma and Lily without Ruby. But she had promised herself and promised Martin that she'd do this. And so, two days after returning from New York, Emma took a train to Salisbury and then walked across the town to the address she'd memorised. It was a small Victorian terraced house, with neatly painted window frames and a tiny front garden. A rose climbed up beside the door, its early blooms framing the front room window. It was a well-cared-for house. As Emma approached the front door she felt a pang of regret. This, surely, was the kind of house she and Martin might have had. He'd have cultivated the rose, she'd have snipped blooms from it to put in a vase on their mantelpiece. There'd be pretty lace curtains at the window and the door would be painted a cheery red.

She took a deep breath and rapped on the door. Time to meet the people who might have become her parents-in-law.

The door was answered by a small woman with grey hair pulled into a neat bun. She was wearing a darned but tidy dark grey dress and her eyes were red-rimmed. Emma introduced herself and Mrs Seward invited her inside, offering her a seat in the front room, which did indeed have a small spray of roses in a vase on a side table.

'Let me fetch you some tea, Miss Higgins, and then we can talk. It will be so nice to hear from someone who knew my Martin. I'm afraid my husband is out at work.' Mrs Seward left Emma in the front room for a few minutes. Emma looked around. In the middle of the mantelpiece, where she'd have put a vase of roses, there was a framed photograph. Emma stood up to take a closer look – it was Martin, in his steward's uniform, looking a year or two younger than she remembered him. He was smiling, happy, proud. She picked up the photograph and felt her eyes fill with tears.

Behind her, Martin's mother was returning with a tea tray. She placed it on a small table and came to stand beside Emma. 'He was a handsome lad, wasn't he?'

'He certainly was,' Emma replied. She put the photograph back and sat down, waiting while Mrs Seward poured the tea.

'You worked with him, then?'

'Yes. On both *Olympic* and *Titanic*. I don't know if he ever mentioned my name when he was home but …'

The older woman nodded. 'He did, yes. Many times.' She smiled at Emma. 'I'd been very much looking forward to meeting you.'

'And I, you. But I never imagined it'd be like this.' Emma took a sip of her tea as she battled to control her emotions. 'He was a hero, at the end, Martin was. He didn't stop, trying to help people out of their cabins, putting life jackets on children and helping people into the lifeboats.' She took a deep breath. 'Including me. He insisted I go. He pushed me through the crowd to a lifeboat. I didn't want to go without him, but he said I must and that he'd get on another boat.'

She looked down at her hands for a moment then back at Martin's mother. 'I didn't know then that there were no more boats. I'm sorry.'

'Oh, love.' Mrs Seward dropped to her knees besides Emma's chair and wrapped her arms around her. 'You're not to go blaming yourself. It's no one's fault, other than the White Star Line for saying the ship was unsinkable and not providing enough lifeboats. I'm glad you were with him that last day. I'm glad he met you and was happy. And I am so, so sorry you did not have more time together.' She took Emma's face in her hands. 'I think I should have liked to have you as a daughter-in-law.'

Emma hugged her back. 'Thank you. And I would have liked to call you Mother.'

It was a different reaction than she'd had from her own ma, she thought. Ma did blame her, somehow, for not saving Ruby. Though what more Emma could have done for her sister she did not know.

She stayed an hour with Mrs Seward, talking through memories of Martin, crying together, laughing together, and leaving her with promises to come again, one day when Mr Seward would be home from work and when Martin's sister could be there too, with her little ones. She left Salisbury knowing she had made lifelong friends and feeling glad that she had taken the trouble to visit.

A few days later Emma had found herself a new job – back at the Star Hotel where she'd worked before going to sea. It offered less pay, but was on blessed dry land. She was employed to take room service orders to guests, turn down their beds, and tidy their rooms. Much as she had done before starting work on the *Olympic*. Sometimes it felt as though the last year had never happened. But then she'd remember that Ruby was gone, and Martin was gone, and nothing could ever be the same.

At home, life went on much as before. The only thing that seemed different to previous visits home was that there was no longer any need to worry about what Ruby was up to.

Emma worried about Ma instead. She seemed older, somehow diminished. Greyer and quieter. It was almost impossible to raise a smile from her. She still took in mending and washing, even though now Lily was older and no longer suffering from bouts of ill health Ma could have gone out to work.

'No, lovey,' she said, when Emma suggested it once, thinking that if Ma could get out of the house and meet people it might lift her spirits. 'I prefer to stay in my own home. There's memories of my Ruby in every corner here, and I want to hang onto them.'

Increasingly, it was Emma and Lily who did the shopping and ran other errands. Ma was isolating herself from everyone. She would sit in the kitchen with a bit of sewing, peering at it with her fading eyesight, or in the back scullery washing clothes, and she'd ask the girls to deliver the sewing or laundry back to the customer when it was done. 'I don't want to see them, lovey,' she'd say. 'I can't stand their looks of pity. It breaks me.' As the weeks went by she seemed to shrink still further into herself, her eyes dark and sunken, her face gaunt and the worry lines deeper than ever.

'What's happening to her?' Lily asked Emma, as they walked home from the shops with a basket of groceries on Emma's day off. 'What sickness is this?'

'Grief,' Emma replied. She had felt it herself – a black cloud that constantly threatened to envelop her, that made her want to simply stay in bed and let the world continue without her.

After a few months, the time felt right for Emma to move into Ruby's room and allow Lily more space. She enlisted Lily's help to clear out Ruby's things. It was heartbreaking going through her clothes, keeping a few things that she or Lily thought they might wear, packaging up the rest for charity. Ma came upstairs while they were clearing the room and stood for a minute watching them.

'Is there anything you … would like to keep?' Emma asked, but Ma shook her head.

'I have my memories of my darling girl. And her photograph. They are all I need.' Ma turned away, and went to her own room, closing the door.

She was doing that frequently these days – taking to her bed in the middle of the day, napping. The grief was consuming her, bit by bit. Emma stared for a moment at Ma's closed door, wondering whether to go in, offer tea, sit with her for a while. But when she'd done this before, she'd been brushed away. Ma blamed her still, she thought, for Ruby's death. She'd never say so outright, but Emma could see it, in her eyes. She should have done more. Somehow she should have kept Ruby safe, got her on a lifeboat, brought her home. Ma was wasting away, grieving for Ruby and it was all Emma's fault. She returned to Ruby's room, where Lily was cleaning inside the now-emptied wardrobe.

'It'll be nice for you to have a room of your own again,' Lily said, and Emma smiled in response. 'I'm sorry Ruby and I weren't better friends,' Lily went on. 'She never seemed to take much notice of me. I think she resented that I needed so much of Ma's attention when I was sick. And I was jealous of her spending time with you – I wanted you all to myself. I was just a child.'

Emma hugged her, unable to answer without more weeping. Lily was still a child, but she'd grown up so much in such a short time.

The following day Emma was leaving work when she spotted a familiar figure waiting outside the hotel's staff entrance. He was leaning against some railings, a straw boater perched on his head and a cigarette dangling from the corner of his mouth, just as he had been when Emma had seen him once before. As she exited the building he pushed himself upright and came to walk alongside her.

'Emma Higgins, isn't it? I heard you were working here. Wanted to see you. Sorry to hear about Ruby – she was a great girl, she was.'

Harry Paine. Emma stared at him for a moment, unsure how to respond.

'Listen, can I buy you a coffee? Wanted to talk to you, and here's not so good. It's about to rain.' He gestured up at the sky, where indeed a black cloud was gathering.

Emma's initial instinct was to tell him to go away, why would she want to talk to someone who had caused her family so much heartache? If it wasn't for him, Ruby would still be alive. But she couldn't help wondering what he possibly had to say to her, and there was only one way to find out. 'All right,' she said, guardedly, following him along the street and to a Lyons corner-house, the same one she'd sat in with Ruby, in another lifetime.

Once installed at a table with a coffee each, which Harry paid for, he took a deep breath. 'Couldn't believe it when I heard Ruby had gone on the *Titanic* and drowned. I'm honestly so sorry to hear that. I liked her a lot, you know.'

'She thought you loved her,' Emma said, unable to stop herself. 'She was devastated when you brushed her off.'

'I … I never lied to her. I was going to leave Dee. And be with Ruby. But then Dee told me there was another baby on the way. And … you must see, don't you? I couldn't leave Dee when she was expecting, and with all the other kiddies to look after. Wouldn't have been right.'

Had Harry known that Ruby was expecting a baby also? Would Ruby have even told him, when she'd already decided to leave town? Emma suspected not. 'None of what you did was right, Mr Paine. It wasn't right to even start a relationship with my sister.'

He took a sip of coffee and lit another cigarette before speaking again. 'Here, she didn't go off on the ship to get away from me, did she? I didn't drive her away, did I?'

'Yes, I think you did. She loved you, she told me. When you dropped her she didn't want to be here in Southampton any more, where she might bump into you on any corner.'

He looked down at his coffee cup for a moment. 'I should have left her alone. Never meant to drive her away. Poor girl.'

'You ruined her reputation. She was spat at, in the street. Her friends all dropped her.'

He shook his head. 'People are so small-minded, aren't they? I've had some of that myself.'

He deserved no comfort from her, Emma thought. None at all. She sipped her coffee and remained quiet, watching him as his discomfort rose. At least he seemed genuinely sorry for his part in Ruby's loss. If it hadn't been for him, Ruby wouldn't have signed on with the *Titanic*, and Martin and Emma would have stayed with the *Olympic*. The world now would be a very different place for them all.

'So, um, are you all right? You and your mother, and don't you have another sister too? Keeping all right, are you?'

She raised her eyes to his and held his gaze until he looked away. Were they all right? Having lost Ruby, with Ma wasting away through grief, how could they possibly be all right? But she had no desire to open up to this man. 'I suppose … we are as well as we can be expected to be.'

'Terrible thing, the ship going down. I knew two chaps who were on board – stokers they were. Both lost. Good chaps, they were. Then I heard Ruby was on board.' He frowned, then looked back at Emma. 'Here, how come she drowned and you didn't? Weren't you together? Wasn't it women and children first?'

'It was. I couldn't find her, when the ship was sinking. And believe me, Mr Paine, I tried to find her. In the end I had to hope she'd got on a lifeboat that'd been launched earlier. I was on the last one to launch. Not that it's any business of yours.' She was furious now, but determined not to cry. 'I thank you for the coffee and now I must get home. It is not your fault Ruby died but it was certainly because of you that she decided to take the job on the ship.'

She stood up and put on her coat. 'She wasn't going to come back, you know. She was going to stay in New York, and have her baby there. Your baby.' She watched the colour drain from his face, then left the coffee shop before he could say anything more.

Chapter 21

Harriet

A few days after the phone call from Davina, Harriet made a decision. It had been preying on her mind since talking to Davina. She took out a pad of writing paper – one she'd had for about fifteen years; it was so rare for her to write letters these days – found a pen and sat herself at the kitchen table to write to her brother, Matthew. Usually she only sent Christmas cards with a printed round-robin letter tucked inside covering the year's news in a brief, superficial way. And she'd sent him a death notice when John died. Matthew had sent a letter of condolence card in return, but had not attended the funeral. To be fair, as Harriet had thought at the time, Matthew lived a long way off – in a small village on the Cumbrian coast. And, as he'd written in his Christmas card to her, he'd had a hip replacement operation that year. Maybe he'd still been recovering from it when John died.

But now, even Davina was taking small steps to be closer to the family – if you could term a phone call every three weeks being 'closer' – and the more Harriet researched her ancestors the more she felt she should get in touch again with living relatives, while she still could. John's sudden death and Jerome's illness had brought it home to her how precarious life was and how quickly things could change. She should seize the moment. Maybe Matthew had stories he could share, that ought to be recorded for future generations. Her daughters had grown up largely without their uncle in their lives – he was just a shadowy figure who occasionally and inconsistently sent them each a cheque for a fiver at Christmas, and who'd visited briefly once or twice.

In her early days with John they'd gone north to stay with Matthew for a few days every year. Then the girls had come along, travelling became more difficult especially as Sally had a tendency to be car-sick, and Matthew's cottage was not big enough to put them all up. She and Matthew had simply drifted apart over the years. He could have come south to visit her more often, she supposed, but then again, had she invited him? If she was honest with herself, she knew that she hadn't – she'd just assumed if he wanted to come he'd invite himself. Matthew had never married, and although he'd had a long-term partner who'd died a few years back he'd had no children. She'd thought perhaps they no longer had anything much in common.

But they had – their shared childhood. Their memories. It was just that not seeing Matthew had become a habit. Over the years contact between them had dwindled to almost nothing until it was the norm; it was just how things were, and somehow she'd accepted that.

The same thing had happened with Davina. Although it had been a much more dramatic cut-off, over the years Harriet had become gradually and reluctantly used to not seeing her daughter. That wasn't to say she didn't wish things could be different. She did, of course she did, with all her heart. She'd do anything to have Davina back in their lives – but it wasn't up to her. It wasn't in her power to bring Davina back.

She could, however, do something about her relationship with Matthew. She sighed, took the lid off her pen, and began writing.

Dear Matthew

I thought I'd write to you, even though it's not Christmas (!) to update you on some family news. Firstly, I should get the bad news out of the way. My grandson, Jerome (that's my older daughter Sally's child) is seriously ill with leukaemia. He has had chemotherapy but it is not working, and now the doctors are looking for a bone marrow donor for him. Of course this is all terribly worrying for all of us, especially for Sally and her husband Charlie, but we are hoping and praying for the best.

In other news that might interest you, I have begun researching our family tree. This was sparked by finding a photograph in amongst Gran's old things, that shows she had two sisters. Did you know that? I always thought she only had one, but you were older and perhaps you might remember more of her stories? The sister I didn't know about, Ruby, drowned when the Titanic sank. I had no idea we had any family connection to that tragedy. I am adding all the details I find to a family tree on the Ancestry website and if you are interested, when I'm finished, I can send you a link to it.

Last month I went on a cruise with my friend Sheila – just a short one that criss-crossed the Channel, but it was a lot of fun and we are talking of doing it again next year. John never liked the idea of being on a cruise ship so it is something new for me to do.

I am in the process of thinning down my possessions and selling the house. It is far too big for one person and so, despite it holding so many precious memories of my life with John, it is time to move on. As soon as I have a new address I will of course let you know.

Do you use email? It would be far easier to keep you updated via quick emails. It took me ages to find this writing paper!

My email is harriet.wilson71@gmail.com. I would love to hear back from you. We are not getting any younger, and

perhaps because of Jerome's illness and John's death I'm finding
I want to gather my family close while I can.

I hope you're keeping well.

Love from your sister,
Harriet.

When she'd finished writing, she read it back through a couple of times. Yes, it hit the right, jolly, chatty tone but with the serious underlying message that she'd hoped for. It might spur him into replying, if for nothing else, to wish Jerome well.

She found an envelope, put the letter inside and addressed it. They'd got on so well as children and teenagers. Surely there was still something there that they could build on? It was, she knew, at least as much her fault as his.

There was a postbox almost directly across the street from her house. She padded across, still in her slippers, and posted the letter. There. She'd taken the first step – now it was up to Matthew. A memory surfaced – of a 12-year-old Matthew refusing to go with a friend's family to see a film unless Harriet could come too. The film was Disney's *Sleeping Beauty*, and while she'd guessed that Matthew wasn't all that keen to go anyway, it not being his kind of film, he'd taken a stand and insisted Harriet be allowed to come too, even though they'd not get home until after her bedtime. 'I want my sister with us,' he'd said, putting his skinny arm around her shoulders, 'otherwise I'd rather stay home with her.' Their parents had agreed in the end, smiling indulgently at their son as he ushered his little sister into the friend's family car and promised to look after her. That film had been her favourite for many years, and she'd enjoyed re-watching it on VHS with Sally and Davina years later. Matthew had admitted afterwards that he'd hated it, but was glad he'd managed to give her the opportunity to see it.

Back inside, she put the kettle on and smiled at the memory. He'd been such a dear brother to her, in those days. And now they were in their early seventies, perhaps they'd be able to renew that friendship? It was worth a try. It would be lovely to see more of him again.

Harriet was still drinking her coffee when the doorbell rang. On the doorstep were a bright-eyed couple she judged to be in their forties, and her estate agent. She blinked, and inwardly cursed herself for not remembering there was a viewing booked. The house was not as tidy as she liked it to be when people were coming to look at it. Nevertheless, she plastered a smile on her face and ushered everyone in. The estate agent would handle the tour – she knew it was best for her to keep quietly out of it and let the potential buyers walk around the house at their own pace without her breathing down their neck.

'This is Mr and Mrs Cannon,' the estate agent said, and they all shook hands.

'I'll be in the kitchen,' Harriet said, 'if there are any questions.'

'Thanks,' the female half of the couple said. 'This looks like a lovely house. Can't wait to go around it.' She smiled, and the smile looked genuine. Harriet wondered if possibly these buyers really were interested and not just curious time-wasters, as most of the other viewings had been so far. She nodded in response and went into the kitchen, leaving the door open wide so they knew they could come in and look round whenever they wanted.

As the tour progressed, she could hear murmurings from the couple. It sounded as though they liked what they saw. She fiddled about, washing her coffee cup and a few other things that had been left, wiping down the kitchen table and putting things away. At least she could make the kitchen look present-able before they came in here. Though the floor could have done with being mopped.

When they finally came into the kitchen, ten minutes later, the couple's eyes were shining even more brightly and they were smiling broadly.

'Oh, this is perfect,' Mrs Cannon said. 'A lovely size, and I always wanted a kitchen with a big table in it where everyone can gather. We have three kids,' she said to Harriet, 'and we're desperately in need of more space.'

'Plenty of space here,' Harriet said. 'We only had two kids – girls. But it was a very happy family home.' Until Davina walked out, of course.

'We've two boys and a girl. That garden looks a good size. There's space for a trampoline. Ellie's been pestering us for one for ages.'

Harriet smiled at the idea of the house being brought back to life by a lively family. John would have been happy with that too. She suspected that had he lived, they might well have been starting to talk about downsizing by now, anyway. She crossed mental fingers that this lovely couple might decide this was the house for them.

'May we go outside?' Mr Cannon asked, and Harriet nodded, crossing the kitchen to unlock the patio doors that led out to the garden. She slid it open. It was a fine, sunny day, and although the garden was in need of a bit of attention its potential was obvious. She stayed in the kitchen while the couple wandered around out the back, and the estate agent stayed with her.

'This seems to be a very positive viewing,' he told her. 'I have high hopes something may come of it. What's your situation now, in case they ask? Do you have a property lined up?'

'Ah, not yet, no. Tell the truth, I haven't really begun looking seriously. But I thought this house would take ages to sell, whereas there's plenty of the kind of property I want, so I'll have a wide choice. I will begin searching.' Harriet blushed as she said this, praying that her lack of action finding a new home wouldn't hold up the sale or mean that she lost these buyers. Well, that was her plan for the next few days then. Maybe Sheila would come and look at some houses with her. She couldn't ask Sally, whose time was completely taken up with caring for Jerome now.

'You're all right – there'll be plenty of time, but it's probably worth making a start,' the agent said, as the couple stepped back inside. They were discussing where they'd put a shed, and whether the space at the end would make a good vegetable plot or whether that should go at the side, behind the garage. It was always a good sign when potential buyers were planning how they would live in the house, imagining themselves already in possession.

'This is a lovely house,' Mrs Cannon said. 'It looks cared for, as though you've been very happy here. I guess you'll be sorry to leave.'

Harriet nodded. 'I will, yes. But it's too big for one person. Time to move on.'

Mrs Cannon stepped forward and took Harriet's hand. 'If we buy it, I promise you we'd take very great care of it. It'll be as loved as it obviously has been by you and your family.'

Harriet bit her lip. There was nothing she could say in answer to that, that wouldn't make her cry.

Once the Cannons had left, Harriet took out her laptop, planning to get started with some house-hunting online. She found an online estate agent, plugged in some details as to her requirements, desired location and budget, and soon had a long list of potentials. She ruled out upstairs flats with no lift – not sensible as she was getting older and her knees sometimes twinged on stairs. Ground-floor flats then? Did she really want a leasehold or would she prefer a freehold property where she'd be fully in control? Victorian terraces, originally two-up, two-down but now with attic conversions and garden extensions? Modern boxy houses on small plots? Three-bed semis built between the wars – which in some cases weren't much smaller than the house she was selling.

'There's too much choice,' she said to the kitchen walls. 'I honestly have no idea.' If only John had still been around. It would have been fun discussing with him, going to view properties, choosing one together for their old age. She tried to imagine what sort of place he'd have gone for. Maybe that was what she should do – buy the sort of place they might have bought together. After all, if they had decided to sell up a couple of years ago, she'd have been widowed in a house he'd have helped choose.

'You'd have gone for a bungalow, wouldn't you, John?' she muttered. 'Yes. That's it. You would have.' A house on one level, that was easy to care for. Not too big, but with space for visitors and space in the attic to store the things she could not bear to part with. She narrowed her search criteria and began looking in more detail at the list of two-bedroom bungalows available near to Sally. There were about half a dozen on this website – a more manageable number to consider.

She was just reading the details of one when the laptop pinged to show an email had arrived. It was from the Ancestry website, alerting her to a private message sent to her from another member. Intrigued, she clicked on it to open it, and as she read the message her jaw dropped open in astonishment. How could that be? It turned everything she thought she knew about her family on its head.

Chapter 22

Emma, 1914-16

Since the summer, Britain had been at war with Germany. Some scuffle in the Balkans had escalated alarmingly and now it seemed that all of Europe was involved in the conflict. Huge numbers of troops were being sent to the Western Front, and there were calls for men of fighting age to sign up and do their bit. Kitchener's poster was everywhere, and almost daily there were troops marching through Southampton streets; excited young men hoping they'd see some action.

In Emma's street, several young men had been lost on the *Titanic*. They'd have signed up, she thought, had they survived. News came that Harry Paine had joined up, leaving his wife and five children alone. Emma hoped for his family's sake that he'd stay safe and return home to them. He'd calmed down, by all accounts, since Ruby's death. He'd become a family man, spending much more time with his children. 'Best thing that ever happened to him, your Ruby drowning,' Mrs Williams had said, patting Emma's arm as though she'd intentionally sacrificed her sister to make a point to Harry Paine. The woman at least had the good

208

grace to blush and apologise once she realised the implication of her words. But the damage was done. Emma had to turn and walk away quickly, before she lashed out. She did not need the likes of Mrs Williams reminding her of Ruby's loss. She still felt it, all too intensely, every minute of every day. She'd failed in her promise to Ma. She hadn't been able to keep Ruby safe. If only she hadn't let her go drinking. If only she'd searched harder for her when she first felt the ship hit the iceberg. If only … The guilt was eating away at her, and no matter what she did, she couldn't throw off the feeling that it was her fault Ruby had died. And every time she looked at Ma – grey, ageing, always tired – it served as a reminder of her failure.

As autumn progressed into winter and the opposing troops dug themselves into trenches it became clear this war was not going to end quickly. Lily was now 15 and had left school.

'I'm going to train to be a nurse,' she announced to Ma and Emma one evening, as they sat at the kitchen table, finishing a dessert of tinned peaches and custard. 'If the war goes on no one will want to stay in hotels, and I want to do something useful, for the country. They say there will be lots of injured soldiers being sent back from the front line. If I can help save them, they can return to their families.'

Emma smiled at her sister. 'What a lovely thought, and such a kind thing to do.' How typical of Lily, to be thinking of others as she decided upon a career. She was the sweetest child ever. Unlike Ruby who had generally thought of herself first.

'I've heard they're sending nurses to the front line,' Ma said, with a sigh. 'Don't you go, Lily. It'd be dangerous out there. Lord knows I've lost one daughter, and losing another would finish me off.'

'I won't go to the front,' Lily said. 'That's only military nurses. I'll be a civilian nurse.'

'They're sending those Voluntary Aid nurses too,' Ma said accusingly.

'That's not me, though. I'll be paid, once I'm trained up. It'll be all right, Ma.'

'You'll get hurt. You'll leave me all alone in my old age, I know it.' Ma heaved herself up from her chair and went to sit in the front room.

This was how Ma always was these days, Emma thought. Always fearing the worst, terrified that Lily or Emma would come to some harm, talking as though they were taking risks on purpose, to spite her. She'd never got over the loss of Ruby. 'She'll get used to the idea,' Emma said to Lily. 'I think it's wonderful of you.'

'I have to do what I can,' Lily said. She stood and began stacking the plates. 'I can train here in Southampton, so I won't need to leave home and can still help out, with Ma and everything.'

'Thank you,' Emma said. Ma was increasingly frail these days. Although she was just over 50 years old she seemed much, much older. Ever since Ruby had died, it was as though something had died inside her too. She'd stopped taking in any laundry though she still did small amounts of sewing. Emma and Lily did all the cooking, shopping, and housework, leaving Ma to sit quietly, as she so often did, alone with who knew what thoughts running around her head. She no longer ever left the house. 'Lily, I'll clear up tonight. You go and sit with Ma, reassure her that you won't be in any danger.'

'All right.' Lily hugged Emma. 'Thank you for being the best sister ever.'

Emma squeezed her in return. 'I'd do anything for you, you know.'

Lily smiled. 'And I would, for you.'

The war dragged on throughout 1915 and into 1916, with the newspapers bringing depressing news of countless casualties daily. Emma had changed jobs – she was now a cleaner at the Royal South Hants hospital, the same one in which Lily worked as a nurse. Lily had tried to persuade Emma to train as a nurse also, but Emma was reluctant. She was better at caring for rooms than sick people, she argued, and it was important to keep wards spot-less. At least working in the same building she would occasionally come across her sister, and when their shifts coincided they were able to walk to or from work together.

It was in the early autumn of 1916 when Lily announced that she was volunteering to work on board the various hospital ships that had been requisitioned and were being used to collect injured soldiers from points around the eastern Mediterranean.

'I feel I can do more good closer to the front line,' she said. 'There are so many men stranded in makeshift camps out there – they must be brought back and cared for. Several ships have been going back and forth. They need more nurses, and I want to do this.'

'You're going to sea,' Ma said, looking up at Lily with tired, sad eyes. Ma was lying on the settee in the front room – it was where she spent the bulk of each day, simply napping the hours away. She no longer took in any sewing work. Emma and Lily brought her meals to her there, and left bread and cheese within her reach when they went out to work. Often the bread and cheese remained untouched.

'Yes, Ma, I am. To help out with the war effort. It is the best thing I can do.'

'But I lost my Ruby when she went to sea.'

'Oh Ma. This is different. We won't be sailing across the Atlantic, just around the Mediterranean. It's perfectly safe.'

'There was that ship, the *Lusitania* – it was torpedoed. How can you say it's safe?' Ma closed her eyes as she spoke, as though keeping them open was too much effort.

'But I'll be on a hospital ship, marked with a red cross. No one would torpedo a hospital ship. It'll be perfectly safe.' Lily leaned over and kissed her mother. 'I wouldn't go if I didn't feel I had to, Ma. But I must do *something*.'

'All right, if you must. You are grown up now, and I must not stand in your way. Will Emma stay home to look after me?'

211

'Of course I will, Ma.' It was Emma's turn to kiss her mother.

What was wrong with her? Ma seemed to be wasting away. She was grieving still, for Ruby. She'd lost her favourite daughter, the lively one, the one she'd always said was most like herself. And she seemed not to be able to move on from that. She ate less and less, and sometimes it seemed as though the very act of swallowing was more than she could bear.

Emma had suggested they call a doctor to see her, but Ma shook her head. 'We can't afford a doctor. Anyway there's nothing wrong with me that a doctor can fix, I'll tell you that for nothing.'

'But they might be able to do something. There are doctors we know at the hospital – Lily might be able to persuade one to call on you for no payment ...'

'No, lovey. I don't want a doctor.' Ma had sighed. 'I just want my Ruby back, and that I cannot have.' She'd turned over then on the sofa, her back to the room, signalling the end of the conversation. A moment later she was asleep again.

'It's as though she's lost the will to live,' Lily said later, when Emma told her about the conversation. 'She's just lying there waiting to die. Oh, Ems, what can we do?'

'We could bring a doctor round despite what she said? We could ask Dr Thompson, perhaps, he always seems like a lovely chap when I've passed him in the wards. Maybe there's something we can do to help her ...'

Lily nodded. 'I'll talk to him, at least. If I describe her symptoms he may be able to advise us even without seeing her.'

Lily did speak to Dr Thompson, and reported back to Emma a couple of days later. 'He's so busy, but he'll try to call round. We can introduce him as a friend, perhaps. Meanwhile we're to make nourishing soup that's easy to digest, and feed her that, and try to find something to interest her. Another nurse gave me a couple of magazines. I'll give her those.'

But Ma wouldn't look at the magazines, saying they hurt her

212

eyes. And although she tried the soup, she would not finish even a small bowl of it.

Dr Thompson called two days later. He left his doctor's bag by the front door, and Lily went to make him tea while Emma showed him into the sitting room where Ma lay on the settee.

'Hello, Mrs Higgins,' he said. 'It's so nice to meet you – Lily has told me a lot about you. How are you feeling?'

Ma made an effort to sit up, pushing back the knitted blanket that was tucked around her. The doctor jumped to his feet to help her, but she feebly pushed him away and then glared at him. 'What did you say your name was?'

'Doctor – I mean, Mr Thompson. I'm … a friend of Lily's.'

'Doctor? From the hospital?'

He sighed and nodded, glancing apologetically at Emma. 'Yes, I am a doctor. Lily asked me to come to check on you. She's worried.'

Ma rolled her eyes and lay back down. 'I'm not well, that's true, but I don't want no doctor prodding at me. Sorry, Dr Thompson. My daughter has you here against my will. I'd ask you to finish your tea in the kitchen and leave me in peace.' She waved her hand dismissively.

Dr Thompson stood and went through to the kitchen, followed by Emma. 'I cannot force her to let me examine her, I'm afraid. Don't worry about the tea, Lily. I must hurry away now. Keep feeding her hearty soups, with plenty of water in between, maybe with a little sugar stirred in. Let her rest if that's all she wants to do. Talk to me again if she complains of any pains. There is not much else I can advise.'

'Thank you anyway,' Lily said, as Emma showed him to the door. She went back to the kitchen after he left, to find Lily sitting at the table, head in hands.

'I won't go,' Lily said. 'On the hospital ship. I shall stay here and help you with her.'

'Oh, Lils, are you sure? It was your dream. I can manage …'

'I'm staying, Ems. I fear … Ma might not last long. You can see it in her eyes. She's … giving up on life.' Lily brushed away a tear.

Emma went to sit beside her, wrapping an arm around her sister's shoulders. Lily was right, she thought. Ma might not have long. 'Well, if you are sure … it'll certainly be easier to have two of us here … in the coming weeks.'

'Weeks?' Lily sounded aghast.

'Months. However long it is. She might rally yet.'

'She might.' Lily wiped her eyes, and stood. 'I'll make her some sweet tea. And there's a biscuit she can dunk in it. We'll do what we can for her, won't we? And I'll tell her I'm not going away.'

As Emma spoon-fed her mother dinner that evening, she noticed Ma was struggling to swallow. She only managed a couple of mouthfuls before turning her face away.

And this became the norm – Ma ate less, talked less, and began to physically fade away as the days went on.

A few weeks later as Emma sat at her side, reading to her, Ma reached out a shaky hand and began opening and closing her mouth in an effort to say something. Emma broke off from her reading. 'What is it, Ma?'

'L-look after … Lily. P-p-promise.'

'Of course I will. You're not to worry, Ma.'

'If she g-goes on a sh-sh-ship. You g-go too, l-lovey. T-take care … of her.'

'You want me to go to sea again? Even after …' Emma stared at her mother.

Ma nodded, slowly, weakly. 'L-look after her. I tr-trust you. Promise me.' She reached out a shaky hand to Emma, who gave it a gentle squeeze, battling back tears. Ma trusted her. Despite the situation, despite Ma's illness, Emma felt a weight drop from her shoulders, at the realisation at last that Ma didn't blame her for Ruby's loss.

But Ma was asking her to go back to sea. Emma had said she

never would, not after the *Titanic* … Ma wanted her to promise, and Lily was so intent on taking a job on a hospital ship to do her part for the war. Emma had failed Ma before – she had not kept Ruby safe despite her promise. Maybe this was her chance at redemption. Make this promise; ensure Lily's safety even if it meant overcoming her own fear of getting on a ship again. She'd be able to live with herself once more.

She turned her gaze back to Ma, Ma's eyes watery and pleading. 'I promise, Ma. I'll keep Lily safe no matter what.'

'Th-thank you.' Ma's mouth twisted in what Emma supposed was the nearest she could manage to a smile, and then her eyes closed and she drifted off to sleep.

Emma watched her for a moment, her chest rising and falling, her breathing becoming noisy. She put the book down on a side table and went out to the kitchen to make a pot of tea. Lily was at work. Emma needed a moment of reflection. So now she'd promised to go back to sea, when the time came after Ma was gone. In some ways it made sense – rather than stay in the Southampton house alone, she'd be with Lily, making a difference, helping with the war effort. And, as Lily had told Ma when she'd first had the idea – a hospital ship in the Mediterranean was a far safer place than a liner in the north Atlantic. Maybe Lily would only do one voyage, and feel that was enough. It would be all right. And if she did this thing, she'd have kept her promise. She'd do it in Ruby's memory.

Two weeks later, with Ma's breathing becoming more and more laboured, both girls sat at her side in the evening. Emma caught Lily's eye and gave a tiny shake of her head. She watched her sister bite her lip to stop the tears from falling. Ma slipped into a coma, her breaths grew less frequent, uneven and ragged, and then there was one last shuddering intake, exhalation and then … nothing.

The girls sat quietly at her side, each holding a hand, for a few minutes. 'She's gone,' Lily whispered, and Emma nodded.

'Yes. It was peaceful. We can be glad of that, at least.' She tucked the blankets up around Ma's chin, not wanting just yet to cover her face. 'I'll go … for the undertaker, tomorrow.'

Somehow, neither of them wanted to leave the front room that evening. They sat until the early hours beside Ma's dead body, talking in low voices about what needed to be done, reminiscing on the good times before Ruby died, when Ma was fit and healthy, and even before then when Pa was alive and they lived on the Isle of Wight.

'It was that ferry, you know,' Emma told Lily, 'the ferry across to Cowes that we took when I was 4, when we first moved to the island. Before you were born. That was when I first decided I wanted to go to sea.'

'And you did.' Lily smiled sadly.

'And I shall again,' Emma said, glancing at Ma as though she expected a nod of approval.

'What? When? I thought …'

'When you go on the hospital ship, I shall go too. They'll need cleaners as well as nurses. I shall get myself a job alongside you.' Emma smiled what she hoped was a confident smile.

Lily crossed the room and hugged her. 'Thank you. It will be nice not to be alone. And I know Ma would have wanted us to stay together. I've heard there's a call for nurses and staff for voyages to the eastern Mediterranean this autumn. Shall we apply for jobs on those?'

'Yes, we should. Which ship is it, do you know?'

'A White Star ship, called the *Britannic*,' Lily replied.

Emma felt dread clutch at her heart but she forced herself not to show it. *Britannic. Britannic!* Why did it have to be that ship, of all the liners available? *Olympic* and *Titanic*'s third sister ship.

Chapter 23

Harriet

I am delighted to find someone in England whose family tree overlaps with my own. I always knew my grandmother was English but she was not in contact with any of her English family, and as a child I didn't think to question her about it or ask for their details. I realize now I should have paid more attention to her stories of her younger life – isn't that always the way? From what you've entered on Ancestry I think you and I may be second cousins. My grandmother was Ruby Higgins, and she was a survivor of the Titanic *disaster of 1912. She came to New York aboard the* Carpathia *and never went back to England. I would love to hear back from you, and hear any tales you remember from your own grandmother.*

Robert Connolly, Oakland, New Jersey

Harriet had to read the message several times before it sank in. So Ruby had not died on the *Titanic*, even though she was listed as lost. Somehow she had survived and stayed in New York, and had a family. Harriet couldn't help but wonder why she had never gone back to Southampton. Had she fallen out with her family, perhaps? Presumably Emma and Lily and their mother had not known Ruby had survived – they must have believed she was dead. They'd even put a notice in the paper – Harriet recalled seeing that fact on the *Encyclopedia Titanica* website. Emma had been rescued. Harriet's research had found that all survivors were picked up by the *Carpathia* – so why had Emma not found Ruby on board the rescue ship? Harriet recalled a scene near the end of the film *Titanic*, where the character Rose hid under a shawl, turning her face away, as her hated fiancé called out her name on board the *Carpathia*. Could Ruby have deliberately hidden from Emma? Perhaps they'd argued. It was a harsh thing to do to your sister. Harriet knew the lists of survivors and dead were not a hundred per cent accurate, and there was disagreement about exactly how many people had been on board the *Titanic*. So it was possible that somehow Ruby's name had not been added to the list of survivors and instead she'd been presumed dead. No, not possible – it *must* be what had happened. Robert Connolly, her second cousin, was living proof.

She considered how best to reply, and in the end simply responded with her email, phone number and the words: *Hello second cousin! How wonderful to hear from you! Yes, I think we have an awful lot to talk about. Are you free to chat, perhaps via WhatsApp if you use that? Harriet Wilson.*

Within minutes a reply arrived with Robert's phone number. She entered it on her phone and set him up as a WhatsApp contact, sending a first message. With the time difference to New Jersey and the cost of international calls to the US, using WhatsApp for calls would work out much better. Robert replied to her message, suggesting a call later that day – evening in UK time, mid-afternoon for east coast US. Harriet responded with a thumbs-up and grinned. How exciting, finding a whole branch of the family she hadn't known existed! She couldn't wait to hear what Robert remembered of his grandmother's stories. Meanwhile, she spent some time jotting down notes of her own memories of Gran's stories. Robert would certainly want to hear them.

At the agreed time that evening, with a glass of wine to hand for fortification purposes, Harriet called Robert via WhatsApp, on a voice-only call. He answered quickly, as though he'd been waiting with his phone in hand.

'Hi there, cousin! Shall we make this a video call, or would you rather not?' His voice was confident, friendly, with an east-coast American accent. She imagined him saying *cawfee* for coffee, *Noo Yoik* for New York, etc.

'Hello! I'm happy to do a video call if you are.' Harriet touched the relevant button on her phone and propped it up against her fruit bowl, hoping that the angle was not too unflattering. As Robert's picture appeared, she saw a pleasant-faced man with scruffy grey hair and a neatly trimmed beard. He was wearing dark-rimmed spectacles that gave him the look of a kindly professor. She judged him to be a similar age to herself, perhaps a little younger.

'Well, look at you, ma'am! My English cousin – I am mighty pleased to make your acquaintance!' Robert gave her a mock salute and she laughed, already warming to her new relation.

'You too! I must admit, I was extremely surprised to get your email. I thought Ruby had died on the *Titanic*.'

'Yes, I saw you had put a date of death as April 1912. I nearly pointed that out in my first message to you.'

'She's listed as a victim of the disaster all over the place,' Harriet said. 'To tell the truth I only found out about her existence recently.' She recounted the story of coming across the photo in her grandmother's old sea chest, and of seeing Ruby's name on the list of the *Titanic*'s dead at the exhibition and on the *Encyclopedia Titanica*.

'Really? I've only ever glanced at that. Guess I should send them a correction,' Robert said, his eyebrows raised. 'We always knew Grandma had been on the *Titanic,* so I never felt the need to read through survivors' lists and all. She talked about it plenty, how it had been her escape – excuse me, ma'am, I hope it doesn't upset you, but Grandma said she'd had a hard time with her family back in England.'

'It's all right – it's over a hundred years ago. I'm longing to hear all you can tell me about her. At two generations removed I won't be offended if you tell me she thought my gran was a right cow.'

'A right cow!' Robert repeated, with a chuckle. 'What a wonderfully English insult! She used to say she felt misunderstood. Bossed around a bit. As though nothing she did would ever be good enough. She wanted a clean break.' He cleared his throat. 'I think too, though she kept a little quiet about it, there may have been some scandal involving a man. Certainly my aunt was born within just five months of her arriving in New York.'

'Oh! So she must have been pregnant when she left Southampton!'

'I believe so, yes. So, let me tell you what I remember of her stories. They're family legend. She was on one of the first lifeboats to be launched. When her lifeboat reached the *Carpathia,* a first-class passenger from that ship offered her the use of his cabin. She never left that cabin, until they reached New York. The passenger looked after her.'

'That was kind of her.'

'Him. It was a man – he was named Douglas Connolly.'

'Connolly?' Harriet frowned, putting two and two together.

Robert chuckled, a warm, throaty laugh. 'That's right. My grandfather. They must have hit it off on the ship. When they arrived in New York he offered her a room in his apartment in midtown Manhattan. He looked after her while she had her baby, in return for her "keeping house" for him. I always thought that might be a bit of a euphemism. We suspect Grandma batted her eyelashes at Grandpa from the moment she boarded the *Carpathia.* She was very beautiful as a young woman, and she could certainly turn on the charm when she needed to. Anyway, a couple of years later they married and then had two children together. My father was the youngest. My grandfather brought Ruby's first child – my Aunt Margaret – up as his own.'

'He sounds like quite a man.'

That chuckle again. 'He was nice enough, what I remember of him. I think he was simply crazy in love with Ruby. He'd do anything for her.'

'Do you remember much of Ruby?'

'I do – she lived until I was in my late twenties. She was a real character. Forceful, lively, a woman who knew her own mind. Grandpa worshipped her but I think he didn't always have an easy life with her – she could be quite demanding. Everything we did as a family we'd do with her in mind – making sure she'd be happy and looked after ahead of worrying about anyone else. But we all loved her, and when she died at the age of 91 we were all devastated. It felt like the heart had been torn out of our family.'

'Wow. She sounds awesome. My gran was quite different – quiet, kind, caring, but happy to fit in with everyone else. She was probably the least demanding person I knew, but everyone was always happy to do anything for her. She was a very wise woman, always able to offer good advice. I still hear her in my head at times.'

'Ah, that's awesome. Did she tell you stories of her younger life? I guess not so much, if she never even told you she had a sister she thought she'd lost on the *Titanic*.'

'She did – but as a child and young woman I didn't really pay as much attention as I should have. I remember her talking about her later career on the *Olympic* – she worked on the *Olympic* on and off until it was retired in the 1930s. So did my grandfather, and they'd leave my mother, who was born in 1925, with my paternal grandparents if they were both at sea together. She always said she couldn't work on another ship, so once the *Olympic* was taken out of service, she took herself out of service too. She'd laugh when she said this, but thinking back, there was always a kind of wistfulness about her when she spoke of life on board ship. I thought that was just because she missed it, but perhaps she was thinking of her lost sister.'

'You believe she always thought Ruby had perished?'

'She must have. Otherwise, in all those trips to New York on the *Olympic* in the Twenties and Thirties, surely she would have tried to find her?'

'I guess so.'

'Also, the family put a death notice in the local paper. Do you remember Ruby talking much about her English family?'

'Hmm.' Robert scratched his beard. 'She did talk about them a little. I remember her saying her mother was poor but hardworking. Her father died when she was quite young. Her sisters – ah yes, I remember something she used to say when we asked her about them – "one bossy, one sweet as sugar". I don't remember which was which. But she'd been adamant she had to have a clean break from them all, and never wanted to contact them. "They wouldn't understand, and they'd never forgive me," she used to say. Grandpa used to just listen in silence, looking sad. I had the impression over the years he might have tried to persuade her to contact her mother at least, and let her know she was alive and well, even if she didn't want to stay in touch with them. He could never talk her into anything she didn't want to do, though. No one could.'

'Did she remain living in New York?' Harriet asked.

'Yes, she and Grandpa owned an apartment near Central Park. I used to love visiting as a child, taking the subway in from New Jersey. It seemed such a glamorous place to live – there was a concierge at the front desk and an elevator with a brass concertina door you had to pull across manually. They lived on the sixth floor and there was a stunning view over the park.'

'Sounds lovely – and a far cry from the Victorian terraced house Ruby grew up in,' Harriet said.

'Grandpa was well off. He'd inherited money from his father. Say, I'd love to come over some time for a trip to England. I've only been to London on a brief visit twenty years ago. Perhaps if I come over, I could come to Southampton and take a look at Grandma's old place, if it's still there. Maybe you and I could meet up for a coffee?'

'I'd love that! I don't live far from Southampton so could easily meet you. It's a nice city. The Higgins's house is still there, according to Google Street View. It's nothing special, just a typical Victorian terrace. We've hundreds of thousands of houses like that in this country. You'll be surprised how small it is!'

'All right! Well, ma'am, I'm afraid I must go now, as I have errands to run this afternoon and I imagine it is getting late over there in England. It has been tremendously exciting to chat to you, long lost cousin! Let's stay in touch by WhatsApp and I'll let you know when I've booked my trip to England.'

'Yes, please do! Lovely to talk to you, too. Hope to see you soon.'

Harriet ended the call with a broad grin on her face. What a wonderful second cousin she had! He seemed like a genuinely nice man and she hoped his plan of coming over for a visit would work out. She had the impression he had plenty of money so hopping on a trans-Atlantic flight wouldn't be a big deal to him.

It had been quite a momentous day. The estate agent had called earlier, saying that Mr and Mrs Cannon had put forward an asking-price offer for her house. They clearly wanted it badly – they'd only viewed the house that morning. Harriet had accepted, and now the pressure was on to find somewhere she could move to.

Harriet had to share all her news with someone. She had found a bungalow she wanted to view, and the estate agent had set up an appointment for the following afternoon. She phoned Sheila.

'Need you, Sheila,' she said, when her friend picked up the phone. 'Lots to tell you, plus I need your opinion on a house.'

'Ooh, a viewing?' Sheila squealed. 'You know I said I'd come any time to look at possibilities. I love nosing around houses.'

'Two o'clock? I'll pick you up. I'm to meet the estate agent at the property.'

'Sure, perfect. And what's all the news? Is Jerome any better?'

'He's still the same, poor little mite. The search for a donor is ongoing.'

'Aw, bless him. Hope they find one soon.'

'Also, I have a buyer for my house.'

'Fabulous! Well, we must work hard to find you a suitable new home then!'

At two o'clock, Harriet picked up Sheila who was wearing a fake leather jacket in an alarming shade of green. She'd dyed her hair a bright orange since Harriet had last seen her. 'Look at you, brightening up the day,' Harriet said. 'Who cares if we have grey skies?'

'Well, that's what I thought,' Sheila said as she climbed into the car. 'So, what news?'

They drove to the bungalow – further from the beach than her current home but still within walking distance, she was pleased to note. Once there and sitting in the car outside waiting for the estate agent, Harriet filled her in on what she'd learned from Robert.

'So Ruby lived! That exhibition listing her as dead was wrong, then.'

'Not just that. All the websites, every list I've found online. A newspaper notice in the *Southern Daily Echo* in 1912 that her family placed. She was pregnant, it seems, and wanted to make a fresh start somewhere new. Perhaps her family didn't approve of whoever her boyfriend was. Ah – see, that fellow looks like an estate agent.'

A young man in a shiny suit was locking his Vauxhall parked on the other side of the road. Harriet climbed out of her car and looked across at him. He smiled and approached her, hand outstretched to shake. 'Mrs Wilson? James, from Winkworth. We spoke on the phone. Nice to meet you. Are you ready to go in?'

'Yes, thanks. This is my friend Sheila who's going to have a look round with me.'

'Nice to meet you, Sheila. Always wise to bring someone with you for a viewing,' Jamie said, as they crossed over to a bungalow with a neat front garden and block-paved driveway. He unlocked the front door which was on the side of the house, explaining that the elderly owner had moved into a nursing home. 'So there is no onward chain.'

Harriet and Sheila followed him into a surprisingly spacious hallway from which all the rooms were accessed. Two bedrooms at the front. A bathroom with separate toilet opposite the front door, and to the rear, a large sitting room and a kitchen-diner. A conservatory had been added at the back, accessed from the sitting room. The garden was small, a little overgrown as though the owner had not been able to care for it for a couple of years, but there was a patio that looked as though it'd be a pleasant place to sit on a sunny day.

'Kitchen's nice,' Sheila said, and Harriet nodded. The cupboards were painted cream, New England style. The floor was tiled in a dark grey vinyl. The bathroom was plain white, and while the bedrooms and sitting room weren't decorated to her taste, it was nothing that a few pots of paint and new carpet couldn't fix.

'What do you think?' Sheila pressed, as Harriet had said nothing as she went around.

'It's very probably perfect,' she replied quietly, but as Jamie grinned she realised he'd heard and was seeing pound signs flashing up before his eyes.

They wandered around a little more, checking out the garden and garage, looking at the house from the outside, asking Jamie to lower the loft ladder so they could have a peek in the attic. Harriet was pleased to see the attic was fully boarded. She'd be able to continue storing all her mementos. She'd need to get rid of a lot of furniture to fit in this house – but that was the point of downsizing.

As they left the property and shook hands with Jamie, he glanced at Harriet expectantly. 'I'll be in touch,' she told him, not prepared to make any commitments right there and then.

'Right-o. Well, I look forward to hearing from you, and if there's anything else I can do for you – we have several other bungalows on our books if you would like to see them ...'

'Yes, thank you. I'll be in touch,' she said again, and she and Sheila headed back to her car.

'Well?' said Sheila once they were in the car and Jamie had driven off.

'I'm going to buy it,' Harriet said, grinning.

Chapter 24

Emma, 1916

Ma's funeral was a sad and sombre affair. All the neighbours turned out, as did many of Ma's old clients for whom she'd sewed, mended or washed clothes over the years. Each of them shook Emma's hand as she stood at the graveside, lamenting how hard it must be for the two young women to come to terms with the death, especially after losing their other sister. All agreed Ma had been taken far too soon, and enquired what were Emma and Lily planning to do, with the house, with their lives, now?

It was at the funeral that Mrs Williams, never one to miss an opportunity to pass on some gossip, informed Emma in an almost gleeful tone of voice that she'd heard from Dee Paine that Harry Paine had been reported killed, in one of the many pushes in the battle to take the river Somme. 'It's his just desserts,' the old woman said. 'After the way he carried on with your sister, with his poor wife in the family way at the time as well. He's got what was coming to him. I expect you're pleased to hear this news.'

'His poor wife's a widow and his children are fatherless. No, I am not at all pleased to hear this news.' Emma was disgusted.

'Harry Paine made some mistakes in his time – leading my sister astray was one, certainly – but he was not all bad and did not deserve this.' She turned her back on Mrs Williams and walked away before the other woman could say anything more, or see the tears that brimmed in her eyes.

She joined Lily who was standing, head bowed, at the graveside still. Standing beside her, she slipped an arm around Lily's waist, and her sister leaned her head on Emma's shoulder. 'Just us now, lovey,' she said, and Lily turned to stare at her.

'That was Ma's word for us. Sounds so odd when you say it.'

'Sorry, Lils. I won't use it.'

'It's all right. When you said it, just for a moment it felt like you were Ma, and she's still here watching over me, but through you.'

Emma smiled and squeezed her sister tighter. 'And she is, Lily. I will always be here for you. I promised her.'

'And I promised her I'd follow my dreams and never shy away from life's challenges,' Lily replied. 'She made me swear that, in her last few days.'

The mourners were dispersing, and it was time for Emma and Lily to return to the house. It felt so empty, without Ma's presence in it. Lily went into the sitting room and began pulling the sheets and blankets off Ma's bed and folding them, stacking the pillows and cushions she'd used.

'Leave that, Lily,' Emma said. 'We can do it tomorrow. For now, let's sit in the kitchen with a cup of tea and relax. There's time enough for everything else.'

To her surprise, Lily, who'd been so strong, so resolute throughout Ma's illness and death and the funeral, broke down sobbing, and allowed herself to be steered into the kitchen to sit at the table. 'There now, lovey,' Emma said. 'Let it all out. You've been so brave through it all. I'll make tea. You sit there.'

'It's Ruby. It's her fault,' Lily sobbed.

'I know. Losing her and then Ma ...'

But Lily shook her head. 'I mean ... if Ruby hadn't died Ma

228

might not have become ill. That's what started it all, isn't it Ems? If Ruby hadn't carried on with that man, if she'd listened to you and gone on the *Olympic*, if she'd stayed with you on the *Titanic* and been saved ... Ma would still be here.'

Emma was surprised to hear a touch of venom in Lily's voice. Her two younger sisters had never got on very well – Ruby had resented Lily for being ill and needing so much care, and Lily had resented Ruby for paying her too little attention when she was growing up. But it was hardly Ruby's fault that she'd died, and that her death had in part led to Ma's death, was it?

'Ah no, Lils,' she said. 'We can't blame Ruby for what happened to Ma.'

Lily sniffed and wiped her eyes. 'I know. But in a way, I do, a bit. It's wrong to, but I can't help myself.'

Poor Lily. She was only 17, and had already dealt with so much in her short life. Emma was so proud of her. Ruby would have reacted differently, she knew. Ruby would somehow have blamed Ma for getting ill, for forcing her to change her plans. She'd have resented having to nurse Ma. Emma felt guilty for thinking it, but if she was truthful she was glad she'd had Lily at her side during these last months and not Ruby. Her youngest sister, who they'd always treated as a bit of an invalid, had proved herself to have a deep, hidden strength.

A few short weeks after Ma's funeral word came that both girls had been accepted for work on the *Britannic*. Lily as a junior nurse and Emma on general cleaning duties. Her previous experience at sea had helped her secure this job.

They'd cleared Ma's things from the house, and had found a lodger – a fellow nurse from the Royal South Hants hospital – whose rent for Ma's old bedroom helped cover the bills. And they'd acquired all the items they'd need on board ship. Privately, Emma had spent a lot of time in quiet contemplation of what was ahead of her, trying to remember her excitement at going to sea and suppress her fears and the nightmares that had dogged her since the *Titanic*. It was hard, but she was ready. She'd be doing a good, worthwhile thing – better than serving rich, fussy passengers. And she felt sure that once she set foot on the ship the old thrill of being at sea would come back.

At last the day came, and Lily and Emma bade farewell to their lodger who promised to take care of the house, and set off for the familiar walk to the docks. Emma gasped as the *Britannic* came into view. She looked exactly like her sisters *Olympic* and *Titanic*, only in different livery. She was painted white, with a large red cross on her bow and a green stripe running her length. But there were still the four backward-sloping funnels, the elegant proportions, the promenade decks, just as she remembered. It'd all be very different on board, she guessed. No chandeliers or plush carpets, no walnut panelling or sumptuous upholstery. All that grandeur on the *Titanic* that was now at the bottom of the ocean. The *Britannic* had been requisitioned as a hospital ship before she'd had a chance to be fitted out as a passenger liner. She'd made a few trips to fetch injured troops already, so routines would be established and Emma and Lily should be able to quickly slot into place. Thankfully it was not the ship's first trip. Emma knew she could not have coped with being on another maiden voyage.

As they approached the gangway Lily caught Emma's hand. 'So, this is it. Are you all right?'

Emma bit her lip, and nodded. The truth was, she was a mess of conflicting feelings. Pride that she was helping the country and also keeping her promise to Ma. Relief that she would not be separated from Lily. Excitement at the thought of being at sea once more, doing a job close to the one she had always loved. And fear – gut-wrenching, mind-numbing fear that the *Britannic* would meet the same fate as her sister. *There are no icebergs in the Mediterranean*, she kept telling herself. She allowed herself to be led on board by Lily and ushered to the cabin the two of them

230

would share for the next few weeks. It was almost identical to those on the *Olympic* and the *Titanic*, and she arranged her things in the wardrobe just as usual, trying not to remember when she and Ruby had all too briefly shared a cabin.

She placed the photo of the three sisters by her bedside. This had been Ma's copy. Lily had left hers at home. Perhaps, Emma thought, Lily had left it behind because it would be too much of a reminder of all that they had lost. But for Emma, having that photo in its usual place helped her accept the idea of being at sea once more.

They had very little time to organise their cabin, for the ship was due to sail soon and they needed to tour the ship and be advised of their duties. As they mustered in what Emma recognised as the space that had been a first-class dining room on the other two ships, Emma noticed a familiar figure across the room.

'Violet! I did not expect to see you here! Violet, this is my youngest sister Lily. Lily, I worked with Violet on the *Olympic* and ... the other one.'

'Lovely to meet you, Lily. I remember your other sister, Ruby, too, God rest her soul. And how wonderful to see you again, Emma? Are you a VAD nurse too?'

'Lily's a junior nurse, not voluntary, and I'm on general duties. Cleaning, mostly. Isn't it odd seeing the ship set up like this?' Emma gestured to the functional tables and chairs that furnished the room. 'Have you done any voyages on the *Britannic* before this one?'

Violet shook her head. 'No, this is my first. I've just completed training as a VAD nurse. And yes, it's very odd to see the ship kitted out like this. But I believe it works well as a hospital ship. Ah ... here's Captain Bartlett to address us all.'

The girls fell quiet as they listened to the Captain – a gruff man, without the charisma of Captain Smith, whom Emma had served under on the *Olympic* and who'd then been lost when the *Titanic* went down. They heard that the plan was for the

Britannic to set sail the next day, along the English channel, across the Bay of Biscay and round Spain, through the Straits of Gibraltar into the Mediterranean. There was a refuelling stop planned at Naples, before the ship steamed on towards Greece. The wounded servicemen were to be picked up from Moudros on the Greek island of Lemnos.

'We might have rough seas on the first few days,' the Captain said, 'but once we are past Gibraltar it should be calm. This is the ship's sixth voyage, and I am fully expecting it to feel quite routine. Many of the crew have been with us before, so thank you for returning, and welcome to those who are new to *Britannic*. That is all.' He nodded and left the gathering. The nurses were then taken off for on-board training, and Emma went with the rest of the ship's crew to start on her duties. Her work would be harder than it had been on the *Olympic* in some ways – there'd be long hours and many areas to clean – but also easier as she would not be at the beck and call of demanding passengers. And it would be a more meaningful job.

The ship left Southampton as scheduled, and Emma felt a pang of sadness as she realised that this time she was leaving no family in the city; no one to come back to. And then she looked at the excited face of Lily and knew that she was doing the right thing. 'I'll take care of her, Ma,' she whispered, as the ship inched away from the docks, pulled by the same tugs that had been used by both of *Britannic*'s sisters. As they sailed down Southampton Water just as on earlier voyages Emma was out on deck, pointing out the landmarks to Lily. Passing Netley she indicated the enormous Royal Victoria Military Hospital. 'Look, I've heard that's now full of recuperating soldiers. Some that we pick up on this voyage will be sent there to complete their recoveries, I expect.'

'Yes, I think you are right,' Lily said, as the huge building passed by on their port side.

The journey to the Mediterranean passed without incident,

and the crew and nurses were kept busy with preparations for the soldiers. Passing Gibraltar, Emma spent some time on deck, gazing at the view to both port and starboard. There was the coastline of Spain on the one hand and the mountains of Morocco on the other – Africa! This was why she'd loved her job on the *Olympic*. Seeing new places, travelling across the world. She resolved that once the war was over she would return to sea as a stewardess once more. Boarding the *Britannic* had helped her get over her fear of life at sea. Maybe she'd be able to get a job on liners plying different routes – to the Far East, perhaps, to India, China, Australia ... There were so many places in the world, and she wanted to see as many of them as possible.

Emma and Lily found themselves often sitting for meals at the same table as some other crew members – a couple of pleasant-faced young seamen, who regaled them with tales of their past adventures and their future dreams. 'I was going to join the Royal Navy,' one of them, a red-haired fellow with a cheeky smile said, 'but then I decided to stay in the merchant navy. This job's perfect – I've always worked for White Star and now I get to do my bit for the country.'

'Were you on the *Britannic*'s earlier trips?' asked Emma. She liked this fellow – his name was Frank Perkins, he said.

Frank nodded. 'Yes, this is my third. They're satisfying journeys – there's a real sense of purpose to them. I'm hoping I can stay with *Britannic* until this war's over, then go back to *Olympic*.'

'Oh – I was on *Olympic*!' Emma tried to remember if she'd ever met Frank before. Surely she'd have remembered such bright ginger hair and twinkly blue eyes? Although back then, of course, she'd only had eyes for Martin.

'Really? Lovely ship. I joined it after its refit in 1912.'

The refit, Emma knew, had been to increase the number of lifeboats and make the bulkheads extend higher up the ship, so an accident like the *Titanic*'s could not sink it. 'Ah – I worked on it in 1911 and then ...'

'*Titanic*?' His voice softened and his eyes were sympathetic.

Emma nodded. She'd only just met him. Too soon to tell him about Ruby.

'How long until we reach Moudros and begin taking on the wounded?' Lily asked Frank, and Emma smiled at her, grateful for the change of subject.

'Few days, if the weather holds. We're due to dock at Naples and take on coal and fresh water first. Won't be allowed on shore though.' Frank pulled a sad face, which made both Emma and Lily giggle. Emma noticed Frank flash Lily a look that suggested he was pleased to have made her laugh.

That night, Lily lay on her back on her bunk, musing. 'That Frank, and his friend Peter – what did you think of them?'

'They seem nice,' Emma said. 'What did you think?'

'Mmm. I liked them both. Frank's really sweet. Peter's very good-looking.'

Emma smiled to herself as she moved about the cabin, folding clothes and putting things away. It was the first time she'd heard Lily show any interest in a man. Or men, she mentally corrected herself. Well, there would be no time for any flirtations or shipboard romances once they had picked up their patients.

'Which of them did you like the best?' Lily was asking her.

Emma considered. 'Frank, I think. He seems so … open and genuine.'

'How does he compare with your Martin?'

Emma sat down heavily. Over the years since the *Titanic* she'd confided in Lily about her first love, feeling the need to talk to someone about him. Lily's quiet sympathy had helped her come to terms with his loss. 'Oh, I don't know. I can't compare one person I hardly know, with someone who died over four years ago. I'd have to spend more time with Frank.'

'Do you think … you might? I mean, when all this is over …'

Emma felt herself blushing. She'd never so much as looked at another man since Martin. It seemed disloyal to his memory.

But eventually, she supposed, it would be time to move on, and perhaps step out with someone else. After the war was over, as Lily suggested. But with Frank? 'I don't know, Lily. Honestly, we've only just met. Maybe Frank doesn't like me in that way at all. Or maybe he likes you more.'

'Me?' Now it was Lily's turn to blush, Emma was pleased to see. 'Why not? You're beautiful.'

'Ah, get away! I am not. You're the pretty one.'

'Ruby was the pretty one,' Emma said quietly, and Lily nodded.

'She was, indeed.' She raised a glass of water she had on her bedside cabinet. 'To darling Rubes, forever in our hearts.'

'To Rubes,' Emma said, raising her own glass of water. *And to Martin*, she thought, *and to all those who perished on the Titanic. May such a tragedy never strike again.* 'I wish,' she whispered, 'I'd never persuaded Ruby to take a job at sea. Then she'd …'

'Don't think like that,' Lily said firmly. 'We go forward from where we are. There's never any point wishing things had happened differently.'

Emma smiled at her sister's wisdom. 'You are right, Lils. Thank you.'

A few days later they were docking at Naples, taking on coal and fresh water just as Frank had said. Emma stood on deck and gazed out at the jumble of rooftops backed by the cut-off cone of Mount Vesuvius. Another country, another place with a long and glorious history. Storms kept them in port longer than planned. There was no chance to go onshore but she was happy to have had this tiny glimpse of Italy, and promised herself that one day she would return. There were more glimpses to come – when the weather improved at last, they steamed down the coast of Italy and through the Straits of Messina, before heading out into the open sea again. Soon they'd be picking up their passengers, doing what they'd come out here to do, and Emma was looking forward to knowing that she was doing some real good in the world.

Chapter 25

Harriet

Two days later, after a second viewing of the bungalow with Sally (Jerome being left with Charlie as it was the weekend), Harriet put an offer on it, for a little under the asking price. It was accepted immediately. Suddenly it all felt very real.

'Well done, Mum,' Sally said, after Harriet had made the phone call to the estate agent following the second viewing. 'So pleased you are getting yourself sorted out. I wish I could help more, but the bungalow you picked with Sheila is perfect.'

'It is lovely, isn't it?'

Sally nodded, and Harriet was horrified to see there were tears in her eyes. 'Sorry, Mum. I'm just a bit sad, I suppose, that I wasn't able to come and see it with you the first time, and you had to take Sheila instead. I feel like I'm letting you down. I should be a better daughter.'

'You are being a wonderful daughter,' Harriet said, giving Sally a hug. 'You've done so much for me. And honestly, I'll manage this move perfectly well on my own if I need to. I love having you to help but you have more important things to worry about.'

Sally sniffed and wiped her eyes. 'Well, I have some time now, so is there anything I can help with?'

'A few boxes to go to the charity shop,' Harriet said. She could have taken them herself, but had held them back for precisely this moment – so that Sally could feel she was doing something useful.

'I'll take them when I leave,' Sally said. 'And now you know where you're moving to and how much space you will have, you can start deciding on what furniture to keep and what to get rid of.'

'Yes. I thought I'd go round and put Post-it notes of different colours on items.'

'Good plan,' Sally said.

Harriet smiled. Of course it was a good plan – it had been Sally's suggestion originally.

Sally needed to leave – she didn't want to stay away from Jerome too long. And Harriet had loads to be getting on with. She helped load the boxes for charity into Sally's car, waved her off, and then went to fetch a pack of Post-it notes to make a start on her furniture decisions. Just then a bleep from her phone alerted her to an incoming email, and she decided to check that first.

It was from Matthew, replying to the letter she'd sent him. A long email that deserved her full attention. She made herself a quick cup of tea, and opened her laptop so she could read it on a larger screen.

It was long, chatty, full of news and reminiscences of their shared childhood, full of regret that they hadn't seen each other for so many years. Matthew thanked her for getting in touch, said that yes (obviously!) he did use email and would love to use it to be in more regular contact with her. He said too, that he was planning a trip southwards in a couple of months, and would love to spend some time with her then. *After all*, he went on, *as you say, we are not getting any younger. Let's enjoy each other's company while we still can.*

Harriet read the email twice. It was wonderful – it made her feel as though she'd regained her brother. She immediately emailed

237

back, thanking him, saying she was looking forward to seeing him when he came south and of course he was welcome to stay with her if he liked, and asking when would be a good time for a chat on the phone? She pressed Send, then sat back to finish her cup of tea, smiling with satisfaction and wishing it could be that simple to rebuild her relationship with Davina.

As planned, Harriet spent the rest of the day going round the house armed with pads of various coloured Post-it notes. Yellow for items to keep in the new house. Pink for things to offer to Sally and if not wanted, sell. Blue for anything to be free-cycled now. She'd need two beds, not four. Her own wardrobe and chest of drawers, and another chest for the spare room. The bookcases, obviously. One sofa – not the three she currently had. The dining room table and chairs would have to go, but the kitchen set would fit nicely in the new place. She tried to visualise the furniture in each room of the bungalow. No doubt some wouldn't look right and she'd need to replace it, but the main thing was to take enough with her to allow her to live comfortably. She could buy new furniture if needed when she decorated each room.

Strangely, she found herself far less sentimental about the furniture than she had been about the boxes of bric-a-brac and mementos. Even items she'd chosen with John in the early years of their marriage – they'd done their job, had their day, and she felt ready to part with them. If John had been still with her and they were down-sizing together, they'd still have been parting with the same items. That thought gave her comfort and made it all much easier.

It didn't take too long, and she was happy with her choices. Next job was to advertise the items she wanted to give away on Freecycle. Anything that wasn't taken by that method would have to go to the tip. She took photos of the pieces and spent a couple of hours adding posts to her local Freecycle group. It was good to think there was a chance her unwanted furniture would find new homes with people who needed it.

The next day, she phoned Sally to say the job was done and emails from Freecycle members were already flooding in. It looked like all the items would be taken.

Sally sounded breathless as she answered the phone. 'Mum! Hi, er, hold on, just ... putting the kettle on. Think I need a cup of tea. Probably something stronger but ...'

'What's happened, love?' Harriet felt a pang of fear. Was it Jerome? Had something happened?

'Nothing bad, don't worry, in fact ... the opposite ...' There was the sound of a tap running, a kettle being filled and flicked on, a cupboard opening and a mug put onto the counter as the kettle began to rattle and hiss. 'Good news, Mum. They think they've found a donor.'

'Oh my God that's amazing news!' Harriet couldn't help herself from squealing.

'Isn't it just! Dr Windletter called to say a match had been found, and the person was happy to donate, and they'd sent them all the forms and stuff, and were beginning the process. I've to take Jerome into hospital – he needs to have more treatment to prepare his body for the donation. But Mum ... something positive at last, and I can't ... I just can't ...' She began sobbing.

Harriet's heart went out to her – she could imagine Sally's emotions were a mix of relief that a donor had been found, concern about what Jerome had to go through, fear that the treatment might not work or go wrong somehow. But yes, it was positive.

'Love, I'll come round. You sound like you need a hug.'

'I have to get Jerome ready. They want him in hospital today, to begin the preparatory treatment. Tests and scans and whatnot at this point, and that play therapy they mentioned ...'

'I'll help. I'll drive you there.'

'Charlie's coming home. I just called him – his boss has given him the day off.'

'That's good. Let me come round, darling. I'll do what I can to help. You just sit with your little boy for now, I'll come, and help you pack whatever needs to go with him to hospital.'

Sally agreed, sniffing, and Harriet rang off, grabbed her handbag and car keys and set off to Sally's. She arrived just as Charlie did, and she rushed over to hug him. He looked stressed yet excited – just as they all felt.

'Good news about the donor,' she said as she greeted him.

'Yes, very exciting. Sally's in a state.'

'I know, I was speaking to her on the phone. That's why I've come over.'

'Thanks, Harriet. We really appreciate all you do for us, you know.' He squeezed her and together they went inside. Charlie went straight to Sally while Harriet went to find Jerome, who was lying on the sofa tucked under a knitted blanket, half-heartedly watching a Disney film.

'Hey, soldier,' she said, sitting down beside him and stroking his arm. 'How are you feeling?'

'My legs hurt,' he said. 'And Mum says I've got to go to hospital again. And stay there. I want to stay here.'

'Yes, pet, you do need to go to hospital. Did Mummy tell you there's a new treatment that will make you better, but you have to be in hospital for them to be able to do it.'

'Yeah, she said.' Jerome's attention was fixed on the TV. 'Nanna, will I be there in the night?'

She sat beside him and put her arm around him. 'Yes, you will.'

'On my own?'

'I think Mummy will see if she or Daddy is able to stay with you. I am not sure what the arrangements are. But there will be nurses that will be your friends, and there will be other children there too.'

'Can I take Mr Bungle?' Jerome pulled the bear out from under his blanket and held it tightly to his face.

Harriet smiled. 'Of course.'

'How long will it be?'

'I don't know exactly. I expect when you get there the doctors will be able to tell you how long.' Harriet knew that if you didn't know the answer to a child's question it was always better to answer honestly than make something up.

Jerome nodded in response. 'I will ask the doctor. He will know.' He sounded wise beyond his years, but his next question broke Harriet's heart. 'Nanna, if this treatment doesn't work, what will happen next?'

'This will work, pet. I've looked it up on the internet. It always works.' OK, so this time she had lied, but the odds were good.

'Why didn't they do it first then?' Jerome turned to look at her, his eyes wide.

'Because it's quite difficult to do, so they wanted to try easier treatments first. Sometimes the easier treatments are all that's needed. But it seems you're special, and you need the bigger treatment.'

He smiled a little, and then turned his attention back to the Disney film. Harriet kissed his dear little head, fuzzy with the growth of new hair since he ended the last cycle of chemotherapy, and went in search of Sally. The fact Sally had kept out of the sitting room told Harriet her daughter was not composed enough for Jerome to see.

Sally was upstairs, in her bedroom, where she and Charlie were sitting on the bed, arms wrapped around each other. 'Let me do the first night,' Charlie was saying. 'You're in no fit state. Then I'll at least be able to tell you what to expect.'

Sally shook her head. 'It should be me. I'm his mum.'

'And I'm his dad.' Charlie looked up at Harriet. 'What do you think, Harriet? I'm just not sure Sally's up to staying with Jerome in the hospital. They said one of us can – during the first stage while they prepare him for the transplant.'

'Ah, good. He was asking about that. I wasn't sure.' Harriet glanced at Sally, who was clearly working hard to get a grip on herself. 'Sally, love, it's a good thing that's happening. And the preparatory treatment – it's chemotherapy, isn't it? Jerome's an old hand at that. Then the actual transplant is just done via the central line that they'll already have put in place for the chemo.'

Sally sniffed and nodded. 'The main danger is that his immune system will be knocked for six while he's undergoing the treatment. We can't stay with him then – he'll be in isolation. And Charlie – I think I should be the one to stay with him up till that point. I'll be all right. You can't do it – you have to work. And better for one person to stay all the time than have us coming and going, risking bringing infections in.'

'Are you sure – it won't be easy ...'

'I'll be all right. Honestly, don't know why I've crumpled this morning. It's just such a big step – something I've been longing for, and here it is. At last.' She wiped away the last of her tears and went through to the en-suite bathroom. Harriet heard the sound of a tap running – Sally was obviously washing her face.

'She'll be OK,' she said to Charlie, putting out a hand to him. 'She's strong. Now, you go and see your son, while I help Sally pack.'

'Thank you. Best mother-in-law ever,' Charlie said, smiling at her. He looked more hopeful than he had done for weeks, Harriet thought. It was good to see. They still had tough times ahead, but there was more hope now than there had been for a while.

The morning passed quickly as Harriet helped Sally pack a few things for her and Jerome's stay in hospital. 'I've been asked not to take too much,' she said. 'But Charlie can bring changes of clothes as I need them.'

'Main things are your Kindle, your phone, charger, purse, toiletries and nightwear. And for Jerome, most important is Mr Bungle and his iPad.'

'Six-year-old with an iPad,' Charlie said, shaking his head.

He'd originally been against their son having electronics but they'd given in when Jerome's diagnosis came through, and they realised he was going to spend long periods in hospital or sick at home. 'But thank goodness he has one. It can keep him occupied for hours.'

Harriet wasn't needed to take them to the hospital, as Charlie wanted to go, and stay there for the afternoon at least. Harriet promised to visit Jerome the next day. 'Nanna will bring you a little surprise,' she promised him, as she helped buckle him into his car booster seat, firmly clutching Mr Bungle. 'You be good, now.' She smiled brightly at him, and was pleased to get a little worried smile in return.

She waved the family off, and went back into Sally's house to wash up their breakfast things, vacuum the sitting room, straighten the beds, and any other little job she could think of. Anything to make it a little easier for Charlie who'd be coming home to an empty house that evening.

Chapter 26

Emma, 1916

They'd crossed the Ionian Sea and were steaming up through the Greek islands. Every now and again land was visible one side or the other. Their destination, Moudros, where thousands of wounded servicemen were waiting for them, was on an island further on, in the Aegean sea. To reach it the ship had to navigate a route past the Greek mainland – almost within sight of Athens! – and between islands.

There was a good atmosphere on board, as they prepared for the wounded. Emma had deep-cleaned endless cabins, made up beds, stocked each room with basic supplies. The crew sang as they went about their work, and the nurses completed training courses. The weather was mild and sunny. Emma found herself enjoying being at sea once more. It was in her blood, she thought. She was glad that Lily's ambition and her own promise to Ma had brought her back to life on board a ship. It felt good, it felt right.

'I have dressed so many pretend wounds,' Lily told Emma, as they prepared for bed one evening in late November. 'I will be very pleased to be dressing real wounds – making an actual difference and really helping people. It sounds awful, I suppose – those poor soldiers. But I am looking forward to having them on board and them knowing they are on their way home.'

Emma slipped her nightgown over her head. 'I know what you mean. I'm looking forward to it too. This is so different to when I've worked on ships before.'

Lily crossed the cabin and hugged her. 'Ems, are you still happy you came? It was a lot to get over, after *Titanic*. Violet told me she'd considered giving up sailing too.'

Emma smiled. 'Yes, still happy I came. It feels good to be helping. And Violet can't have considered giving up for long – she told me she was back on *Olympic* only a few weeks after *Titanic* sank. She's a braver woman than I am.'

'Oh! Gosh, if it was me, I'd have stayed home for the rest of that year at least.'

'I suppose she needed to earn money, like the rest of us. Well, come on now, Lily, we need to get to bed. Tomorrow's a big day.'

The following morning dawned sunny and warm, and the girls were at breakfast, piling their plates high with eggs and bacon and toast from a buffet in what should have been the first-class dining room. They were about halfway through eating, when Emma spotted Violet enter the room.

'She's late for breakfast,' Lily said, waving at their friend.

'She'll have been at Mass. She's Catholic, and it's some sort of feast day today, so ...' Emma broke off speaking, as there was a deafening roar, a shudder that seemed to pass all the way through the ship sending their breakfast plates crashing to the floor and Violet staggering against a pillar.

'What was that?' Lily said, her eyes wide and frightened.

'Bloody hell. I think we've hit something.' Emma got to her feet and clutched at her sister. How could this have happened again? There were no icebergs ... but the sound had been different, more like an explosion.

Violet staggered over to them. 'We've been hit, I'd say. Torpedoed or something. Or a mine. We need to get to the lifeboats.'

'Hit? Oh God, no!' Lily's hand shot to her mouth. 'And the lifeboats … are there …'

Violet took hold of Lily's shoulders and held her. 'There are plenty of lifeboats. After *Titanic*, they have made sure there are enough lifeboats for everyone on board, and the ship is far from full. Thank goodness we don't yet have the servicemen on board – that would have made things a lot more difficult. Look, I'm just popping back to my cabin for my coat. You two, get yourselves on a lifeboat and I'll see you later.' She hurried away from them.

All around, everyone was on their feet, talking quietly, moving towards their stations, getting on with what needed to be done to evacuate the ship. It was so different to the *Titanic* disaster – this time there was a definite sense of urgency, of knowing what needed to be done and done quickly, and just getting on with it right now. Perhaps because there were no passengers on board, perhaps because the explosion and that shudder had left no doubt whatsoever that the ship was in grave danger. Emma took Lily's hand. There was no way she was letting her sister out of her sight, not this time, until they were safely on board another ship or on land. 'Come on, we need to go.'

'How long have we got?'

'I don't know, maybe an hour or so, we don't seem to be listing yet.' Emma pulled her sister towards the stairs.

'I'm in my slippers, I need a coat,' Lily said, and Emma considered. They'd have time to fetch things from their cabin. Violet was doing so too. It would be all right. Inside she felt strangely calm. She'd been through this before, and she'd survived. And this time, there would be no frantic searching for her sister. She had Lily's hand in her own, and she would not let go. She would never let go.

They hurried through the galley-ways to their cabin, where they put on their life jackets. The years since 1912 felt as though

246

they'd never happened – here she was, putting on a life jacket in her cabin, trying not to think about what the next few hours would bring. Emma helped Lily on with her jacket, and then passed her her coat.

'Coat over the top. In case you need to take it off – it's easier if the coat's on top.'

'Why would I need to take it off?'

In case you end up in the water, where the coat will drag you down ... but Emma did not want to worry Lily with that thought. 'Well, it just fits better with the life jacket underneath. Come on. Leave that alone. We need to go.' Lily had begun tidying up – and Emma remembered how she'd done exactly the same, back on the *Titanic*. She caught Lily's hand again but her sister pulled back.

'Just need to put my shoes on.' With that done, at last they began making their way up to the boat deck. The ship had begun to list a little to starboard, but there was no sign of water on board yet. They met Violet heading up the stairs too, and the three joined forces. Violet had her apron folded up on itself, the bottom of it tucked into her waistband.

'Why have you done that?' Emma asked her, pointing to it.

'I've a few important things in there. Hopefully this will keep them safe.'

'Important? Like what?' Lily asked, and Emma guessed she was wondering if there was anything back in the cabin she should have brought out. To her surprise, Violet blushed as she answered.

'A precious ring, from someone I care about, and ... a toothbrush.'

'A toothbrush!' Despite the critical situation they were in, Emma could not stop herself from laughing. 'Why on earth?'

'After the *Titanic*, on the *Carpathia*, I was unable to get hold of one. So I decided I would never again be parted from my toothbrush.' Violet thrust her chin defiantly into the air, which made Emma laugh all the more.

'Ems, we are on a sinking ship, and you are laughing at a

247

woman who's saving a toothbrush,' Lily said, and now it was her turn to hurry them along, up the stairs and onto the boat deck.

'We're late!' Violet gasped, and the three girls leaned over the side to see dozens of lifeboats already in the water, rowing frantically away from the ship.

'Why are we steaming forward?' Emma said, remembering how the *Titanic* had cut its engines immediately after the impact, and the ship had floated calmly as it slowly filled with water. The *Britannic*, however, seemed to be on full steam ahead.

'Captain's trying to reach shallower water, and ground the ship,' a crewman told her. Then he shouted, 'There are women here!'

Emma realised the people on deck still waiting to get into lifeboats were all men. There were far fewer women on board – the nurses plus a few female crew like herself – and they'd obviously all come straight up and got into the first boats. She felt hands grabbing her, pulling her through the crowd to the front, and it was all she could do to keep hold of Lily's hand. Violet was pushed through too and they were helped onto the next lifeboat. It was filled with crew men, the three of them being the only women on board.

Lily was whimpering quietly, and Emma squeezed her hand to calm her. 'It'll be all right. We'll be lowered down, and once in the water the crew men will row us away from the ship. We'll be safe, we're on the lifeboat.' And we're together, she wanted to add, feeling a surge of relief that she had kept Lily with her, got her onto the lifeboat. This was how it should have been on the *Titanic*.

But they were not safe yet, she knew it. Once the boat was full, the crew began lowering it down the side of the ship. *Britannic* was now listing to starboard severely, and their port-side lifeboat scraped its way down the side of the ship, catching at one point on an opened porthole before freeing itself with a jolt.

The lifeboat hit the water hard, sending them falling into the middle of the boat. How well Emma remembered this moment from leaving the *Titanic*! The crew men got their oars out quickly and began rowing. The lifeboat was heavy and hard to manoeuvre and rowing seemed to make little difference to their position as the water churned around them. *Britannic* was still steaming ahead. Emma was clutching Lily's arm, and Violet, sitting on the other side of her, also had hold of her hand. They were safe, they were in the lifeboat, it was a mild day in the Mediterranean with land in sight – so different to the ice of the north Atlantic. They'd soon be on dry land.

And then Emma saw the people in the lifeboat lowered just before theirs were all abandoning it – jumping into the water and swimming away. 'What are they doing?' she screamed. 'Why are they getting in the water?'

The crew of her lifeboat looked where she pointed, and then frantically shouted. With horror Emma realised that the lifeboats – theirs included – were being sucked towards the fast-revolving propellers at the rear of the ship, where they would surely be chopped into pieces by those enormous steel blades. No amount of rowing could get them away from the ship. Their only chance was to abandon the lifeboat and swim for it …

Chapter 27

Harriet

During the following weeks, Harriet's life fell into a pattern of working on house-move related tasks in the morning, eating a quick lunch, and then going to the hospital for the afternoon visiting hours. Often as not she'd call in at a toy shop or sweet shop and buy something small for Jerome – an activity comic, a set of Lego figurines, a pack of chocolate buttons. Anything to see his eyes light up and to give him something to look forward to. She brought things for Sally too – magazines, a tube of expensive hand cream, bars of her favourite Green and Black's chocolate. Anything to make life a little better for her during this difficult time.

Jerome had got through the first part of the preparatory treatment. He'd borne it all well, and had made some friends in his ward, with whom he played or watched TV daily. Sally had spent many nights at the hospital – but not all. One day Jerome had said to her, 'Mummy, why don't you go home and stay with Daddy tonight? He must be lonely, and I'll be all right on my own.' It had broken Sally's heart but she'd done as he suggested and the unbroken night's sleep had done her good.

Harriet had to wear protective equipment when she visited him – a mask that Jerome laughed at, saying she looked like a bank robber, and robes he said made her look like one of the hospital cleaners. The treatment was suppressing his immune system so it was essential to keep him protected from any germs she might be carrying.

There came a day when Sally told her she could no longer visit, as his immune system was now too weak to risk it. 'It's parents only now, for short visits only. I can't stay overnight any more. And he'll not be allowed to play with other children in the ward. They've even had to give Mr Bungle an antibacterial bath.' She looked strained as she said this, and Harriet hugged her.

'Just remember, it's one step closer. They have to knock out his immune system so that his body will accept the bone marrow transplant. So, although it's hard, it's just a step along the way. Soon they'll do the transplant and then his recovery can start.'

On the day of his transplant, Harriet spent the day keeping busy to take her mind off what was happening to her little grandson. She cleaned her house from top to bottom. She made lists of people to contact with her new address. She phoned solicitors and estate agents to chase progress, and kept everyone on the phone far longer than was necessary, just to chat and stop herself wondering how Jerome was getting on.

It went well, Sally told her later that day. Ten days later his white blood cell count had recovered to the point that he was allowed visitors again. Harriet went to see him, taking a small Lego model as a gift.

'So, you had your big transplant,' she said to him, brightly. 'How was it?'

He rolled his eyes. 'It was *borrrring*. I had to just lie still while they put stuff in through here.' He showed her the central line that led to an artery near his heart, through which the doctors had been administrating chemotherapy drugs as well as the bone marrow stem cells themselves.

'But now that's done, that's another step closer to going home,' Harriet told him.

To her surprise Jerome shrugged. 'I don't mind it here, now that you're allowed to visit me and bring me presents. It was boring when no one was allowed to come and I wasn't allowed to play, but it's all right now. I don't have to do anything like make my bed and tidy my room and stuff like I would at home.'

Harriet laughed. 'No, I suppose there's no chores for little boys in hospital. What about school?'

'I miss my friends but not the lessons.'

'I'm trying to teach him a little when he's well enough,' Sally said, 'but I'm not much good at it. Still, we do some reading practice, don't we? And I found some supposedly educational games for his iPad.'

'Don't worry. He'll catch up. He's a bright lad,' Harriet told her.

Sally smiled. 'By the way, I've asked Dr Windletter to put me in touch with the bone marrow donor. I'd like to write and thank them, and send a photo of Jerome.'

'That's a lovely idea.'

There was hope. Plenty of it. Jerome was responding well to the treatment. The doctors were talking about a discharge date, after he'd had the necessary course of treatment to ensure his body didn't reject the transplant. They were due to remove his central line within days. He'd need more treatment, but it could be done as an outpatient. And with luck tests would soon show he was cancer-free, able to resume the normal life of a 6-year-old. Harriet was well aware it was a long haul yet – most children with leukaemia took a year or more to recover and problems could recur at any stage of his life – but things were looking much brighter than they had for months. Thank goodness for that anonymous donor, whoever he or she was. They'd saved Jerome's life.

Davina sent a text a couple of days after Jerome's transplant. Harriet was surprised – she'd never had a text from her younger daughter before. Davina still managed to hide her phone number on the text – she used some kind of app to block the number – but it meant Harriet could reply to the text. She had a way of contacting her daughter, for the first time ever since she'd left home.

How is Sally's kid? Has he had the bone marrow transplant yet? Been thinking of you all. D.

Harriet replied immediately. *Jerome had transplant 2 days ago. Went well. Now having follow-up treatment. Looking good – we are hopeful.*

She didn't dare do more than answer Davina's questions. If she added any more Davina would back off. But a second text came back quickly.

Sounds good. Keep me informed, please.

Will do xx

Harriet smiled as she sent that last short text. Those little kisses she'd been able to add – it was a tiny thing, but it was the nearest to affection she had been able to show her daughter for so many years. She could now text Davina whenever she liked. Davina had actually asked her to do so – at least with any news about Jerome. It was a step in the right direction, and it allowed Harriet to raise her hopes, just a tiny bit, that they might be able to build bridges, just as she was doing with Matthew at last. 'Give her time,' John had always advised, 'and she'll come back when she's ready.' Was Davina, just possibly, ready now?

At last, Jerome's white blood cell count was high enough, and he was deemed well enough, to return home. He first extracted promises from a tearful Sally that he would not be expected to tidy his own room, for at least a month. 'I'd have promised him anything,' she told Harriet, '*anything* to have him back with us. It just feels so wrong to have your child away from home for so long.'

Harriet baked Jerome a cake for his homecoming. Chocolate, covered with chocolate butter cream, and decorated with Smarties.

'Next time you come to visit me,' she told him, 'it'll be in my new house.'

'Will there be cake?' he asked, through a mouthful of his homecoming one.

'I don't see why not,' she replied. It was so good to see him happy and well again. He wasn't yet back at school, but once his energy levels returned and his blood counts improved further, he would be allowed to return.

The chain of house-buyers was a short one, with first-time buyers at the bottom, then Harriet's buyers, and she was buying an empty property. Everyone wanted to move quickly, so the whole process didn't take as long as Harriet had feared. Contracts were exchanged, completion dates were set, she booked a removals company and within a couple of weeks of Jerome's return home from hospital, all systems were go. Charlie, bless him, took a day off work so that he could care for Jerome while Sally was with Harriet, helping with the move.

'So glad to have you here today, love,' Harriet told her, when Sally appeared in the early morning before the removals company turned up, armed with a flask of coffee and a paper bag of chocolate croissants.

'You're very welcome. I brought coffee in case your kettle was already packed.'

Harriet smiled. Typical of Sally to be so organised and think things through.

The removals company had come the day before to pack almost everything into boxes, leaving the minimum to do today. It had been stressful seeing her rooms dismantled but Harriet knew it was a step forward that needed to be taken. She'd put her most precious belongings in her car so they'd be safe no matter what. All her unwanted furniture had already been disposed of – plenty of delighted young couples setting up their first homes had collected the items she'd free-cycled.

Sally and Harriet managed a quiet cup of coffee before the removal van turned up. Sally updated Harriet on the latest news about Jerome. She smiled, as she reported that he seemed better by the day, and his latest blood tests were looking good. 'Honestly, whoever that donor was I want to hug them,' she said.

'Did you never hear back from Dr Windletter on that?' Harriet asked.

'He forwarded my letter of thanks and photo of Jerome to the person, but it's up to them if they want to get in touch or not.' Sally shrugged. 'If it was me I think I'd want to meet the child whose life I'd saved but I suppose everyone's different. I'm just grateful they agreed.'

The doorbell rang then – the removals company had arrived. Four hefty fellows trooped in, leaving a large van parked outside. They got straight to work, shifting the boxes and furniture out of rooms and packing it tightly into the van. Harriet and Sally hurried to clear up their coffee things, and then began cleaning rooms as the men emptied them. Harriet found she was kept too busy to think about what was happening. She'd imagined feeling emotional on moving day, but there simply wasn't time. And Sally's presence helped. She was so down-to-earth and practical, and the morning flew by. At last as they were hoovering the last room, the removals company foreman came to say the van was packed, and they were off for a lunch break, and would meet Harriet at the new property around three o'clock to unload.

The van left; Harriet and Sally finished up and loaded the vacuum cleaner into Harriet's car, and did a final check around the house. It was strange to see the rooms empty, dents in carpet all that remained to show where furniture had stood for decades, rectangles on the walls like ghosts of the pictures that had hung there.

'Well, Mum. This is it,' Sally said, slipping an arm around Harriet's shoulder as they stood at the door of Harriet's old bedroom. It didn't look like the room she'd shared with John for so many years – not without its furniture and clutter.

'Yes, this is it.' Harriet pulled out a tissue to dab at her eyes. 'I think we've done everything. Best go and drop the keys off at the estate agent then. The new family will be wanting to get in.' Mr and Mrs Cannon, and their three children. She wondered how long it would be before they put a trampoline in the garden, as she recalled they'd promised one of their kids.

She shoved the tissue into her pocket and went downstairs, grabbing her handbag from a peg by the door. Sally followed her out, and Harriet locked the door for the last time, standing back for a moment to look at it, the view overlaid in her mind with a memory of unlocking it for the first time, on the day she and John had moved in. Sally had been a baby at the time, and Davina not yet born. It was their first proper house, with a garden and a garage and an attic – they'd lived in a flat before. Harriet had known they would stay in the house for many years – it had felt like theirs from the very first moment she'd seen it. She realised now that her buyers, the Cannons, had had a similar reaction when they'd viewed the house. She knew they would be as happy in it as she and John had been.

Even so, saying goodbye to the house was difficult, at this final moment. She would probably never set foot inside it again. She put a hand on the door, sighed, and then walked down the garden path to her car. Sally was standing by her own car. Their plan was to have a quick lunch at a nearby café and then get to the new house before the van. Sally would go and order the lunches while Harriet dropped off the keys and picked up the keys to the new place. She'd received the call from her solicitor confirming that the money transfers had all taken place successfully so there were no last-minute hitches.

After lunch, Sally went home and sent Charlie to help Harriet in her place. 'You'll probably need to shift furniture into place,' she'd said, 'and he'll be better able to do it.' Harriet was quietly pleased by this change of plan – she knew Charlie would just position items where she wanted them, whereas Sally would have her own ideas where things should go and would try to boss her around. She suspected Sally recognised her own tendency to take charge and had stepped down at this point on purpose, to reduce the chances of any conflict.

The next hour was a whirlwind of activity, as the removals company emptied the van in what seemed to be record time – far faster than they had loaded it. Furniture was put into the right rooms but not the right places, as Sally had foreseen. Boxes were stacked against walls and on kitchen counter tops. All the stuff that she wanted to store in the loft was stacked in what was supposed to be the spare bedroom. By the time the removers left, with a generous tip from Harriet, she was left wondering if she'd kept too much stuff. She looked around in despair.

'How on earth am I going to sort all this out?' she said. 'There's not even space to build my bed, without shifting loads of boxes.'

'That's a job for tomorrow,' Charlie said. 'Tonight you come and sleep at ours. Sally's roasting a chicken for dinner. Tomorrow's Saturday, and I can spend the day with you making this place liveable.'

Harriet smiled at him. She was exhausted, and so grateful that for today she could just leave the mess and come back to it in the morning.

Chapter 28

Emma, 1916

The men were all jumping overboard and swimming, thrashing, kicking, away from the lifeboat, away from the ship, away from those lethal propellers which were nearer than ever. Surely it was only a matter of moments before the lifeboat would be chopped into pieces, and them with it?

'Get in the water!' Emma screamed, and Violet, staring wide-eyed at the carnage around them, nodded and slipped over the side. 'Lily, now! In the water!'

'I can't swim!' Lily shouted, her voice filled with the fear and desperation Emma herself felt.

'Our life jackets will keep us afloat. Get your coat off, quick. Hold your breath, get in the water and kick, get away from the ship.' There was no time to lose. Keeping hold of Lily's hand she pulled her overboard and they sank together, down into the dark water.

Which way was up? Which way was away from the ship? Lily's hand in hers felt so slight, so vulnerable, but she could not, would not let go. She'd promised Ma. Whatever happened, she had to save Lily. She kicked frantically, and felt them begin to move up, through the water. Her head hit some sort of debris; for an awful moment she thought it was a propeller and it would all be over, but it was an abandoned oar and then her head broke the surface, Lily's too, and they were gasping for breath and the life jackets were holding them up.

The water was not too cold. Emma could swim – as a child in the Isle of Wight she'd swum in the sea many times. Lily could not swim – she'd been too young, too frequently sick to learn. Now, Emma put an arm around Lily's chest under her arms, twisted onto her side and kicked, a kind of side-stroke, her free arm reaching and pulling and somehow making progress away from the ship. There was a sickening crunch as the lifeboat they'd been in just moments before was reduced to matchwood by the propellers, and splinters and shards of wood showered down upon them. Lily screamed and then spluttered as a wave washed over them. Emma could not say anything to calm her sister – all her breath was needed for swimming, getting them as far as possible from the back of the *Britannic*. She tightened her hold on Lily. The one thing she knew was that she would never let go.

She hoped all those who'd been on her lifeboat and the others in the area had got away. She risked a look back, and wished she hadn't. In the trail of the *Britannic* there were streaks of red amongst the debris and foam, and she had to swallow back bile as she realised that not all the debris was wooden – there was a human arm, a torso, the remains of a leg, shoe still on, floating by. Where was Violet?

But she and Lily were steadily moving out of range of the propellers. She twisted to look forwards – she was tiring and needed to plan where she was heading. There were some lifeboats a few hundred yards away, could she make it to them? She kept on kicking, pulling, gasping, groaning. In her grasp, Lily was spluttering now and again as the water washed over her, but she was staying still, clutching Emma's arm that encircled her chest.

That helped, a little. Emma kept swimming, silently cursing her skirt as it wrapped itself around her legs, cursing her corsets that restricted her breathing, cursing her long hair that had escaped its pins and kept plastering itself across her face. But the lifeboats were getting nearer, and she could do this. She had to do this. She thought she spotted Violet a little way off, in the water, clutching a spare life jacket and just treading water, a dazed expression on her face. There was nothing she could do to help Violet. It was all she could do to keep herself and Lily afloat, moving gradually towards the other lifeboats and safety.

Another glance back, and there was the *Britannic*, nose down and stern up. Emma trod water for a moment, holding Lily up, and watched as the great ship went down, just as the *Titanic* had gone under, amid a gurgle and a roar, those propellers still turning even as they were lifted out of the water. It was far enough off to not cause them any harm now.

And she must swim. She must hold on to Lily and reach the lifeboats. She checked how far off they were – they were still standing off a couple of hundred yards from where the *Britannic* had sunk. But now the ship was gone, they might row closer in to look for survivors. Meanwhile Emma could kick and pull and somehow get Lily towards the lifeboats, towards safety.

Her world shrank, until it was just them and the water around them and she'd been doing this, kick and pull, kick and pull, for ever. She remembered her mother's face, as she lay dying and pleading with Emma to keep Lily safe, to look after her. 'Take care of her,' Ma had gasped, summoning all her strength to make sure Emma would promise to protect her little sister. The frantic, fruitless search for Ruby on the *Titanic*. Lily was thankfully still in her arms, her grip on Emma's arm still strong as she lay in the water, her back against Emma's hip, pushing her down so that every now and again the water closed over Emma's face and she had to kick harder to surface again, gasping for breath. Her legs were aching now, her arms tired, every muscle was calling to her to stop – just stop, let go, drift down to sleep in the dark water – but no! She had to save Lily. Lily was all that mattered.

'Here, love. Grab a hold of this.' A stick, something, an oar, perhaps, was thrust towards her, hitting the side of her face. A new pain in her cheek temporarily blotted out all the other pains and made her feel dizzy, the sea spinning around her, waves washing over her.

'Grab it, love.' A gruff male voice – who was it? Sounded like Martin but he was dead, he'd gone down with the *Titanic*, hadn't he? She'd been to his mother's house and talked about him.

'Hold tight, I'll pull you in.' Lily had let go of her arm, and something was tugging her away from Emma, and Emma was screaming, grasping, trying to find her sister again but she couldn't focus and her head kept going under, and her mouth had filled with water. Her legs were as lead, she could kick no more, and Lily was gone from her reach.

Someone was screaming, calling her name. The wooden thing, the oar, hit her once more on the head. She grabbed for it but it was just floating in the water and drifted away from her. Someone swore and all Emma could think was that there was no call for such language and where was Lily? She'd promised to keep Lily safe, she'd promised Ma. She'd failed with Ruby, she had to save Lily, and now she'd let go of her, and where was she? Lily must have sunk, she must be down there in the depths somewhere. She tried to reach down for Lily but she was so tired. There was no strength left in her arms or legs, and her head was pounding. Her movements made her flip over, onto her front, and now her face was in the water. She forced her eyes open to look for Lily in the dark depths but there was nothing there. She tried to lift her head but a wave sent a gush of water into her mouth, down her throat, and she was choking, coughing, and there was no strength to cough, no strength to breathe, and it was all just simpler to stop altogether, but wh-where was Lily … Lily …

Lily

'Here, love. Grab a hold of this.'

Lily felt the oar across her body, and let go of Emma's arm to take hold of it. Emma would be able to swim better without having to hold her up too.

'Hold tight, I'll pull you in.' She didn't recognise the voice and with her wet hair plastered across her face she could not turn to look. But she held tight as instructed, and felt herself pulled swiftly through the water until her head bumped into something and she realised she was beside a lifeboat. Then strong arms reached down and hauled her on board where she collapsed in the bottom of the boat, gasping for breath.

'Emma! My sister, you need to get her too!'

'Shit, she's knocked the oar out of my hand,' a voice said. 'She's drifting – we need to get over to her.'

'With one oar?' another man said. 'It'll be difficult. Oh Christ. She's flipped over.'

Lily pulled herself upright, pushed her hair back from her face and scanned the sea for Emma. She was about thirty feet away, the lost oar floating near her, and as the man had said, she was face down in the water. 'Why is she face down? Why doesn't she lift her head?' No one answered her – the men in the lifeboat were organising themselves to paddle the boat with their hands and the single remaining oar, towards the drifting body of Emma. Lily watched, terrified, willing her sister to raise her head and take a breath. At one point it looked like she was trying to, but her head only lifted a little way and not far enough for her to breathe, before she flopped back into the water. It was clear she was exhausted.

At last – it felt like hours but couldn't have been more than a couple of minutes – the lifeboat was in reach of both Emma and the dropped oar. Men were reaching into the water and grabbing hold of Emma's clothing, life jacket, hair – whatever they could reach. They turned her over and Lily gasped – Emma's face was blue, her eyes open and staring, her lips swollen.

'Pull her in. There's still a chance …' someone said, and Lily thought, a chance? Only a *chance*? 'Get that oar too.'

A moment later Emma was lying in the bottom of the boat, and a man – one of the doctors who'd been on board – was kneeling beside her, pressing on her stomach, rolling her onto her side to let water drain out of her mouth, checking her pulse. Lily stuffed her fist into her mouth to stop herself from screaming at him to save her, save Emma, bring Emma back to her.

'It's no good,' said one of the men, and Lily groaned in anguish. But the doctor – bless the doctor – kept on working on Emma, refusing to give up hope while Lily crouched beside him, holding her sister's hand, rubbing it, wishing there was some way she could push life back into her.

At last the doctor sat back on his heels and shook his head. Another man passed him a shirt, and the doctor placed it gently over Emma's face.

'Nooo! She can't be … she's my sister!' Lily threw herself down by Emma's side and held her cold, wet body, willing her sister to wake up, push the shirt off her face and sit up smiling.

'Lily, come here, there's nothing you can do for her.' Warm arms went around her and lifted Lily up onto a seat. To her surprise Lily realised it was Frank Perkins – the red-haired crewman they'd befriended. She let herself be held by him as she sobbed, her head against his chest, his arms wrapped tightly around her.

'There's another woman – there, look!' The cry went up and at once two crewmen grabbed the oars and began rowing hard. Very soon it was Violet Jessop who was being hauled into the lifeboat. She cried out in sorrow when she saw Emma's body lying in the keel and then took a seat beside Lily.

'I'm so sorry,' she said, putting a wet arm about Lily's shoulder.

Lily turned to thank her, and then saw Violet's head was bleeding. There was also a deep gash on her leg. 'Oh, Violet, you are hurt!'

'Am I?' Violet asked, and Lily noted the uneven dilation of her pupils. Violet was concussed. Lily switched into her nurse persona, thanked Frank for the comfort, and set about patching Violet's leg and head as best she could. Working alongside the doctor she then checked the rest of the boat's occupants, trying to keep her eyes averted from the body of her sister that lay in the bottom. Stay busy, Lils, she told herself. Keep busy, keep working, don't think about it.

By the time she'd done what she could for the injured, she realised the crew had rowed to land – they were approaching a small harbour on an island. Some of the other lifeboats from the *Britannic* were there too, discharging their passengers onto the quayside. Some people were being carried off on makeshift stretchers.

Soon it was their turn, and crew from the other boats together with locals from the island were helping them onshore. Two Greek men carried Emma's body, taking it into a nearby building where she was laid on the floor alongside a few other bodies. A woman brought a blanket and covered her up, crossing herself and murmuring a few words in her own language as she did so. Seeing Lily standing there, sobbing, the woman approached her and put a gentle hand on her arm. She said something – Lily had no idea what – but then led her back outside, a short way up a lane towards a village and then into a small whitewashed cottage – her home, Lily assumed. There, the woman showed Lily to a tiny bedroom, and indicated that she should take off her still-wet clothes.

She did so, feeling overwhelmed by the kindness of these strangers, and numbed by what had happened. It did not seem real. It could not be real. She found herself half-believing that Emma would be in the next room, and in a moment they would meet in the Greek woman's kitchen and talk about their experiences.

Once undressed, she slipped on a loose cotton nightgown that hung on the back of the door, and then, almost unaware of what she was doing, she instinctively climbed into the little bed, pulled the covers up over her and turned to face the wall. How had this happened? How could it be that she'd lost both her sisters, at sea? And how could Emma have died while saving her? She realised that she owed her sister her life. Emma had not let go of her, the whole time they were in the water. Closing her eyes, she imagined she could still feel her sister's arm, strong and comforting, across her chest.

Lily woke some hours later, to the sound of voices in the next room. English voices. She got out of the little bed and found her clothes, dried and neatly folded, awaiting her on a chair. Quickly dressing, she opened the door to find Frank Perkins talking to her hostess, with another man acting as interpreter.

'Ah, here she is. Well rested, I hope?' Frank said, and the understanding and sympathy in his eyes made her want to cry again. But she held back. Now was not the time.

'Yes, thank you. This lady has been very kind.' She smiled at the Greek woman, who smiled back, dipping her head in acknowledgement.

'Well, I have good news. There is a British ship coming to pick us up. It will be here later today.'

'I don't even know where we are,' Lily admitted.

'We're on the Greek island of Kea. While we wait for HMS *Foxhound*, your nursing skills could be put to good use, if you are feeling up to it?'

'Yes, of course. I must do my bit.' She thanked her hostess once more, and followed Frank out of the cottage. *Keep busy, Lils. Keep working.*

Back at the quayside, people were bustling about, tending to a number of injured crewmen. Some were seriously wounded – missing legs or arms, clearly they had come off worse in the battle with the propellers. Some had minor injuries, perhaps from falling into lifeboats. Violet was there, tending to a man with a terrible injury to his leg – his foot was gone. Lily felt guilty for sleeping while Violet, although wounded herself, had got to work.

Violet briefly wrapped her arms around Lily, squeezing her tightly. Lily leaned into the older woman's embrace gratefully, but too soon Violet pushed her gently away. 'Best thing you can do for your sister now is help me with these men. Emma's gone, but we might be able to save some lives, here.'

Lily took a deep shuddering breath and nodded. 'Of course. What can I do?'

'Help me with these dressings,' Violet said to her, passing her some pads and bandages and kneeling beside the injured man. Lily knelt down beside her to patch the man up.

'I'm dying, aren't I?' he said to them.

Lily thought he probably was, and began to say something soothing, but Violet told him sternly, 'No, you're not going to die, because I've been praying for you to live.'

Once the man was seen to, the girls were asked to help cut up life belts to make more dressings, and Lily was kept busy for the next couple of hours until the rescue ship arrived. She was thankful for the activity, which helped keep her mind off her loss. She went into the building where the dead lay one more time, knelt for a moment by Emma's body and said her farewells. 'I'll never forget you, Ems. I love you. Thank you for saving me.'

Emma's remains, along with the others who had perished, would be picked up and buried in a British war cemetery later, she was told.

The rescue ship turned out to be a destroyer, to her surprise. She'd imagined another requisitioned liner. On board HMS *Foxhound* the crew were warm and welcoming towards the *Britannic* survivors. Fresh clothing – mostly male of course – was provided.

'What I want most is a decent meal,' Violet said, eyeing up a sailor's jumper.

Lily was hungry too, but realised that Violet had missed

breakfast that morning, as she'd been at Mass. Was it only that morning that they'd been on board the *Britannic*? The crew handed out cups of hot chocolate which was something, at least. Emma loved hot chocolate, Lily thought, and she found herself looking around for her sister before remembering, with a shock, what had happened.

The day was still not over. They were transferred to another ship, then taken to Piraeus on the Greek mainland, and put in a hotel. At last, a meal, though Lily did not feel she'd be able to manage much. Before eating, Lily was amazed to see Violet cleaning her teeth in a bathroom. 'Where on earth did you get that toothbrush?' she asked.

Violet smiled. 'It's mine. Remember I had a few things tucked in my apron? Amazing that it all stayed in there, despite me being in the water. And now I have clean teeth.'

Lily turned away before Violet saw the tears springing to her eyes. Violet had clean teeth, but she, Lily, had lost a sister.

They didn't stay long at Piraeus – soon a hospital ship, already packed with wounded soldiers, arrived to take them on to Malta. Here they were classed as 'distressed British seamen' and told that arrangements were being made for a homeward journey mostly via land through Italy and France, it being thought that the *Britannic* survivors had had enough of ships. Violet seemed happy on Malta – although her leg injury still gave her pain, she managed to meet up with a brother who was stationed there. 'We've been sight-seeing today,' she told Lily one evening. 'It's so good to spend time with William.' Then she'd stared at Lily, as though suddenly remembering that Lily had lost her sister, and she'd clamped her mouth shut and turned away, embarrassed.

Lily was trying not to think about her loss. It was better to remain numb, and just get through each day as best she could, finding things to occupy her so that she could not dwell on her loss. There would be time enough back in Southampton to grieve, when she returned to her old family home – the last remaining Higgins sister. The last of the entire family.

Frank was a great comfort. He spent most of his time with her, not always talking, but just being there, helping her, taking care of her. His gentle, sympathetic presence was slowly helping her come to terms with all that had happened.

'I'll do everything I can for you,' he promised. 'You've lost so much. Let me help you.' And she was happy to let him help, to lean on him emotionally and sometimes physically, as they waited for news of how they were to be repatriated.

Chapter 29

Harriet

By Saturday evening Harriet was once again exhausted but happy. Charlie had spent the day with her as he'd promised, and the bungalow was now habitable. He'd worked first on her bedroom – putting together her bed and wardrobe and placing her chest of drawers and smaller furniture items where she wanted them. They'd then unpacked boxes, put sheets on the bed and hung clothes in the wardrobe.

'Bathroom next – it's a quick win,' said Charlie over a cup of coffee, and indeed it was. Two boxes to empty – one of toiletries and one of towels and bathmats and it was done.

The kitchen took longer, as decisions had to be made as to where to put everything but eventually it was done, and the pile of emptied and flattened boxes in the garage was growing. The removals company would come to collect them in a week.

In the evening, after Charlie had gone, Harriet spent a while unpacking books and arranging them on her bookcases, but stopped halfway through, exhausted. She dug out a bottle of wine, opened it, and decided to spend an hour or so relaxing before attempting to sleep in her new home. She picked up her phone to check for any messages. There was a text from Sally hoping that all had gone well and promising to call the next morning, and there was a WhatsApp message from Robert.

On my way over to England. Will take a few days – travelling via QM2 as it seemed most appropriate. Will dock in Southampton on Friday. Hoping we can meet soon after that if you are free?

She quickly replied: *Wonderful way to travel – QM2 is a marvellous ship! Am having small house-warming party on Saturday. You're invited!* She added her address and grinned when he quickly responded with a thumbs up. It would be fun to meet him and swap stories about their grandmothers.

On Monday the postman brought Harriet a clutch of 'welcome to your new home' cards. One from Sheila, one from Sally who could have brought it by hand on moving day or sent it with Charlie, but who'd thought (as she wrote in the card), it'd be fun for Harriet to get some post at her new address. And the third was from Matthew. They'd been in regular contact via email since she'd written that first letter to him, and they'd spoken on the phone a couple of times. In the card he'd written that he would be in Bournemouth a couple of days later, and would she like to meet up? He suggested the bar of the hotel in the town centre where he was booked in – it was one Harriet knew well, only a couple of miles from her old house. She emailed him immediately to accept.

She dressed on Wednesday in a loose dress and a casual jacket – nothing too formal but a step up from her usual jeans and fleece combinations. She drove to the hotel, arriving in good time for the afternoon tea he'd suggested. Matthew was already waiting for her, sitting at a small table for two in a bay window at the far end of the hotel bar. He was reading a newspaper – the *Guardian*, she noted, the same one he'd always read – and he hadn't spotted her yet. She paused for a moment while still around ten metres away.

There he was. Matthew. Her big brother who'd always looked out for her, whom she'd worshipped. Whom she'd missed, so much. He looked up, peering over the top of his glasses, and grinned when he saw her, folding his paper and standing up.

'Harriet! I can't believe it – after so long!'

She walked quickly across the bar, and as she reached him she held out her arms and fell into his as though they met up every week. He squeezed her tightly, and she kept her face buried for a moment against his chest, while she brought her emotions into check. 'Matthew! My dear old brother!'

'If I'm old, then so are you,' he said, as he released her and they sat down.

'I'm refusing to count 70 as old,' she said with a laugh.

'Quite right too! Well, shall we order? I thought we could have a proper afternoon tea – little sandwiches, cakes, and scones. My treat.'

'Sounds delightful!' Harriet was thrilled by the way they seemed to be slipping straight back into the friendship and closeness they'd had as children and teenagers. It was possible, then, to pick up and rebuild a relationship that had been allowed to founder.

They chatted for hours – updating each other on their lives over the last many years. Matthew's long-term partner had died a couple of years earlier – not long before John. Harriet's heart went out to him as he talked about his loss. She'd never met Matthew's partner – Greta had just been a name on the Christmas cards – but he'd loved her and lost her.

'We've both missed out on getting to know each other's partners properly,' Matthew said. 'I'm sorry for that. It was my fault.'

'Let's not talk about fault,' Harriet said, reaching a hand across the table to him. 'We both could have tried harder.'

She invited Matthew to her house-warming party at the weekend. 'Sally will be there, and your great-nephew Jerome. Please come. They'd love to see you.'

'I'd like to do that,' Matthew said.

Harriet smiled. 'There's one other family member who should be there on Saturday too. A second cousin we didn't know we had.' She updated Matthew on her family tree research, and how she'd come across Robert on the Ancestry site. 'To think we never knew anything about Ruby's existence! To be honest, I can't remember many of Gran's stories. I wish I'd listened more. I know she talked a lot about her time working on the *Olympic* but she never mentioned her sisters had been on the *Titanic*. I only really remember her talking about events from the 1920s on.'

Matthew nodded. 'I do remember her stories – probably more than you as I was interested in history. But she never talked about the *Titanic* or Ruby. She talked about Emma a lot – I think as a young child she'd worshipped Emma and then of course Emma saved her life.'

Harriet frowned. 'I vaguely remember something about that but not the full story – do you know it?'

'It was on the *Britannic*,' Matthew said, then paused as he took a sip of his tea – their third cup of the afternoon. 'It was used as a hospital ship during the First World War, and they were both working on board when it hit a German mine and sank. Their lifeboat was being sucked towards the propellers so they jumped overboard, but Gran couldn't swim. Great-Aunt Emma kept her afloat, towed her away from the ship and got her into another lifeboat but she was exhausted and somehow ended up drowning.'

'That is so sad.' Harriet was silent for a moment, imagining Gran in the second lifeboat, knowing her sister had saved her at the cost of her own life. 'So selfless of Emma. But how can she have got Gran into another lifeboat then drowned herself? Could no one have pulled her into it?'

'Gran was a bit unsure what happened, but she remembered lots of shouting, and an oar being lost, and Emma floating away face down, unconscious. By the time they retrieved her she was gone.'

'What happened then?'

'The lifeboat rowed to the island of Kea where the injured were treated. Gran helped nurse some of the wounded. Imagine that – having just lost your sister but still trying to help other people.' Matthew stared out of the window for a moment then turned back to Harriet. 'I went there, you know. To Kea, and then to Piraeus on the Greek mainland where Emma was buried in a British naval cemetery along with other casualties of the *Britannic*. I was on holiday in Greece, doing a bit of island hopping and I decided to take a trip there and see if I could find Emma's grave. There's a small plot with a gravestone. I bought flowers and laid them on her grave.'

'That's lovely. I'm glad you went, and that she's not entirely forgotten. I suppose we wouldn't exist if not for her heroism. That's a sobering thought.'

'Yes. Remember Gran had been sickly as a child, with tuberculosis. That's why she never learned to swim, she always said. I always found it amazing that she went back to sea after losing her sister in that way. Even more remarkable now that we know she thought she'd lost two sisters.'

'What a story,' Harriet said. 'Thank you for telling me all you remember. I can update it all on the Ancestry website, and make sure it's all captured for future generations. Maybe I'll even pull together a little book and self-publish it. Just for the family, I mean.' She was thinking of Davina's daughters. If she never got to meet them, having their family history written down might be something they could treasure, in time.

She'd been in the bungalow two days when the next phone call from Davina came.

'Harriet? Hi. Just calling to see how things are going. You're due to be moving house around this time, aren't you?'

'Davina! Moved in a couple of days ago. More or less unpacked now – Sally and Charlie helped me with it all. It's been a busy few days.' She told Davina about her meeting with Matthew

273

– cautiously as she didn't want it to sound as though she was pushing Davina into meeting up. She knew that would serve only to push her daughter away.

'That's lovely news,' Davina replied, and Harriet wondered if she could detect a slight wistful tone in her voice.

'He's staying in Bournemouth for a few days, and I think he might come to my little house-warming party on Saturday. He's lovely. I'm just sorry ...' She'd been going to say she was sorry they hadn't met up often when Sally and Davina were children, but stopped herself in time. It would come across as though she was criticising Davina for keeping away. Sometimes it was very difficult to avoid stepping on all the eggshells that lay strewn between them.

'Sorry we didn't get to see more of him years ago?' Davina said, as though she'd read Harriet's mind.

'Well, yes. That's what I was thinking. Oh, and someone else interesting is coming on Saturday.' Harriet told Davina about Robert and his forthcoming visit to England.

'Quite a reunion,' Davina commented. 'Well, I hope the party goes well. So, how's Jerome?'

'So far so good, as I told you by text. He hasn't rejected the transplant, which is good news, and seems to be responding well. He's stronger every day. It's all very hopeful now, at last.'

'Good ... I'm so glad.'

There was something about the way she said this, the hesitation, the little catch in her voice, that made Harriet frown. 'What is it, Davina? Is there something you're not telling me?' Fears of news that Autumn or Summer were suffering from the same as Jerome flooded through her mind while she waited for her daughter to answer.

Davina let out a long sigh. 'OK, so I suppose I should come clean. Hadn't quite decided but ... James thinks I should. I ... I became a bone marrow donor.'

'You signed up for the registry? That's great. So did Sally.'

'Um, more than that. I donated. I ... well, I contacted Jerome's consultant, got myself tested, and it turns out I was a match. It's rare for an auntie to be a match but somehow luckily I was, and ... I donated bone marrow. To Jerome. It was ... a bit painful if I'm honest, and took me longer to recover than I'd thought, but all worth it, of course, if it's given him a chance.'

'Davina, that's ... oh my God. That's marvellous.' Harriet found tears pouring down her face. 'Can I ... can I tell Sally it was you? She's been asking the consultant if she could be told who the donor was.'

'I know. He forwarded her letter to me. And a photo of Jerome.' There was a catch in Davina's voice as though she too was holding back tears. 'It was a beautiful letter, Mum. Made me ... cry a little. I'd forgotten Sally could be so ... lovely. Warm. Yes, you can tell her. Probably better if you do, before I ... see her again.'

'Before you *see* her?' Harriet whispered, as though repeating the words too loudly might make them disappear and Davina would deny they'd ever been said.

'James thinks, and I guess I do too – it's time – that we should ... pay you a visit. All of us. See if we can ... start again.' She sniffed, loudly, and Harriet heard sounds of her pulling a tissue out of a box.

'A visit! Oh Davina!'

'Would we be welcome? I mean, after everything ...'

'Oh love, do you even have to ask?' Harriet felt as though her heart was stopping. Davina, and the girls, visiting; a new start – it had been her dream for so long. 'When were you thinking?'

'Don't know, soon, I need to make arrangements. So, yeah, tell Sally, and love to Jerome, and ... tell her I forgive her. For that day in Weymouth.' She sniffed loudly. 'And you, of course. I know it wasn't you, it was all down to that Lucas bloke. Anyway. I'll tell her myself. Guess I need some forgiveness from her too ... for not being there ... Anyway, see you, Mum.' Davina hung up before Harriet had the chance to say anything more, but those

last three words seemed to hang in the air like the sweet scent
of roses. *See you, Mum.* She sat down, allowing her tears to fall,
and imagining her younger daughter *here*, in her new home,
with Sally, with Jerome and her two granddaughters … a family
again. A proper, extended family, just as she'd always dreamed of.

Chapter 30

Lily, 1920

The war was at long last over. The Spanish flu had been and gone. Lily had spent the years since *Britannic* working in the Royal South Hants hospital once again, caring for repatriated injured servicemen and later, caring for the victims of the flu. Thankfully she had not succumbed herself. But she had been kept very busy throughout – busy was good, as it helped her deal with her losses.

She'd kept the house – the little terraced house she'd grown up in, that still held so many memories of Ma, Emma, and Ruby. With two lodgers – both nurses she worked with – it was easy enough to pay the bills.

And now, she was 21, the war was over, the epidemic had diminished, and Lily found herself to be tired of nursing. She no longer wanted to deal with the sick and dying. She had given her all to the job, and it had taken its toll on her. But what else could she do?

It was in the summer, while she considered alternative careers, that she had an unexpected visitor, one Saturday afternoon. There was a knock at the door, and Lily put down the duster she'd been using, patted her hair and went to answer it.

'Frank! My word, what a surprise!'

'Hello Lily. I was in town. Just got off the *Olympic*, and thought I'd come to see how you are.'

Frank had written to her a few times over the last four years, and she'd written back, courtesy of whichever hospital ship he'd been working on. But she had not seen him since their return to Southampton in early 1917, after the long, mostly overland, journey back from Malta. His family lived in Bristol, and his few breaks between voyages were spent there. And now, here he was on her doorstep!

'Come in! Excuse the state of me, I was cleaning, but let me make you some tea. And I have some shortbread I made yesterday, if you'd like some?'

'That would be wonderful,' he said, following her inside. Her sitting room was in upheaval as she'd been shifting furniture around to clean behind it, so she had no choice but to take him to the kitchen, with more apologies, but his broad grin showed he didn't mind in the slightest. 'The kitchen is the heart of the home, I always say. And you've a lovely, welcoming one. So, how are things with you? You're looking well, I must say.'

Lily found herself blushing at this. Frank was as open and charming as ever, and his hair seemed a brighter ginger than before, if that was even possible. The years had made him look older, more grown-up, but as handsome as ever. 'I'm very well,' she replied. 'You're working on the *Olympic* now, did you say?'

'Yes, she's just gone back into service as a passenger liner after a refit. She's my favourite ship, so I'm very happy. You're still nursing? Are you enjoying it?'

Lily sighed and turned away as she poured water from the kettle into the tea pot. 'Actually, not any more. I've been wondering about giving up nursing, though I don't know what to do instead.'

'You might work on a liner,' Frank said. Lily turned back to him and put the tea pot on the table. There was a hopefulness in his gaze.

'Ah, I'm not sure I could do that. Not after … all that's happened. Liners have not been kind to this family.'

'No, of course. I'm sorry. I should not have said it. It's just … I cannot think of anything I'd like more than to work alongside you again. You know, our old friend Violet Jessop has signed on for the *Olympic*.'

'Has she?' Lily found it easier to respond to his last statement than the earlier one. She'd love to work alongside him too, but could she really return to sea? 'I would have thought, after surviving both *Titanic* and *Britannic* she'd never want to set foot on a boat again.'

'She says the sea's in her blood. She's made of stern stuff, that woman. And she likes the *Olympic*.'

'Emma liked it, too.' Lily fell silent as she poured the tea, imagining what Emma would have done, if it had been she who survived *Britannic* instead. She'd have done as Violet had, Lily concluded. She'd have gone back to sea, signing on with the *Olympic*. She'd loved life on board ships so much.

'I wish I'd had the chance to know Emma better,' Frank said. 'She was a remarkable woman.'

'She saved my life.'

'I know.'

They'd had this conversation several times over the last few years – while travelling home, and then by letter. Lily had always thought it implied that Frank might have wanted to become closer to Emma if she'd lived. But now, here he was, sitting in her kitchen, and he'd said something about working alongside her again. She eyed him over the rim of her teacup. That twinkle was still in his eyes, undimmed by the war years. She liked him too. She always had, and their shared experiences, plus the years of letters, had confirmed this and brought them closer. She'd thought of him as Emma's, but maybe … he could be hers? If she could bring herself to apply for a job on the *Olympic* – taking up where Emma left off. It wouldn't be the worst future she could imagine. She'd enjoyed sailing on the *Britannic*, before it hit that mine.

'You know, I think I might apply to White Star. Do you think I'd stand a chance?'

Frank's grin was in danger of splitting his face wide open. 'I think you certainly would. They employ a few medical personnel.'

Lily shook her head. 'No, I'd rather be a stewardess, like Emma was. In a way, I'd be doing it for her. She loved the sea, too.'

'That's a lovely thought. I fear it's too late to sign on for the next voyage, but the *Olympic* is due back in Southampton in three weeks. May I visit you again, then?'

'Of course! And you can show me where I need to go to sign on.'

'I would like nothing better. Your shortbread is delicious, by the way.'

Lily smiled. 'Thank you.'

Three weeks later, Lily had finished working her notice period at the hospital and had been successful at an interview with White Star. She was to be a stewardess working second class, just as Emma had, and she had signed on to work on the *Olympic*'s next crossing to New York – following in her sisters' footsteps. Her lodgers would take care of her house, and both Frank and Violet had also signed on.

Violet met her on the day she boarded, with her new sailing trunk, her uniform and her discharge book, and her copy of the picture of herself, Emma, and Ruby. Violet was delighted to see her. 'White Star ships don't seem right without a member of the Higgins family alongside me. So glad to have you on board. As it's your first time as a stewardess, anything you need, anything you want, you just ask me.'

'Thank you,' Lily said. To tell the truth she felt a little choked with emotion, as she walked the galley-ways of the ship. It all looked vaguely familiar from her short time on the *Britannic*, but it was more than that. It was knowing Emma had been here before her.

'One odd thing I wanted to tell you,' Violet continued. 'On my last voyage, when I was in New York, I had a brief glimpse of a woman who looked the spit of your sister Ruby. Very strange, it was. I wanted to run after her, but of course it couldn't have been her. Just someone with the same hair colour and the same way of walking.'

'How odd. But when you think, of all the people in the world, there's bound to be someone who looks like her,' Lily said, wondering why Violet was telling her this. It was no comfort to hear there was someone who looked like Ruby walking around New York, when her sister was at the bottom of the north Atlantic.

'Of course. But just for a moment I wondered – did she survive the *Titanic* somehow? She really did look like Ruby. The woman, whoever it was, went into an apartment building overlooking Central Park. I could show you which one, if you wanted to call and see if it really was her?'

Lily considered this for a moment. Could it be possible that Ruby had survived? Perhaps she still had a sister, after all? But if so, then it was clear that Ruby had wanted to stay away from the family, for her own reasons. Lily had been just a young girl when Ruby had left on the *Titanic*, but she'd been vaguely aware that Ruby was in some sort of trouble with a man. If she had survived and wanted to contact her family, then she could have done so at any time. It had been eight years since the *Titanic* disaster. She knew where to send a letter to. But she hadn't done so.

Lily realised that if it was indeed Ruby, living in that apartment block in New York, then if she went to see her she'd have to tell her sister about Ma and about Emma. That would not be easy.

'Thank you, Violet. But it can't be her, and I'd hate to get my hopes up. If it is her, she can get in contact with me if she wants to. I'm still at the same address. If she doesn't, she must have her reasons for not wanting to. If she comes back, I'm here, with open arms. If not, well, it's up to her.'

Violet nodded. 'I think that's wise. I was probably wrong

thinking it was her. Well, come on, we've a few hours to spare before we sail, and I believe a certain young man is looking forward to spending his spare hours with you on this voyage. Shall we go and find him, after you've sorted out your cabin?'

'Yes please!' Lily was so looking forward to seeing Frank, even though she'd seen him just two days before, when the *Olympic* had docked and he'd come to her house. They'd gone for a walk on Southampton Common, and about halfway round, he'd taken her hand in his as though it was the most natural thing in the world to do.

'Well, I'll leave you for now – see you up on the promenade deck in twenty minutes?'

'All right, see you then.' Lily went into her cabin and set to work unpacking.

When she'd finished putting everything away, she took out her photo of the three sisters, and placed it beside her bed, so it would be the last thing she saw at night and the first thing she saw when she woke up each morning. Thankfully she hadn't taken it with her on the *Britannic*. Her sisters smiled at her from the frame, as though telling her she was doing the right thing. And as she looked forward to the voyage ahead, her free hours to spend with Frank, her chances to see new places in the world, Lily knew that the past with all its sorrows and losses was behind her and that there was much to look forward to, for the first time in years.

Chapter 31

Harriet

Sally arrived early on the day of Harriet's house-warming party, to help prepare food and arrange the furniture. There weren't too many coming – Charlie would bring Jerome later, Sheila was coming, and Harriet had asked a few of her new neighbours. And of course, Matthew and Robert. 'My guests of honour,' she said to Sally, as they arranged bowls of olives and crisps on side tables.

'I'm looking forward to meeting Uncle Matthew again. It's been too long. And to think one day Jerome will get to meet his auntie – his life-saver.' Sally took a deep breath. Harriet knew that her daughter found herself feeling overwhelmed every time she thought about what Davina had done.

It had been an emotional moment, when Harriet had gone round to see Sally and Charlie, and told them about Davina's last phone call. Jerome had been in bed, and Harriet had sat in the living room with Sally and Charlie as she told them the news. They'd listened in astonished silence, and as she told them about Davina's donation of bone marrow tears had begun to stream down Sally's cheeks. She'd made no attempt to stop them.

'And Davina said she'd like to meet us all. Start again, she said. I don't know when, but she said soon. Her new man, James, has been a good influence it seems. It's he who's encouraged her to be more in touch with us.'

'She's still my sister,' Sally whispered. 'She stepped forward when we needed her. I'd like to see her, and be able to say thank you in person. I'd love to see her again.'

Charlie put his arm around Sally. 'It's quite a thing she's done. We're amazingly grateful. I want to thank her too.'

'And say sorry for … that day,' Sally said.

Harriet reached a hand out to her daughter. 'She said she forgives us for that. She's sorry too, for all the occasions she missed.'

Sally smiled. 'We've grown up at last, haven't we?'

Harriet had not heard again from Davina, so there was no news as to when she was planning to visit. But it was enough to have that ahead of them.

And now, there was the party to prepare for. It was to be an afternoon and early evening affair – Jerome wouldn't be able to stay late and he'd said he most definitely wanted to be at Nanna's new house party. Thankfully he was well enough, though Harriet had decided to keep the spare bedroom free and ready for him in case he needed to rest. Guests had been asked to arrive from three o'clock, and it was Sheila who arrived first, a bottle of champagne clutched in her hand.

'Now then, before anything else, you and I are going to have a glass of this beauty together. You've taken an enormous step moving here, and I know how hard it has been for you to do this without John, and with everything else that's been going on.' She went through to the kitchen, found the champagne flutes and opened the bottle with a flourish, pouring three glasses. 'Sally, you have one too. You deserve it, love. And we've a lot to celebrate, eh girls?'

'We certainly have,' Harriet said, and took a glass. She clinked it against Sheila's and Sally's, but before she could take a sip the doorbell rang and she was busy ushering in her new neighbours, making introductions, passing round drinks. Sheila took up position in the kitchen as chief barmaid, while Harriet stayed near the door as a stream of visitors arrived – neighbours from both sides and from across the street.

Charlie came with Jerome, who was holding an enormous bunch of flowers. 'For you, Nanna. I wanted to buy you a Lego model of a house but Dad said you'd like these more.' He shrugged, as if to show he'd never understand adults.

'Oh my, they are absolutely beautiful,' she exclaimed, kissing both Charlie and Jerome. 'I'll put them in a vase of water so they last a long time.' She bent down to whisper to Jerome. 'I'd have quite liked the Lego too, but how about you show me which model it was, and I buy it for you instead? We could build it together.' His face lit up with a grin as he nodded frantically.

Another batch of neighbours arrived, bringing a couple of children of Jerome's age. They were instantly awed by his bald head, and the three of them happily went off to play in the garden. Charlie watched with Harriet as Jerome ran after the others, giggling. 'It's amazing to see him like this. So much better. He'll be tired later, and he won't be able to keep it up, but look at him, playing, having fun, like any other child.'

'It's lovely to see,' she agreed.

Robert arrived next, filling the small house with his larger-than-life presence, his good humour, and his guffawing laugh. He enveloped Harriet in a huge bear-hug, clearly delighted to meet her in the flesh. She felt as though she'd known him for years as they'd had several video calls over WhatsApp since first getting in touch with each other.

'It's so lovely to have you here!' she told him. 'I expect it'll be difficult to have a proper chat today but as you're staying in Southampton for a few days we'll have plenty of chances. I can easily drive over.'

'Hey, I've hired a car so I can drive over to you too! I want to explore the whole area – the New Forest, the beaches, everything. It's real beautiful over here.'

'I'd love to be your guide for some of it.' Harriet took his arm and led him around, introducing him to Sally and Charlie, and then Sheila, who immediately wanted to know every detail of his Atlantic crossing on the *QM2*.

'We just had a short cruise on that ship,' she told him, 'to Rotterdam, Zeebrugge, and Guernsey. I'd love to sail to New York. Just like the old days before trans-continental flights.'

'It was marvellous,' he said, 'and I spent so much time imagining what it must have been like on the great ships of the past, that Harriet's and my grandmothers worked on.'

'Robert, my brother Matthew is coming today,' Harriet told him. 'So you'll meet another second cousin soon. I'll introduce you.'

'Awesome. Extending my family even further.'

Harriet heard the doorbell ring, and left Robert chatting to Sheila. This time it was Matthew. She hugged him, feeling slightly overwhelmed that her brother was here, in her house, taking his place as part of her family. She swallowed hard, blinking, anything to try to stop the tears that threatened. Matthew seemed to understand, for he squeezed her tightly and then released her, smiling.

'Sis! It's good to see you again. What a wonderful little bungalow. So perfect a place to live. I should really do the same – my house is too big and too much work, and it'd be great to have a smaller place. You've totally inspired me. So, shall I go to the kitchen for a drink? If you've a can of beer that would be perfect …'

His stream of chatter gave her the chance to compose herself, and she smiled back at him gratefully. 'Yes, my friend Sheila was doing the drinks but she's now chatting to our second cousin Robert – I told you about him? – so I probably should get your drink myself. We have beer. Lager or a bottle of craft beer?'

'Oh, a craft beer, thank you.' He sounded delighted, and Harriet suddenly remembered that he'd always been a fan of real ale and micro-breweries. She fetched him the drink, and as she handed it to him she realised Sally was on the patio, looking in at them with curiosity. 'So, come and say hi to your niece. I think she was only about 15 when you last saw her.' She grabbed his hand, pulled him through the patio door and introduced him to Sally.

'Uncle Matthew! Fabulous to see you again! You're just as I remember, although it must be twenty years, so I guess I've changed a bit!' Sally shook his hand and then leaned in to kiss his cheek. She tipped her head on one side. 'You know, I think I can see the family resemblance. Something about the shape of your eyes reminds me of my sister, Davina. And your face shape is the same as Mum's.'

'Ah, we both got that from our father,' Matthew said, and Harriet nodded.

'I was going to say you're the spitting image of Dad.'

'And you remind me so much of our Mum,' he replied. 'It's nice to be reminded.'

Harriet looked around at her party happily. She wasn't expecting any more guests, and everyone she'd invited had come. A happy couple of hours passed, with the children playing tag in the garden, while Charlie watched, keeping a watchful eye on Jerome. Sally and Matthew were getting to know each other, and Sheila and Robert were deep in conversation. Harriet spent time mingling, talking to her new neighbours who all seemed friendly as they sat in her living room, chatting and laughing. She wandered out to the hallway and as she glanced through the window beside the front door she realised a taxi had pulled up outside, and someone was getting out. A man, with two children, and a woman ...

Holding her breath, she opened the front door and walked up the driveway while the man paid the taxi driver. She stared at the woman, the children, and then the woman again. Tall, blonde, elegant, tanned, and staring back at her, her mouth gradually reshaping into a broad smile. Harriet took a step forward and clutched at a gate post.

'Harriet? Mum? God, you don't look a day older,' the woman said. She also stepped forward but there was still a couple of metres between them – a short distance but a wide gulf of years of misunderstanding and regret.

'Davina! Oh my God, Davina!' Harriet reached out her right hand, still clinging to the gate post with her left as though she might drown in her emotions if she let go. Davina made another step forward and took hold of Harriet's hand. Contact with her daughter for the first time in fifteen years – it made her fingers tingle and a rush of warmth spread through her. 'Oh, Davina,' she said again, pulling her daughter towards her into an embrace, wondering too late if that might be a step too far. All these years of learning not to push things with Davina, all the care she'd always taken not to push her away – all that was gone like driftwood on the tide as she revelled in the feel of her youngest child in her arms once again.

And Davina was sobbing on her shoulder, her body heaving, her arms clutched tightly around Harriet like a drowning woman. All those years apart, all those missed opportunities to make memories together, all of it washed away in a torrent of tears.

'Mummy? Is this our granny?' A small hand was tugging at Davina's sleeve, and Harriet reluctantly pulled away a little to see that the smaller of the two girls was standing by. Her sister was hanging back a little, beside the man who must be James.

'Summer?' Harriet said, and the nearer child nodded. 'Yes, I'm your granny. It's amazing to meet you.' She held out a hand, not knowing whether to hug her granddaughter or shake hands, but Summer made the decision for her, wrapping her little arms around Harriet's waist. She leaned over, resting her cheek on the top of Summer's head, breathing in the scent of apple shampoo. Out of the corner of her eye she saw James give the other girl an encouraging little nudge, and then Autumn was there too, in a group hug. Autumn was almost as tall as Harriet, and darker haired, looking so like Sally had as a teen that for a moment it felt as though the years had rolled back and it was her daughters she was embracing, not her granddaughters.

'When you said you would come, I didn't expect it to be today – it's my house-warming party,' she said to Davina, over Autumn's shoulder.

'I know. You said on the phone it was today. I guess Sally's here, and I thought I'd meet you both at once.' Davina gave a short laugh and a wry smile. 'I don't make it easy for you, do I?'

'No. You never have,' Harriet replied, also smiling. 'Well, then, we should go inside and find Sally.' She let go of her grand-daughters, but was delighted when Summer's hand slipped into her own.

'Yes. Oh, and this is James,' Davina said, and he stepped forward to kiss Harriet's cheek.

'Lovely to meet you at long last,' he said. Harriet squeezed his hand in gratitude at his part in bringing her family back together.

As they headed back up the driveway, the front door opened and Harriet's neighbours appeared, thanking her for the party but explaining they had to leave now and they'd see her soon, if she needed any help she should just call on them. She thanked them for coming, knowing she'd need to explain about her tear-stained cheeks at some later date.

Inside there was only family and Sheila left. Someone had washed up most of the dirty glasses. Harriet led Davina through the house to the garden, where Sally was sitting at the patio table with Charlie. Jerome was sitting on the grass picking daisies. Autumn and Summer immediately, instinctively went to him, flumping down beside him and joining in with him. Sally stared at Davina in astonishment.

'Davie? Oh my God, Davie!' She clamped a hand to her mouth as Charlie put a supportive hand on her shoulder.

'Hey, Sal. Yes, it's me. I suppose I should have given some warning, but you know me …'

'Yes, I know you,' Sally said as she got to her feet and came around the table to stand before her sister. 'Mum, did you know she was coming today?'

'No. I've just had the same surprise as you,' Harriet said. She was watching carefully. Her daughters had had a prickly relationship, and they'd hurt each other badly all those years ago. But now after all that had happened – Davina's return and her selfless donation of bone marrow – surely Sally would forgive her, as Davina had forgiven Sally?

There was quiet in the garden, the only sounds being birdsong and a little murmuring from the children, as everyone watched this momentous reunion. Slowly, as though dazed, Sally reached out a hand to Davina just as Harriet herself had done a few minutes before. Davina reached back, and then they were in each other's arms, crying and hugging, and all that had gone before was past and they were simply two sisters who loved each other.

Matthew had come out and now stood beside Harriet, his arm loosely draped across her shoulder. 'Davina back in your life now too?'

She nodded. 'Yes.'

He smiled. 'Wonderful.'

'Shall I make everyone tea, or is it time for more champagne?' Sheila asked the group at large.

'Tea for me, I think,' Harriet said.

'Champagne!' Davina and Sally answered in unison, and then turned to each other and laughed.

Harriet went inside to help Sheila with the drinks. By the time they'd finished and were distributing cups and glasses, people had migrated around the house. Matthew and Robert were in the conservatory, swapping memories of their respective grandmothers. On the sofa in the sitting room, Charlie and James were getting to know each other, discovering a shared love of rugby and talking about Munster's chances in the weekend match against Perpignan. The children had also come inside and Harriet found them in the spare bedroom. Jerome was lying on the bed, clearly tired out from the day, cuddling Mr Bungle tightly. Summer was sitting at the foot of the bed, with Davina's old teddy that Harriet had rescued from the attic clutched in her arms. Autumn was telling them both a story. Harriet watched for a moment, catching Autumn's eye. Her older granddaughter smiled shyly at her but continued with her story, tucking a knitted blanket gently around her young cousin as his eyes began to close.

Outside, sitting at the patio table, were Sally and Davina. They were close, their knees touching, and every now and again one would put her hand on the other's arm, as if to be reassured that yes, her sister was really there, in the flesh. As Harriet watched, Davina said something and Sally threw back her head and laughed, then Davina joined in.

Sheila put two glasses of champagne in front of them, then passed a mug of tea to Harriet. 'Look at you,' she said. 'Not so long ago you were crying on my shoulder about your family being so small. Now look, you have a huge family, all around you. Brother, cousin, daughters and grandchildren. You'll have no need of me any more.'

Harriet hugged her. 'I shall always need you, to keep me sane. But yes, I feel so grateful to have them all here now.'

'It's your doing,' Sheila said. 'You kept lines of communication open with Davina, you never gave up on her. And it's paid off. Now you reap the rewards.' She leaned closed to Harriet and nudged her. 'You'll be wishing you'd kept the big house now, for all this lot.'

Harriet laughed. 'It would have helped for this party, certainly! But I know I am going to be very happy here.'

John was not there to see it, but somehow Harriet could feel him beside her, happy that she had pulled her family back together. In a way it was his doing. His death had been the catalyst for her to contact Matthew. And following his mantra – *love is always open arms* – had helped bring Davina back at last. There was work to be done, things to be discussed, but they'd manage it. They'd all made those first steps, hugged each other, learned to laugh together again, and everything else would follow. They were family.

Author's Note

This book began life as a conversation in the pub with my brother Nigel. He was telling me he'd just bought a book about the *Olympic*. '*Titanic*'s sister ship,' he explained. 'Actually there were three sisters – *Olympic*, *Titanic*, and *Britannic*.' He went on to tell me that the *Britannic* had been used as a hospital ship in the First World War and had hit a German mine. But it was those words, 'three sisters' that had sparked my imagination – three ships, three girls, two shipwrecks … I knew from that moment on that I would write a book from this idea.

Almost as soon as I began researching, I came across Violet Jessop, whose memoirs were posthumously published as *Titanic Survivor*, edited by John Maxtone-Graham. She did indeed serve on all three ships, as described in this novel, and her memoirs were invaluable to me. While my sisters are of course fictitious, almost everything Violet does was taken from her book. I decided to put my girls on the same lifeboats as Violet for both of the shipwrecks. The details of Violet holding an unknown baby on the *Titanic* lifeboat, and the disaster with the lifeboats on the *Britannic* are all real events, as is her tending to an injured sailor on the Greek island of Kea and telling him he wouldn't die because she'd been praying for him. (He did indeed survive, and Violet met him again in Italy on her journey back home.)

My own experiences of cruise ships are sadly very limited to date. As a child I grew up within sight of Southampton Water, and often stood at the end of our road to watch the *QE2* go out. Her foghorns, often sounded on leaving port, would sometimes wake me up. For my fortieth birthday, my husband booked me a surprise weekend cruise on the P&O ship, *Aurora*. We only sailed from Southampton over to Zeebrugge and back but it was glorious. In researching a suitable short cruise for Harriet and Sheila, that had to start from Southampton, I came across the one on the *QM2* that they take, and now it's on my bucket list to do that.

I wrote this novel during the 2020 pandemic, working from my home in Bournemouth. The cruise industry was hit very hard, and several ships were anchored in Bournemouth bay for the duration. They came and went, but *Aurora* was there much of the time, and the *QM2* paid us a few visits too. Between writing this novel and ship-spotting from our local cliff top, I turned into a bit of a ship-nerd. I blame my brother – he kicked all this off with his talk of sister ships!

Acknowledgements

Many thanks to my editors Abigail Fenton and Dushi Horti for their invaluable help with this novel. Thanks also to my brother Nigel Thompson, who loaned me a pile of fascinating books about *Olympic* and *Titanic*, as well as providing the initial spark that started me off on this story.

Thanks to my son Connor who listened to me talking through my plot ideas, and who came up with the idea for one of the twists. I hope I've written it the way you thought it would work – you will need to read it to see!

As always, thanks to my son Fionn and husband Ignatius for being beta readers and providing me with some early feedback.

Thank you to all at HQ – copy editors, proof readers, cover designers – all do a superb job bringing my books to market. And thanks to the readers who keep buying them!

Last but by no means least, huge thanks are due to my friend Lor Bingham, who also acted as a beta reader for this book. Your detailed notes and comments, especially regarding the cancer storyline, were an enormous help. I hope I have got these sensitive sections right.

Keep reading for an excerpt
from *The Secret of the Château* …

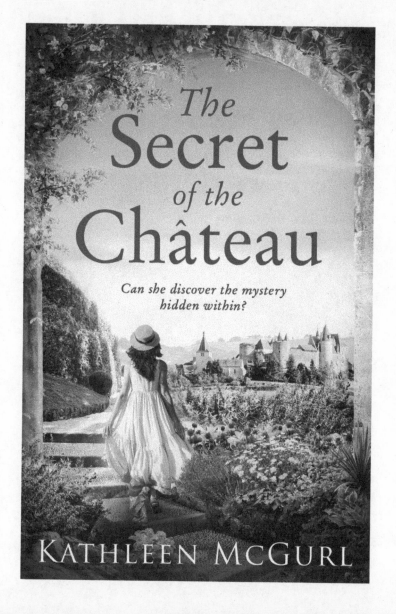

The
Secret
of the
Château

*Can she discover the mystery
hidden within?*

KATHLEEN McGURL

Keep reading for an excerpt

from *The Secret of the Château* ...

Prologue

Pierre, 1794

Pierre Aubert, the Comte de Verais, could see the mob coming in the distance, up the track towards the château, brandishing flaming torches, shouting and chanting. There were perhaps fifty or more men, in their rough brown trousers and loose shirts. Most of them were carrying weapons – farming implements, sticks, pikes. He clutched his young son close to his chest, hushing the child and trying to ignore the pains that shot through him as he hurried along the path that led away from the château, towards the village. The girl was ahead of him, holding the baby. They had to get the children to safety first; only then could Pierre concentrate on saving himself and his wife.

Catherine. His heart lurched as he recalled her white, frightened face as he'd hurriedly told her his plans. If she did what he'd told her, she'd be safe from the mob, and soon the family would be reunited and they could get away. Into exile, into Switzerland.

France had changed over the last five years or so. The old ways, the *ancien régime*, had gone. There seemed to be no place in this new France for the likes of Pierre and Catherine. In the past it had been their class who ruled, but not anymore. If this mob caught them, they'd be imprisoned, summarily tried, and very likely executed – by guillotine.

But the mob would need to catch them first. Pierre had received a warning and was a good way ahead of them. The men hadn't reached the château yet, and they wouldn't find Catherine there. She was safe for now, and he'd return to her later. It would all work out.

It had to. It was their only chance.

Chapter 1

Lu, present day

It all began one drunken evening at Manda and Steve's. We were all staying with them for the weekend, as we often did. Three of us – that's me (I'm Lu Marlow), my husband Phil and our mate Graham – had arrived on Friday afternoon, and Steve had cooked a stupendous meal for us all that evening. We'd all brought a few bottles of wine, and I admit by the time this particular conversation began over the remnants of dessert we may have all had a tad too much to drink.

'What are you going to do, now you're retired?' Phil asked Steve. Steve had been forced to retire early – given a choice between that or relocating to Derby. ('Nothing against Derby,' he'd said, 'but we've no desire to live there.') He was aged just fifty-nine. We were all fifty-eight or nine. We'd met forty years ago, during Freshers' week at Sussex University and had been firm friends through rough and smooth ever since.

Steve shrugged. 'Don't know. I didn't want to stop work. Not quite ready to devote myself to the garden yet.'

'He needs a project,' Manda said. 'Something to get stuck

301

into. He's lost without a purpose in life. House renovation or something.'

'But your house is beautiful,' I said. 'It needs nothing doing to it.' We were sitting in their dining room, which overlooked the garden. They'd bought the house over twenty years earlier when their daughter Zoe was a baby. Zoe had recently sent Manda into a tailspin by moving to Australia on a two-year work contract. They'd done up their house over the years, turning it from a tired old mess into a beautiful family home.

'Yes, and I don't see the point of moving house just to give me something to do,' Steve said. 'More wine?' He topped up everyone's glasses.

'Can you get any consultancy work?' Phil asked. 'I've had a bit, since I got my redundancy package.' He'd done a few two-week contracts, and a part-time contract that lasted three months.

'Probably. But it's not what I want.'

'What *do* you want, mate?' Graham, who we'd always called Gray, asked.

Steve looked out at the rain that streamed down the patio doors. 'Better weather. Mountains. A ski resort within an hour's drive. Somewhere I can go fell-running straight from the house. A better lifestyle.'

'Relocating, then. Where to?'

'I fancy France,' Manda said.

'Yeah, I do, too.' Phil looked at me, as if to gauge my reaction. First I'd heard of him being interested in living abroad – we'd never talked about anything like that. We went to France or Italy a couple of times every year on holiday – always a winter ski trip (Phil's favourite) and usually a couple of weeks in the summer exploring the Loire valley, the Ardeches, Tuscany or wherever else took our fancy. Very often these holidays were with the other three people sitting round the table now.

'France?' is all I managed to say. An exciting idea, but my life was here in England. Even though there was less to keep me here, since Mum died. I imagined visiting Steve and Manda in France for holidays. That'd be fun.

'I like Italy,' said Manda.

'But we don't speak Italian,' Steve pointed out.

'We could learn …'

'Where in France?' Gray interrupted, leaning forward, elbows on the table. I knew that gesture. It meant he was Having An Idea. Gray's ideas were sometimes inspired, sometimes ridiculous, always crazy.

Steve shrugged. 'Alpes-Maritimes?'

'It's lovely round there,' I said. Phil and I had had a holiday there a couple of years ago, staying in a gîte in a small village nestled among the Alpine foothills. We'd gone walking in the mountains, taken day trips to the Côte d'Azur, dined on local cheese and wine and all in all, fallen in love with the area.

'It is lovely,' Manda agreed. 'But I'd hate to move somewhere like that and be so far from everyone. Bad enough having Zoe on the other side of the world but if I was a plane ride away from all our friends too – you lot, I mean – I'd hate that.' She sniffed. 'You know I hate flying.'

'We'd all come and stay often,' I said with a grin, 'if you got a house somewhere gorgeous like that.'

'We'd move in,' said Gray. I looked at him quizzically and he winked back.

Steve laughed. 'Ha! I'd charge you rent!'

'Maybe we should all just chip in and buy a place big enough for all of us,' Gray said. 'Sell up here, buy ourselves a whopping great property over there that's big enough for all our kids to visit us, and retire in style.'

There was laughter around the table, but Gray looked at each of us in turn. 'No, really, why don't we? Makes perfect sense. It'd be more economical overall – shared bills and all that. Property is cheaper there than here – at least cheaper than it is in the south of England. And imagine the lifestyle – we'd be out cycling and

303

walking, skiing in the winter, growing our own veg. We should do it now, while we're still fit enough. None of us have jobs to keep us here anymore.'

'We could employ a cleaner,' Manda said, ever the practical one.

'And a gardener. And a chef.' Phil grinned.

'We could keep chickens and have fresh eggs every day.' Steve's eyes lit up. He's such a foodie.

'I'd get a dog.' I'd always wanted one.

'Can I have a horse? Let's get a place with stables,' Manda said, to a bit of eye-rolling from Steve.

'It'd need somewhere to store all our bikes,' Gray, our resident cyclist, chipped in.

'There needs to be plenty of spare rooms for guests. Our kids would want to come to stay.' Me, again.

'Imagine at Christmas! All of us together – we'd have a ball!' Steve said – actually, if he wasn't a bloke, I'd have said he squealed this.

We were all speaking at once. The idea had taken shape, invaded all of our minds, and yes, the quantity of wine consumed had helped but as the conversation went on, I could see it taking root. At some point Gray and Steve both pulled out their phones and began searching for properties to buy.

'You can get an eight-bedroom château for about a million euro,' Gray said, peering at a list of search results. 'That's about the right size for us five plus visiting kids.'

'We could afford that, if we all sold our houses here. That's two hundred thousand per person. Your place is worth, what, six hundred thou?' Steve looked at me and Phil.

'About that, yes. And the mortgage is paid off.'

'So you two put in four hundred, that's euro not pounds, and you'd still have a huge wodge of cash over. Manda and I do the same, Gray puts in two hundred.'

'Look at this place! It's got a medieval defensive wall!'

'This one's got a tower, like something from a fairy tale.'

'Rapunzel, Rapunzel, let down your hair!'

'Who's Rapunzel? Steve's bald as a coot, can't be him!' Manda teased.

'You, dearest! Always wanted you to grow your hair long!'

We were passing phones around, looking at the various large properties currently on sale across France. There certainly seemed to be a lot of intriguing-looking châteaux that were within the ball-park price range Steve had suggested. It was a fun evening, and as we indulged ourselves in this little fantasy of selling up and moving to France together we laughed and joked and I felt so happy and comfortable with my friends around me.

It'd never happen, of course. It was just a bit of a giggle, a way to spend the evening with lots of laughter. That was all. We were all far too settled in our current homes and towns. And I, for one, was not good enough at French to be able to manage living abroad.

We'd met during Freshers' week, the five of us. We'd all gone to the Clubs and Societies Fair, and had signed up for the Mountaineering Club. The county of Sussex does not actually contain any mountains of course, but the club arranged weekends away travelling by minibus to north Wales, the Lake District, Brecon or the Peak District for camping, walking and climbing trips. The first meeting of the term was at the end of Freshers' week, where first-years were welcomed and the programme for the term was laid out. I signed up immediately for a trip a fort-night later to Langdale in the Lake District. So did Manda, and we agreed to share a tent. By the end of the meeting we were chatting with the other first-years – Phil, Gray and Steve – and the five of us decided to go on to one of the student bars for a beer. And that was it. We bonded. We were practically inseparable from that moment on, sharing digs during the second and third years, although it wasn't till after university that Phil and I finally paired up, closely followed by Steve and Manda.

'No one left for me,' Gray had said, with a mock-tremble of his lower lip. He was best man at both weddings. And there was never any shortage of girlfriends for him throughout the years. Melissa was the one who lasted longest. They never married but had two daughters together before splitting up when the kids were little. Gray shared custody of the girls with Melissa, having them for half of every week throughout their childhood. He was a great dad. Then there was Leanne who lasted a while, but Gray's commitment phobia sadly finished that relationship in the end.

Phil and I had two kids as well – our sons Tom and Alfie. And Manda and Steve had their daughter Zoe. All were now grown-up, finished with university, earning a living, flying high and happy in their chosen lifestyles. They didn't really need us much anymore, other than for the occasional loan from the Bank of Mum and Dad.

So the five of us were all pretty free, free to do what we wanted with life. We were still young enough to be fit and active, although Phil was a bit overweight and not as fit as he ought to be. We were old enough to be financially secure. We were all recently redundant or retired. Our kids were grown-up and independent. We had no elderly parents left that need caring for – my mum was the last to go of that generation.

So I suppose if we had been at all serious about upping sticks and moving to France, it was the right time to do it. But of course we weren't serious, and in the morning we'd all be dismissing it as a joke, a good giggle but nothing more. At least I hoped so, as I lay searching for sleep in Steve and Manda's spare room that night. I didn't want to move to France.

I was the last one up next morning. That's not unusual – I've never been a morning person. The others were sitting in the kitchen, drinking coffee while Steve organised breakfast. All the men in our little group are great cooks. And Manda can bake amazing cakes, cookies and breads. It's just me who's a klutz in the kitchen.

'Morning, Lu,' Steve said. 'The full works for you this morning? Phil said you were still out for the count.'

'I was. And yes please.' I scanned their faces. Was everyone wondering, as I was, whether the conversation last night had been serious or not? Or had they all forgotten it after a night's sleep? The latter, I hoped.

Phil put out a hand and pulled me to a seat beside him. 'All right? There's fresh tea in the pot. Want some?' He didn't wait for an answer but picked up an empty mug and poured me a cup, adding just the right amount of milk. The advantage of thirty years' marriage is that we know exactly what the other person likes and needs. I smiled a thank-you at him and sat down.

'How're everyone's heads?' I asked.

'Surprisingly all right,' Gray replied. 'Think we drank about eight bottles between us so we've no right to feel good this morning. Not at our age.'

'Speak for yourself, Gray.' Manda gave him a playful punch on the arm. 'You may be knocking on a bit but I'm still only fifty-eight.' She'd always been the baby of the bunch – youngest by all of two months.

The banter was all very well, but I was dying to know. Were they about to start house-hunting in the Alpes-Maritimes? Or anywhere in France for that matter. I hoped not. Steve was busy flipping fried eggs, and Manda was taking trays of sausages and bacon out of the oven and putting them on the table. There was a bowl of cooked mini tomatoes, racks of toast and a pan of sautéed potatoes. I couldn't help but grin. A good old fry-up the night after a skin-full of wine was my favourite thing.

Could you even get bacon and sausage in France?

It was as we finished eating, as Manda was making more coffee and I began stacking plates to load the dishwasher, that Steve spoke up. 'So. This house in France. Are we going to do it, then?'

'Were we serious?' Phil asked.

'I was,' Gray chipped in, as he munched on the last of the toast.

'You're never serious,' Manda told him.

'Well' – he waved the crust of his toast at everyone – 'I was last night. Honestly, it'd be awesome. We could breakfast like this every day!'

'We'd be fat as fools in no time,' I said. My stomach gave a lurch. If they all wanted to do this, I couldn't be the one to spoil the party. Not now. It'd all fizzle out soon enough anyway.

'I'm up for it,' Phil said, looking at me with a raised eyebrow, and I swallowed and nodded. 'Er, yeah. Sure.'

'Manda and I discussed it this morning, while we waited for you lazy lot to show your faces,' Steve said. 'We think we could make it work. Manda needs something to take her mind off Zoe being away. Phil needs a healthier lifestyle. Sorry, mate, but you do. And you, Lu' – he nodded at me – 'need to do something for yourself, after all your years caring for your mum. As for me, I need a project. So I'm happy to do the legwork.'

No one was better than Steve at organising things. He'd been a project manager in a finance company for years and was good at it. And he spoke better French than the rest of us.

'What about me?' asked Gray. 'What do I need?'

'A new hunting ground,' Phil said, with a wink. 'Maybe you'd meet the perfect woman in France.'

'Mmm, I like the sound of that!' Gray laughed.

'Well then,' Phil said. 'Let's go for it!'

There was much cheering and clinking together of coffee mugs, and by the time I had that dishwasher loaded Steve had opened his laptop and begun a search, and a shortlist of potential properties was being drawn up. I watched them crowded around behind Steve and smiled. It would probably all come to nothing, but in the meantime I had to admit it was fun dreaming and planning. In the end the whole thing would no doubt just fizzle out, thankfully, but I wasn't going to be the one who said no to it. Not while they were all so excited.

*

Phil and I discussed the idea on our drive home later that day.

'Moving to France, eh? At our age! Great idea, isn't it?'

I bit my lip for a moment, not sure how to respond. It was one thing going along with the excitement when we were with all the others, but surely I should be honest about my misgivings with my own husband? 'Yeah. Lovely idea, but I can't see it actually happening, can you?'

Phil glanced across at me and frowned. 'Don't see why not. You know what Steve's like when he gets his teeth into a project. There's no one better than him at getting things organised and done.'

'Do you really think we should do it? Sell our house and everything?'

'Well, what's the alternative? Neither of us are working anymore. I'm not ready to just vegetate in front of daytime TV for the next thirty years. So, yes, I think we should put our house on the market as soon as possible. We've been saying we should thin down our possessions ready for downsizing anyway. This'll force us to actually get on and do it. And living with Steve, Manda and Gray will be awesome. It'll be like being twenty again – regaining our youth!'

'Ha. Except we are nearly sixty. But I agree, we do want to downsize and release some equity. So we might as well get on with sorting our stuff out. I reckon the boys will take some of the spare furniture. And it's probably time I threw out all their old schoolbooks and nursery artwork.'

'God, Lu, have you still got all that?'

I grimaced and nodded. 'In the attic. About five boxes of it.'

Downsizing. Not moving to France. That's all I'd agreed to, wasn't it?

So the following week I began clearing the attic, while Phil started on the garage and arranged for valuations from estate agents. We cleaned and tidied ready for the agent's photographer, and then put the house on the market. It felt good to make a start on this – we'd been talking about selling up for at least a year.

A week later we heard that Gray already had an offer on his place, and that Steve was away in France looking at potential properties.

'Already!' I said to Manda, when she phoned to tell us. I couldn't believe they were really this serious about it all, but it looked like Steve was, at least. My heart lurched. I'd accepted the idea of selling our family home, but moving abroad was a much bigger step, one I didn't entirely want to take.

'He spent days online scrolling through endless possibilities, then two days ago said to me it'd be easier to be "on the ground", and next thing I knew he'd booked a flight to Nice.'

'Didn't he want company?' I asked. I'd have thought he'd have taken Manda or Gray with him.

'I think his plan is to whittle his short list down to a proper shortlist – there are over a hundred on it at the moment – and then let us have a look at the details. Then if any really stand out and we're still all keen, we can go en masse to view them.'

'Sounds good.' The rest of us hadn't the first idea how to buy property abroad, but Steve would have looked it all up already, spoken to suitable people for advice, and would know exactly what he was doing. He was a born project manager.

'Lu, I'm so excited about this, aren't you?' Manda said. I detected a tiny bit of worry in her voice, as if she was frightened Phil and I might have had second thoughts. She was right – I'd been having second thoughts all the way through. But I refused to be the one to spoil things.

'Definitely! Just can't wait to get on with it now!' I forced myself to sound enthusiastic. Whatever happened, I was not going to put a dampener on it. There was still a strong chance the plan would fall apart.

'Phew! I told Zoe, too. She thinks it's a great idea. I was worried, you know, that she'd somehow think we were abandoning her ...'

'But she lives in Australia – actually you'll have moved a little closer to her!'

'I mean more that when, or God help me *if*, she comes home to England, we won't be there.'

'No, but you'll be a short flight away. And she can come "home" to France. Home is where her heart is.'

Manda answered with a little wobble in her voice. 'You're right. It's the only thing that worries me, though. That our kids won't like it.' She took a deep breath. She'd struggled with empty nest syndrome ever since Zoe first left home to go to university. 'What do Tom and Alfie think?'

This was my chance. I could offload to Manda here, now, tell her my misgivings about the whole project, using the boys as an excuse, perhaps. She'd talk to Steve, and maybe it'd all be quietly put to bed, for surely if we weren't all happy with the idea, we shouldn't do it? After all, moving to another country is a big step, at any time of life. But no. I wasn't going to be the party pooper. They'd never think quite the same of me again if I did that now. And I was still convinced the plan would die a natural death if I just let events run their course.

I smiled, to make my voice sound happy. 'They're delighted. Tom sees it as a base for cheap holidays. Alfie's dictated we need to have a swimming pool, and a butler serving iced cocktails at all hours.'

'Fair enough. I'll let Steve know the new requirements.' We had a giggle about this, before going on to talk about Gray's house sale.

'Steve and I have said he can move in here if need be, if his sale goes through really quickly. Actually that'd give us some capital for a deposit, if we need it. It's all working out, Lu. We've got the skiing holiday coming up, then it's possible we might be ready to move in the summer!'

Well, I hoped Phil and I would be ready to move by the summer. But with luck, not to France.

Dear Reader,

We hope you enjoyed reading this book. If you did, we'd be so appreciative if you left a review. It really helps us and the author to bring more books like this to you.

Here at HQ Digital we are dedicated to publishing fiction that will keep you turning the pages into the early hours. Don't want to miss a thing? To find out more about our books, promotions, discover exclusive content and enter competitions you can keep in touch in the following ways:

JOIN OUR COMMUNITY:

Sign up to our new email newsletter:
http://smarturl.it/SignUpHQ

Read our new blog www.hqstories.co.uk

https://twitter.com/HQStories

www.facebook.com/HQStories

BUDDING WRITER?

We're also looking for authors to join the HQ Digital family!
Find out more here:

https://www.hqstories.co.uk/want-to-write-for-us/

Thanks for reading, from the HQ Digital team

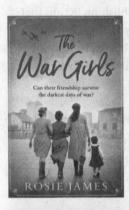

If you enjoyed *The Lost Sister*, then why not try another sweeping historical fiction novel from HQ Digital?

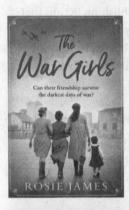

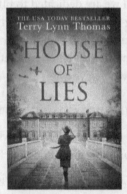

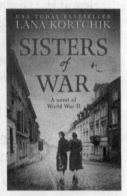

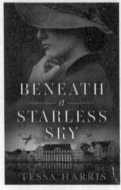

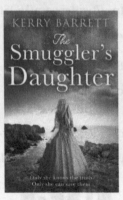